Drew contemplated the enigma before him. She couldn't possibly be telling the truth. No gently bred woman would allow her hair to flow with such abandon from her kerchief. No gently bred woman would loosen her bodice with two men mere feet away. No gently bred woman would have survived the passage over. If she was an earl's daughter, he was a king's son.

Still, no common born female would know how to read and write.

No common born female would speak in such a refined manner. No common born female would have asked for a washbowl instead of a bucket.

"Are you, by any chance, the *illegitima*   clean of an earl?"

She gasped. "How dare you! Why, you wouldn't know the queen of England if she were staring you in the face!"

"Answer my question."

"I shall not dignify that question with an answer."

Brushing her skirt to the side, she swept past him and set off down the path—in effect, dismissing him. Well, by trow, he was the master here.

The sooner she understood that, the better.

A BRIDE
MOST
BEGRUDGING

Books by Deeanne Gist

A Bride Most Begrudging
The Measure of a Lady
Courting Trouble
Deep in the Heart of Trouble
A Bride in the Bargain
*Beguiled**
Maid to Match
Love on the Line

* with J. Mark Bertrand

A BRIDE
MOST
BEGRUDGING

DEEANNE
GIST

BETHANY HOUSE
a division of Baker Publishing Group
Minneapolis, Minnesota

© 2005 by Deeanne Gist

Published by Bethany House Publishers
11400 Hampshire Avenue South
Bloomington, Minnesota 55438
www.bethanyhouse.com

Bethany House Publishers is a division of
Baker Publishing Group, Grand Rapids, Michigan

Printed in the United States of America

ISBN 978-0-7642-3060-8

Scripture quotations are from the New King James Version of the Bible.
See "Author's Note."

17   18   19   20   21   22   23   7   6   5   4   3   2   1

For my dearest friend and precious savior,
Jesus Christ.
Oh, how I love you. Cherish you. Rejoice over you.
I praise the One Who Is.

ACKNOWLEDGMENTS

O ne's first novel is like one's first baby—an almost surreal experience that delights and frightens all at the same time but is treasured forever. The journey has been long and full of adventure. Many have been there from the beginning, others have walked part of the way with me, and yet others were waiting at the finish line. To all of you, I pray that God will bless you tenfold to how you have blessed me.

A heartfelt thank-you to my college sweetheart and husband, Greg Gist, who is my dream come true. I have been so incredibly blessed to have landed such a treasure. I love you most of all.

My parents, Harold and Veranne Graham, have been instrumental in their support and encouragement, not only during my writing career, but from the moment I entered this world. Thank you for your unconditional love, for sharing your wisdom with me, and for introducing me to Jesus Christ. May He shower you with blessings.

Thank you to my critique partners, Heda Christ and Anne Dykowski, for your hours upon hours of devotion, skill, and input. Every time I pick up *Bride*, I think, *Heda told me to put that there*, or *Anne suggested I do that*, or *Golly, I'm glad they made me redo this part*. You are diamonds of the first water. Words cannot express my gratitude.

The folks at Bethany House have been an absolute dream from the moment they received my manuscript to the moment *Bride* hit the shelves. Dave Long, your enthusiasm, dedication, and inspiration have made me want to be the very best I could be. Thank you for stepping out there and making a difference. My editor, Julie Klassen, is the best editor ever—of course, she's the *only* editor I've ever had, but there are some things one just *knows*. And I look forward, Julie, to sharing many more laughs and confidences and books with you. Thank you for your wonderful insight and input. You are a gem.

And a huge and hearty thank-you to Richard Alvarez for choreographing my fight scene, to Ted Simon for giving me a crash course in Housebuilding 101, to Victor Belfi for helping me with the math puzzles, to Richard Curtis for believing in me, and to Ron Smith for managing me. Any mistakes made in regards to fighting, housebuilding, or problem solving are completely and totally mine.

God bless you all.
Love, Dee

PROLOGUE

DEPTFORD, ENGLAND
APRIL 1643

Saints above, girl. What are you *doing* here?" the shackled man hissed.

Lady Constance Morrow rushed those last few steps across the upper deck. "Please, Uncle Skelly, don't scold me. I couldn't let you leave without saying good-bye."

"It's only for seven years. Now get off this blasted shallop."

She touched a hand to her throat. How could she leave? He'd been much more of a father to her than the earl. Perhaps he felt shamed by the shackles clamped tight around his wrists and ankles.

Her heart squeezed inside her chest. He looked as if he'd aged ten years since she saw him just three short months ago. She might not have even recognized him had he not spoken out.

An unhealthy gray pallor replaced the rosy glow she had grown so accustomed to seeing in his cheeks. And his pride and joy—the pure white beard and mustache he'd kept meticulously trimmed and groomed—grew in great abandon about his face.

But his green eyes were still crystal clear and, at the moment, absolutely furious.

"But *America*," she exclaimed. "It's so far away and wild and heathen."

"It's better than being dead," he growled. "For love o' the king, girl, this ship is not interested in men only. Those colonists need breeders, and the captain chained a whole store of female felons in the hold for that very purpose. You have no business being on board. Where is your maid?"

"I easily escaped from her. Besides, the captain would not dare allow a member of his crew to touch an English gentlewoman."

"He'd dare that and more. All the other well-wishers have long since left, so there is no one on board that can check his actions." He swiveled to look behind him and when he turned back, near panic lit his eyes. "Quick," he cried. "He has seen you!"

Who, she thought. *The captain?* She grabbed the front of her skirts, poised for flight, yet did not move. Releasing the expensive silk, she clasped Skelly's hands in hers. His irons clanked.

"Oh, Uncle. I can't bear this." Her eyes pooled with unshed tears. "I will not let the submissions to your *Diary* go unanswered. I will keep the publication going while you are away. It will be ready and waiting for you upon your return. You have my oath."

"Have you not heard a word I've said? You must leave *this instant*. The captain of this ship is a villain and a

coward. It will go the worse for me if he catches us together, and I'd just as soon avoid a flogging. Now, *go*."

She paled. "Oh! I'm sorry. I had no idea."

She glanced across the upper deck. The captain's huge
silhouette advanced, his crisp stride unaffected by the
sway of the vessel. Her hairs stood on end. "I love you,
Uncle," she whispered frantically. "My prayers are with
you."

Picking up her skirts once again, she turned and hustled toward the gangway.

The captain whistled. An unkempt sailor posted just
feet from her took two long steps. He grabbed her forearm.

"Release me at once!" she demanded.

The man's dark leathery face formed a grotesque
imitation of a smile. "I think not, maiden."

She increased her resistance. He grabbed her other
arm. She tried to jerk free. He tightened his hold. She
slammed her heel onto his booted toe. The heel broke off.

He snarled, grasped her around the waist, and hauled
her clear off her feet, slamming her against his side.

"What's this, Cooper?" The deep voice barely registered in her panicked mind. She could not believe they
would be so bold.

She squirmed. Nothing happened. She kicked. Nothing happened. She bit his arm, gagging at the repelling
taste of his sleeve.

His grip loosened. Encouraged by this tiny bit of success, she bucked and kicked with increased vigor. He
swore. The air suddenly quit reaching her lungs.

The shallop lurched. The rigging creaked.

"What have you?"

"I'm not sure, Capt'n," her captor responded. "A little bird trying to fly the coop, looks like."

The captain fingered her hair. "And a red bird, at that."

She yanked her head away from his touch. "You'll hang for this!" Her threat came out pathetically weak. She struggled for air. "I cannot breathe."

The sailor's pressure did not let up. She labored to stay conscious as her vision began to fade.

"Arman!" the captain shouted.

She jerked her eyes open at the command.

"Sir?" Another voice filtered up the gangway.

"What conveyances are on the dock?"

Her lungs were on fire. She opened her mouth, gasping. A thimbleful of air entered. She needed more. Much more.

"A hired hackney, sir." This, again, from the gangway.

"Anyone in it?"

"Just the driver, sir."

Her eyes refused to stay open. Icy prickles bombarded her fingers, toes, arms, and legs. Yet her hearing still functioned perfectly.

"Take her below with the others."

The captain's quiet words produced seconds of pure terror before blackness overtook her.

ONE

The gown they gave her fit too closely. It displayed her figure with humiliating clarity, but perhaps that would work to her advantage. She had lost so much weight, she couldn't imagine any farmer wanting to invest in such a sickly looking woman.

Several tobacco planters had been on board already to examine the "cargo." The men stood chained on one side of the upper deck, the women on the other. The men were being sold as indentured servants for seven or fourteen year terms, depending upon their sentence.

But the women were to serve a lifetime sentence. They were to be purchased as brides. One bride in exchange for 120 pounds of tobacco leafage, the colony's cash crop.

All except Constance, that is. She had been placed alone up on the half deck, her wrists and ankles shackled, the first mate standing guard behind her right shoulder. The captain was asking two hundred pounds of tobacco for her. Ridiculous.

Her gaze drifted over the indentured men. Uncle Skelly was not among them, of course. How could he be?

Only twice during the voyage had the captain allowed the women onto the upper deck for fresh air. The first time up, she'd passed Uncle Skelly on the mid deck. With a collar and padlock about his neck, they had chained him not only to a board but to three of the most abominable creatures she had ever seen. Jail fever consumed one of those creatures.

The second time up, she had found Uncle Skelly's place on the board eerily vacant. The first mate, Cooper, had confirmed her fears. Skelly Morrow was dead.

Constance swallowed the rush of tears that even now accumulated in her throat at the memory.

"Look lively, maiden. Here comes a'one," Cooper snarled.

She stiffened as a young farmer of but a score or so years approached the half deck. He looked at Cooper, nodded slightly, then turned to her.

She jerked back when he captured some strands of her hair between his long work-roughened fingers. The captain had not allowed her to wear a headcloth this morning. He'd insisted on having her hair loose and uncovered around her shoulders and back.

This display was nothing short of blasphemy. A woman's hair was sacred and a recognized symbol of her maidenhood, only to be worn free while speaking wedding vows.

She'd never felt so naked in her life. Her hair wasn't soft and silky like other women's. It was wild and thick with tightly coiled ringlets that seemed to multiply when unbound.

The bay breeze picked up, causing her hair to swirl around her face. She tried again to free herself from the man's grasp.

"Easy, miss. I'll not hurt you," he said.

His voice was kind, as were his eyes. He did not rake her with an offensive look nor handle her roughly. If he asked to see her teeth, though, she'd be most uncooperative.

Below, two men captured her attention. One was a dark-haired farmer with a straw hat in his hand. The other was blond and had been on board the ship during the passage over. He'd not been a prisoner, nor had he been a crew member. She'd learned he had paid an extraordinary fee for his passage to the colony, a place he claimed as his home.

The pair singled out Mary, the woman who'd been chained next to Constance the entire voyage over. They spoke with Mary, checked her teeth, and had her walk the length of the deck and back.

The captain approached them. More words were exchanged. The bargaining had begun. In a few minutes, Mary's fetters were removed and she left the ship with the blond man, while the dark-haired farmer signed a voucher for the captain.

Constance tapped down her panic. Mary was more than a fellow prisoner. She was Constance's only friend.

Of a sudden, the captain pointed to Constance and the farmer turned in her direction. He narrowed his eyes, finished his transaction with the captain, and headed to the half deck.

She returned her attention to the young man in front of her. He still had hold of her hair, but he was focused on Cooper.

" . . . a gen-u-ine lady, she is," the first mate was saying.

"Then why was she transported?" the man asked.

"Oh, we didn't ask questions. Not our job to ask questions."

She rolled her eyes.

"You have papers for her?"

"No, he does not," Constance replied.

Cooper grabbed her arm. "Keep quiet, missy, or you'll be the sorrier for it."

"Looking for a bride, Gerald?" The dark-haired farmer had reached the half deck.

The man who must have been Gerald released her hair and jumped back. "Drew! No, not at all."

"Is she for sale?" Drew asked Cooper.

"Aye, mate."

"As a tobacco bride?"

"Aye."

Drew turned back to Gerald and raised an eyebrow.

"Now, Drew, it is not what it appears. I was merely curious."

"You gave up the right to be curious the moment you married my sister."

Gerald's face filled with color. "Actually, it was you I was thinking of," he sputtered.

Drew lifted both brows this time.

Gerald swallowed. "I, uh, just thought if you found someone of an, uh, acceptable nature, you might be interested."

"And you deem this female acceptable?"

Gerald paused. "They say she is a lady of the realm, Drew."

"She has red hair, and I absolutely abhor red hair."

She stiffened. Gerald's face suffused with color. Although her hair was more auburn than red, Gerald's hair was almost orange, it was so bright.

"Your pardon. I did not know."

"Well, well, well. What have we here? Looking for a bride, Master O'Connor?" A scrawny, slovenly man with more teeth missing than not swaggered onto the half deck.

Tension bounced between the three men. Drew put on his hat, shifted his attention to Constance, and tipped his brim. "If you will excuse me, miss." He, along with his brother-in-law, moved past her, past the man with the missing teeth, and past two other farmers now approaching the half deck.

The scraggy man watched them leave and ejected tobacco-colored saliva onto the wooden planks as he followed their progress.

"Emmett," greeted one of the advancing farmers. He and his companion both had great bushy black beards, jolly faces, and rounded bellies. Perhaps they were kin.

"Woodrum," Emmett said, then turning to her, grabbed her cheeks and squeezed until her mouth gaped open. "Well, would you look at all them teeth. Why, she's got a mouth full of 'em. How's the rest of her, Cooper? You patted her down?"

She reared back, trying to grab his arm, but the chains around her wrists and waist restricted her movement. He tightened his grip. The rank smell of him took her breath away, and if he'd had any fingernails at all, they'd have cut half-moons into her cheeks.

"No damaging of the goods, matey, until after you buy her," Cooper said. "Pat all you want, but don't be leaving any bruises."

She stiffened. Emmett released her with a shove, and she would have fallen backward if the big man called Woodrum hadn't caught her elbow. Once she was steady, he relaxed his hold, then let go of her completely.

Emmett raked his gaze up and down her frame, rubbing his hands against his puny chest. "Why's she up here away from them other brides?"

"She's one of them ladies of the realm, she is," Cooper responded. "And she'll cost you a few more tobaccy leaves than them others."

"What proof you got fer yer claim? I say she's nothing more than a quail plucked right off them London alleyways." He eyed her again. "She shore got what it takes to do the job, and I ain't gonna be paying out a bunch of sot weed for used goods."

Woodrum scratched his cheek. "How much are you asking for her?"

"Two hundred pounds," Cooper answered.

Emmett harrumphed. "Of tobaccy? You'll not be gettin' two hundred pounds for a light skirt."

"She's a gen-u-ine lady, mate, but no bloke's a forcin' you to claim her. We already got us a bid for her, we do."

Emmett furrowed his brows. "From who?"

"Drew O'Connor."

Woodrum and his silent companion looked at each other, caution evident in their expressions. Emmett's eyes took on an unnatural brilliance. Constance didn't know what game the first mate was playing, but she would hold her tongue for now.

"O'Connor, you say?" Emmett asked. "How much did he offer?"

"Two hundred."

"Then why's the maid still here?"

"She has to be paid for in tobaccy only. No vouchers. The capt'n wouldn't release her or take her off the block before collecting payment. O'Connor went to collect his sot weed."

As far as she knew, that was an outright lie, but she couldn't be certain.

The merciless sun beat down upon them. Sweat trickled down Emmett's face and into his snarled beard. "Well, ain't that interesting." He wiped his hands against his backside, then looked to the first mate. "May I?"

"Help yourself," Cooper replied.

Emmett reached for her.

She leaned away from him. "Touch me, and I'll see you flogged before the morrow's sun appears on the horizon."

Emmett's eyebrows shot up to his hairline. "Ho, ho! Would you listen to that? A saucy one, ain't she?" Cackling, he rubbed his hands together.

Constance tensed.

"Leave off, Emmett," Woodrum said, grabbing Emmett's arm. "It's clear that she is healthy and there is no padding beneath her garment."

Emmett's lip curled. "What's it to you, Woodrum?"

"Either up Drew's wager or keep your hands to yourself."

"I ain't makin' no bid till I test the goods."

Without taking his eyes off Emmett, Woodrum handed his hat to his companion, removed his coat, and relinquished that as well. He slowly began to roll up his sleeves.

The man's belly may have been round, but his arms

and chest appeared to be solid rock. "You'll not touch her unless you pay for the privilege."

Smelling a fight, the farmers on the upper deck had begun to crowd close.

Emmett slowly lowered his hands. "Two hundred twenty, Cooper. I'll give you two hundred twenty pounds for her."

"Two twenty-five," Woodrum countered.

It was time to speak up. "Gentlemen," she interjected, "this is really all quite unnecessary. I am not a tobacco bride. I am the daughter of an earl. The captain kidnapped me and is trying to sell me unlawfully. As soon as the governor comes aboard, I will have an audience with him and will then be freed and on my way back to London."

Her statement, made during one of those unfortunate moments when every person in the crowd, for whatever reason, is silent all at once, carried across the entire breadth of the ship.

The quiet that followed her pronouncement was fraught with shock. On the heels of that, a huge swell of laughter and guffaws from the whole company of men rose to alarming levels. Even Woodrum was amused.

"Oh, she's a wicked one, she is," Emmett cackled. "Where's the capt'n?"

The crowd parted, and the captain took the steps two at a time. Woodrum and his friend receded into the crowd.

Emmett grasped the captain's hand. "I'll give you a whole hogshead for her, capt'n, and while my field boy rolls it down here, I'll be celebrating at the meeting-house."

The captain pursed his lips for a moment, then broke into a grin. "Three hundred pounds it is, then. Gentlemen, Goodman Emmett here has purchased himself one high-born bride."

The men roared their approval and surged forward, encircling Emmett. He put an X on the voucher and exchanged it for a receipt from the captain. The excitement escalated and the crowd pulled Emmett off the half deck and further away from her. He twisted around. The depraved promise in his eyes projected itself into her very soul.

Bile converged in her throat. She was going to be sick. Forsooth, she was going to be sick right here, right now.

Help me, Lord, help me. Where is the governor? Where are you, Lord? Please, please. Help me.

As one, the company moved from the ship to the shore. And on, she supposed, to the celebration.

Chills from within shot through her body, causing a series of bumps to erupt along her arms and legs. Then an all-consuming anger at the incredible injustice of it all made her blood surge. Her resolve solidified and she focused in on the captain.

"How *dare* you!" she cried. "You will not get away with this. Mark you, if you do not arrange an audience with the governor at once, I will create a commotion of such magnitude they will write legends about it."

The captain did not even bother to acknowledge her. "Throw her back in the hold, Cooper," he said over his shoulder as he descended the steps.

She filled her lungs with the intention of letting out a scream the likes of which would not be ignored. Before she could release it, the first mate squeezed a band of skin between her neck and her shoulder.

Debilitating pain cut off her scream and buckled her knees. She crumpled to the ground. Cooper did not let go but followed her to the floor. She whimpered, trying to pull away from the torturous vice his fingers created.

His hot, foul breath invaded her ear. "Not one sound, dovey. Not one."

TWO

Constance lay shivering and alone belowdecks. Darkness entombed the hold. Midnight had passed, but morning was still more than a few hours away.

She felt certain the men's celebration was over, for the balance of brides had been picked up long ago. All except for her.

She tried not to let desperation fill her. If the governor had put in an appearance, it was after Cooper had forced her back into the hold and secured her to the wall. With that opportunity gone, she knew there would be no other. At least not anytime soon. And by the time she did see the governor, it would be too late.

She would belong to a man. An odious, vulgar man who inspired revulsion, loathing, and horror. A man who, in the eyes of this colony, would have complete dominion over her. Who would have the right to do with her as he saw fit.

Her stomach clinched and she pushed herself up off the rough planks and heaved once again. Nothing left.

She'd managed to hold her fears at bay until the last

bride had been led to her doom. When the trapdoor had closed behind that poor woman, it was the first time in over eight weeks that Constance had been completely alone. And it terrified her. The dark, damp, malodorous deck that had felt so cramped and hemmed in now loomed over her with a soundless assault.

The irons around her waist and wrists weighted her down. Collapsing onto the slats, she vaguely heard the scurrying of a rat echo off the walls of the hold. A fresh rush of tears spilled from her eyes.

Have you heard my cries, Lord? Have you destroyed my enemy? Is that why I am still here?

As if in answer, the squeak of the trapdoor reached her ears just as light from a lantern reached her eyes. She covered her eyes with her arm, the clanking of her chains ricocheting around her.

The heavy tread of the mate clomping down the steps sent her heart into a terrible gallop. She curled into a tight ball. *Please. Please. Spare me, Lord. Rescue me. Please!*

The crewman's smell reached her before he did. "The call to reckoning has come, wench. Up with ye, now. Yer man's arrived and it's anxious he is to take possession of ye."

In a pig's eye, she thought. A great calm settled upon her. She slowly unfurled, pulled herself into a sitting position, and looked up to see who had the late night watch. Arman. A beastly excuse of a man.

He removed the lock attaching her to the wall and pulled the chain from around her waist. Grabbing the irons around her wrists, he yanked her to her feet. The room swirled round, but Arman gave her no time to gain her sea legs.

She stumbled. He shoved her forward. She fell hard on her knees, pain shooting up her legs to her back and neck.

"Get up," he snarled, jerking her back to her feet. "You'll not be playing yer high-and-mighty games with me, missy. Ye might work yer wiles upon Cooper, but yer nothin' more than a hen to that struttin' rooster on the uppers, and if ye think to be givin' him or me any troubles, it'll go the worse for ye."

She kept her face expressionless, but she would not cooperate with Arman or the rooster. And she was prepared to do whatever it took to free herself from the knave.

When they made the upper deck, she scanned the area for the despicable Emmett man that had purchased her. He was not there. Instead, Arman led her to stand in front of the dark-haired farmer they called Drew O'Connor.

What was he doing here? Was he to take her to Emmett? But, no, it had been clear those two were not on friendly terms. Confusion clouded her thoughts.

"Remove the fetters," O'Connor said.

"I wouldn't advise it, sir. The dove has been a bit of a trial."

O'Connor scrutinized her. "A strong gust of wind would knock her over. From what I hear about the victuals you serve the felons, I would imagine she's too weak to put up much of a fight."

Arman stiffened. "She was fed."

"Um. Let me guess. Pease and loblolly?"

"Once a day."

"Remove the fetters," O'Connor repeated.

"You remove 'em."

O'Connor snatched the keys from Arman's hand and reached for her wrists. She jerked them back.

He paused. Moonbeams glanced off the ship's metal bell, throwing his features into dark relief. "Do you not want to be released?"

"I, of course, want to be released, but not only from these irons. I want to be granted my freedom. The captain of this ship kidnapped me. I did not come here voluntarily as a tobacco bride, nor am I a felon."

"Then how is it you stand before me bound with shackles?"

The irons surrounding her wrists rattled as the wooden deck shifted beneath her feet. "My uncle was a prisoner on this ship. I came to bid him good-bye—"

"Lies," Arman growled.

"Hold, man," O'Connor snapped. "I'll hear what she has to say."

A whisper of hope flickered within her. "My uncle was sentenced to seven years of indentured servitude for not subscribing to the king's supremacy. By the time I learned of his sentence, he was already on board the *Randolph*. I hastened to this vessel. No sooner had I located Uncle Skelly than the captain grabbed me and threw me in the hold."

"What of your escort?"

She hesitated. "I escaped from my maid's watchful eye. Had she known of my destination, she never would have permitted it."

"And the other visitors on board? Surely someone saw this atrocity occur?"

"The last of the visitors were leaving by the time I arrived and boarded."

"Did not your driver notice you failed to return?"

She sighed. "I hired a hackney. My own driver is loyal to my father and would not have brought me to see Uncle Skelly. I'm sure the captain saw to my hired conveyance for me."

O'Connor arched a brow. "You were alone?"

Looking aside, she nodded.

"On the docks?"

The disbelief in his tone brought her chin up. "Uncle Skelly was like a father to me. He'd raised me since my mother's death. I was hardly more than a babe. My real father didn't bother to make an appearance until he needed me for a marriage alliance. An alliance I refused to accept."

"Who's your father?"

"The Earl of Greyhame." The tackle creaked and whined against the water's pull but held the slaver fast to the dock.

O'Connor glanced at Arman. "I'll speak with the prisoner she calls Uncle Skelly."

Arman snorted. "There ain't no such person."

"He's dead." The words fell flat from her lips. She still couldn't quite believe it. Forcing down the lump in her throat, she contemplated the vast watery cemetery beyond the dark horizon. "He didn't survive the passage over."

O'Connor scratched the back of his head, knocking his hat askew. "Let me make sure I understand this. You came to the docks *alone* and boarded a ship of felons just to give your uncle a peck on the cheek? An uncle who is, for all practical purposes, nonexistent?"

She jerked her focus back to the matter at hand. "He died!"

"How convenient." O'Connor straightened his hat, his narrowed gaze quickly sluicing up and down her body before resting upon her face.

She returned the favor. His bronzed skin was too dark, his blue eyes too pale, his jaw too square.

That jaw tightened. "I suppose you will now tell me peers of the realm no longer dress in the manner they used to."

She fingered the lacings digging into her waist. The bodice was ridiculously tight. "This gown is not mine."

"No? You mean you wore someone else's clothing when you came on board to visit your notorious *uncle*?"

"Certainly not."

"Then where are your clothes?"

A good question. Before they docked yesterday, all prisoners were expected to bathe. On the upper deck. In the open. She had resisted, of course. But with the help of another sailor, Arman had stripped her of her clothing, shoved her into a filthy barrel, dumped a torrent of salt water atop her, then yanked her out by her hair.

She had kicked and bit and clawed until the captain shoved an unfamiliar bodice, skirt, and headcloth into her arms. No chemise. No stockings. No shoes.

Clutching the items to her frame, she had questioned the absence of the undergarments and the soiled condition of the clothing. In response, the captain threatened to take them back and leave her with nothing.

It was then she had demanded the return of her diary. It lay in the pocket of her old skirt. The captain's eyes had narrowed. The diary would be returned to her in exchange for a more satisfying sport with the men, he had said, starting with him.

She was shrewd enough to know when to retreat. Remembering that retreat fed her anger. She tipped her head toward Arman. "Ask him."

O'Connor turned to him. "Where are her clothes?"

"Below."

"Bring them to me."

"They're rags, matey, and not fit for man nor beast, they ain't."

"The clothing, if you please."

"I want my diary back too," Constance said.

Arman's black eyes impaled her.

"I'll review any belongings she brought on board," O'Connor interjected.

Arman spun around and headed toward the companionway. O'Connor stopped him. "Tell your captain I'll have a word with him as well."

The rhythmic lapping of the water against the shallop accentuated their sudden silence. O'Connor did not look her way. Standing with his head bowed and shoulders slumped, he rubbed his eyes. His sleeveless leather jerkin covered thick, broad shoulders. Its laces opened at the chest, revealing a well-worn shirt underneath, while a cloth pouch hung from the leather belt at his trim waist. Full breeches fastened just below his knees, where long stockings hugged muscular calves. Unadorned braid laced up the square shoes on his feet.

At the sound of Arman's return, O'Connor lifted his head and straightened his shoulders. The sailor handed him a wad of fabric.

Stepping closer to a lantern, O'Connor unfurled and examined the once-beautiful silk dress she had worn that long ago day of her kidnapping. His hands, massive and strong, explored the hollows of the garment, gliding over the soft curves custom-made for her alone. The faded green bodice fluttered beneath the ministrations of his adept tanned fingers. An unwelcome burning crept up her neck and into her cheeks.

Finally, he allowed the dress to slither from his hands to the deck. Dragging her attention from the bundle of silk pooled at his feet, she watched him shake out her chemise. Another inspection of seams and construction followed.

He held up the undergarment by its shoulders and squinted over at her. "Are these your things?"

She nodded.

"Did this fit you when you boarded the ship?"

She blushed anew. "It did."

Cocking his head to the side, he scrutinized the chemise again. "You have lost a considerable amount of poundage."

She said nothing. His strapping frame dwarfed the chemise, hanging limp within his grasp. Even so, he was right. The only fullness left on her body was that across her chest, and even that had diminished in size a bit.

As if reading her thoughts, he regarded the area in question. She resisted the urge to shield herself. She had worn gowns at home cut every bit as low as this one without a moment of self-consciousness.

In time, he retrieved the dress from the deck and fingered its finely woven fabric. After checking the pockets, he shoved the clothing beneath his arm. "The diary?"

Arman handed O'Connor a small, worn book. O'Connor spent several minutes studying the publication. "Where is her diary?"

"That's all we found," Arman answered.

"That is the diary I spoke of," Constance said.

O'Connor looked at her. "This is no diary. This is a collection of nonsense."

She bristled. "It is an almanac containing many delightful and entertaining particulars."

He snorted. "For what purpose?"

"It provides me and a great number of other ladies with a wealth of scientific information."

He opened the volume and turned to one of the leaves. Holding it up to the lantern, he read an entry.

> "At London one morning 'neath the sun's shin-
>   ing glow,
> I found my cane's length in its own shadow,
> As I held it upright; 'twas the tenth day of May:
> Now tell me exactly the time of the day?"

He looked at her over the rim of the book. "You must be jesting."

"Can you provide the solution?"

"Nine hours, thirteen minutes, and sixteen seconds into the morning."

She rolled her eyes. "You saw my answer."

"*Your* answer? These are your figures scribbled in the margins?"

"They are."

He threw back his head and laughed. The deep, warm, rich sound of it chafed her ears. She took a deep breath and met his gaze square on.

"O'Connor," the captain shouted. "Back again from this morning?"

Snapping the almanac shut, O'Connor shoved it under his arm with the clothing. He held out his hand. The captain grasped it.

"Good evening to you, Captain. This wench says she comes unwillingly."

The captain glanced at her. "You're here to claim her, then? I'd heard Emmett lost her in a game of chance this afternoon, but I couldn't quite credit it. You have the receipt?"

O'Connor handed it to him.

Her mouth went slack. A game of chance? They bartered for her in a *card game*?

She snapped her mouth shut. *Was this your answer, Lord? This is what you consider being released? But that's not what I meant and you know it! I want to be freed!*

The captain scanned the piece of parchment, then cackling, handed it back to O'Connor. "By trow, Emmett must be sorely vexed. Particularly since he paid out so much sot weed to purchase her." He clapped O'Connor on the back. "What took you so long to fetch her? All the other men have long since collected their brides."

"I had things to attend to."

A suggestive grin spread across the captain's face. "Ah, yes. I'd almost forgotten. You purchased a bride of your own this morning, didn't you? Were so desperate for one, in fact, that you sent your brother clear to England to handpick one for you." He gave a low coarse laugh. "And you're just now coming up for air? Decided you'd like to try this one on for size? Ho, ho! Emmett's going to throw bung by the cartload when he recovers from his drunken stupor!"

Constance's mind whirled. Was the captain referring to Mary? Mary had left with the blond man, but it was O'Connor here who had signed the purchase papers. Oh, poor Mary! Still, O'Connor couldn't very well try and force Constance into a marriage contract if he was already wed to Mary.

"I've not married the woman my brother recommended but merely purchased her," O'Connor said.

Constance's breath caught.

The captain howled. "Oh, that's even better! By my troth, but I can't wait to see Emmett's face when he hears."

O'Connor's nostrils flared. "Where are this female's papers of transport?"

The captain's expression sobered somewhat. "She came on board the vessel with fraudulent letters to the prisoners in an effort to procure their escape. We seized her before her plan could be carried out."

She gasped. "That is untrue!"

She caught a glimpse of suspicion on O'Connor's face. Surely it was the captain he doubted, not *her*?

By heaven, she must locate the Crown-appointed governor of this godforsaken place haste, posthaste. Only then could this unconscionable injustice done to her be righted.

A sinking sensation began in the pit of her stomach. What if she finally managed an audience with the governor and he didn't believe her? She was no more than a warm female body in a colony desperate to be fruitful. What if the governor refused to believe her simply because it suited his purposes, and the Crown's, to have her here?

This overgrown provincial American might be her only chance at freedom. After all, he evidently owned her. So if he believed her story, wouldn't it be within his power to set her free?

The captain regarded her through half-closed lids. "We were given an order from Lieutenant-Colonel Windem to keep her. She is such a rebel as not to be permitted to stay in the mother country."

"How dare you!" she cried. "My father—"

"May I see the order?"

The captain returned his attention to O'Connor. "The order came by word of mouth."

O'Connor tightened his lips. He handed the keys to the captain. "Release her. I am ready to take her home."

The captain moved to unlock the fetters. "By all means. I almost hate to see her go, though. It's a mighty feisty wench she's been, and she can certainly put on the airs. Too bad I didn't join you in your gaming. Maybe Emmett would have lost her to me and I could move to the next port and sell her all over again!"

Stiffening, Constance squared her shoulders. She and O'Connor stared at each other over the captain's bent frame. Sighing, she held her peace and watched the fetters come off.

"Miss Morrow?"

"*Lady* Morrow."

O'Connor offered her his elbow.

"Do you believe I am who I say I am?"

He said nothing. Merely shifted the straw hat resting atop his long sable waves, then once again extended his elbow.

"I need to speak with the governor. Will you take me to him?"

He gave a brisk nod. "Of course."

She looked at his elbow, then back up at his eyes. "When?"

"It's the middle of the night," he said, a touch of impatience flickering across his face. "Not a very good time to ask the governor for a sympathetic ear."

She bit her lip. He was right, of course.

Lifting her chin, she said, "I'll not marry you until I've spoken with the governor."

O'Connor raised a brow. "Have I asked you to marry me?"

"Well, no, but I assumed—"

"Don't assume."

She studied him for a moment, then hesitantly placed her hand upon his arm and accompanied him off the ship.

"We are going to your home?" she asked.

He nodded.

Leaving the shore behind, she and O'Connor zig-zagged through a forest of trees growing, at every foot-fall, larger and nobler than the last.

The sheer number of trees held her speechless. She had heard the colonies held a wealth of timber, yet she hadn't expected such profusion. Even the moon, resplendent in its full phase, seemed to blaze in an unprecedented fashion, providing them with an abundance of light.

At length, they entered a natural alley lined with trees whose circumference hinted at ages of two hundred years or more. Blending together with the shrubs, they arched overhead, forming a bower. Beams of moonlight filtered through its leafy roof, illuminating the pathway hemmed in by the lush foliage and trees.

Closing her eyes, she inhaled. Sweet smelling scents she could not identify filled her. She savored the pure and delicious aroma just before stumbling across a root.

Her eyes flew open as O'Connor grasped her elbow in support.

"Thank you," she said.

"You are all right?"

She flexed her ankle. "Yes."

Carefully placing her foot on the ground, she looked up. Their gazes caught and held.

An owl searching for dinner used his dense downy plumage to fly close to them without making a sound. He hooted his irritation at their intrusion of his domain. Constance squealed, jumping toward the American and away from the piercing screech. O'Connor emitted a grunt of amusement.

She tightened her lips. "When can I see the governor?"

"As soon as I can find the time to take you to his plantation."

"When will that be?"

"Probably in November."

Jerking her elbow out of his clasp, she took a step back. "November! That's five months from now. I can't wait that long. I have to see him tomorrow."

"Impossible."

She gasped. "I demand it!"

"Demand all you want. I've a tobacco farm to run. That takes precedence over running around the countryside on some wild goose chase. Meanwhile, I suggest you acclimate yourself to the fact that by the law of this land, I own you and I will do as I please."

"But, the ship," she sputtered. "The captain. You said, I thought, my lack of papers and . . . Well, you *must* let me speak with him tomorrow."

"Talking with the governor will do you no good. He won't free you without my consent."

"Then give him your consent. Or leave him out of it all together. Pray, just free me and be done with it."

He shook his head. "I am not a fool, little Lady of the Realm. I will send a message to your so-called father. If and when I hear from him will be time enough to release you."

She stilled. She'd hoped for something a bit more expedient than the time it would take for a missive to reach her father. If a message was sent back with the ship, however, her father, even displeased, would send someone as soon as he received word. "You want not to marry me?"

He snorted. "I assuredly do not."

"Will you send a message on the *Randolph* before it sails?"

He gave her a long pointed look before acquiescing. "I will."

He will? *He will*. She smiled. Really smiled. It was the first time she'd done so since this whole ordeal began. Lifting her hands above her head, she leaned her face toward the heavens and twirled in a circle. The kerchief around her head slipped off.

Closing her eyes, she stopped spinning and offered up a word of prayer and thanksgiving. She opened her eyes to find O'Connor frozen in the pathway.

"Thank you," she whispered. "I am truly grateful."

He gave no indication of having heard her.

She searched the ground for her kerchief. She would have a devil of a time cramming all her intractable hair back into it. Scooping up the limp piece of fabric, she hugged it to her chest. Her throat filled. Lord willing, she'd be home for Christmas.

With her arms hiked up to replace the kerchief upon her head, she moved toward O'Connor. When he eyed the uncovered expanse of her neck, her steps slowed.

He remained still, his focus riveted on her person. She surreptitiously tried to adjust her bodice, peeked through her lashes at the man, then winced. The boor's stare held a most unsettling mixture of mortification and fascination.

She stopped.

Studying her intently, he took two hesitant steps toward her, closing the distance between them.

Heavy, moist air pressed against her, smothering her with its warmth. She took a deep breath. "Are you all right, sir?"

"How many years are you?"

"Why, ten and nine."

"You have red hair."

Blinking in confusion, she lifted a hand to the wisps of hair escaping the kerchief's confines. "It's auburn."

"It's red. And you have freckles as well."

She gasped and covered her cheeks with her hands. A pox on those wretched freckles. Even in the shade, she had simply to be touched by a warm breeze and out they'd pop like fireworks exploding in a starless sky. Still, even the sailors hadn't been so uncouth as to mention it.

His brows drew together in a frown. "They're even on your hands."

Jerking her hands down, she straightened. That he could see them by the light of the moon alone made her humiliation all the worse.

He looked from her face to her shoulders to the bare expanse above her bodice. After an almost imperceptible pause, he shook his head and turned back to the path.

She released the breath she hadn't realized she'd been holding. *Of all the ill-bred, audacious, uncivilized individuals,* she thought.

She watched him disappear around a bend in the path. He wasn't as filthy and openly crude as Emmett had been, nor did he fill her with disgust and trepidation the way Emmett had. But the truth was, she knew absolutely nothing about this O'Connor person. Was he trustworthy? Would he really send Father a missive or was he simply humoring her?

Maybe she should go back. Back to the captain and Arman. Back to pease and loblolly. Back to the damp, dank hold that was now deserted.

She shuddered. She couldn't. She wouldn't. And for what? For the off chance the governor would come on board and hear her pleas? The pleas of a runaway bride and possible felon?

What if the captain did indeed simply take her to the next port and sell her once again for a hogshead of tobacco leafage?

She scrutinized the path from whence she had come. Maybe she should try to slip away. The bower-covered alley would be easy enough to follow, but beyond that, she wasn't sure. Where would she go? What kind of wild creatures lurked in these forests? What of the savages she'd heard so much about?

She stood for several more moments in indecision. *What do I do, Lord? What do I do?* No answer was forthcoming.

The croaking, hooting, and howling of the night increased tenfold. A twig snapped a few yards away. There was nothing for it. Raising her chin, she lifted her gown and followed the path Mr. Drew O'Connor had tread.

THREE

Drew emerged from the natural bower into the sudden burst of moonlight. Flooded with a sense of gratification for what his father had accomplished before him, Drew looked upon the one-room cottage where he'd grown up. He took a deep breath, relishing the rush of love and well-being the home induced. Built in the old wattle-and-daub style, it nestled in a clearing amidst a handful of tall girdled trees.

A hint of smoke swirled out of the clay chimney on one end, while a large pile of firewood lay neatly stacked against the other. A hairless rabbit skin stretching across the square window provided a screen, of sorts, for those sleeping inside.

His brother sat on the oak chopping block in the yard, resting his elbows on his knees. Drew smiled to himself. An incurable optimist, that was Josh. If a thunderstorm came, Drew would anticipate a flood, Josh a rainbow.

Drew thought back to how inseparable they'd been as boys, one the perfect complement of the other. As men, their bond made a natural progression to partnership in the tobacco trade. Drew farmed with passion and voracity, while Josh exploded on the factoring market with a natural ability others merely dreamed of. It was good to have his brother back home after this last bout in England.

Josh removed the toothpick from his mouth. Beneath his hat, dark blond hair curled down beyond his shoulders. "Where is she?"

Drew shrugged. "A few lengths back."

Josh frowned. "Did you tell her to stay on the path? Even though it's dark, snakes still frequent the area."

"What's the point? Her chances for survival are next to nothing."

"Not that bad, surely."

Drew dropped Constance's clothing and diary on the bench by the cottage door. "You've forgotten. Not many women make it once they're sold. Only one out of every three. Only the heartiest. Only the strong. More often than not, only the orneriest of the lot."

Returning the toothpick to his mouth, Josh clamped down on the slender piece of wood. "Just because Leah didn't survive here doesn't mean every woman will meet the same fate."

Drew stiffened. "Leah has nothing to do with it."

"That's an out-and-out lie, and well you know it. It's been nigh on three years since her death, well past time you got over it."

Drew picked up Constance's diary and thumbed through it. It was too dark to read, of course, but no matter, for visions of Leah infiltrated his thoughts. Her quiet beauty transformed into a stark lifeless form, pale against the corn-silk color of her hair as they sealed her in a pine box and lowered her six feet into the ground.

A great knot formed in his stomach. He hated to see the spark and vitality snuffed from the redhead as well. With staunch resolve, he closed Constance's diary. All he need do was keep his distance, and perhaps the cessation of yet another life wouldn't affect him. He'd made that mistake once. He wouldn't make it again. "The wench will be dead before one season's passed."

Josh rolled his eyes. "You don't know that."

"Care to place a wager on it?"

"All right," Josh agreed. "If she's still alive after her seasoning, I win and you have to marry her. If she's dead, you win and I'll have to marry her."

Drew tossed the diary back on the bench. "Very amusing and very safe, considering your betrothed is breathlessly awaiting your return to England."

"So she is." Josh rubbed the stubble on his cheeks. "Well, are you going to marry her or not?"

Drew scowled. "Not. She'll just have to be our servant."

"But she's not a servant, not according to the terms for this shipload of women. The women on the *Randolph* were sold as tobacco brides, not as indentured servants, and well you know it. But you didn't want a bride, did you, Drew?" Josh's eyes snapped with annoyance. "No, you've sworn off women forever, so you say, and because of it you sent *me* on some hair brained mission to scour the prisons until I found a woman who wasn't a hardened felon, was being deported, but would be unable to wed." He spit the toothpick out, watching its arched flight to the ground. "Well, I did that, big brother. I found one

Mary Robins, just for you. Wasted weeks upon weeks doing so, in fact."

Drew refused to look away from the anger in Josh's expression. He deserved it and more. His brother had followed his directives with no questions asked, but now all would be voiced and, in fairness, Josh had every right to do so. Therefore, he'd stand here and take whatever his brother dished out—at least for a while.

Josh tightened his jaw. "Then what do you do the first blasted day I get back?" A silence frothed with tension encompassed the glade. "You play recklessly at cards and end up winning a bride. A *marriageable* bride. Now you have two women while others have none." He shook his head, all the bluster and anger seeming to leave him with a whoosh of his breath. "The council won't stand for it, Drew. You're going to have to marry this new one."

Drew stared at his brother with passionless eyes. "No."

Resting one elbow on his knee, Josh searched the wood shavings for a fresh toothpick. "Why not?" Fingering one sliver, then another, he decided on a third. "Aren't you tired of being a virgin? Don't you think a man of twenty-eight years ought to have long since—"

"Enough!" Drew whipped off his hat. "My convictions run a different course from yours. Playing the town bull when you reach England may seem like the ultimate freedom to you, but not to me."

Josh averted his eyes. "I'm not judging you. I'm merely vexed with your pining for Leah. She wasn't your wife— she was your betrothed." He rubbed the back of his neck. "She's dead, Drew. Dead. Why can't you get over it?"

Drew slowed his breathing. "Have you forgotten that

we used to be a family of nine? Have you forgotten the death rate in this settlement? Have you forgotten we're parentless, with only Sally and Grandma left?"

"Don't forget Nellie. She's still alive," Josh said softly.

"True. But she's married now and no longer under my care."

"You haven't answered my question."

Drew tunneled his fingers through his hair. "Would I like a woman to call my own? Of course. But from what I've seen, they aren't worth the trouble."

Unwanted images of Constance bombarded him. He hated red hair, and she was a walking beacon. Yet, heaven help him, when he'd seen her on deck and again when her kerchief slipped off, he'd felt the impact clear to his toes.

And those unsightly freckles. They were everywhere. Still, he'd stood staring at her like a woodcock. By trow, when she'd adjusted her bodice he'd not been able to move, much less breathe.

He glanced at Josh. "I don't want a woman if I have to helplessly watch her, and then our offspring, die."

"Then if not for the benefit of an heir, why are you so set on building a grand plantation home?"

"What would you have me do with all that timber Father had us split last year? It's seasoned now and ready to be used."

"There are plenty who would purchase it from you."

Setting his hat back upon his head, Drew stared at the forest of trees just beyond the clearing. "Father made me promise him I'd build it. Not just any home, mind you. He made me promise to build the one he had drawn up. The one he'd purchased all those nails for. The one with three levels plus a brick cellar."

After a moment of speechlessness, Josh snapped his mouth shut. "When did he extract that promise from you?"

Drew heaved a long sigh. "While you were away. He was on his deathbed, writhing in pain. I couldn't deny him."

A soft breeze grazed his face while stirring the fuzzy leaves of the mulberry tree on his left. He plucked a cluster of dark purple fruit from amongst the sheltering heart-shaped leaves.

A tiny stream of sweet juicy nectar trickled from his lips. Wiping his sleeve across his chin, he popped another berry into his mouth. The vibrato of a nearby frog suddenly ceased, leaving the clearing strangely quiet.

Josh slapped his hands on his knees and indicated the bower with his head. "Shouldn't she be here by now?"

Drew shrugged.

Focusing on the worn pathway, Josh squinted his eyes. "What did you think of her red hair?"

Drew's jaw tightened.

Josh's eyes lit with amusement. "Would you like to know what she's like?"

He offered no response.

"Spirited. She's very spirited."

Drew flipped the stem of the berry cluster away.

"Of course, throughout the voyage the men and women were kept on separate decks so I didn't spend as much time with them as I did the men. And the men—well, you'll be right pleased with the men I recommended. With them, your house will be constructed before a year's passed."

Drew refused to give in to the baiting. Where was she anyway? She should be here by now.

"Still," Josh continued, "I slipped down to the lower deck fairly often to ensure one Mary Robins was fed." He stretched out his legs, crossing them at the ankles. "They were chained next to each other, you know. Mary and your redhead."

Drew glared at his brother.

"It's true. So, I'm in a uniquely qualified position to know exactly how spirited she is." He pursed his lips. "Actually, she's a bit more than spirited. Indeed, she's a regular hoyden. But I like her. Truly, I do."

At that moment, Constance trudged into the clearing. Drew allowed his gaze to travel from her partially covered hair to the tips of her bare toes. Her faded tunic was coated with layers of grime and far too snug to provide decent coverage.

His brother stood and offered a slight bow. "How do you do, Lady Constance?"

She collapsed onto the stump Josh had vacated, glancing between the two of them. "You are relations? But of course. I should have realized. Well, how do you do?"

The corner of Josh's mouth tipped up. "Fine, my lady. And you?"

"Don't encourage her, Josh." Scowling, Drew turned to her. "We do not use titles here in the colonies. You will be addressed as all the other servants until we hear from your 'father,' if we ever do."

He watched her struggle to tuck an unruly bundle of curls back under her kerchief. "How am I to be addressed, then?"

"Constance."

She gasped. "You cannot be serious. I will not allow it."

"It is either that or wench," he said, eyes narrow. "If

you do not respond to your Christian name, rest assured I will call you by the other."

She compressed her lips. "And what, pray tell, are you to be addressed as?"

"Master Drew."

"I will call no man *master*. I have only one master and He resides up above."

"Well, you have two now."

The cottage door opened and closed. Drew looked back. The woman Josh had contracted for him stood illuminated in the moon's refulgence.

"Mary," Constance breathed.

Jumping to her feet, Constance hurried to the other woman's side. What an incongruous picture the embracing women made. One tall with an aura of strength, the other petite and painfully feminine.

"I'm so glad to see you!" Constance cried.

"Whatever are you doing here?" Mary responded.

Josh cleared his throat. "We've a bit of a problem, ladies. Seems my brother has acquired two women instead of one."

Taking two strides, Drew grasped his brother's arm. "Josh . . . ladies, why don't we step away from the cottage so we don't wake Grandma and Sally." He tightened his grip. "Shall we?"

At the edge of the clearing, he released Josh with a little shove. "Now that you've wagged your tongue, you may explain it to them."

"Explain what?" he asked. "That you accidentally won Lady Constance in a wager? That everyone present, other than our little redhead, knows you never had any intention of wedding Mary from the start? That the

menfolk in the colony are going to hang you by your toes
when they hear? Or that Grandma will do even worse?"

Drew gritted his teeth. "Never mind. I will explain
it to them."

Josh rounded his eyes. "By all means."

"Ladies," Drew began, "I won Constance in a wager
and have no intention of marrying either one of you."

Josh burst out laughing.

"Joshua!" Drew hissed. "Lower your voice. Grandma
might waken, and I have no desire to deal with her tonight over this mishap."

"Certainly," he allowed. "I wouldn't dream of waking
Grandma. Especially not after you went to the extent of
leaving Lady Constance in that hold half the night simply
to ensure Grandma would be well and truly asleep when
you brought her home!"

"Enough!"

Josh clamped his mouth shut, but mirth lurked within
his eyes. Drew gave his attention back to the women.
"Have you any questions?"

"I'd like a bath now, please," Constance said. "You
do have a sponge and bowl I presume?"

Drew tightened his lips. "All the captives bathed before
the ship docked."

"In salt water. It was most unpleasant. Besides, the
boat . . . well, it had a particular stench to it. I thought
once I disembarked the odor would take leave. It didn't.
Unless, of course, it's you I'm smelling and not me."

His face warmed by several degrees. "As it happens,
Miss Lady of the Realm, my dear mother, God rest her
soul, had a peculiar penchant for cleansing one's person
on a regular basis. Josh and I wash every day."

Constance gasped. "Every day! Surely you jest. Why, it's unhealthy to bathe so often. It will extract the oils from your skin and . . . and . . . I don't know what all."

"I'll tell you what all. It extracts the livestock from one's head and the layers of grime from one's person. My mother's been gone nigh on three years, but I haven't missed a dip in the creek any day during the warm weather or any Sunday during the cold."

"Dip in the creek?" she squealed. "You *submerge* yourself in the water?"

"I do."

"That's, that's . . ." She crossed herself.

"We expect the same from our servants."

Josh's eyebrows lifted. Mary fanned herself with her hand.

Constance blanched. "Absolutely not. Under no circumstances will I submerge myself in a creek or in anything else for that matter. I've no objection to bathing. But a sponge and bowl will serve. I will *not*, however, descend beneath water of any kind."

He gave her a parody of a smile. "Care to place a wager on it?"

She looked frantically at Josh. "Is he serious?"

Josh shrugged. "He looks it to me."

Drew held back his smile of satisfaction. "Do you still wish for a bath, little Lady of the Realm?"

She took a slow deep breath. After a moment of silence, she inclined her head. "Yes. But, a bowl and sponge will more than suffice."

He glanced at Josh. "Take Constance to the creek so she can wash her face and prepare to retire."

Stepping forward, Josh offered her his arm. "My lady?"

Drew scowled. Constance hesitated.

"No dunking tonight," Josh whispered. "I give you my word."

Studying his eyes for a moment, she accepted his arm and followed him to the creek.

Drew turned back to Mary. "Did Grandma give you a blanket to bed down on?"

"Yes, sir."

"Good. You'll need to fashion some sleeping ticks haste, posthaste."

"Yes, sir."

He removed his hat to scratch the back of his head, then replaced it. She stood with head bowed, hands clasped. A kerchief hid most of her dark brown hair.

"Why is your head bowed?"

She lifted her face, keeping her eyes downcast. "It's disrespectful to be looking you in the eye, sir."

The moonlight softened features grown old before their time. She probably wasn't more than one score, yet lines creased her forehead and the corners of her mouth.

"Here in Virginia, you needn't worry over formalities such as those. You may look at me, Mary, whenever you please."

Slowly, she swept up her lashes. Huge brown eyes focused on his hat, not quite meeting his eyes. The round pecan-colored orbs were by far her best feature.

"You know I have no need for a bride," he said, then blew a puff of air from his lungs. "I am in need of a woman, though."

Her gaze moved from his hat to his eyes. "I see," she whispered.

He felt the heat creep up his neck. "No, no. You misunderstand. I mean I need a woman to cook, keep my house, keep my garden, and take charge of my young sister."

She lowered her chin. "That will pose no problem, sir."

By troth, he had embarrassed her. "You did know I purchased ten men and plan to pick them up in the morning? They'll be quite hungry."

"I will see to it, sir."

"Thank you, Mary," he sighed.

"Certainly, sir."

"You may return to your slumber."

"Thank you, sir."

He watched her walk to the cottage. Though somewhat gaunt, her tall, straight form gave the overall impression of a woman built from staunch and hardy stock.

He nodded. She'd do just fine. Turning his attention to the well-worn trail, he headed toward the creek.

"Ah! If it isn't the lucky bridegroom," Josh exclaimed.

Drew growled.

Sitting on the bank, Constance twisted around to see if the men would come to blows. Drew looked willing enough. Josh, however, propped his shoulder against a tree.

"Easy, Drew. I was just wondering when the marriage would be performed."

"Vex me no more, Josh, else I'll knock out your brains."

"You last did that when I was only a lad. You wouldn't have such an easy time of it now."

Constance turned back to the creek. Fringed with

trees and a variety of other foliage, the contour of its indented bank dipped and swelled at random. A crudely formed raft moored several feet away bumped against the shoreline.

Nudging her sleeves up, she trailed her fingers through the still water. The night light shimmered across the ripples she'd created. Leaning forward, she splashed a bit of water onto her thirsty skin, relishing its cool tranquillity.

"All I see is a man who needs to be unbuttoning his doublet after supper," Drew sneered.

"Me? Ha! If you're not careful, your guts will surely come tumbling about your knees."

"You impudent, hairy nothing. I've a Herculean stomach."

"Herculean! What rubbish."

Casting a quick glance back at the men, Constance judged the distance separating her from them. Not too close, but not very far either. She shrugged. It would have to do.

Turning her back to them, she loosened her bodice, perched on the bank, and cupped handfuls of the cold, refreshing water into her palms. With care, she poured the water over her face and neck, running her hands across them. It was absolutely divine.

"Consider, you walking gorbelly, I still top you by a good three inches."

"True," Josh agreed. "But what I lack in height, I make up for with nimble feet."

Sighing, Constance began to retie her bodice. Their sparring would surely come to a close soon and she didn't fancy being caught with an open gown. She pulled at the laces with all her strength. She hadn't realized how difficult it would be to do without Mary's help. She pulled again, holding the laces together with one hand and trying to retie the bodice with the other.

"Drew, you're still upset. I would have you at an unfair advantage."

"Humph. Your wit is as fat and lazy as your belly."

Constance heard a chuckle, then a playful whack. She could not close the gap. Frantically she pulled, willing the fabric to come together. "Oh!" she gasped.

One of the laces broke. She stared in horror at the limp piece of cording in her hand, then closed her eyes in mortification. The other half of the broken lace fell out of its housing.

"Lady Constance?"

"Josh, do not address her that way again."

There was a moment of silence.

Biting her lower lip, she tried to pull the bodice together with her hands. In the process, the rest of the lacings loosened. She choked.

"Constance?" Josh asked. "Are you all right?"

She heard a stirring behind her. "Constance?"

"No!" she whimpered. "Stay back!"

The movement stopped.

"What is it?" Drew asked.

She pulled with her hands. It only worsened the dilemma.

"What are you doing?" Drew's voice sounded right behind her.

Crisscrossing her arms, she tucked her chin and hunched over. "Go away." Her plea was muffled.

She heard his knees crack when he bent down beside

her, then felt him tentatively place his hand upon the small of her back. She very nearly fell into the water from the shock of it.

"Are you in pain?" he asked.

"Yes. Go away."

He stayed where he was. "What ails you?"

"Oh, you big oaf. Just go away."

"Constance?" This from Josh, now kneeling on her other side. "Is it your woman's pains?"

"Ohhhhh," she cried. And here she thought the situation could not get any worse.

"Joshua!" Drew cried. "You overgrown puke stocking. Have you taken leave of your senses? Use a little discretion, if you please."

"Oh, a pox on it. She's your blasted bride—you take care of her."

Constance heard the unmistakable sound of Joshua's retreat, then silence. If it had not been for Drew's palm burning a hole through her back, she would have thought he'd gone as well. No such luck.

"Are you in great pain or just a little pain?"

She peeked out from above her arm. "Are we alone?"

He looked disconcerted. "Are you planning on doing me in?"

She smiled despite herself. "Not right now."

"We are alone."

She breathed a sigh of relief. "I have need of your jerkin."

His eyes widened. "I beg your pardon?"

"May I please wear your jerkin?" she asked, lips tight.

"Wear my jerkin? Whatever for?"

"My bodice seems to have fallen apart." Sneaking

out one hand, she wiggled the broken lace between her fingers.

He jumped up and back. "By trow, woman."

Before she could blink, he dropped his jerkin in front of her and turned his back. She stayed still for a moment to assure herself of his intentions. When his back remained turned, she snatched the jerkin off the ground, slipped it on, and stood.

The sleeveless jerkin swallowed her whole. The deep V in the front, however, provided no cover. She turned the garment around. Much better.

The surprisingly soft leather brushed against her. It smelled of sunshine, sweat, and the great outdoors. It smelled of the man who wore it.

"Thank you," she whispered.

He glanced over his shoulder before facing her. "You have it on backward."

Heat flooded her face. "Yes."

His Adam's apple bobbed nervously. "Your laces broke?"

She did not think her face could burn any hotter. Still, she refused to explain to this barbarian her compelling need to wash away all vestiges of her dreadful ordeal. She nodded.

His attention fell on everything but her. He raked his fingers through his hair. "It's too late for a thorough washing tonight. You may have one in the morning, though."

She chewed on her lower lip and wiped her hands on the jerkin. "With a sponge and bowl?"

His gaze settled on her face. "With a rag and bucket."

She took a deep breath. "Thank you. That would greatly please me."

A waft of air swept the path, strewing a few curls across her face and rustling the underbrush around them. A weeping willow's long tassels swayed gently behind him as he rubbed his eyes, muttering, "What folly."

After a moment, he peered at her wearily. "I have no need for a bride. I especially have no need for an additional woman. You'll simply have to make yourself useful as best you can. For now, help with the cooking and upkeep of the cottage."

"I don't know how to cook."

His eyes narrowed slightly. "And why is that?"

"I never had reason to do so."

"No need for food, have you?"

She tipped up the corners of her lips. "On the contrary, I'm quite fond of food."

"But not of cooking."

"It's not a matter of fondness. It's a matter of know-how. I know not how to cook."

"What do you know?"

"Stitching."

"Nothing else?"

"I'm rather talented with numbers."

"Well, praise be. And here I've been worrying you were worthless."

"Quite so."

Drew contemplated the enigma before him. She couldn't possibly be telling the truth. No gently bred woman would allow her hair to flow with such abandon from her kerchief. No gently bred woman would loosen her bodice with two men mere feet away. No gently bred woman would have survived the passage over. If she was an earl's daughter, he was a king's son.

Still, no common born female would know how to read and write. No common born female would speak in such a refined manner. No common born female would have asked for a washbowl instead of a bucket.

"Are you, by any chance, the *illegitimate* daughter of an earl?"

She gasped. "How dare you! Why, you wouldn't know the queen of England if she were staring you in the face!"

"Answer my question."

"I shall not dignify that question with an answer."

Brushing her skirt to the side, she swept past him and set off down the path—in effect, dismissing him. Well, by trow, he was the master here. The sooner she understood that, the better.

Tightening his lips, he took several great strides, hooked his arm around her waist and lifted her up off the ground. She reacted with vehemence—shrieking, struggling, kicking, scratching, and biting. He wasted no time in releasing her.

She whirled around, crouched and ready to spring. "I have been torn from my homeland, chained in a hold with fifty female felons, sold as a bride, and bartered for in a card game. Suffice it to say I am not in the most tolerant of moods. Touch me again and I'll not be held responsible for my actions."

"You most certainly will. I am your master in all things. How you fare here will be the direct result of how I decide to treat you. Because the majority of the women in this settlement are former criminals, the means by which we control them are somewhat barbaric. Before, I never advocated such treatment, but at this moment, I am rapidly reassessing my stand. Do not ever walk away from me when I've asked you a question."

She spun around and marched off. He hesitated only a moment before swooping down upon her from behind. He twisted to take the brunt of the fall, then quickly rolled her beneath him. "Are you the illegitimate daughter of an earl?"

She snaked her arms up between them and pushed with a respectable amount of strength. "I wish that you did itch from head to foot and I had the scratching of thee. I would make you the loathsomest scab in all of England."

"We're in the colonies. Now answer my question."

She spit in his face. Wiping his cheek with his shoulder, he allowed more of his weight to rest upon her and bracketed her cheeks with his hands. She stilled.

"Do not *ever* do that again. Do I make myself clear?"

He saw her gathering the spittle within her mouth. He narrowed his eyes. "I dare you."

Ah. A response at last. She swallowed her spittle.

"Are you the illegitimate daughter of an earl?"

"I am not."

He hesitated. She'd answered his question. He'd won the skirmish. Now he should release her.

He stayed where he was. Of course, the leather jerkin he'd lent her may as well have been a suit of armor, for it completely disguised any curves she might possess. But a single beam of moonlight captured her face in its gentle palm. And he took his time exploring her features at such close range.

If he ignored the freckles, she was really quite comely. Her delicately shaped face was graced with a pert and dainty nose, and never in his life had he seen eyelashes so long. Long and not red, exactly, but a sort of rusty shade, like her eyes.

Oh, but her eyes were something. Big, luminous, and far too intelligent.

She moistened her generously curved lips.

He panicked at the reaction that induced. "I suppose Mary can do the cooking and cottage. You may see to the garden and my young sister."

"You're too kind."

He crooked up one corner of his mouth. Ah, victory was sweet. Rising, he turned and headed down the path—in effect, dismissing *her*.

FOUR

Constance opened her eyes. An exquisite child stared at her with wide-eyed innocence. The moppet's pearl-like complexion glowed with exuberance and charm. Thick jet-black curls fell past her shoulders.

Constance lifted her head.

In an immediate attempt to scramble back, the child plopped to the floor. A puff of dirt billowed around the shapeless sack that served as her dress. Drawn in at the neck and wrists with a narrow cotton ferret, the primitive gown concealed the child's build. If her heart-shaped face and delicate hands were any indication, the garment encompassed a petite frame.

Constance smiled.

Springing to her feet, the child ran out of sight.

Constance allowed her head to fall back on the pallet and sighed. How wonderful it was to wake up in unmoving quiet. No tipping deck that continuously swayed to and fro, no feet sounding on the upper decks, no stifling hold with everyone's irons rattling and banging about.

After a moment, she became cognizant of the household awakening. A whispered exchange. A muted padding from one spot to another. A crackling fire. Turning her head, she glanced toward the fire and discovered Mary hunching over its embers.

Her friend stirred the contents of a peculiar frying pan perched on three curved spiderlike legs. With a thick cloth in hand, she rearranged several wrapped objects sitting amongst the coals.

Dearest Mary. Had it not been for her, Constance never would have survived the passage over. What a pleasant surprise to find the good Lord had seen fit to keep them together. It would make everything so much easier, for both of them. Constance inhaled deeply. The savory trail of the morning's meal drifted to her.

Propping herself on her elbows, she canvassed the rustic cottage. She had seen next to nothing in the darkness of the night before. The light now seeping through a square hole in the cottage's wall provided a bit of visibility.

At one time, this sparse one-room cottage with crudely made furniture would have surely caused a wrinkling of her nose. But compared to the hard deck she had slept upon for these last two months, the complete blackness that filled the hold and the enclosed air soured by the sick, this thatch-roofed dwelling was more like a palace.

A long table with two benches made of split logs, flat side up, sat shoved against one wall. A low platform built into one corner of the room marked the only bed in evidence. Puzzled, she looked for the family's sleeping quarters, but found none. Opposite the bed sat a long wooden trunk. Clothing and utensils hung on a few pegs driven into the walls. She took it all in, her confusion mounting, until finally she noticed a split-pole ladder propped up against a small loft at the far end of the cottage.

The fire popped. Constance turned back to Mary. The fireplace took up one entire wall. Its hearth, made of flat rock, contrasted sharply with the mixture of clay and grass baked around the fireplace's wooden frame. An assortment of implements and pots hung from a beam and littered the hearth.

"You'd best rise, girl."

Yanking the covers to her chin, Constance sat up and twisted around.

A seasoned woman passed behind her carrying an armful of folded linens while the child clung to her skirts. Opening the trunk, the woman placed the makings of some pallets inside. "The men will be in shortly. We need to ready the cottage."

This must be the grandmother Drew had spoken of last night. She wasn't at all like Constance had pictured her. This woman carried herself with grace, holding her head high and proud. Her cheekbones, accentuated by the onset of old age, held an unnatural, but becoming, blush of pink. The child at her skirts hooked an index finger over her nose and thrust a thumb into her mouth.

Releasing the covers, Constance stood and stretched. Her old chemise hung limp on her frame and still smelled of unspeakable odors. After the disaster with her bodice last night, she'd had no choice but to garb herself in the only covering she possessed. With her fingertips, she plucked the chemise away from her body. "I was told I could make use of a bucket and rag this morning."

The woman nodded. "Fold up your pallet, then, and help me arrange the cottage."

Stepping onto the dirt floor, Constance leaned over and picked up the top bed sheet. "You live here?"

"For the time being." The old woman scrutinized her while tying together the two strings dangling from her cap. "I'm Elizabeth Lining, but everyone calls me Grandma."

"A good day to you, Grandma. My name is Lady Constance."

Grandma humphed. "We don't stand on formalities here in the colony. I'll be calling you Constance."

Constance handed the woman the folded spread. She allowed it to unfurl, then refolded it.

"Where are the men?" Constance asked.

"Washing at the creek."

She gave Grandma a quick peek, but the woman acted as if that was indeed an everyday affair. Moving to retrieve the bottom linen, Constance shook it out. Dirt surged upward.

Grandma grabbed the bedsheet. "Mercy, girl. You never shake the linen indoors."

Coughing, Constance rubbed her eye. "Your pardon."

While the dirt was settling, Grandma took the bedding outside.

Constance wasted no time in turning to Mary. "What do you know of our situation here?"

Darting a quick look at the open door and then the child, Mary wiped a hand on the tattered apron she wore around her waist. "The master contracted for me 'cause his married sister is due for a birthing right soon. The grandmother goes to care for her. So I am to care for the two masters, this little tyke, and the men."

"Men? What men?"

"The master bought ten indentured men—two of them brick layers. He's to pick them up from the ship this morn."

"When does Grandma leave?"

Mary shrugged. "They didn't say, but if I was to guess, it'd be right soon."

"Has anything been said about me?"

Mary shook her head. "Not a word, but I'm thinking the grandmother was pretty surprised to see you slumbering on the floor this morn, she was."

"Mr. O'Connor still hasn't told her about me?"

"I don't know, but it seems not. He was gone when I arose and the grandmother was still sleeping."

Constance caught a flash of brown from the corner of her eye, spun toward it, then relaxed. The little girl had wedged herself between the table and wall.

"And what's your name?" Constance asked softly.

The thumb stayed in her mouth. "Sallwee."

"Sally?" Constance squatted down.

Her curls bobbed up and down with affirmation.

"How do you do, Sally?"

The child's brow furrowed. "What's your name again?"

Constance thought a moment, sent Mary a mischievous smile, then looked back at the child. "My Lady."

Sally wound a lock of hair round and round her finger. "That's a lovely name."

"Thank you. Sally is a very lovely name too. How old are you?"

Releasing her hair, Sally held up two fingers. "Thwee."

Grandma reentered and placed the linen in the trunk. "Come, Constance, and help me move the benches and board to the middle of the room."

Constance stood and glanced about the room for the chamber pot. She could see the bed didn't have one beneath it, yet she couldn't imagine anyplace else to keep one. Perhaps they had a privy instead.

She hesitated, then moved to help Grandma. The roughhewn benches weighed a considerable amount. The table nearly did her in. Leaning on its knotted surface to catch her breath, she acknowledged there was no more time to spare. She must ask Grandma where the necessary house was located.

Looking up, the words stuck in her throat, for Drew's broad frame filled the doorway. With sunbeams shooting through the cracks between him and the doorframe, it was impossible to discern his expression.

"What goes here, Grandma?" he barked. "The wench looks as if she's just arisen. The day is calling."

"There were no instructions for this one, so I let her slumber."

Constance could not mistake the accusation in Grandma's tone, but Drew didn't have time to respond, for Sally had run straight to him, forcing him to swing her up into his arms as he stepped into the cottage. The little moppet grasped his face between her hands and kissed him straight on the lips.

Constance marveled at the softening of his features. After giving the child a squeeze, he set her on the ground, then fixed his attention on Constance. Derision replaced the tenderness she'd seen just moments before. "By my troth, woman. Get yourself ready. There's work to be done."

She narrowed her eyes and headed toward the door.

He stepped into her pathway. "Have you developed an affliction? There was certainly none last evening."

She stopped. "Your pardon?"

"What is wrong with your legs?"

"Nothing."

"Do not tell me a falsehood. I can see with my own eyes that you walk with a twist."

An unwelcome warmth crept into her cheeks. She should have gone to the necessary immediately upon rising. Brushing past him, she barely made it beyond the threshold in a seemly manner. Once outside, she half ran, half hobbled to the back of the cottage, then stopped short. The *master* nearly knocked her over in his effort to follow.

She scanned the clearing. Nothing here but a fenced in garden and a chicken coop. Beyond that, a legion of trees, shrubs, and vines caged in the little homestead they'd made for themselves.

"What's the matter?" he asked. "Did you not expect to see a great forest blocking your escape route?"

Maybe it was on the other side of the cottage. She hustled around to the side. He dogged her progress.

Situated a bit beyond the cottage was a crude but sturdy-looking structure. It looked much like a lean-to, but was freestanding. Its wattle-and-daub walls led to a thatched roof sloping downward in one direction. By faith, it was too big for a necessary house.

"What in the devil are you doing?" he demanded.

"It's a morning ritual I have," she answered, squeezing her legs together.

He spun her around. "Well, we have a morning ritual of breaking the fast. So I regret to inform you that my ritual takes precedence over yours. Now get back in that cottage and help with the preparations."

Oh, Lord, forgive my boldness. She took a deep breath. "Where is your house of office?"

He looked stunned. She blushed with mortification.

Throwing back his head, he let out a great howl of laughter. "Is that your affliction?"

"Yes!" she snapped. "Now where is it!"

Swiping at the water in his eyes, he spread his arms wide. "You are looking at it."

It was her turn to be stunned. "Surely you do not mean you have none!"

"That is exactly what I mean. I'll not waste good lumber on a privy when I can dig a hole just past the clearing."

Her cheeks burned again, but she wasted no more than a moment contemplating his revelation. If she found out later that he had lied, there would be the devil to pay. She plunged into the copse.

"Watch out for the poison weed," he yelled.

Poison weed?

"It is three-leafed—much in the shape of the English ivy!"

She quickly scanned the area for any three-leafed ivy.

"If it brushes up against you, you will develop a nasty itching that quickly spreads all over your person!" His chuckle from well beyond the trees riled her shattered sensibilities.

Imagine! Bellowing at her like that and—even worse—*knowing* that entire time what she was attending to. It didn't bear thinking of.

Obstinate man. She should have gone back to the ship last night. And what of last night? Wresting her to the ground in order to obtain an answer from her, then just up and leaving. Barbaric. And the ridiculous question of her legitimacy! Well, by troth, she had set him straight on that issue.

Unbidden, his face loomed over hers within her mind. It had surprised her last night by softening somehow. Much like it had this morning with Sally. And with the softening came the dimple.

She'd studiously tried to ignore it, but there was no ignoring it this morning when he greeted his little sister. Why she'd ever found dimples attractive, she couldn't imagine.

Shaking out the hem of her chemise, she cautiously made her way back toward the clearing, watching for any signs of English ivy.

The lushness of the land cushioned her bare feet. So caught up was she in the bounty beneath her feet, she almost missed a little blackbird scavenging for its morning meal.

Bless me—a blackbird with red shoulders! Slowing her steps, she shaded her eyes while it darted from the forest floor into the dense treetops. By the time she followed its path from oak to cedar to poplar, she'd returned to the clearing.

Drew was, thankfully, gone. Looking down, she took abrupt note of her appearance. She had on only her chemise. Her hair hung down her back in a braid and her bare toes peeked out with each step. She must repair herself at once.

Back inside the cottage, she stood a moment adjusting to the relative darkness. Of all the shadows merging and materializing, it was Drew's that first took shape.

He leaned against the wall, a pail dangling from his outstretched fingertips. "Since Grandma and Mary have the preparation of breakfast in order, you may go and milk the goat."

Milk the goat! She gaped at him before blushing anew at her state of disrepair.

"You'll end up having to do it for her, Drew," Grandma said. "I'll attend to it for now and you can show her some morning when you've more time."

Constance scanned the cottage. Where the devil was her clothing?

Setting down the pail, Drew walked to the wall behind her and plucked the skirt she'd worn last night off a peg. "Is this what you are in need of?"

She whirled around. Snatching it out of his hands, she held it up against her like a shield. He smiled. Sweet heavens, he had not one dimple, but two.

"Where is the bodice?" she asked.

His eyes flickered. "I fear it's not of much use to you. Wear the skirt and chemise without it."

She gasped. "'Twould be indecent!"

He arched a brow. "Not nearly as indecent as if you tried to stuff yourself into that bodice again."

Saints above, these ill-bred colonists would say anything. Even the grandmother's presence did not temper their wagging tongues. "If you've but a length of cord, I can manage fine."

He chuckled. "It's not just a length of cord you're needing but an entire bolt of cloth."

Suppressing a groan, she dropped the issue and quickly searched for a place in which she could dress. Grandma and Mary bustled around the fire. Sally sat on the floor grinding meal with mortar and pestle. Did they do everything together in this primitive little room?

She turned back to Drew. "Be gone. I must dress."

"Miss Constance, Lady of the Realm, have you still not grasped the essence of your position here? I am the master and you are the servant. When you would like to request something of me, I suggest you couch it in the sweetest of terms."

"I am not a lady of the realm."

"That is right. You are a servant. The sooner you accept that, the more pleasant you will find your lot in life here on my farm."

"The devil's dung in thy teeth."

His smile vanished. "You will watch your language."

"I will do as I please."

"You will do as you are told or you will have no privileges."

She narrowed her eyes. "What are you saying?"

"Baths, food, and so forth are privileges awarded to those worthy of receiving them."

She didn't think so. Leaving one's servants in filth and starving them was counterproductive. "Get out. I need to dress."

He stepped forward and gently grabbed her chin. "Lesson number one: Ask with meekness and servitude."

A pox on meekness and servitude. If he were a gentleman, she wouldn't even have to ask. She kept her lips firmly sealed.

"Constance, you were bought and paid for. I have the receipt to prove it."

She jerked her chin out of his hand. "You said you would send word to my father."

"It will be at least six months until we hear back from your father."

She gasped. "Six months?!"

"Six months. Until then, you are my possession."

"Only in your own sluggish brain."

"Dear girl, it is within my rights to marry you at any time. Once that happens, you will be bound to me forever under God—father or no father."

She blanched. It had only been within the last few years that England allowed women a veto in matrimonial affairs. Had this current not penetrated the colonies? She wasn't at all sure.

"Wish you to marry me?" he asked.

"I do not!"

"Then ask me to leave in a proper manner."

In a pig's eye, I will. Hugging the dress closer to her, she opened her mouth.

He gently placed his finger over her lips. "Think, girl, before you speak."

His callused finger abraded her lips. She pushed the offending appendage away. "I wish you to go."

"Phrase it with respect."

Gritting her teeth, she impaled him with her stare. "Will you please do me the honor of leaving the cottage for a moment or two . . ." *you wretched, poisonous, bunch-backed toad*?

"Excellent." Removing a worn but clean homespun dress from a peg on the wall, he handed it to her. "Josh should be back from the creek by now. You may follow the same path as last night for your cleansing in the water. Make sure you return before the breakfast bell is rung. There's some soap on the shelf, there above the trunk."

"What of the bucket and rag?"

"Hanging there, on that peg."

Walking to the peg, she snatched up the bucket and rag. Off the shelf, she removed the soap and dropped the coarse yellowed block into the bucket. "A drying cloth?"

He retrieved a cloth from another peg.

"It's wet."

He nodded. "You have to rise early if you want first use of the drying cloth."

First use? "May I slip on my old skirt before embarking on my excursion, O Great One?"

He narrowed his eyes. "You may."

Zigzagging her gaze between him and the door, she waited. The dolt simply presented his back to her.

Setting her cloth, bucket, and fresh dress on the table, she slipped on the skirt. Drawing close, Mary silently placed a small wrapped bundle inside Constance's bucket. The sweet aroma of fresh bread surrounded the girls.

Constance glanced quickly at Drew. His back was still turned. Grandma bent over the bed tightening its ropes. Sally watched the women with unabashed curiosity, while Constance and Mary shared a smile.

Scooping up the items on the table, Constance marched out of the cottage.

Standing ankle deep in the creek, Constance sluiced the bucket of water over her with an invigorating rush, then lathered her hair and body for the third time. She didn't care if the crude soap stripped off her skin; she wanted no residue from that wretched ship left on her person.

She poured water down her body several more times, then stood with eyes closed, cataloging each part of herself. She felt a droplet of water slide down her neck, hit the upper swell of her breast, then plummet through the valley between. Placing her hands against her ribs, she grimaced at the ease with which she could delineate each one. Pressing her hands lower, she tested the flatness of her stomach, then stopped and circled around her hips and thighs. Yes, she'd lost a considerable amount of poundage, but she was clean. Blessedly clean.

Making her way to the bank, she retrieved her cloth from the bush, dried her face, then raised her chin. The sun wrapped its rays around her, enveloping her with warmth.

Never had she bathed in the daylight hours, much less out in the open. After the dark confinement of the ship, it was precisely the catharsis she needed. Not only did it give her an unprecedented sense of freedom, but it made her feel as if she were sharing this Eden with God Almighty himself.

She smiled. The thought of bathing every day wasn't nearly as daunting as it had been last night. With a satisfied sigh, she wrapped her hair up in the cloth and reached for the dress.

Unlike the dresses she was accustomed to, this home-spun frock was all one piece. The sleeved bodice had been sewn directly onto the skirt, and there was no chemise at all, nor was there need of one. She slipped it on, and though the crude material grated against her skin, never was she more appreciative of a gown. No matter that the sleeves hung below her hands or the hem drug on the ground. The cut of its bodice covered every inch of her while its cleanliness and open-air scent intoxicated her.

She wondered whose it was, then tenderly rolled up the sleeves and made a cursory effort at drying her abundance of hair. It was a useless endeavor. She threw the cloth back over a nearby bush.

At the creek's edge, she wrung out her wash cloth, watching the leftover suds butt up against the bank before scattering and eventually dissipating.

Finding a soft patch of fragrant grasses, she lay down, fanned out her curls, and studied this wilderness called America. A duck squawked at his companion and then dove beneath the water while a bird hovered above the surface, snatching the food away just as the duck reappeared.

She frowned. He should work for his own supper instead of stealing someone else's. She quickly shied away from that thought, but not quickly enough. Not before it transformed for a fraction of a second into *When have you ever worked for your own supper?*

She hastily rolled onto one elbow and turned her attention to the land. A grand maple, shouldering back a prolific beech, craned its limbs over the creek at a gravity-defying angle. Flowers of all kinds and colors grew wild within the grove, their beauty rivaling many richly designed gardens and orchards back home.

Back home. Surely she'd be back home in less than six months. She sighed. Not so for Uncle Skelly. He would *never* make it home. Not subscribing to the king's supremacy usually meant death. But because of Papa's influence, Uncle Skelly's sentence had been reduced to deportation. In the end, it hadn't mattered.

Tears coursed unchecked down her cheeks. As a young-
ster in her aunt and uncle's home, she had spent many
a candle-lit evening advancing her prowess for mathematics under Uncle Skelly's watchful eye. Only he had
understood her insatiable zeal for numbers, for he was
filled with a passion for numbers equal to her own. Or,
at least, he had been. With big dreams and high hopes,
he had seen to the editing of *The Ladies' Mathematical
Diary* every year. Even now hundreds of submissions
from mathematically talented women throughout Europe
would be arriving at Skelly's home.

She'd given her uncle an oath that she would main-
tain the publication until his return. But he wouldn't be
returning. She knew he'd never expect her to fulfill such
a promise under the circumstances. Still, she *wanted* to
carry out her obligation. In his honor. For his honor.

Swiping at her tears, she strengthened her resolve. As
long as she had a breath in her body, she would not rest
until those submissions were answered. She would use
her gift for mathematics so Skelly's dream and *Diary*
lived on. No matter the cost, she would survive in this
land until her father came for her. She must.

A squirrel scampered across the clearing just a stone's
throw from her feet, then froze. Scrutinizing her with his
unblinking stare, he twitched his tail, then spun around
and darted up a young oak. She turned her head, watching him leap from the oak to a larger, more mature tree.

The young oak once again drew her interest. Here
was something new and strong that had survived in this
land. It was about ten yards in height and had a wispy ivy
plant clinging to its trunk. The plant looked nothing like
English ivy but instead held dainty tear-shaped leaves.

She was fascinated with the regularity in which the twining plant encircled the column. If the oak's diameter at the top was, say, six inches and at the bottom one foot and the ivy twisted around the tree so that each twist was approximately ten inches apart, what would the length of the ivy be?

She studied the tender tree and its delicate vine. A soft breeze rustled its leaves and prompted a bird to take wing. She must set a quill to the question as soon as she returned to the cottage.

Burrowing down into her grassy mattress, she unwrapped the unusual smelling bread Mary had slipped her. Taking a bite, she marveled at its taste and texture. She had become so accustomed to the hard, chalky biscuit-bread of the ship that she nearly bit her tongue, so easily did her teeth sink into the bread. And then, by heavens, she needn't even chew, for it immediately melted.

Closing her eyes, she took great delight in the bread, in the sounds around her, and in the sweet smell of God's green earth. As had been the pattern for most of her life during moments of such exquisite pleasure, numbers danced in her head.

She pictured the young oak and its vine twisting its way to the top. If the hypotenuse line that the ivy moves around in equals z, and x equals the distance from the vertex to the top of the first turn—

The sound of the breakfast bell ringing across the countryside brought her back to the present. Finishing off the delectable bread, she stood, reached for both the drying towel and bucket, and headed back to the cottage.

Breakfast actually melted in his mouth. There wasn't a thing wrong with Grandma's cooking, but Mary's? Saints above, Drew had never tasted mush this good before.

"So," Grandma began, "are you going to tell me where Constance came from?"

Drew and Josh exchanged a glance. Here it comes. He'd managed to avoid Grandma thus far, but that brief respite was over. He wiped his mouth with the napkin tied around his neck. "I won her."

Grandma whipped her head around. "Won?"

He grimaced. She was so sensitive about playing cards. He pushed his mush back and forth within the confines of his trencher. Josh was going to be of no help. He and Mary, who together shared a trencher, ate with an unwarranted amount of concentration. Sally, sharing her trencher with Grandma, was oblivious. Constance had not yet returned from the creek.

"Yes," he admitted.

"Won, how?" she asked.

Focusing on his trencher, he took a bite of mush, chewed, and swallowed. "Playing one-and-thirty."

Grandma set her spoon down with meticulous care. "I hope you are jesting."

He slowly shook his head from left to right. Grandma never wasted a moment of daylight. That she would stop eating in the midst of a meal did not bode well. Even Sally began to show an interest in the conversation.

Grandma dabbed at her mouth with her cloth. "What do you plan on doing with her?"

"I know not. She claims the captain kidnapped her."

He took a deep swallow of cider from his wooden noggin. "Says she's the daughter of an earl."

Grandma stilled. "What earl?"

"Greyhame or some such nonsense."

She lifted her brows. "And?"

"And, I told her I'd send a missive to her father. So I'm bound by my word to keep her for the time being."

"For the time being? England is in the midst of a civil war. Have you any notion how long it could take for a missive to catch up with the earl? He'll be moving from one confrontation to another. Why, the girl could be here for a year or more."

"What would you have me do, Grandma?"

"What skills has she?"

Slipping a finger inside the neck of his shirt, he adjusted his collar. "That remains to be seen."

"She has no skills?"

He stiffened. "She stitches."

"Every female stitches. What *skills* has she?"

Propping an elbow on the table, he rubbed his eyes. "She claims to have a talent for numbers."

After a strained moment, he felt his ears and neck burn.

Grandma nodded. "You are being punished for dallying with the devil's books."

"Grandma," he said with a sigh, "they are playing cards, not the devil's books, and simply a form of amusement for me."

She glowered at him. "Pray tell me, are you amused now?"

He looked away. Constance walked in the door.

"Good morrow, everyone," she exclaimed. "Isn't it a

glorious day? Your weather here is quite quaint." She smiled as she hung her wet cloths on a peg.

Grandma untied her napkin. "I'm going to Nellie's."

Drew and Josh looked sharply at Grandma. "For a visit?" Drew asked. "You're going to Nellie's for a visit?"

"Where's a wooden plate for me?" Constance asked, searching the shelves.

Grandma scooted off the bench. "I'm going to Nellie's to stay."

Pulling off his napkin, Drew stood. "You cannot. Who will train Mary? Who will watch Constance?"

"'The Lord is known by the judgment He executes; the wicked is snared in the work of his own hands.'"

"Card playing is not wicked!" Drew insisted.

"Psalm 9:16," she responded.

"I know which psalm it is. David was talking about battles and victories and enemies, *not* card playing."

"'Woe unto them that are wise in their own eyes, and prudent in their own sight.'"

"By my faith, Grandma, you are testing me sorely. Now, sit down and stop this foolishness."

Grandma took two steps forward. "You will watch your tongue, young man. I agreed to train Mary, not some useless woman you acquired by wicked means."

She held up her hands, stopping his denial. "Nay. Talk no more. Nellie's babe is due any day now. She has need of me, and from the looks of this morning's fare, Mary requires no assistance. I am away."

"Grandma, please."

The tension was palpable, causing them all to jump at the pounding on the wooden door. "O'Connor? Come! We have need of your presence."

Drew scowled at the door, then looked at Josh.

Shrugging, Josh rose from the table.

Outside, four of the settlement's most influential men gathered. Drew had known them his entire life—all except for their leader, Theodore Hopkin. The governor, Sir William Berkeley, had left last month for a year's excursion to England. The Crown had sent Hopkin as his temporary replacement.

Well, at least now Drew wouldn't have to make a trip to the governor's plantation. Constance could go ahead and have her audience with him while he was here.

A fifth man stood back and to the side. It was Jonathan Emmett, the man who'd lost Constance last night in their game of one-and-thirty.

Sparing barely a glance for him, Drew looked at the others. "Is there trouble?"

Governor Hopkin furrowed his bushy gray eyebrows. "Merely a concern or two. I'm sure you can put it to rights."

Josh stepped out beside Drew. Sunlight streamed down on their secluded homestead. Oak, pine, hickory, and tulip trees towered behind the councilmen like mounted soldiers reinforcing their leaders. What Drew used to take comfort in beholding now cast a menacing shadow about them.

Hopkin cleared his throat. "Emmett, here, holds some strong accusations against you."

Drew allowed his gaze to slide past Hopkin and roam over those more familiar to him. Morden, a bear of a man, had a heart in proportion to the rest of his body— massive, generous, and malleable. Unfortunately, the preacher was nothing more than a figurehead on this council and rarely offered an opinion on anything.

Kaufman, on the other hand, held a legitimate position but reminded Drew of a thick candle with two eyes and a hook nose—fairly solid looking, but continually melting when things heated up.

Both avoided his scrutiny, while Colonel Tucker looked him square in the eye. It pleased Drew to have him here. The military man was well respected and had been particularly close to Drew's father. If mischief brewed, Tucker would bank the fire.

Hopkin pulled the waistband of his breeches up around the hill of flesh surrounding his gut. "Emmett says you succumbed to drunkenness, assaulted him, and spirited his bride away."

Drew leaned his shoulder against the doorframe. "I joined in the festivities at the meetinghouse. During the course of the day, Emmett made a wager with his bride. I won the wager and have the receipt to prove it."

"He cheated!" Emmett barked.

Drew stood straighter. "I struck Emmett for that comment yesterday. It is an untruth, and many were there to witness it."

Hopkin nodded. "May I see the receipt?"

Josh reentered the cabin to collect the voucher. Tucker's serene gaze met Drew's. Drew relaxed. Everything would be all right.

Returning, Josh handed the piece of parchment to the governor. Hopkin perused the document, then restored it to Drew. "All appears to be in order."

Emmett blustered, then quieted in the censure of the other council members.

Drew folded the document and tucked it inside his

belt. "Care you to share some cider with us? We were just breaking our fast."

Hopkin again pulled up his slipping breeches. "Actually, we've a bit more business."

Drew frowned. A scattering of chickens clucked nervously about the clearing, mirroring his confusion.

Grandma stepped out of the cottage, pouch in hand. She tilted her head in acknowledgment. "Governor. Councilmen." Looking at Emmett, she simply snorted.

"Mistress Lining," Hopkin said. "What are you about this fine day?"

"It's Nellie's time," she answered. "I'm off to tend to her for as long as she has need of me."

"You are away at this moment?" he asked, looking at her bundle.

The morning's light blazed down into her eyes. She squinted over at Hopkin. "I am."

Drew stiffened. "I will escort you, Grandma, if you will but wait until our business here is concluded."

"No need. You have the indentured men servants to fetch down at the wharf. Besides, I'm of a mind for some peace and quiet." She transferred her pouch of belongings from one arm to the other. "Good day, sirs."

Hopkin tipped his hat. "Good day, Mistress. Our prayers will be with your Nellie."

Looking at Josh, Drew tilted his head toward Grandma. Josh reached for her pouch.

She swatted his hand. "Cannot an old woman get some peace when she wants it?"

Josh lifted his brows and turned back to Drew. She must be sorely vexed to scold them in front of the others. Still, he should have expected it. He knew his late grandfather had squandered away his fortune with cards, forcing Grandma and their only daughter to come to the colonies. Though neither Grandma nor his mother had ever bemoaned their life here, Grandma always lost her perspective where cards were concerned. With an almost imperceptible lifting of his shoulders, he motioned Josh to let her go.

She wasted no time in presenting them with her back. "Don't know what all the uproar's about," she muttered, setting off down the path. "I'm not in my grave and don't plan to be anytime soon. If I wish to walk to Nellie's by myself, then so be it."

Listening to her litany, Drew felt a pang of remorse. He waited until her voice drifted off on the breeze before turning his attention back to Hopkin and the council, who were busy murmuring amongst themselves. He glanced at Josh, who shrugged in a gesture of bafflement.

"O'Connor?" Hopkin cleared his throat. "Seems the situation is more serious than we realized. 'Tis a sign from God that we arrived when we did."

A sign from God, indeed. Drew crossed his arms in front of his chest and leaned back against the cottage's frame.

"How many women have you living under your roof?" Hopkin asked.

Drew adjusted himself more comfortably against the cottage. "At the moment, two."

"I see," he said through pursed lips. "And when are you and your brother planning to marry them?"

Drew stilled, as did Josh. "They're servants," Drew replied.

A babble of voices broke out amongst the council.

Emmett's scrawny frame bristled. Hopkin held up his hands for silence. "These, uh, *servants,* they are of breeding age?"

Drew narrowed his eyes a margin or two. "They are."

Hopkin yanked down on his doublet. "And they are unmarried?"

Uncrossing his arms, Drew pulled slowly away from the cottage. "What are you getting at?"

Hopkin twisted his breeches up to his midriff. "And they are residing in this dwelling with you, Joshua, and your baby sister?"

Drew stiffened. "Where would you have me keep them, Hopkin? With the goat?"

The governor reddened.

Tucker quickly stepped forward. "Hopkin, I recommend the council discuss this matter at length before taking any undue action."

"Undue action?" Emmett screeched. "We dare not leave these immoral creatures with the unattended ladies fer even a moment. No tellin' what deviltry would take place in our absence."

Josh grabbed Drew's forearm, forcing him to check his inclination to knock out the few teeth left in Emmett's mouth.

"Enough!" Tucker exclaimed. "You are not a member of this council, Goodman Emmett, and have no voice here. Be silent."

Emmett narrowed his eyes.

"Hopkin," Tucker continued, "I insist we discuss this more thoroughly."

Hopkin wiped a bit of spittle from the corners of his mouth. "There is not much to discuss. These men are living in a climate that breeds corruption. Regardless of the character you insist they have, the fact remains that they find themselves in this situation through their own unsavory actions. That alone makes me question your opinion of their character."

"Unsavory?" Tucker asked. "The whole settlement was playing cards yesterday. Shall we pay them all a visit this morning as well?"

"Do not patronize me. No other man in this colony lives with unmarried females in an unsupervised fashion. Your outspokenness troubles me greatly. Perhaps I need to write our gracious king and suggest a replacement or two." Hopkin met each councilman's eyes in turn. "Any other objections?"

Drew looked to Tucker's colleagues for a show of support. None was forthcoming.

Expelling a wad of phlegm from his mouth, the governor turned back to Drew. "Under no conditions will the council of this settlement allow you to harbor these women in a licentious fashion."

Drew's breathing grew deep. "There is nothing licentious in keeping a cook and a woman to watch Sally."

"There is if you defile 'em!" Emmett shouted.

The council broke out in more murmurs. Tucker grabbed Emmett's shirtfront.

"Call them out here," Hopkin demanded over the confusion. "We would have a look at these *servants* you keep."

"And if I refuse?"

Silence fell upon the group. Tucker's grip on Emmett loosened.

"O'Connor, we would have a look at these servants

or you will stand before this council on charges of misconduct and risk losing all you and your father before you have worked for."

Drew's jaw tightened. Constance and Mary stepped out of the cottage. There was no doubting they'd heard every word through the cottage's uncovered window.

Drew clinched his fists as Hopkin's gaze crawled over each woman's body with slow deliberation. The chirping chatter of the blue jays and playful antics of the squirrels mocked him and the others gathered in the clearing.

Hopkin shifted his attention back to Drew. "You and your brother will either marry these women or you will have your arms broken and your tongues bored through with an awl. Then you will be banished from Virginia, relinquishing any privileges of freedom in this country. Fornication will *not* be tolerated by this council."

FIVE

Dumbfounded, Constance could only stare at Hopkin.

"Morden? Have you your Bible?" he asked.

The large man with rounded cheeks and troubled blue eyes stepped forward. "I have it."

"Then let us get on with it." Hopkin turned to Drew. "Decide which woman you will wed and which your brother weds."

Drew's face cleared of all expression. "I agree to marry one, but Josh cannot. He is betrothed, with the contract negotiated and signed."

Hopkin narrowed his eyes. "Betrothed to whom?"

"Lady Hannah Eastlick of Bowden," Josh said.

Astonished, Constance snapped her attention to him.

"Why would a lady consent to marry a simple farmer?" Hopkin sneered.

"I have the contract," he replied.

"I would see it."

Josh stepped inside the cottage, then returned with contract in hand.

Hopkin briefly reviewed it. "The date set is not until next spring."

"I plan to return for her after the tobacco's been harvested and packed."

Hopkin handed the contract back. "I like it not. Even with your brother married, the situation asks for wrongdoing."

"Be that as it may," Drew interjected, "I will be eligible to chaperon once I wed. I choose Lady Morrow." He turned to face her. "Will you be my wife?"

"I cannot." She turned quickly to the governor, bobbing in a curtsy. "Governor Hopkin, I am Lady Constance Caroline Morrow, daughter to the Right Honorable the Earl of Greyhame, My Lord Randall Christian Morrow." She reveled only for a moment in the startled silence that passed before she continued. "The captain of the *Randolph* kidnapped me. I am not a felon, nor was I commissioned to come here voluntarily as a bride."

Hopkin lifted his brows. "Kidnapped? I heard nothing of a kidnapping." He turned to Drew. "What do you know of this?"

"The captain had no transport papers for her, and Lady Morrow claims he took her by force."

Emmett shoved his way to the front. "What! More likely than not, she's a lady's maid trying to better her position here."

"Perhaps," Drew said. "Perhaps not. But can we take the chance? What happens if she is indeed the Earl of Greyhame's daughter? We would have the king's displeasure for certain."

"After Marie Bernard's escapade? I think not," Emmett argued.

Hopkin frowned. "What escapade?"

"Miss Bernard was a lady's maid to one of the queen's women," Emmett said.

"What has that to do with us?"

Emmett hooked his thumbs beneath his armpits. "Miss Bernard filched a valuable jewel from one of the royal apartments and was sentenced to death fer her trouble."

"Get to the point," Hopkin urged.

"Well, due to some fancy talkin' by her former mistress, the sentence was changed to transportation. Miss Bernard was deported and sold right here in Virginia to Goodman Bushell. After a brief time, the girlie escaped and made her way up to Watertown."

"And?"

Emmett rocked back on his heels. "This is the inter'sting part. Thinking herself well and truly free, she claimed the title of Princess Jeannette Francoise Sophie, declaring herself a sister of our dear queen."

Hopkin snorted. "How could anyone mistake a runaway for a princess?"

"Miss Bernard was a wily one, she was," Emmett replied. "She'd planned to run, so she hid away a few jewels and a medallion portrait of Her Majesty. It was some impression she made. Even promised promotions to them fools up there." His matted beard quivered. "Well, her game was up when Goodman Bushell's messenger came, raising a loud hue and cry fer *her serene highness*."

Constance felt the councilmen eyeing her. Nay, judging her. If she had managed to have a private audience with the governor, she felt she could have convinced him of her situation. But she'd been around her father's friends enough to know when men and their political decisions are under the watchful eye of others, they very rarely make sound choices.

She sighed. There was naught to do but focus on Emmett and hope her exasperation over his tale was evident.

He cackled, then patted his rail-like frame. "She was hauled from her fine quarters in Watertown and back to Bushell's, where she's servin' the rest of her term."

"If you're so certain Miss Morrow is no lady," Drew asked, "then why did you pay a whole hogshead for her?"

Emmett jutted out his chin. "'Cause a lady's maid is better'n some filthy felon."

Josh straightened. "Are you maligning Miss Robins?"

Emmett took a step back. "No, I'm just saying this talk of kidnapping is pure nonsense, and the girlie in question should be given back to me."

Back to him? Emmett thought to get her back? Absolutely not. She wouldn't allow it.

"Enough, Emmett," Hopkin said. "Let me consult with the council."

The governor and his men stepped to the edge of the clearing for a brief conference, their voices rising and falling in waves.

Constance bit her lip. They must take Drew's word on the matter. What other choice did they have? Mary glanced at her with a tight smile.

Walking back to the cottage, Hopkin hitched up his breeches. "You may keep Miss Morrow until her story can be investigated, but meanwhile, you'll have to marry this other one."

Drew's shoulders stiffened. "Miss Robins?"

"Yes."

Drew and Josh exchanged a look.

Mary paled, then took a quivering breath. "I cannot marry, good sir."

Hopkin scowled. "What's this?"

Mary visibly swallowed.

"Speak up, girl!"

She jerked, stumbling back a step. "I'm already married, I am."

"What a great bunch of tripe," Emmett exclaimed. "If I can't have back the one I originally bought, then at least let me have this wagtail. By trow, just give her to me and be done with it!"

"Married!" Hopkin roared. "To whom?"

Mary looked at her feet. "'Tis true. My man was press-ganged into the Navy two years past. I ain't seen nor heard from him since."

"She lies!" Emmett screeched.

"He cannot marry her, Hopkin," Colonel Tucker insisted, looking to the other councilmen. They nodded their encouragement. "Even with the tiniest chance at truth, the sin of marrying one while still married to another would be too great. It is out of the question."

Hopkin whirled on Mary. "How did you get on a bridal ship if you were already wed!"

Mary cringed, falling back several more steps. Josh moved forward, partially shielding her with his body. "She's a felon, Hopkin. Her sentence was deportment. She'd no choice in the matter."

"What do *you* know of this?"

"Only that I contracted her for Drew and when we arrived at the cottage, she told my brother what she just told you."

Hopkin's face mottled. "What was your husband's name?" he barked to Mary.

Josh laid a hand against her waist, pressing her ever so slightly forward.

"Obadiah Robins," she answered.

"That could be anyone," Emmett cried. "Her brother or father or anyone."

"Occupation?" Hopkin asked.

"A street sweeper."

"Oh, fer—" Emmett murmured.

"How long were you married?"

"Four years."

"Children?"

"Two."

"Where are they?"

A discernible pause. "Dead."

This last was said barely above a whisper. Constance clasped her hands together. Poor Mary. It was clear she didn't want to talk about it.

"Why were you in Newgate Prison?"

"I was accused of committing perjury, sir."

"She was forced to testify against a lord," Josh said. "The lord's influence decided the outcome of the trial before Miss Robins ever stepped into Old Bailey."

Hopkin turned to Josh. "If I want any more of your input, I will ask for it."

Hopkin's anger was there for all to see, building as if it were a living, breathing entity. He turned to Drew, searing him with his gaze. "I am this close to banishing you, your brother, and your bawd-strutting women." He pointed his pudgy finger directly at Constance. "That one. You will either marry that one or sell her back to

Emmett. And if I hear one single dispute from your lips, it will mean the end of your freedom here in the colonies, and not only yours by troth, but every member of your family's—extended or otherwise."

Tension radiated from Drew's frame.

"Morden, open your Bible," Hopkin ordered. "We've wasted enough time."

"Excuse me," Constance whispered.

Drew's head slowly pivoted toward her, along with the rest of the men present.

"Might I have a word with you?" she asked Drew.

His eyebrows lifted.

"It will only take a moment . . . sir."

He looked past her to Josh. Josh shrugged. Drew turned to Hopkin. "May I have a word with the lady?"

"It's highly unusual."

"So is this whole situation," Drew replied.

"You have two minutes."

Nodding, Drew propelled her into the cottage. Once inside, he held his finger over his lips and indicated she go to the corner of the cottage furthest from the door and window. She barely noted Sally's napping form before turning back to him. "I have a proposition for you," she whispered.

"By my faith, get on with it."

"Do you want to marry me?"

"I want to keep my tobacco farm, and I want not for my family to be banished," he answered.

"Good. Here is what I propose. You provide me with the protection of your name until my father can be notified. I, in turn, will help you around the farm. Of course, I would . . ." She averted her eyes.

He frowned. "Explain yourself."

Fingering the sleeve of her gown, she moistened her lips. "Well . . . what I mean to say is we'd be married in name, but we wouldn't, we needn't—" She took a deep breath. "What I'm trying to say is, well, we would forgo . . ." She twirled her hand in the air, indicating one corner of the room.

He turned toward the corner, espying the bed. His cheeks filled with color. "Marriage is not taken lightly here in the colonies. When a ceremony is performed, it is meant as a covenant with God until our deaths."

She reinforced the folds at her gown's waist. "Well, yes, of course. But, surely, under certain conditions, the marriage can be reputed?"

"O'Connor!" Hopkin yelled. "Your time is up!"

Drew rubbed his eyes.

She grabbed his sleeve. "Do you agree?"

His gaze found hers. There was no shielding of his expression this time. His eyes were filled with reluctance, determination, and unmistakable frustration.

"Go in after him!" Emmett screeched.

Drew turned and stalked out of the cottage. Picking up her skirts, she followed.

"Open your Bible, Morden," Drew said.

She surveyed the formidable group of men. Forsooth. It appeared that like it or not, she would be married this day. Still, exacting a promise of abstinence from Drew *before* the ceremony was much more likely than after.

She pinched his arm. "Answer my question."

He scowled.

"Give me your word, Mr. O'Connor," she whispered. "I've forced my papa to cancel five marriage contracts so far. If you wish to avoid a scene, I suggest you agree to my terms."

His shocked expression spoke volumes. Of course, five contracts was a bit of an exaggeration. She must pray for forgiveness immediately after the ceremony.

Tightening his lips, he nodded.

"Josh," Morden said gently, "go and collect your mother's wedding band. We have need of it."

Josh hesitated only a moment before doing as asked.

Morden moved his attention to Drew. "She must be married in her hair. Please loosen it."

Her mouth went dry. After a long, tense moment, Drew cupped her chin and turned her toward him. Clearly, he was distressed. Whether from the thought of loosening her hair or from placing his mother's ring on her finger or from the very act of wedding her, she knew not.

He tugged the strings of her cap and slid the covering from her head. Her braid tumbled down her back, its end brushing against her waist. She felt her heart thump loudly against her breast.

Josh returned to the glade, and Drew handed him her head cloth. Drew's eyes, however, never left hers. He stood as such for an inestimable amount of time.

"You must finish it, son," Morden prompted, his voice low and kind. "You know it is to hang completely free."

Still he made no move. He simply waited. Waited, she realized, for her permission. The heart that had near jumped from her chest before, now slowed in gratitude. He, of course, knew this marriage was not a real one. And to loosen her hair in such a manner should be the privilege of her future mate. So he waited.

She felt her face relax a bit. She had no desire to see

him and his family banished simply because the preacher was going to insist her hair be worn in the manner it should for such an occasion.

She pulled her braid across her shoulder, letting her hand run the length of its tight coil before allowing it to hang free.

His gaze followed the path of her hand. His Adam's apple bobbed. Lifting the tail of her braid, he took a tentative step toward her, then began to unravel her hair. His knuckles inadvertently brushed against her. She jumped. He froze, then much more carefully continued with his task.

As he neared the top, she tucked her chin to better accommodate him. When all was in readiness, he spread his fingers wide and ran them through her tresses, draping them across her shoulders and breasts.

She raised her chin. His blue eyes had darkened by several degrees. Her breathing grew labored.

Morden cleared his throat. She and Drew centered their attention on him.

"Dearly beloved, we are gathered together here in the sight of God, and in the presence of these witnesses, to join together this man and this woman in holy matrimony. . . ."

She looked about the clearing. Even if it was temporary, she wanted to take special note of her wedding day. She almost gasped aloud when she caught sight of a doe, with a spotted fawn at her heels, well beyond the clearing. The doe, stretching her neck and perking her ears, stood transfixed.

" . . . was ordained for a remedy against sin, and to avoid fornication; that such persons as have not the gift of continency might marry, and keep themselves undefiled members of Christ's body . . ."

As the deer and her fawn loped out of sight, Constance turned back to the preacher. His words had captured her attention.

"The ring."

He held his Bible out in front of Josh. Josh placed the gold band upon the Book, and the preacher delivered it to Drew. Taking her left hand, Drew slid the warm metal onto her fourth finger, retaining hold of her hand even after the task was complete.

"Wilt thou, Andrew Joseph O'Connor, have thee . . . uh . . . oh my. Pardon me, dear, but what was your proper name again?"

She stiffened. Drew entwined his fingers with hers.

She took a deep breath. "Lady Constance Caroline Morrow, daughter to the Right Honorable the Earl of Greyhame, My Lord Randall Christian Morrow."

Morden balked for a moment, then cleared his throat. "Well, now. That's quite a name. For these proceedings, I will make use of your forename and surname."

"As you wish," she replied.

Morden pulled at the collar of his shirt. "Wilt thou, Andrew Joseph O'Connor, have thee, Constance Caroline Morrow, to thy wedded wife? To have and to hold, to love and to cherish, to comfort, honor, and keep, as long as ye both shall live?"

Drew's serious blue eyes turned to her. "I will."

She swallowed. He gave her hand a gentle squeeze.

"Wilt thou, Constance Caroline Morrow, have thee, Andrew Joseph O'Connor, to thy wedded husband? Wilt thou obey him and serve him, love, honor, and keep him, forsaking all other, keep thee only unto him, so long as ye both shall live?"

Her throat swelled. What was she doing? It had sounded so simple in the cottage. *Oh, Lord.* She looked from Drew to the preacher to the governor and back to Drew.

Easing into a smile, Drew covered their clasped hands with his free one and turned her toward him. "It's all right, Constance. The Lord says, 'Fear not, for I am with you; Be not dismayed, for I am your God. I will strengthen you, yes, I will help you, I will uphold you with my righteous right hand.'"

She stared at him in wonder. What manner of man was this Andrew Joseph O'Connor?

"I will." The words were out before she even realized she'd said them. He rubbed his thumb lightly across her knuckles.

Morden started. "Yes. Uh, very good. Uh, forasmuch as Andrew Joseph O'Connor and Constance Caroline Morrow have pledged their troth either to other, I pronounce that they be man and wife together." He closed his Bible. "Those whom God hath joined together let no man put asunder. Amen."

This was wrong. It was wrong to declare such vows when she had no intention of keeping them. It was wrong to trick these men who, in their own disillusioned minds, merely thought they were protecting her virtue.

She searched Drew's features for a clue as to what his thoughts were, but to no avail. He'd certainly surprised her with his words and gentleness. Was it genuine? Yes. She believed so. She hoped so.

Her throat ached. It was all so unfair, for both of them. And what would happen to him when the council found out about their subterfuge? Would his arms be broken? His tongue bored through with an awl? Would he lose his farm anyway? Whatever happened, it would be all her fault. Her eyes pooled.

"Our Father, who art in heaven, Hallowed be Thy name . . ."

Drew's rich baritone voice joined in with the others assembled. She moved her lips to the prayer, yet no sound came forth. Cradling one side of her face, his thumb swiped at the tears now trickling down her cheek.

" . . . And lead us not into temptation, but deliver us from evil. Amen."

A warm breeze caressed her, swirling a tendril of hair. He hooked the tendril with his finger and pulled it from her face.

"You may kiss thy bride."

She widened her eyes. That too? They must do that too? Time stood suspended, then he cupped her face with both hands and slowly lowered his lips to hers. She slid her eyes closed.

The softness of his mouth barely registered before a peculiar heat spread from their kiss, down her neck to her shoulders and throughout her body. Her lips parted in surprise.

Oh, sweet saints that be. She'd not been hugged or held for so very, very long. But this, this was so much more and so absolutely heavenly.

His hands moved to her back, pulling her closer. She brought her hands up to his arms, crinkling his sleeves within her grasp.

"Drew."

The voice came from far away.

"*Drew!*"

She clung to him as she felt him tense and pull back. He placed his hands about her arms and gently disengaged himself. When her vision cleared, it was to find him holding her at arm's length, his face bright with color.

Mortified, her gaze traveled over an entire group of flush-faced men. Stepping back, Constance felt her own face heat, then turned as Josh grazed her sleeve.

He touched his cheek to hers. "Welcome to the family, Mistress O'Connor."

"Thank you."

"What about Miss Robins?" Emmett inquired petulantly.

Hopkin took a deep breath. "Drew will clarify the particulars on her, Emmett."

"How?"

He shrugged. "He can send word with the captain."

"The captain of the *Randolph*?" Emmett cried. "He'll not bother himself with that."

"I'll pay him for his troubles," Drew said.

"I just bet you will," Emmett sneered. "If the price is right, the captain'll do anything. Including lie and report whatever you pay him to report. No, the captain is out of the question."

"Now you're willing to admit the captain is a liar?" Drew asked. "Where were these objections a few moments ago when my wife's claim of nobility was questioned?"

"I admitted the captain would lie about the lady's status," Emmett retorted. "He might know full well she's a maid yet claim she's a lady just to line his pockets."

"He might also have kidnapped her and claimed she was seized according to his orders," Drew snapped.

"Enough!" Hopkin exclaimed. "Either way, Emmett has the right of it. The captain is not trustworthy. I recommend Joshua go abroad and investigate the matter."

"Josh!" Drew exclaimed. "Absolutely not. I am about to expand my farm into a plantation. I've ten indentured men awaiting me at the wharf as we speak. The harvest is due to be cut before the month is out. I need Josh here."

Hopkin squared his shoulders. "I have wasted enough of my time and the council's time this morning. Joshua will either investigate the marital status of Miss Robins or he will marry her."

"This is outrageous!"

"Hopkin," Tucker interjected, "you are being unreasonable."

Hopkin whipped off his hat. "And I am done with your constant interference. Joshua and Miss Robins are both young, healthy persons. Confining them on this farm for the next eight months is more temptation than I am willing to afford them."

"I'll marry her," Emmett said.

"She's not for sale," Drew growled. "I need her here to cook."

"You have your *wife*," Emmett snarled.

Drew took one step forward. "If you refer to my wife in that tone again I will lay you out flat."

"I'll leave on the *Randolph*," Josh stated.

Drew whirled around. "A fie upon it, Josh, what are you saying?" He appeared at a loss for words before determination settled into his expression. "Have you forgotten there's a civil war raging in England?"

"I've not forgotten," he said. "I've also not forgotten the woman I'm pledged to."

"We can appeal this," Drew countered. "I am married and a suitable chaperon. They cannot force you to marry as well."

"Appeal to whom?" Josh asked. "The whole blasted council is standing right here. Besides, think. While I am investigating the whereabouts of Mary's husband, I can also notify the earl about Constance's kidnapping. He's bound to be frantic."

Drew combed his fingers through his hair. "But it's already late June and the *Randolph* is empty with nothing here to load. Josh, she'll be sailing up and down the coast and maybe even to the West Indies before she's full. Add that to the months needed for locating Greyhame and Robins, and you are sure to be tardy. What then? What if you return too late to factor our tobacco harvest? With no broker for our tobacco, the whole year will be lost and our plans for a plantation with it."

"I'll be back come spring," Josh said. "In plenty of time to transport and sell our tobacco."

"But the war!"

"I'll be back."

Hopkin tapped his hat down on his head. "So be it. Councilmen, our business here is concluded. Let us away."

Drew's lips thinned with visible anger.

Colonel Tucker extended his hand to Drew's. "I'm sorry. I'm as unhappy about this as you are."

Heaving a sigh, Drew accepted Tucker's hand. "You did what you could, and I thank you for that."

Tucker nodded and turned to join the other men. Constance watched them follow Hopkin like a flock of crows. The king would hear of this as soon as she returned home.

Home. She glanced at the man who had pledged his life to hers. His brother wouldn't be back until spring? Sweet saints above, would she ever return home? Surely there was a regular schedule with ships arriving every third week or so.

She furrowed her brows. If they were all slavers, though, she had no desire to risk boarding another without protection. And she certainly had no desire to go to the West Indies.

Straightening, she pushed back the bothersome curls surrounding her face. She would return to England. She must. For Uncle Skelly. For the women of Europe. For herself.

Drew rubbed the back of his neck. His rugged muscular body shifted beneath his shirt. She swallowed. *Dear Lord, please let Josh return before spring.*

SIX

"Are you my gamma now?" Sally asked.

Constance continued to slice her carrots. Ah, how to explain this? "No, dear. I'm . . . well . . . your sister, I suppose."

Sally's violet eyes widened. "I used to have sister. She got real sick. She went to heaven."

Constance paused. "I'm sorry."

"Mama and Papa live there too."

"I see." Constance laid down her knife. "What was your sister's name?"

"Sister."

Constance blinked. "Oh. I have a sister too."

"She live in heaven?"

"No, she lives in a place called England. It's not quite as wonderful as heaven, but almost."

"She call you 'Sister' or 'My Lady?'"

Constance bit her lip. "She calls me 'C.C.'"

"Sissy?" Sally's eyes lit up. "I call you Sissy too?"

Placing her hand on top of Sally's, she gave it a gentle squeeze. "That would be lovely."

An enchanting smile spread across the child's face. With it came two charming dimples.

Constance picked up the knife and glanced at Mary, who bustled around the fire. Due to the council's visit, they were late in preparing the midday meal and Mary had not stopped moving since Drew and Josh left to retrieve the indentured men.

"Knives are very dang'russ."

"Yes," Constance agreed. "Don't ever touch one."

"Or I might hurt me? Like you did?"

Constance nodded, glancing at two of her fingers, now wrapped with strips of cotton. It wasn't that cutting vegetables was so difficult; it was just that the gold band on her fourth finger kept drawing her attention away from the knife. The ring's presence not only startled her every time she noticed it, but it also reminded her of the man who had placed it there.

The knife slipped yet again, barely missing her finger.

Sally gasped. "You better let Miss Mary cut the yun-yuns."

"You mean *onions*."

"Yes. Yun-yuns."

Constance swiped a sleeve across her face, trying to shove back the curls blocking her view, and concentrated on her task. "Well, I'll strive to be more careful. Otherwise I might run out of chemise."

Sally eyed the old chemise crumpled upon the bed. "I think you'll run out of fingers."

Mary scurried over to collect the carrots, waiting while Constance scooped up her slices and dropped them into the iron pot. "I'll set these over the fire, then show you how to cut them 'yun-yuns.'" She turned and winked at Sally. "After the noon meal, we'll boil that chemise, we will. I have a feeling she'll be needing it again, and the smell of it hurts my nose."

Sally giggled as Mary struggled with the pot of carrots in one hand while pinching her nose with the other.

By the time Drew and Josh arrived with the new men, Mary had prepared a hearty vegetable soup with enough corn pone for all. The men servants were weak, filthy, and hungry. They partook of their meal in the clearing, then deposited the empty trenchers they shared in the pails by the door.

Constance watched as, by degrees, they filed in front of the cottage and faced Drew, awaiting his instructions. Josh stood at Drew's left, while she and Sally were instructed to stand behind him and to his right. Mary picked up the pails of dirty dishes and headed to the creek.

Fetid shirts and britches hung on the men like rags on a cord. None wore shoes. Their newly shorn hair stuck in odd angles from their heads, while their grim faces displayed pallid complexions beneath a night's growth of whiskers.

She recognized none of them. Her thoughts had been of Uncle Skelly on the trip over and she had taken little notice of the other men during her brief jaunts to the upper deck.

"Eight of you are to serve a seven-year term," Drew started, "two a fourteen-year term as per your contracts. For the most part, we will be harvesting tobacco. I also have plans to build a three-level house come November.

"I will clothe and feed you well and, for now, you will

sleep in the tobacco barn. When the big house is built, you may have this cottage as your living quarters."

He clasped his hands behind his back, his shadow stretching beside him in the still morning light. "At the end of your terms, each of you will receive an acre of land along with corn and new clothing. I will show you your land tomorrow. If you wish to work it on your free day, you may do so. Good behavior and hard work will be the price of seeds and tools for your land."

Constance looked from one indentured man to another, noting their guarded expressions. And no wonder. Drew's manner was in sharp contrast to that of the ship captain's. They had received nothing but barking orders and immediate retribution on the ship. To now have the lure of owning land dangled before them must be a bit suspect. She tilted her head, guessing it would take a while for them to accept their master's word as truth.

"Whatever price your crop brings will be yours to keep. I will hold your monies in an account with your name. If you want to save it, you may have the whole of it come the end of your term. If you want to use it to purchase supplies or sundries, you may give me the list and I will purchase them for you."

He took to pacing in front of the men. "You will not be working in the fields alone. I will be there working beside you. Any man who works harder than I will be given a bonus at the end of the season."

He stopped. The trees whispered. The hens clucked. The men kept their focus fastened on him. "I have plans for a great plantation. You are coming in at the best possible time. If you perform your tasks well and efficiently, you will act as leaders for the next group of men I purchase. Are there any questions?"

The men were silent.

He strode back to his brother. "You have already met my brother, Master Joshua, on the *Randolph*. He is my factor and will be leaving for England with the ship."

Moving to stand behind Constance and Sally, he placed one hand on Sally's shoulder and rested his other on Constance's waist. "This is your mistress, along with my sister, Miss Sally. Members of my family and household are to be treated with the utmost respect."

Mistress. He may have agreed to an in-name-only marriage, but no one else would suspect it as such. For he had not hesitated in the introduction of her as his wife and even placed a possessive hand to her back. She kept her expression neutral.

He took several steps forward and spread his feet. "If it is escape you have in mind, let me assure you, I will track you down. The punishment for attempted escape in Virginia is thirty-nine lashes of the whip. Have no doubt that I will catch you and administer them. Personally."

The men said nothing.

He relaxed his stance. "This morning you will worm and weed the fields. This afternoon, you will help as needed around the clearing with any light work Mistress O'Connor or my servant, Miss Mary, asks of you, but you will stop before the sun sets. You are all in need of rest and good food. I will see you have it before I expect you to put in a full day's work. Any questions?"

There were none.

"Fabric with which to clothe you should be arriving in port in about two weeks. Until then, I fear you must make do with what you have." He adjusted his hat. "Let us away to the creek where you can wash, then we will head to the fields."

As promised, Drew worked the men throughout the rest of the morning, then had them do light chores around the cottage. Though they were hesitant to speak freely, he hoped a sense of camaraderie would soon form. After a sumptuous supper, they could barely move, so, disregarding the sun still perched in the sky, Drew allowed them to retire.

Lighting his pipe, he then helped Constance carry the dishes to the creek for their washing, early evening shadows trailing behind them as they walked. He carried the heavy pots filled with noggins, while she held a pile of trenchers.

"What's that?" she asked, indicating a flowering tree covered with creamy globular blooms in a setting of huge glossy leaves.

"A magnolia."

"Lovely. And there are so many of them." She inhaled deeply. "Umm." Setting down her load, she moved to the tree, breaking off a flower and pressing it to her nose.

The rich fragrant perfume of the magnolia drifted to him. He took a deep breath, then surveyed his land, trying to see it through her eyes. Thinking back to the two years he'd spent at Cambridge University, he recalled what few trees they'd had abroad. Here, there was enough wood to supply all of England and more.

"How did the men do?" she asked.

He hesitated a moment. "In the fields?"

"Yes."

"Surprisingly well. They seem to have reconciled themselves to their stay here and give every indication of turning into fine workers. I don't think any of them will run."

"No?"

He smiled. "Well, they thought about it when I told them we would wash every day. Still, I don't think any will try to escape. Josh has a great knack for discerning a person's character. It appears his instinct didn't fail him. The men he advised me to purchase were exactly what I needed."

"That's why he was on the transport ship?"

He studied her for a moment. "You saw him?"

She nodded. "He took pains to smuggle as much food and drink to Mary as he could."

"Um. He did the same for our men. It has made their adjustment to me and the farm much easier."

She fingered one of the creamy petals cupped in her palm. "Did he smuggle food only to those particular men?"

He frowned. What prompted that question? "There was one other man he had chosen, but who died on the passage over."

She slowly lifted her gaze. "Who?"

He shrugged. "I know not. Why?"

Taking a deep breath, she laid the flower on top of her stack of dishes, then picked them up. "My uncle was on that ship."

"Ah, yes. *The uncle.*"

She stiffened at his sarcasm, and he felt a pang of regret. Regardless of whether she had told a falsehood, he should've kept to his own counsel until he knew for certain.

Removing the pipe from his mouth, he readjusted the hat on his head. "I'm sorry."

She bit her lip. "So am I," she whispered.

They walked the rest of the way in silence.

When they reached the creek, he set the pots on the bank as a feeling of contentment flowed through him. The closing of the day was upon them, and despite the disastrous morning with the council, things were going well. It appeared his plans for a plantation would still bear fruit.

Propping himself against a birch tree, he placed the pipe in his mouth, inhaled deeply, and blew a series of smoke rings above his head. His practiced eye scanned the water's edge looking for the animals that met there to feed and hunt. The busy crossroads joining the creek and forest lay unusually still, as if sensing a human presence. Picking up a rock, he skipped it across the water. The ripples disrupted the glistening surface of the creek as the sun began its final descent in the west.

He turned to watch Constance clean the trenchers. She sat perched on the bank, her eyes rounded and focused on him.

"What?" he asked.

"Aren't you going to help me?"

"With what?"

"These dishes."

He snorted. "Have you taken leave of your senses? I've already carried the pots down here for you."

"You mean I'm ordinarily expected to carry them myself?"

"Of course. My sister Nellie did it all the time. I only got in the habit of it when Grandma took over."

"So you carried the pots for your grandmother, then sat against that tree and watched her cleanse them?"

He frowned. "This is one of my favorite times of day and your screeching is chafing my ears. Please cease."

Her lips parted. His gaze was inexplicably drawn to them. Their sweet taste, along with the incredible softness of her appalling hair, reared itself in front of him. Clamping down on his pipe, he inhaled too quickly and began coughing.

She dropped the trencher in her hands, rushed over and whacked him on the back. He jumped up and scrambled to the creek, but the trencher was already floating away. Seeing no other alternative, he splashed in after it, still coughing.

He made it back to the bank, wet, still gasping for air and, with eyes watering, fell to his knees.

"Smoking is really a nasty habit," she said, pounding him on the back several more times.

"You dropped the trencher," he wheezed.

"Yes. And I truly appreciate your heroic effort in fetching it. Thank you."

He took a deep breath. She reached out to whack him. He grabbed her wrist and held it loosely within his grasp.

"Do not hit me again."

She blinked. "I wasn't hitting you. I was assisting you in your breathing."

"Constance, I have no food caught in my throat. What are you trying to knock out? The smoke?"

She bit her lower lip. "Oh. Your pardon."

He released her wrist. "You dropped the trencher."

"You said that already, and I thanked you quite prettily for retrieving it."

"Do not *ever* drop a trencher. We've only a few as it is."

"Why do you not use porcelain or silver?"

"I'll not waste money on such as that. Trenchers do just fine."

"Oh. Well, maybe you need to make some more while I cleanse the dishes instead of slouching against that tree."

He handed her the trencher. "Clean it."

She looked down at it. "I'd say this one has already been cleaned."

"It's been rinsed. Now it needs to be cleaned."

"How?"

He frowned. "What do you mean, 'how'? You scrub it. How else?"

She looked around at the pots and other trenchers. "Scrub it with what?"

He tossed the trencher down. "With sand. Have you no power within your brain?"

She straightened. "I have never before scrubbed dishes." Back rigid, she fell to her knees on the bank, grabbed a handful of muddy sand, and scrubbed.

He located his discarded pipe and again settled back against the tree.

"I've never heard of such a thing," she began. "To clean the dishes, you rub dirt on them. It's absurd." She dunked the trencher into the water, then dunked it again.

He tightened his mouth. The tobacco in his pipe was wet. Turning it upside down, he tapped it out.

"How's this?" she asked. "Is it clean, or do I need to get it dirty again?"

He looked over at her. She had pushed up the sleeves

of her gown in order to wash. Her arms were covered with freckles.

"Run your hand across it," he said. "If it's grimy, rinse it some more. But you shouldn't need to scrub it again."

She pushed the curls away from her face with her shoulder, then ran her hand across the trencher. Frowning, she dunked it back into the water.

He sighed, looked at the stack of dirty trenchers, then the sun lowering in the horizon. They were going to be here all night.

Pulling away from the tree, he grabbed a trencher and knelt beside her. When he finished, she snatched it from him and ran her fingers over it.

"It's grimy," she said and handed it back to him.

He looked at her with disbelief. "It's perfect."

Slowly, a smile crept onto her face. "Easy, now. I was merely jesting."

Jerking the trencher back, he dropped it to the side and started on another. The sloshing of the trenchers continued as they worked in companionable silence. In the distance, a woodpecker tapped out a staccato beat while a persistent dragonfly patrolled the shoreline, briefly lighting on the old raft before resuming his restless flight.

Drew had cleaned five noggins, two trenchers, and both pots before she'd finished her fourth trencher. Grabbing it from her, he proceeded to finish the last one. Rolling down her sleeves, she stood and watched.

"Well," Josh said, "isn't this a pretty picture."

Dropping the trencher in the creek, Drew jumped up and whirled around.

Constance quickly reached in and retrieved it, shook

the water off, and handed it to him. "Do not *ever* drop a trencher. We've only a few as it is."

He ignored her. "What do you want, Josh?"

Josh eyed Drew's sodden breeches but said nothing of it. "I came to say good-bye."

"Good-bye?"

He nodded. "We're going to Nellie's. I need to say good-bye to her and Grandma. I'll leave from there in the morning."

"*We're* going to Nellie's? Who's *we*?" Drew asked.

"Mary, Sally, and I."

"Why are Mary and Sally going?"

Josh darted a glance at Constance. "Because."

Drew frowned. "Because, why?"

"Because it's your wedding night, you beetle-headed knave," he said, rolling his eyes. "Why do you think?"

Drew reddened. "It's not necessary."

Josh lifted an eyebrow.

Drew grabbed Josh's arm and propelled him several yards down the path, well out of Constance's hearing. Still, Drew waited to speak until she'd turned and began stacking the clean noggins inside the pots.

"We're not to have a *real* marriage, if you will."

"What are you talking about?"

Drew lifted his hat and settled it back on his head again. "I'm merely providing Constance with the protection of my name to satisfy the council. When her father returns, she plans to have the marriage terminated."

"On what grounds?" Josh asked, obviously appalled.

"On the grounds that she was forced into marriage and on the grounds that the marriage hasn't been consummated."

Slapping Drew on the back, Josh laughed. "You gor-belly. I almost believed you for a moment."

"I'm deadly serious."

Josh paused. "No. Surely you jest. Drew, look at her. She appears to be endowed with all a woman should have and more. If you but bridle her and slip her some sweets, she'll be eating from your hand long before I return."

"You overstep yourself, Josh. That is my bride you speak of."

"A bride most begrudging, it seems."

"Even so, you'll hold a civil tongue in your head when you refer to her. I've given her my word on the annulment matter and that's an end to it."

"Given her your word? To abstain until I contact her father? But I won't be back for eight extremely long months. Why would you do a fool thing like that?"

"Because she might not die before you return, and if she doesn't, I do not want to contend with the possibility of offspring, much less a wife."

"This was *your* idea?"

"Of course not. It was her condition for marrying me."

A myriad of expressions crossed Josh's face. "Sweet saints above. In the cottage . . . Is that what she wanted to discuss with you in the cottage before the ceremony?"

Drew blew a puff of air from his lungs. "Yes."

"By trow, never have I heard of anything so absurd. 'Tis folly for sure."

"Probably, but leave Mary and Sally just the same. There is no need to take them."

Josh shook his head. "Everyone in the colony knows it's your wedding night. Regardless of what the situation is, you must at least pretend to have a real marriage or no telling what Emmett will stir the council to do."

Drew drug his hand down his face. "A fie upon it."

"Mary and Sally will go to Nellie's with me tonight. I will send them back come morning."

Drew sighed and extended his hand. "Best so."

Josh grabbed his brother's hand. Leaning forward, the men embraced.

"Godspeed, Josh, and be careful. I'd appreciate your returning to factor my tobacco. If you get caught in the crossfire of that war, it will really put a cramp in my plans."

Josh chuckled and pulled away. "I'll be home come spring."

Drew nodded.

Josh strolled back down the path to Constance. "Take care of him for me, Lady Constance. I do not want to be a plantation owner. Being the second son suits me quite nicely."

Standing, Constance smiled. "He'll be fine. You have the letter I wrote for my father?"

He nodded. "I have it."

"When do you leave?"

"On tomorrow's tide."

"So soon?"

"The seaworthy old girl's anxious to go looking for cargo and has no reason to linger here."

Constance clasped her hands together. "Well, then. Have a care."

He lifted her clasped hands to his lips and kissed them. "I'll find him, Lady Constance."

She took a deep breath. "Thank you. And Josh?"

"Yes?"

"Please, call me Constance."

He crinkled his brow. "Sally gets to call you Sissy."

She smiled. "Sally is three years old."

A wicked gleam entered his eyes. "Yes, but I'm better looking."

Constance's laugh tinkled out across the clearing. "Hurry back, Josh."

He tipped his hat. "I will, sister."

Turning, he passed by Drew and bumped him to the side with his shoulder. "Try not to pick the lock before I return," he whispered, winking before sauntering up the trail.

Drew glanced toward Constance. The sunlight at her back outlined the curves hidden beneath Nellie's old dress. He swallowed. *Dear God, please let Josh return before spring.*

SEVEN

The moon and stars lit up the night sky with abandon, showering some of their beams on Constance. Leaning against a girdled tree, she greeted Orion. He stood as stalwart as ever, raising his club for a kill, while his brilliant belt housed that mighty sword. She looked a bit to the left and, yes, there was Venus dazzling in the rectangle of Gemini. High above and to the right of Orion shone Jupiter.

With these old friends joining her, she could almost pretend she was in her flower garden back home. Almost. But sooner or later, she'd have to bid her friends goodnight and go inside that cottage. With him.

She glanced at the cottage door. Why had he allowed Josh to take Mary and Sally with him for the night? Had he misconstrued her rather warm response to his wedding kiss? She hadn't meant to respond at all. But respond she did and with not just a little enthusiasm.

She readjusted the hem of her sleeves. Something intense had flared between them. Most likely, it was a product of the excessive tension. Still, whatever the reason, it couldn't happen again, and if he'd arranged for an empty cottage with a reckoning in mind, she would have to persuade him otherwise. Fortifying herself, she turned and entered the cottage.

Due to the heat outside, the fire in the hearth was small and gave off little light. He sat on a bench in front of the fire, smoking a churchwarden pipe, its long stem protruding a couple of feet from his mouth.

"Where are the candles?" she asked.

He slowly expelled a stream of smoke. "What need have you for a candle?"

She dabbed at the moisture around her hairline. "I'd like to work in my diary."

"The cruse is on the shelf, but it drips, smokes, and smells so bad, we never use it."

"The cruse? With grease? You've no candles?"

"No need for them. When darkness falls, the family usually retires."

"But the family isn't here."

He took a long drag from his pipe. "No, they aren't."

He'd removed his hat at some point, and the glow of the fire framed his dark curly hair with bluish highlights.

"Where's my diary?" she asked.

"In the cedar chest."

She glanced in the direction of the chest but saw nothing. The cottage was shrouded in darkness.

"Have you any parchment?"

"Why don't you just go to bed, Constance? You're bound to be worn out."

"Yes, I should be, but for some reason I'm wide awake."

He lowered his pipe. "Me, too."

She barely caught his murmured words. Stretching her

arms out in front of her, she headed toward the chest. At least, she hoped she did. Her hands made contact with the wall. Moving along its rough surface, she methodically felt up and down.

"What are you doing?" he asked.

"Looking for the chest."

He sighed. "It's too dark. You'll never be able to find the booklet inside that chest without some light."

"Then where's the cruse?"

"No, you'll simply have to wait."

Tears immediately sprung to her eyes. This day had been almost more than she could bear. Too much had happened too fast. If she could just work on an algorithm, everything would fall into place for her. Swallowing, she continued her search, then jumped when she felt his hand encircle her wrist.

"Come and sit down, Constance. If you cannot sleep, then sit by the fire. Even if you found your diary, the fire would not give off the light you'd need."

"Yes it would." She pulled back her hand.

He paused. "Are you crying?"

"Don't be ridiculous. Why would I be crying?"

"No reason I can think of, but that never stopped my sisters."

"Well, I'm not one of your sisters."

A great swell of silence encompassed the cabin. "No," he whispered, "you're my wife."

She swallowed. "Why did Josh take Mary and Sally with him? Didn't you explain?"

"I explained."

"Then why?"

"Appearances. Emmett. The council."

"Who could we possibly be trying to impress with appearances? I've seen no neighbors."

"We've neighbors, Constance. They just live a good distance away. Still, word always seems to get around."

"But what does it matter? Who would care?"

"The council. Emmett. Me."

"But I'll be leaving soon. Why, I could take next month's ship. There's no need for me to wait for your brother."

He shook his head. "This isn't London, Constance. Ships are few and far between here. But even still, you'll be going nowhere until I've confirmation about your background from Josh or until your alleged father himself shows up."

She sighed. Her background again. "This is such a mess."

"Um."

They stood in the darkness. Her eyes had long since adjusted, but she still couldn't make out his expression. She could smell him, though—that now familiar mixture of male, sunshine, and tobacco. His breath tickled her face. She took a step back. "I think I will sit down."

After settling herself on the bench, she suppressed the urge to scoot to its farthest edge when he joined her.

"What's in your diary that was so important?"

"I wanted to work on an algorithm."

He stretched his long legs in front of him and propped his hand against the bench, leaning away from her. "Did you now?"

She wet her lips. "Yes."

"And which algorithm would that be?"

Placing her hands on either side of her knees, she grasped the bench seat. "I saw a fly in the cottage today."

He tapped the stem of his pipe against his lips. "Now, that's an algorithm I've never heard of."

She slid him a glance, then turned back to the fire. "I also saw a spider."

"My, what a busy day you've had."

She allowed herself to relax a bit. "Let's assume this cottage is 21 feet long, 10 feet wide, and 10 feet high. On the middle line of one of the smaller side walls and 1 foot from the ceiling is a spider. On the middle line of the opposite wall and 9 feet from the ceiling is a fly. The fly, being paralyzed by fear, remains still until the spider catches it by crawling the shortest route. How far did the spider crawl?"

He readjusted himself on the bench. "Whatever was your father thinking to indulge you in the area of academics?"

She drew a circle in the dirt floor with her toe. "He was too busy with his business interests to take much note of my activities, and by the time he realized Uncle Skelly had seen to my tutoring, it was too late."

"What of your mother?"

"She died when I was three. I've no recollection of her. But upon her death, one of my sisters and I were sent to Uncle Skelly and Aunt Katherine's country home." She tucked a loose curl at her nape back into her cap. "Since my aunt and uncle never had children of their own, they devoted much of their time and love to us."

"But what possible purpose could you have had for an education? Particularly in mathematics? 'Twas pure folly."

"Pure folly? But why?"

"Well, I would venture to guess that if your time had

been spent exclusively on skills of a female sort, you'd be safe at home. Instead, you maneuver your way out of five marriage contracts and get kidnapped as well. No, it's my guess your father rues the day you learned your letters and numbers."

She flushed. "Five contracts was a bit of an exaggeration. It was only two."

"Only two? Well, then. That makes all the difference."

She stiffened. "My education encompassed what every woman is expected to know."

"Such as?"

She lifted her chin. "Piety and needlework. Catechism and the Bible. Civility, of course, was instilled by two gentlewomen and a French woman."

"And the more secular subjects?"

"Uncle Skelly hired tutors for me."

"What all were you taught?"

She shrugged. "I don't know. Several things. Latin, French, rhetoric, logic, mathematics, geometry, writing, spelling."

"Your poor father. When did he find out?"

"When I was thirteen."

He grimaced. "What did he do?"

"He fetched me home. I'd have had to go home anyway, though, since a marriage contract he'd made for me was about to mature. Having long before transferred my affection to my aunt and uncle, I went rather unwillingly."

"And now?"

She looked into the fire. "Now, I'm quite fond of Papa."

He pulled his feet back and propped his elbows on his knees. "Let us see. How far from the ceiling was the fly?"

"Nine feet."

"Nine feet. And the spider was one foot below the ceiling, correct?"

"Yes."

He took several drags from his pipe. "Have you figured a solution for your puzzle?"

She shook her head. "I do much better if I can draw pictures."

He set his pipe down. "All right." Bending toward the fire, he scooped up a handful of cold soot and spread it out. "Sketch away."

For a space of several beats, she considered him. Unable to resist, she found herself on her knees beside the pile of soot. Sketching out the cottage and insects with her fingers, she sat back. "What do you think?"

He pursed his lips. "I think I should come up with my solution and you should come up with yours. Then we can compare them."

She looked from him to the soot and back. "All right. When do we compare?"

"How long will it take you to come up with an answer?"

"How long will it take *you*?"

"I already have one."

She gasped. "You lie!"

He grinned. It was a two-dimple grin. She hastily looked down at the soot.

"How long will it take you?" he asked.

She shrugged. "Five minutes."

"Done."

She smiled. "Then go sit over there with your own soot."

Chuckling, he moved to the opposite end of the hearth. She had already started scribbling in her ashes.

Twenty minutes later, she sat back. He was still crouched over his soot.

"Your time is up," she said.

He straightened. "Humph. It's been up for some time now. I was simply giving you some extra."

She suppressed a smile. "What's your solution?"

"You first."

She narrowed her eyes. "How will I know you aren't stealing my solution?"

"How will I know you aren't stealing *my* solution?"

"I'll explain how I came about my answer."

"As will I."

"It's 30.48 feet."

He shook his head. "It's 31 feet."

She clapped her hands together. "You're wrong! I win."

"I think not. You are wrong and I win."

"The route the spider took was 30.48 feet. I'm sure of it."

"Well, then, would you care to place a wager on it?" he asked.

She nodded. "All right. If I'm wrong, I'll wash all the dishes tomorrow evening. If you're wrong, you'll wash them."

"Ha! That's no bargain for me. You're supposed to wash them anyway."

"Then what do I have that you want?"

A coal from the fire shifted. He considered her. Had she worded it any other way, that blessed kiss from this morning would never have crossed his mind. Now he was at a loss to think of anything else.

His gaze moved to her lips. He hadn't expected them to taste so good, her to feel so soft. And her response. Sweet Gemini. Had she walloped him in the stomach, he'd have been less surprised.

She cocked her head. "Is there nothing I can do as a forfeit?"

The implication set his blood pumping. "A kiss."

He heard her quick intake of breath. "I thought we had an agreement."

"A kiss does not a marriage make."

She nodded. "According to my papa, it does."

Shifting, he pulled at his pant legs. "How did you arrive at 30.48 feet, Constance?"

"I like not the conditions of the wager and withdraw from play."

He arched his eyebrows. "You concede defeat?"

"Certainly not!" She fluttered a hand about her neckline, then rested it in her lap. "Cease jesting with me, Drew."

The sound of his name flowed off her lips like the finest of wines. "I'm not jesting in the least."

"Then let us choose another prize."

"I've already chosen. I want a kiss. If you win, you may choose what you want."

A vein in her neck jumped. "A week without washing supper dishes."

"I think not."

"Then I think not about your prize." She smoothed her hands along her skirt. "I say 30.48 feet and a week without washing the supper dishes."

He pursed his lips. "I say 31 feet and a kiss, given freely."

She glanced at her drawings in the soot. "Done."

His body's reaction was swift and profound. "Done."

He closed the distance between them and knelt down on one knee beside her. She visibly swallowed before she pointed to the spider's route drawn in the ashes, along with a triangle.

"The horizontal leg of the right triangle is 21 + 1 + 1. The vertical leg is 5 + 10 + 5," she explained. "Its distance equals the square root of 23 squared plus 20 squared. That makes the hypotenuse of the right triangle—and the path the spider took—30.48 feet," she finished, running her finger along the projected path of her spider.

He studied her drawing and figures. She'd taken the cottage and unfolded it in her drawing, then connected the spider's location to the fly's in one straight line. From there, she had figured the length of the line by drawing a right triangle.

He should have thought of that. It was so simple once he saw it. He tightened his jaw. Now, not only would he have to wash the dishes for a week, but she'd know he wanted a kiss. He slid his eyes closed. *Heaven help me*.

A beat of silence. "How did you come up with 31 feet?"

He opened his eyes. "The wrong way."

She moved nary a muscle.

He made no attempt to hide his emotions. "You'd better get yourself in your pallet, wife. Right hastily."

Her gaze skittered to the bed and back. "I don't get the bed?"

By my troth, could she not see what a state he was in? "Not unless you intend to share it with me."

She scooted back. "I think I'll go make my pallet now. Good night, Drew."

There it was again. His forename. He watched the darkness of the cottage swallow her, then heard an *oomph* and a soft expletive. He knew the moment she found the cedar chest. After some muffled sounds, all was still.

"Drew?" Her address whispered across the room.

He stiffened. "Yes?"

"I'll be needing something to wear to church tomorrow."

He expelled the breath he'd been holding. "We won't be going to church until Christmas Day."

She gasped. "What?!"

"No one does. It's too far and none can afford to lose a full day in the fields every week."

"Then why in the world were they so sanctimonious about us, to the point of forcing marriage?"

He took his time in answering. "I'd like to say that just because we don't attend church regularly doesn't mean we aren't expected to live Christian lives. But the truth of the matter is, I'd two females in a settlement of men desperate for wives. I imagine they couldn't stand the thought of your being single yet out of their reach."

"But marriage only made me further out of reach!"

"Go to sleep, Constance."

He heard her mutter and flop around in her pallet, and then everything settled into silence. If anyone had told him a week ago he'd be married today, he'd have thought they were in their altitudes. If anyone had told him he'd be spending his wedding night on the opposite side of the room from his wife, he'd have thought the drunkard was addled as well.

Tapping out the contents of his pipe, he stirred the

fire's embers, then looked again at her scratchings in the soot. She may not be an earl's daughter, but she wasn't common born either. So exactly what did that make her?

Your wife, whispered the inner recesses of his mind. Slamming a lid down on that thought, he made his way to the bed.

EIGHT

The sun, amidst streaks of pink, yellow, and orange, barely peeked over the horizon. Yet Josh's attention rested not on nature's glorious display but upon Mary. Kneeling on the ground behind Nellie's cottage, her fingers moved with dexterity as she plucked chicken feathers from the hen he'd wrung earlier.

"Mary, I must away. Have you a moment?"

She paused, then carefully placed the feathers in a pouch beside her. "I do."

"When I reach England, I will inquire into the whereabouts of your man."

"Yes, Master Josh."

He frowned, then squatted down in front of her. "Your man's name is Obadiah Robins and he was a street sweeper?"

"Yes."

"When did you see him last?"

"It was the spring of '41, it was."

"And when he didn't return home, you made inquiries?"

She traced a feather with her finger. "No," she whispered.

Well, now, what was this? Settling on the ground in front of her, he rested an arm across his upright knee. "When did you discover he'd been press-ganged?"

"It was with friends, he was, when the deed took place. One of the men managed to escape. After he came out of hiding, he told his wife, who then informed me of Obadiah's mishap."

"Who did the deed?"

"I know not."

His brows drew together. "But the man who returned would surely have known."

She wet her lips. "Yes."

"Then how is it you do not?"

"I asked not." With quick jerks, she plucked the feathers again.

He tilted his head to the side. "You asked not?"

The pace of her work increased. There could be only one reason a wife wouldn't seek out her man. "Obadiah was an unsuitable husband?"

No response. Unsuitable he was, then. "I must still attempt to find him. I've given my word to both Drew and the council."

"I know," she breathed.

Fire and torment, he hated this. "The man who escaped, know you his name?"

"Arnold Parker. A peddler of oatcakes, he was."

"How many men were taken, other than Obadiah and Parker?"

"I know not."

"You were in London at the time?"

"Yes."

He watched her for a moment. It was a good thing that chicken was already dead, the way she clenched it with every pluck. Reaching out a hand, he covered hers. "It will help me in my dealings with Obadiah if I know of his unsuitable traits."

Her face tensed. She made no move to enlighten him. He released her. "I must guess then?"

She said nothing.

"Well, I would suppose he either took mistresses, was a slug-a-bed, or overindulged in drink."

She reddened. "I asked not and cared not about the women. He never missed work, and tipping the cup was not his way."

"Then what?" he asked, rubbing his eyes.

She remained silent. His hand stilled. Beatings. He knew many a man who beat his wife. His father had never once raised a hand in anger, but there were count-less who did. "He mistreated you?"

Color drained from her face, yet she continued with her task. He tensed. "And the children?"

The quickening of her task was her only response. He waited. "Mary? Did Obadiah mistreat the children?"

Silent tears began to fall from her eyes. "Yes," she choked, so softly he barely heard it.

His nostrils flared. Placing his hands on either side of him, he leaned forward. "How did your children die?"

With total disregard to preserving the feathers, her pace became frenzied. He took her chin in his hand and raised it. "How did your children die?"

Her face was pale, her eyes hollow. "Obadiah had no patience for the crying. Quite mad it would drive him. I placed myself between him and the babies, but the more I did, the more vexed he became. Until one day, his anger, it turned into rage."

He slid his eyes shut. *Wretched cur, when he's found it will go the worse for him.*

Her body slumped. "I tried to stop him, I did, but . . ."

Removing the chicken from her lap, he tenderly reached for her. She came to him without resistance.

The pinks and oranges of the sky had been chased away by the sun, now shining its full glory upon them. A nearby whippoorwill repeatedly whistled the rendition of his name.

How long they embraced, knee to knee, torso to torso, he knew not. Eventually, she tensed.

He released her. "I promise you. Never again will Obadiah lay a hand on you in anger."

Her gaze flew up. "No, Josh. You mustn't confront him. It will only make it worse, it will."

"My word's been given."

She touched his arm. "Obadiah can be ruthless, and his ways are not fair."

"Thank you for the warning."

"You understand not. Where his property is concerned, it's unreasonable he is. Why, he'll kill you just for mentioning it."

"We'll see."

Her eyes welled up again. "I'll not be having another death on my hands. And if you don't have a care for my feelings, then what of your bride's? She'll not be thanking me for the demise of her man, that's for certain."

He frowned. "You wound me with such a lack of confidence. He never will lay a heavy hand on you again and that's an end to it. As for Hannah, she has nothing to do with it."

"Nothing to do with it. Nothing to do with it. What's she like, this Hannah of yours?" After a shocked pause, her face flooded with color.

He widened his eyes, hesitated, then sought to put her at ease. "Ah, how to describe Hannah?" He pursed his lips. "She reminds me of Mama's porcelain cup. Delicate, fragile, refined."

"And beautiful?"

He shrugged. "Yes. She's quite lovely."

She reached for the chicken. A breeze stirred her thick maple hair, while white feathers floated around her.

Glancing at the sun, he noted the time. He needed to go. Stalling, he gathered the runaway feathers and deposited all but one into the pouch resting at her side. "Well, I must away before the captain leaves without me."

Keeping her chin tucked, she said nothing.

He stroked the downy fringe of the single plume in his hand. "Aren't you going to say good-bye?"

"Good-bye, Master Josh."

"Josh," he corrected.

She shook her head. "Master Josh."

"You called me Josh a few moments ago."

She glanced up. "Did I? I wasn't, I mean, I didn't—"

He placed the feather against her lips, effectively stopping her words. "It's all right. I simply want you to continue with that form of address."

She sat still, her gaze riveted to his. With slow deliberation, he drew the feather to her jawline, following its sleek curve to her ear, then up to the widow's peak forming the juncture from which her heart-shaped face began. With the gentle slope of her nose beckoning, he ushered the feather to its tip. Her lashes swept down.

Ah, don't hide those lovely eyes from me, dear Mary. He skimmed the feather across her lids. They twitched, then opened. Extraordinary.

He grazed the rosy buds of pink blooming along her cheeks. What pleasure God must have taken in creating her. She held a subtle beauty, enhanced by her very nature.

Her lips parted. He guided the feather to them, tracing their enticing shape. He hesitated. Tempting as it was, he had no business kissing her, not when he had another awaiting him back in England.

He transferred the feather from her lips to his, brushing it lightly across his own. She swept her lashes down, then resumed her plucking.

Slowly, he stood. "Good-bye, Mary."

"Happy wedding, Master Josh," she whispered.

Tucking the feather safely into his cloth pouch, he noted the bittersweet taste her good tidings had caused.

Stirring a batter of cornmeal, salt, and water, Drew determinedly kept his back to Constance as she brushed out her hair in long, slow strokes. The color of it hurt his eyes this early in the morning.

He turned to pluck a cloth from a peg by the fireplace, then paused. She was no longer kneeling by the chest, nor was she anywhere in the cottage.

He glanced at the door, propped open with a rock. He'd given her another old dress of Nellie's this morning, and she'd been anxious to change. A movement up by the rafters caught his attention.

There she knelt, with her back to him, probably thinking the loft's shadows hid her from view. Not so. She lifted her dress up over her head. His breath caught.

He should turn around. He should leave her to do as she would. Instead, his gaze lingered, moving down to her waist where it curved in and then flared out at her hips. Those hips disappeared in the blanket she'd wrapped around her lower body.

He held himself perfectly still. He'd given his word not to bed her, but he'd never said anything about this. It was implied, though, and he knew it.

He swallowed. She'd probably never gone without underthings in all her born days. He'd never really realized until now that she wore nothing underneath the flimsy homespun dress. When the next ship came through, he'd be sure to get her some stockings, at least, and maybe some shoes.

With the help of God Almighty, he forced himself to turn back to the fire and spread some hot ashes over the hearthstone. He poured batter on top of the ashes.

Moments later, she stepped up beside him. "What are you making?"

"Ash cakes."

"But you're getting them dirty."

"When the batter cooks up, you simply lift them up and brush off the ashes."

He demonstrated how to do the first one, allowing her to do the rest while he poured more batter onto some fresh ashes. "Take that first batch out to the men," he said, "and tell them to help themselves to anything down in the orchard."

When she returned, he had another batch ready. "I'll take these out. You grab a trencher, dust those last few off, and we'll eat in here."

He returned to find two trenchers on the board. "Who's eating with us?"

She blinked from her place at the table. "No one."

"Then why are there two trenchers?"

"There are two people."

He picked one up and returned it to the shelf. "No need to wash two when we have use for only one."

Settling himself on the bench next to her, he said grace, then popped several cakes into his mouth.

She sat with her hands in her lap. "We're to eat with our fingers?"

He chewed a moment more, then swallowed. "Stabbing ash cakes with a knife might prove to be a bit futile."

She wet her lips. "I see."

Polishing off more cakes, he suppressed a smile. First no privy, then no bed, now no utensils. He'd make a colonist out of her yet. Reaching for his noggin, he downed the rest of his cider. "Mary and Sally should be back sometime this morn. In the meanwhile, please see to your chores."

She lifted her brows. "Chores? What would you have me do?"

Taking off his napkin, he stood. "You know—weed the garden, wash the utensils, gather the eggs, that sort of thing."

He stepped out of the cottage, grabbed a large iron pot, and reentered. "Here are some turtles I caught yesterday." He set the pot on the board. "We'll eat them for our midday meal. If Mary doesn't return within an hour, you'll need to chop off their heads, then drop them—shell and all—into boiling water." He plucked his hat off a peg by the door. "See you at noon."

Constance stared at the large pot beside her. After several moments, she leaned over to peek inside. The turtles were not only huge but alive. She would never make it until spring.

Thoughts of Uncle Skelly and his diary intruded. She took a deep breath. Yes, she would. She would, by heaven, make it until spring. She must. *But Lord, I'll need your help!*

Wiping moisture from her forehead, she tugged the oversized skirt from under her feet. Before this day was through, she would alter these dresses Drew had given her. Meanwhile, she would make good on her commitment to enjoy a daily bath.

The sun had gotten a jump on her by the time she returned from the creek clean, refreshed, and beaming with pride over the dishes she'd scrubbed. Wouldn't Drew be pleased?

With a tune on her lips, she carefully stacked the clean dishes in their proper places and stoked the fire. Making a wide circle around *the pot,* she scooped up a basket and headed to the chicken coop.

Situated on the southeast corner of the clearing, the chickens were imprisoned behind a rudimentary fence. The twilled wooden barricade, comprised of thin rails passing over and under sturdy posts, encircled their little house and yard. Stepping through its gate, she paused as chickens came from all quarters. Ugly creatures. "I've come for the eggs."

The hens clucked.

She backed up a step. "Yes. I don't blame you. I'd be vexed as well. Therefore, I will only take a few. Would that be acceptable?"

A large, particularly ugly gray-and-white rooster crowed loud and long.

"Ah. You must be the master. Well, I see not what you're complaining about. You're not the one that's done the laying now, are you?"

The rooster took four more steps toward her and crowed again.

She scooted down the fence line, making her way to the hen house. "Easy. I meant no offense. Pay me no mind. I'll be but a moment and then will leave you in peace."

The ornery creature charged. Shrieking, Constance swiped the basket in front of her. The other chickens in the coop yelped while the rooster fluttered its wings and tried to flog her again.

She screamed without ceasing, bandying her basket about like a sword. Before she could manage to escape, the monster caught the calf of her leg with its spurs. She knocked him to the side with her basket, allowing just enough time to put herself on the other side of the gate.

He flew against it, crowing. She screamed again as she fumbled to secure the latch. The hens raced around the coop squalling and flapping their wings.

Jerking up her skirt, she could see nothing but blood running down her calf. "Oh, you awful, awful creature! Look what you've done. Why, I'll have your head for this. Don't you doubt it for a moment!"

The rooster continued to crow and spread its wings. With a running leap, it managed to lift itself off the ground. Constance screamed and scrambled back, but despite its efforts, the cock couldn't get higher than midfence.

"It's supper you'll be tonight, you worthless clapper-dudgeon," she hollered from a safe distance. "Mark my words. When the *real* master gets home, we'll just see whose side he's on. It's the mistress you've flogged and, so help me, I will savor every bite I take of your wretched hide!"

Spinning around, she limped to the cottage, back straight, head high. The eggs would have to wait.

Once inside the cottage, she jerked her chemise off a peg and ripped a goodly portion from its skirt. Plopping onto the bed, she lifted her dress for another look. What a nasty mess and oh, how it throbbed.

She bound the wound tightly, all the time visualizing that awful bird on a spit over tonight's fire. She knotted the ends of the rag together, then took a deep breath. She could have been killed. What if she hadn't been able to get out of that pen? What if the gate hadn't opened? What if it hadn't closed? Her entire body began to shake.

None of this should be happening. She should be safe at home, where she knew the rules and how to get around them. Certainly, the war had disrupted everyone's life, but this . . . this place with its barbaric ways and uncivilized people. No telling what might happen to her.

I want to go home, Lord. Home. Where the faces are familiar. Where I am loved and protected and cherished. Where we eat real food and sleep in real beds. Where I have shoes and stockings. Candles and parchment.

On the heels of that prayer, though, came not peace,

but anger. Pure, unadulterated, full-blown anger. And with it a great urge to unleash it on the men who had done this to her.

She spied *the pot*. Narrowing her eyes, she rose from the bed in search of the kitchen knife, then made her way to the table with only the slightest of limps, the weapon hanging heavily from her hand.

Rolling up her sleeve, she took a fortifying breath, then plunged her free hand into the smelly water. The reptiles retreated into their shells. The turtle she grasped displayed a perfectly geometrical design on its back. Fascinating.

With the tip of the knife, she tapped what could be construed as the turtle's shoulder. "I dub thee," tap, "Sir Hopkin," tap. "Governor of the Virginia Colonies." Looking at the specimen with contempt, she lifted her chin a mite. "Because of the shirking of your duties and your treacherous behavior toward countless unsuspecting women, I sentence you to die, by beheading."

She held Sir Hopkin high for all to see while she marched him out of the cottage and into the clearing. Dusting off a place in the yard, she set him down.

He did not come out. Typical, the lily-livered fiend. "Come, Sir Hopkin. Take your due like a man, even though all know you to be a spineless, arrogant, useless knave."

Nothing. She frowned. How did one make a turtle come out of its shell? Squatting down beside the animal, she studied its design. The sun climbed higher and beads of moisture formed at her hairline before Sir Hopkin deigned to poke his uglisome head out.

She whizzed the knife down. He withdrew faster than

she imagined possible. She took a deep breath. Her leg ached, her anger simmered.

After spending a good part of the morning trying to behead Sir Hopkin without success, she swiped him up off the ground, marched—well, *limped*—back into the cottage and threw him into his watery home. The turtle soup would have to wait. Cursed animals.

She rubbed her leg, then set out for the garden. It, too, was encircled by a fence woven together with shaved tree limbs. Her expertise was cutting and arranging flowers. Tilting her head, she studied the chessboard of variegated pieces. No flowers, only herbs and weeds. But which were which? She sighed. The gardening, it seemed, would have to wait as well.

Returning to the cottage, she stoked the fire, set a pot to boil and then reached for the dress she'd worn yesterday. Taking it outside, she proceeded to alter its dimensions.

When Drew arrived home it was to find Constance sitting prettily in the middle of the clearing wearing a dress that actually fit, while sewing on another.

The chickens in the coop squawked, the garden remained unchanged, and no smoke came from the chimney.

"Constance?"

"Drew! Oh, thank goodness. You're home." Struggling to her feet, she limped toward him.

He frowned, but only for a moment. She'd done something drastic to her gown. It looked nothing like the ones Nellie wore. It was tasteful and modest, covering every inch of her, but simultaneously accentuating all the dips and swells of her person. "What did you do to Nellie's old dress?"

Looking down, she held out the skirt of her dress with two hands. "I made a few alterations."

She slid the skirt back and forth, causing the fabric to brush from one side of her torso to the other, then lifted her attention. "I left a little room in it, though. I'm still not myself, after the voyage and all."

His gaze remained on her face, trying to banish the image of even larger proportions filling out her dress. "You are exceptionally fast with a needle."

"Yes, I am."

"Mary and Sally have been delayed."

She released her skirt. "Why?"

"Gerald sent word that Nellie's time is upon her."

"Gerald?"

"Nellie's husband."

She frowned. "Oh dear. Perhaps I should go and collect Sally?"

"No. You'd get lost. Why have you not weeded the garden?"

"I know not which are weeds and which are herbs."

"You've never gardened?"

"Only flowers."

He nodded. "And the eggs?"

Her features clouded. "Your rooster attacked me. Please wring his neck for me and we'll eat him for supper."

"What did you do to make him attack you?"

Her eyes grew wide. "What did I do? What did *I* do? That worthless cock attacked me and you want to know what *I* did? I'll tell you what I did. I screamed so loud they could hear me all the way back home. Then I smashed him with my basket. Then I told him he'd be dead before nightfall. That's what *I* did. Now what are *you* going to do about it?"

He rubbed his forehead. No one could be that inept. Even Sally could collect eggs. "Well, I'm not going to wring his neck. That's for certain."

She gasped. "Why not? I could have been killed!"

"You provoked him."

"Provoked him! I did not do one blessed thing to your precious rooster! I went into that coop, announcing my intentions to gather eggs, and he came at me full speed."

"You announced your intentions? What do you mean, you announced your intentions?"

She paused. "I walked in and told the chickens I planned to gather the eggs."

"What else did you say?"

She propped her hand on her waist. "Drew, you are testing me sorely."

"What else did you say?"

"I don't remember. I might have insulted it a time or two, but this is absurd. It didn't understand me!"

"You were crowing in his yard."

"Your pardon?"

"You were crowing in his yard. Roosters use their crow to establish territory and are very sensitive about it. If you went into the coop and started blathering about this and that, then there's no doubt he took it as a threat. You didn't let him win, did you?"

Her face registered what could only be shock. "If you are suggesting that I was to stay inside that yard and fight it out with him, then yes. I let him win. But ultimately, when his neck is wrung, the win is mine."

He lifted up his hat then resettled it on his head. "Come. I'll show you how to win."

"No. I'm not going back inside that pen with you or anyone else. Not until Mr. Meanie is on a spit."

Mr. Meanie? Suppressing a smile, he veered toward the chicken coop. She stayed where she was.

"You don't have to come in, Constance. You may watch me from the other side of the fence."

Her basket lay on its side where she must have dropped it in her scramble to freedom. Drops of blood littered the clearing. Frowning, he turned back toward her. "You are all right?"

Her lips thinned.

Body O'Caesar, he thought, *I should have asked that earlier*. Sighing, he entered the coop. "Hello, children, Mr. Meanie. How do you fare this day?"

The chickens squawked. The rooster ruffled his feathers.

"See you how Mr. Meanie is already becoming provoked?"

She gave no response.

"So. You've taken to attacking defenseless women, have you? Well, I've not checked the damage yet, but you'd better hope it's not too severe. It's displeased I am that you attacked my wife. You're to treat her with respect."

The cock began to dance around him.

"What? Like you not my crowing in your yard? Then come and get me, you scurvy fellow. Do your worst."

As if on cue, the rooster struck. Drew jumped to the side, making a swipe at its feet, but missed. They circled each other. Drew sang, adding a jump and a jig with each verse for good measure.

> Here's to the maid with a bosom of snow;
> Now to her that's as ripe as a berry;
> Here's to the wife with a face full of woe,
> And now to the girl that is merry:
> Let the toast pass,
> Drink to the lass,
> I'll warrant she'll prove an excuse for the glass.

As he expected, the popular drinking ballad infuriated the rooster. Crowing with displeasure, he charged. Drew swiped again and, snagging the cock's feet, lifted him into the air, upside down. "There you have it, Constance. How to establish territory. I will hold him like this while I crow in his yard for a while longer, and when all the blood has settled in his head for a moment or two, I will release him. I, also, will have won."

"You're not going to kill him."

He paused. She had made her way to the edge to the fence and rested her arms atop it.

"No. I'm not."

"Why not?"

"We need the eggs."

"There are two other roosters in the coop."

He glanced at the other cocks, pecking at the ground in the yard. "If I kill Mr. Meanie, one of those would then establish itself as cock of the walk, and you'd have to deal with that rooster as well."

"Don't they fight amongst themselves?"

"These three roosters have grown up together, but if

I introduced a new rooster into the yard, a fight would ensue."

She nodded once and turned to leave. He hated it when she dismissed him like that. He'd told her once already never to walk away from him in the midst of a conversation, and he'd meant it. Now he'd have to deal with her again on the issue. Pig-headed woman.

He waited a few more minutes before releasing the bird, then watched as Constance's Mr. Meanie wove around jiggling his head.

Letting himself out of the coop, Drew headed toward the cottage. He needed to have a look at her injury.

NINE

She should have known he wouldn't kill the rooster. Food-producing animals were too valuable in this wilderness to be terminated for the mere offense of attacking one's guests. It wasn't as if he liked the rooster more than her, it was simply a matter of practicality. So why was she harboring such hurt feelings?

Hearing Drew's approach, she allowed the hem of her skirt to fall before continuing to rub her calf.

"Why are the turtles not cooking?"

From her perch on the edge of the bed, she tried to suppress her irritation. "How do you make a turtle come out of his shell and stay out long enough to behead him?"

He took off his hat and hung it on a peg. "You hold a stick in front of the turtle and coax him to bite down on it."

She stopped her massage and looked up at him. "I'd never have thought. I did keep the embers—Oh!" Jumping from the bed, she began to work the fire. He, in turn, grabbed the pot of turtles and left.

When next she saw him, he had one pot of headless

turtles and one bucket of fresh milk. She, thank goodness, had accomplished a thing or two herself—the fire was going and a pot of bubbling water hung above it, steam surging from its mouth.

"Drop the turtles into the water, and then I'll show you how to pound Indian corn into samp for the midday meal."

Had anyone asked her if she was squeamish, she'd have vehemently denied it. But always before, her meals had been set before her, cooked and seasoned to perfection. She knew, of course, she was eating animals, but she'd never given much thought to the specifics of their preparation. As she looked into the pot of bleeding headless turtles, she wondered if the pleasures of mealtime were forever lost to her.

Drew appeared to have assembled all that was necessary for the samp. She swallowed with effort, forcing her stomach back down where it belonged, then dispatched with the turtles. The *glub, glub, glub* of their descent nearly did her in. "What's samp?" she gasped.

"The most expedient meal I could think of. You simply pound corn, then pour milk on top before serving."

She tossed the last turtle in, then quickly turned to mortar and pestle, pounding corn with a vengeance.

"You're making a mess, Constance. Slow down."

She slowed. With the two of them working together, they had a goodly portion pounded in no time.

"Now, let us have a look at your injury." Standing, he offered her a hand up.

The gash was in a most improper place. "It's fine, thank you."

"I'll have a look anyway."

She wanted to refuse, but if she did, he might very well remind her that as her "husband" he had a right to look at much more than just this injury. She walked to the bed and sat, skirt down, knees and ankles together, hands locked on her lap.

"Where did he catch you?"

"Above the ankle."

A pause. "How far above the ankle?"

She willed the blush to go away. "A good two inches."

"I have a need to see it."

"I hardly even feel it anymore."

He glanced at the hem of her skirt. "What did you treat it with?"

"I wrapped it."

"No comfrey?"

"No."

He left the cottage, and she let out a sigh of relief. *Thank you, Lord.* At least she'd been spared that indignity. She started to rise, only to plop back down when he returned with a plant he'd obviously just pulled from the garden. She watched him rinse its roots, wrap them in a rag, and crush them with a rock.

"Show me." He knelt before her, focusing intently on her skirt.

Her stomach churned again, and though this sensation was entirely different from the one she'd fought down before, it was no less disturbing. She extended her injured leg and gathered a bit of her skirt at the knee, inching the hemline upward. She felt him release the knot of her bandage and unwrap it, slowing only when he came to where the cloth stuck to her abrasion.

She sat still, watching his bent head covered with that

magnificent black hair, now matted down from his hat. She curled her fingers.

He immediately paused and glanced up at her. "This pains you?"

Heavens, he was a handsome man. She searched desperately for some flaw and could find nothing. The darkness of his skin and the crinkles the sun had put there actually added to his appeal. The eyes searching hers seemed bluer every time she saw them. The last time she'd seen them so clearly from this range was on their wedding day, just before he'd kissed her. She had closed her eyes against them then. She couldn't make herself do so now. "Your pardon?"

"Is the pain great, then?"

This had to stop. She could not sit here and ruminate over this temporary husband of hers. She was only here until Papa came for her, and she was less important than the rooster. "There is no pain at all."

"Your hands are fisted."

She immediately unfurled them as she felt the blood rush to her face. "I'm just a bit nervous."

"I'll be gentle."

She swallowed and gave him a slight smile. "I know."

"Then why are you nervous?"

She said nothing but knew the moment he realized the source of her unease, for his face too turned red and he quickly saw to his task. He finally managed to free the bandage. "It's bleeding again. I'm sorry. It's just that the claw mark is located such that I can't easily reach it."

"Oh, your pardon." She twisted her leg, but she could tell he was still having difficulty. After a few moments, though, he had the bleeding stopped.

"I need to put some comfrey on it."

She nodded.

He didn't move.

"What is it?" she asked. "There is a sting to it?"

"No, no. It will provide relief almost immediately."

"Then what's wrong?"

"I'm not sure how I can apply it to the back of your calf and then bandage it without loosing a great deal of the powder to the floor."

"I can do it."

He shook his head. "No, you'd have even more difficulty than I. No, what I need is for you to . . . to lie face down on the bed, please."

Neither of them moved. She allowed her skirt to fall to the floor. It was one thing to sit on the edge of the bed and have him look after one limb. It was something else entirely to lie prone on the bed and have him lift her dress and attend to her.

"I'll do without the roots," she said.

"I've already picked and crushed them. Besides, it needs the healing powers of the comfrey. That blasted rooster cut into you rather deeply, and being new to the colonies, you're more susceptible than most."

"Susceptible to what?"

"Death."

Well. That was certainly blunt. And, thankfully, made modesty seem rather trivial. Best of all, he'd just insulted the rooster. She swung her legs up onto the bed and rolled over. Her skirts were hopelessly twisted, but before she could fix them, he'd loosened them and flicked them up to her knees. She buried her face in the bedding, ignoring the outdoorsy smell of him there beneath her nose.

The comfrey roots did indeed feel wonderful. He said not a word as he worked over her, placing the powder on her injury, covering it with something soft and fuzzy, then rewrapping it with the rag. He maneuvered her leg as if it was of no import, lifting it, bending it, placing it on the bed. When the rag was knotted, she felt him glide his fingers along the edge of the bandage, smoothing it. Her stomach clenched, her heart skipped a beat, she forgot to breathe.

Was it a caress or simply a doctor seeing to his patient? She dared not move, for if it had been an innocent gesture, she certainly didn't want to overreact. And if it hadn't been? It *must* have been.

The smoothing stopped, yet she still felt his weight on the bed. She jerked when he took hold of her skirt, then called herself ten kinds of a fool, for he'd paused then in the midst of lowering it. Before releasing the hem, his fingers slowly brushed against her ankle. She spun over, landing on her back, plucking her skirt from his fingertips.

A mistake. Now she lay stretched out on his bed, facing him while he sat beside her, his eyes three times darker than they'd been before. He leapt up, grabbed his hat from the peg, and strode from the cottage.

She draped her arm across her eyes and took in great gulps of air. He *was* attracted to her. There was no denying it now. She'd seen that look on the men who'd asked for her hand in marriage and some who had not. The difference was *her* reaction. Instead of boredom or aversion, she felt every nerve in her body standing at attention—some nerves more than others.

What if he changed his mind and decided to exercise

his husbandly rights? She lowered her arm to her side. She'd not be granted an annulment, that's for certain, and that would be the end of the *Ladies' Mathematical Diary*. Heaving herself up out of bed, she put the samp in bowls, hearing for the first time the indentured men in the yard.

The men seemed to enjoy the simple midday meal. Drew allowed them a moment's rest so he could give Constance a tour of the garden. He explained what each plant was and how it was used before rounding up his men and leaving.

The indentured men were to view the land they could claim at the end of their service. It was located on the very edges of his property and would require some time to reach. Upon his return several hours later, he found the garden weeded, the yard swept, and the smell of turtle broth floating on the air.

Removing his hat, he entered the open cottage door and came to a dead stop. A clump of lavender blossoms roosting in Mama's old porcelain cup sat in the center of the board and the movables hanging from the various pegs had been organized. All the clothing hung on one wall, the utensils on another.

Constance sat by the hearth, scribbling in the soot with a stick. She obviously hadn't heard him come in. Staying where he was, he allowed his gaze to roam over her person, his thoughts returning to when he'd dressed her leg. She had freckles there too, but lighter. And her skin. So smooth, so soft. Heaven help him, he'd tried to remain detached, had even pretended in his mind's eye doing such a thing for Gertard Jarvis. But all that had done was point out the lushness of Constance.

He'd spent much more time at the task than it required. It wasn't until he'd lowered her skirt that he realized how tense she'd been. Even still, he'd wanted one last touch. She'd near flown off the bed when he'd lingered a bit long at her ankle. All set to apologize, the words stuck in his throat when he looked into her eyes. It was not disgust he saw there. Far from it.

He took a deep breath and pushed that image, along with the one of her dressing in the loft, to the far recesses of his mind.

Lord, I cannot open myself up to her. No matter the silky skin, no matter the apparent attraction she may or may not have for him, no matter that she was his wife. It was of no consequence.

He allowed himself to remember the grief, the pain, the numbness he'd experienced as this land stripped loved one after loved one from him. Then Leah. The land had taken Leah a mere a week before they were to wed. He'd vowed never again to become involved. He'd meant it then and he meant it now.

"More spiders and flies?" he asked, his voice lower than he'd intended.

She squealed, then laid a hand against her chest. "I didn't hear you." She glanced at the window. "Where are the indentures?"

"Setting traps. What are you working on? More spiders?"

Shrugging, she set her stick down. "How did it go with the men?"

It was a wifely question. One she'd asked before, as if she had a real vested interest.

He hung his hat on a peg. "I'm glad I took them. It's the first time I've seen any animation amongst the group."

Brushing off her hands, she rose. "That's good."

"It's a start." He noticed the embers. "You kept the fire going."

She glanced at the pot hanging over the ashes. "Yes."

Yes, indeed. The pot was heating. The yard was swept. The cottage was spotless. But the eggs were still in the hen house. "You ready to gather some eggs?"

She studied him for a moment. "Do I have a choice?"

"No."

She moistened her lips. "Then I guess I'm ready."

He gave her an apron to wear, telling her to tuck it up and form a pouch for the eggs. They entered the chicken coop together, neither saying a word. The chickens rushed toward them and he could see Constance was skittish. He gathered the eggs. She, sticking close, placed them in her apron. Mr. Meanie gave them no notice.

At suppertime, the indentured men were not animated exactly, but certainly more relaxed. Rather than sitting stiffly alone, looking at nothing but the food they consumed, they now lounged about the clearing, some sitting, some leaning on an elbow, but all grouped in clusters of three or more, quietly visiting during their meal. Constance moved amongst them, enjoying the hum of their conversations superimposed over the drone of the forest's insects.

She'd acted as hostess to many meals, but never had she derived such pleasure from compliments and requests for seconds as she had this evening.

Although gutting the turtles was most disagreeable, she found she actually enjoyed preparing the soup. Never mind that Drew stood at her side, guiding and tutoring her through each step. No, her sense of pleasure came from a task completed from its earliest stages to its last.

"Might I 'ave another serving, Mistress?"

She turned to find an empty bowl extended to her by a set of bony arms. In between those arms were a bony face, a toothy grin, and a head of wild blond hair.

The men had reluctantly introduced themselves to her this morning when she'd given them ash cakes, but she was terrible with names and couldn't remember any of them. "Certainly, Mr. . . . ?"

"Pott. Samuel Pott, mum." He reached up to tip his hat, but of course there was no hat to tip.

She curtsied with a smile and fetched him a second serving.

"Ah, thank you, Mistress. It's a feast the king 'imself would be 'appy to 'ave."

"You're most welcome, Mr. Pott."

"Call them by their first names, Constance."

She glanced over to see Drew issuing this command while taking in more bowls for second servings. So magnanimous was she at the moment, she chose to ignore this bit of rudeness. Still, she must at some point remind him never to correct her in front of the servants. "You're most welcome, Samuel."

She looked down to see Samuel had turned as pale as death, and all the indentures stopped in midmotion.

Drew might have missed the slight he'd just given her, but the men didn't and they expected her to retaliate in kind—toward Samuel.

This was only their second day away from the ship, and she knew only too well how they felt. That they were relaxed at all was indeed an impressive recommendation of Drew's ability with them.

She knelt down so as to be on Samuel's eye level. "You've nothing to fear from me or my husband. If you serve us well, you will be treated well."

Lowering his lids, Samuel nodded.

She cocked her head. "You know, I've six sisters and three brothers—all of them older than me but one. You remind me somewhat of my oldest brother. He quite enjoys his soups and chowders and has a fine set to his shoulders, very much like you. Therefore, I'll not be forgetting your name again, Samuel. Please forgive me for doing so this time."

He'd raised his gaze in the midst of this, and although she hadn't drawn a smile from him, she hoped she'd restored at least some of the casual mood from before. "Oh, no, mum. There's nothin' to forgive, there's not. But I'm much obliged, I am."

She nodded and stood. At a rustling in the brush, she turned to see Mary and Sally trudge into the clearing. "Mary! Sally!" Waving, she rushed over to them. "I'm so very glad you're back. Care you to have some turtle soup?"

Mary shook her head. "No, thank you. Grandma fed the both of us before we took leave, she did. It's sitting down for a moment I'd like to be doin' now."

"Well, let's go inside and sit, then." She looked down

at Sally. "And what of you? Would you care for some soup?"

"Nellie has a baby!"

"A baby! How very wonderful. And how very wonderful it is to see you." She extended a hand to Sally, but before the child could grasp it, she caught sight of Drew and ran squealing into his arms.

Propping her on his hip, he joined them. "How's Nellie?"

"Fine," Mary answered. "It's a big lusty boy she's had."

"No problems, then?"

"No, sir."

"What did they name him?" Constance asked.

"They didn't."

"They're waiting for the baptism?"

Mary shook her head. "They're waiting until he's three."

"What?" Constance exclaimed.

"More often than not," Drew explained, "the children here never see their third birthday. So most people in the settlement distance themselves from the little ones."

"How dreadful! Surely you didn't do that to Sally?"

He tightened his lips. "I've never been able to distance myself."

"Well, I should think not."

He set Sally down. "It's not something I'm proud of, Constance." With that, he spun around and returned to the men.

"Of all the ridiculous . . ." She turned to Mary. "Come. Tell me of your visit."

TEN

With the conclusion of the meal, Mary oversaw Sally while Drew and Constance headed to the creek with the soiled pots, bowls, and noggins.

Once there, Constance set the bowls down on the bank. A feeling of contentment flowed through her. She'd made it through her wedding night without mishap. She had two dresses that fit her reasonably well. She'd completed several chores throughout the day. And best of all, her wager of last evening would bear its first fruit tonight. She didn't have to clean the dishes.

Propping herself against the birch tree, she regarded Drew from beneath her lashes and barely suppressed a smile. He tore into the dishes as if he wrestled the devil himself, his shoulders flexing, his arms tensing.

His mood had deteriorated by great degrees the closer and closer they'd come to supper's end. Then he'd said not a word—nor even glanced at her—during the entire walk down here. His stance had been rigid, his jaw tight.

Picking up a pebble, she fingered it for the slightest of moments before trying to skip it across the water. It fell with a dissatisfying plop, causing a chain of circular ripples to break out across the creek.

He paused for a moment before continuing with his task. Drawing up her knees, she wrapped her arms around them. "I was wondering . . . if a hen and a half laid an egg and a half in a day and a half, how many eggs would seven hens lay in six days?"

He stopped scrubbing the bowl, holding it still beneath the water. Slowly, he looked over at her, blue eyes dusted with dark thick lashes.

She smiled and propped her chin onto her knees.

He offered no smile, no dimples, no response. He simply remained crouched on the bank, staring at her.

"I have more if you'd rather try a different one."

"You have nine brothers and sisters?" he asked.

She raised her brows. "Yes. Yes, I do."

He turned back to his chore. "How many are still alive?"

"Why, all of them."

"I thought you were raised by *the uncle*."

"I was, along with Rebecca, my younger sister. But Papa fetched me home, remember?"

"Ah, yes. For the marriage contract that you refused."

"That's correct."

"And all those siblings were there waiting to take you into their bosom."

She shook her head. "No, they'd already married and left home. But Papa loved to gather them all under his roof as often as he could."

He stopped working again to look at her. "Tell me of them."

She looked at the stack of dirty bowls, then the sun

lowering in the horizon. Heavens, they would be here all night at this rate.

Pushing herself up, she retrieved a bowl and knelt beside him. "My two eldest sisters were married by the ages of twelve and thirteen. Papa had contracted for my other sisters when they were even younger."

"I'm sure he thought he was acting in their best interests."

"Yes, God bless him, he did. Unfortunately, the moral integrity of the groom was immaterial, for wedding into nobility was of utmost importance."

"Women can't be choosing their own husbands, Constance. It would be a disaster."

"Financially, maybe. But I'd rather live simply and be cherished than live luxuriously and be mistreated."

"Surely it's not as bad as all that."

"You haven't met my sisters' husbands."

Their elbows brushed. "Tell me."

She set the clean bowl down next to an assortment of animal tracks stamped into the shoreline, each one unique, yet all coexisting in order to survive. She picked up another bowl. "Leoma, the eldest, wrote to me of her husband's unkindness. I saw for myself that Arietta was beaten. Kristina, the most intelligent of us girls, was bound to a drunken lout. Doreen suffered silently with her spouse's philandering, and Jocelyn, pregnant with her eighth child, was temporarily deserted by her husband."

"That's only five sisters."

"Rebecca's husband stuck her in a musty old country home and hasn't allowed her out nor any visitors in." Constance eyed his empty hands. "You're a bit sluggish with your chores this evening. If you can't visit and work at the same time, I will tell you no more."

He raised a brow. "I've already washed twice the amount you have. I was simply allowing you time to catch up."

She picked up a noggin and handed it to him. "You're too kind. Prithee, continue with your task."

He dipped the noggin in the water. "What did your brothers do to the men who abused your sisters?"

Constance harrumphed. "Norval was busy marrying one of the queen's maids-of-honor and was sent to the continent just after the wedding. Rogan fought an unsuccessful duel over another maid-of-honor, and Foley had made himself so free with the pleasures of town that, consequently, he was unable to consummate his marriage, as all of London learned the next day."

"The devil, you say."

"Yes. Not exactly the kind of men to take an undesirable brother-in-law to task. They'd be more likely to befriend him."

He took the last bowl from her. "How did you manage to make it to the age of nineteen without being forced to marry?"

Scooting away from the bank, she rolled down her sleeves. "I think Uncle Skelly must have refused to send us home, for Papa had to personally come and fetch Rebecca and me."

He stacked the bowl with the others, then picked up his pipe. "How old were you?"

"I was thirteen. Rebecca was ten."

He settled himself against a tree. "What happened?"

She wrinkled her nose. "Well, Rebecca did just as

Papa told her. I, however, was not some ten-year-old child easily cowed into submission. Still, Papa moved forward, welcoming the viscount's son with open arms. The young man had barely set foot in the house before making his address to me."

Catching a movement on the far side of the creek, she gasped, then pointed at the brown furry creature sporting a black mask across its eyes and black rings on its tail. The bizarre animal dipped his dinner into the water before washing it off with his paws.

Drew watched it as well, not turning back to her until it finished and lumbered out of sight. "The savages call it an *aroughcoune*."

"I shall call it a bandit."

He humphed, then took a long pull from his pipe. "So, was this suitor's address so bad, then?"

She allowed a fleeting smile to cross her lips. "Oh, no. He was quite eloquent in his address and declared an extraordinary passion for me." She studied her nails. "Unfortunately, my aversion for him was extreme. Three weeks later he deserted the field." She looked up, and they exchanged a quiet smile.

"What happened then?"

"Well, my refusal put Papa in a rather untenable position. My rejection was embarrassing for him but not the least of his worries, for it appeared to others as if he couldn't make good on his business transactions, thus damaging his credit. Hence, he resolved I would yield . . . or else."

Drew's massive hands cradled his pipe, brushing its stem against his lips. "What did he do?"

She smoothed her skirt. "Well, you are aware, I'm

sure, that women have now been granted a veto in matrimonial affairs. The woman must, of course, have weighty grounds for her refusal. Still, a veto is a veto."

His hand stilled. "Did you have weighty grounds?"

She looked at him askance. "Mr. Fenton said that no wife of his would participate in mathematical pursuits."

The beginnings of a smile touched his lips. "But surely your father exerted his wishes."

"Oh, he tried. He certainly tried. First, he cut off my allowance. That was of little consequence, though, for I simply bought whatever I wanted and had it charged to my future husband—whomever that might turn out to be. So then, he engaged the entire family, hoping they would wear down my resistance. All my brothers and sisters, along with my dearest friends, did most diligently entreat me to give in." She shrugged. "I simply told Papa that no marriage could be consummated without my consent."

A dimple appeared as one side of his smile grew. "That sounds familiar."

She gave him a quelling look. "It wasn't as desperate as Papa made it seem. I still had at least five more years before I'd be considered a full-fledged spinstress."

"So what happened?"

"Well, Papa, you see, had already passed his seventy-third year, and he felt it imperative that I find a match, even if it meant breaking this one and starting all over. So that's exactly what he did."

"Your poor father."

"Poor father! Your sympathies, kind sir, are quite misplaced. Five weeks later he had a new set of marriage articles." She stuffed bits of stray hair back into her cap. "It was not the first time Papa had tried to ally himself with Lord Milburn through a marriage contract, and I represented his last chance at securing this coveted connection."

"Did your father take out the veto clause?"

She bit her lip. "He couldn't, but he did alter his contract. This time he made sure he would not be penalized financially if I refused the suitor, and he stipulated there would be no cash down until the wedding day."

Drew stretched out his legs, crossing them at the ankles. "And what were your 'weighty grounds' this time?"

"The man was fifty years my senior."

"'Tis not uncommon, that."

"'Tis disgusting."

He chuckled. "That's all relative, my dear."

She shrugged. "That was about the time my brothers diverted Papa's attention. When Norval married the queen's maid-of-honor, it opened up a whole new London for the family. I quite adored his wife, Emma, but then the war broke out and it split our family as sure as an ax splits a log. Even now one brother fights another." Lowering her lashes, she swallowed. "Anyway, I was left to my own devices for a good while."

"Thus you found yourself kidnapped and forced to marry an American."

She looked out over the waters, now reflecting the deep purples and pinks of the sunset. "It's been an adventure, that's for certain."

"It could cost you your life, yet. Going on that ship without escort was foolhardy in the extreme."

"I needn't a lecture," she said, standing, "from you or anyone else."

He stood as well, his expression darkening. "Listen well, Constance. Until your father comes, I am responsible for you. Therefore, you will curb your rebellious behavior. One act of foolishness here could result in your death."

She bristled. "And what would you care? Seems it would make your life a great deal easier if I weren't around."

"It would reflect badly of my character if you did something dull-witted."

His character? She snatched up the bowls. "Well, we can't have that now, can we?"

She started to leave. He grabbed her arm. "Do not ever walk away from me in the midst of a discussion, Constance."

They stood nose to nose, cocooned in the aroma of his tobacco. She hugged the bowls to her. "And if I do?"

"Try me."

A burning devil take him. "Why are you so angry all of a sudden? Is it because you've just realized I am who I say I am?"

"You've had an entire ship's voyage to concoct whatever stories you wished."

"I couldn't possibly have made all that up and you know it. That's the whole reason you questioned me."

He stood quietly, his eyes searching hers. At long last, he spoke. "The fact of the matter is, I think I do believe you. It's the only thing that makes sense."

"Do you, Drew? Do you really believe me?"

He loosened his hold on her arm and rubbed it slightly where he'd squeezed it. "Yes, Constance, I do. If I didn't I think, God help me, I'd have already bedded you."

Her breath caught. The light caress on her arm captured

her full attention. She scrambled for something to say. "And my title?"

Releasing her, he tapped her chin and picked up the other dishes. "You are Mistress Drew O'Connor until your father arrives and I can give you into his safekeeping."

Her heart surged. Heaven help her, how could she stand this until spring? "Just send me home on the next ship."

"We've already been through this. Besides, it would be too dangerous. Knowing you, you'd do something dull-witted and then I'd be held responsible."

All tender thoughts fled as exasperation surged to replace them. "*You* take me back, then."

"Don't be ridiculous. I can't leave. You'll have to wait until Josh returns." He glanced up at the dark sky. Gone was the sunset, replaced instead by the iridescence of the moon and stars. He scanned the path ahead of them. "Watch your step. The moon's shadows can be deceiving."

Lifting a corner of her skirt, she nodded, then turned. The night sounds shrouded them as they walked side-by-side to the cottage.

In the following week, the household fell into a comfortable pattern. Mary rose before dawn to prepare breakfast while Constance saw to Sally. After the men left for the fields, Constance and Sally did simple chores until Mary shooed them off so she could complete the tasks she deemed necessary.

"Let's go boo-ee picking!" Sally exclaimed one morning, basket in hand.

Constance frowned. "I've not seen any berries around here. Have you, Mary?"

"No, mum. There's sure to be some, though, and I'd be pleased to make you up some flummery."

"Have you been berry picking before, Sally?"

"Yes, with Gamma! I show you." Sally grasped Constance's hand, pulling her from the cottage.

Despite her concern at the twists and turns they took through the forest, they did indeed come across several shrubs covered with very small white berries. Sally picked one, rubbing its waxy coating between her fingers. Constance touched one to her tongue.

Sally seemed to find that quite amusing. "You don't eat bay boo-eez!"

The child began picking even as she spoke, her confidence such that Constance soon found herself reaching for more. She marveled at the abundance of berries, and the two of them filled the basket with a minimal amount of effort.

On their way home, they encountered a huge magnolia tree as wide around as Constance was tall. The ground surrounding it lay barren, for the mighty tree's roots drank up a great deal of the earth's nourishment and its abundance of intertwining branches and leaves kept any sunlight from filtering through.

Setting their basket down, Constance walked around the base of the tree, basking in its majesty. Sally followed, balancing herself on one root before hopping to another.

Constance tipped her head back, experiencing a moment of dizziness as she tried to see all the way to its top. "Imagine, Sally, if this were the paw of some giant creature, its head reaching as high as the heavens, its mouth holding two thousand teeth."

"Then *we'd* be ants."

She looked back at Sally. Intrigued, the two squatted down, searching for the insect in question. "Do you see any?"

Nodding, the child pointed. "Look! Maybe if we tell them we nice and they tell their ant friends, they won't sting us no more."

Constance chuckled, then froze as just a few feet behind Sally she saw a pair of very brown, very big, very bare feet. She slowly stood and placed herself between Sally and what she now saw was a very-bare-all-over boy of about ten or so years. Thank the good Lord he hadn't grown into those feet yet.

He wore not one stitch of clothing and had shaved the entire right side of his head. A crown of spiky black hair ran down the center of his scalp, and straight black hair flowed to his elbow on the left side. He had none of the paint markings on his body that she'd heard so much about, nor did he have the requisite loincloth. Ten years old or not, he was almost as tall as she and the first naked male body she'd ever seen in her life.

Her face burned as she tried to find a place for her eyes to rest. They honed in on a bow and sack of arrows slung over his shoulder. No sooner had she registered this than he laid them on the ground in front of his feet.

Well, at least it didn't appear as if he was going to shoot them, but it didn't look as if he was going to leave anytime soon either.

She heard Sally stir behind her. "Sally," she said with cool authority, "stay right where you are and do not move."

All was silent behind her. She didn't want to risk taking her eyes off of the savage to look at Sally, but a kernel of panic formed at the child's immediate acquiescence. "Sally, take hold of my skirt and give it a tug if you understand me."

She expelled a breath of relief at the answering tug. The boy stepped over his weapon, advancing slowly.

You will curb your rebellious behavior. One act of foolishness here in the colonies could result in your death. Drew's words rang again in her head. The boy was unarmed at the moment, but even so, she wouldn't have much of a chance against those young wiry muscles.

She briefly thought to send Sally racing but didn't know what the boy's reaction would be, nor did she know how many others were at this very moment hidden amidst the forestry watching. That, more than anything else, kept her immobile.

The boy's face held no expression. No signs of anger, friendship, curiosity, ill will. Nothing.

He stood before her now, a mere inch or two shorter than she. He reached up and she jumped. A flicker of disapproval ran across his face.

She had to calm down. She would wait until she had an inkling of his intentions, then go from there. Meanwhile, she'd do well to use her age to whatever advantage she could. She lifted her chin a mite and cocked an eyebrow.

He pushed in her cheek with one callused finger, then continued with his poking on her nose and chin. She decided to poke his cheek, nose, and chin. She'd gotten in no more than one poke when he jerked his head back and swatted her hand, his shock evident.

She widened her shoulders, stood to her full height,

and gave him her best glare, right down her nose. He seemed amused at that but disliked it mightily when she swatted *his* hand away.

After verbalizing what she assumed was a command, he tugged loose the strings of her cap. Saints that be, she trusted poking each other's faces was not some kind of mating ritual. No, she must get a hold of herself. He was but ten years. She hoped.

"Sally, if I tell you to run, then you run as fast as your feet can carry you to . . ." Where to send her? Supposing other savages were at the cottage or were on their way? "Do you know where your brother and the men work, Sally?"

"Yes, Sissy."

Her seriousness surprised Constance, but she didn't take time to question her good fortune. "That's very good. Then, if I tell you to run, you are to fly to Drew and tell him an Indian is with me and Mary might be in trouble. Tug my skirt if you understand."

She felt the answering tug. The savage had now pulled the cap from her head. There was no masking his astonishment. He tentatively touched her hair as if it might burn him. Then he spoke to her in an unintelligible tongue while gesturing toward her hair. It was clear he wanted it down.

Drew's litany returned with vigor. *You will curb your rebellious behavior.*

Perhaps cooperation might indeed be the wisest course. She loosened the coiled braid at the back of her head, pulling the plait to rest across her shoulder. The boy sucked in his breath, lifted the end of her braid, and led her like an animal to his sack of arrows.

Tales the English traders recounted of scalps that hung on lines stretching between two trees assailed her. When the Indian removed one of his arrows, Constance filled her lungs. "Run, Sally, run! *Now!*"

She heard the child scrambling away. The boy jerked Constance's braid, a string of gibberish coming from his mouth. The language might have been foreign to her, but the tone and scowl on his face were universal. Tears sprung to her eyes at the force of his jerk. His gaze shot to Sally before returning to her and voicing his displeasure again.

When he took to shaking his arrow in her face much like a mother scolding a child, a surge of anger spurted through her. With Sally gone, it was between the savage and herself. If he thought for one minute she'd meekly let some naked whelp have her scalp or anything else, he was in for a surprise. With a strength borne from fear and backed up with prayer, she shoved the young warrior right off his feet. Unfortunately, he still had hold of her braid. She went right down with him, gasping from the pain.

He quickly rolled atop her, pinning her arms beneath his knees. She bucked and kicked and squirmed. "Get off me, you poor, base, rascally, cheating, lack-linen toad! You'll not get one lock of hair without a fight, the likes of which you've never seen before. *Now, get thy brown nakedness off me!*"

When she reduced her struggles to catch her breath, she saw that the boy had a huge smile across his face. He said something to her, nodded his head in agreement with himself, and said it again. He then, without a by your leave, lifted her braid, chopped off a good six inches with his arrow, and jumped to his feet.

The shock of it held her immobile for no more than ten seconds before she was on her feet, running after him. He'd already grabbed his bow and arrows and was darting off into the forest.

"Come back here, you cutpurse! Come back here so I can hack off a length of your hair and see how you like it!" The boy was as swift as a rushing river and out of sight before she'd even finished her outburst.

Grabbing the sudden stitch in her side, she stopped and sucked in gulps of air. Thank heavens she'd sent Sally away. Her rich dark hair would have been much more of a prize for him. As her heartbeat slowed, she rubbed her sore head, then lifted her newly shorn braid.

How dare that heathen do such a thing. Never had she taken a pair of scissors to her hair. She might not care for it too terribly much, but it had been with her for nineteen years and she'd not planned on giving it up anytime soon.

Sally is alone in the woods.

The thought whipped through Constance, sending her heartbeat back up to a horrendous speed. Worse yet, Constance had no idea where the tobacco fields were and therefore, no idea which way Sally had headed. Whirling around, she raced toward home. Drew and several of the men met her before she'd even made it a quarter of the way.

"Sally?" she cried.

Scanning the forest around her, Drew slid to a stop. "Sally's fine. They have left?"

Relief poured over Constance before being replaced by fury, the likes of which she didn't even try to suppress. "How should I know? One minute we were relaxing under a magnolia, the next minute some knotty-pated youth was waving an arrow in my face."

Drew had the men fan out to check the area while keeping a few to watch his back.

She lifted up her shortened braid. "Look what that impudent goat did! He whacked off my hair!"

Drew fingered her hair, but held fast her gaze.

"And I thought those savages wore clothes! He had not one stitch on. Why, I understood that even the less important ones wore grass and the like, but this one must have been in the lowest of the classes, for he wore not one single blessed thing. He was naked, Drew. *Naked*. And with Sally right there and he not the least bit concerned about it. What's the matter with these Indians? Haven't they heard they're supposed to cover themselves? Just how backward are these heathens?"

The men returned with no sign of any Indians. Drew sent them back to the fields, all the while fingering her braid. "He was a youth, then?"

"Yes, thank God, but he was a sturdy one. When I shoved him down, you'd have thought that little chest of his was made of armor."

"You shoved him down?!"

"Of course! You think I'd let some runny-nosed young-ster scalp me without a fight?"

Cursing under his breath, he quickly surveyed the area again, grabbed her hand, and started jogging home. "We needs must go."

She threw a glance behind her. "Are they after us?"

"I hope not."

She put a hand to her head but didn't slow. "My cap. In the confusion I left it and the basket of berries behind."

"Where?"

"By a big magnolia tree."

"We can't go back now. I'll fetch them later when I can better ascertain the situation. Now hush and concentrate on the path. I want you not to stumble."

They made it home without further incident, but she could plainly see Drew was worried. Mary put a pot of cider on to warm then sifted dirt from some floured corn.

Sighing, Constance lowered herself onto the edge of the bed, allowed Sally to climb into her lap, then watched Drew pace the cottage floor, musket in hand.

His face was creased, his mind far away. She tried to catch his attention, but he was having none of it. If he didn't stop soon, though, she'd become dizzy just from watching.

Pulling her braid across her shoulder, she unraveled it, wincing at the tenderness in her scalp. Sally placed a thumb in her mouth and snuggled against Constance's shoulder. Thank goodness the child was safe. Shaken, maybe, but safe.

Constance combed her fingers through her own hair, swallowing back her tears as she looked at its jagged edges. She could have been killed, so what were a few inches of hair? The tears, however, continued to threaten.

Drew stopped his pacing and stood, watching her closely.

She rubbed a lock between two fingers. "The boy had no hair on one side of his head. Is that some sort of punishment they use to control ill-behaved boys?"

"No. The Powhatan men shave the right side of their heads to keep it from becoming entangled with the bow-string when they're preparing to shoot."

"What of the women?"

"The unmarried girls have the front and sides of their heads shaven but allow the back to grow long. The married women allow all their hair to grow."

"Are they pretty?"

"Beautiful. Of an exquisite and delicate shape. Had they fair skin . . . well."

Constance shifted uneasily on the bed. "Sally wanted to pick bayberries."

He took to pacing again. "You should have found plenty. They're everywhere right now."

"What do you use them for?"

"Candles, soap, that sort of thing."

"Oh. Well, Sally handled herself rather remarkably for a moppet of her age."

He looked at the child, a suggestion of a smile crossing his lips. "You've Grandma to thank for that. She prepared all of us for danger from the moment we learned to talk."

"How? How do you teach a three-year-old such a thing?"

"You'll have to ask Grandma."

He moved to the square hole cut into the cottage's wall, surveying the area outside. "Constance?"

"What is it?" She ceased to breathe. "Do you see something?"

He shook his head. "No, not right now. But I want you to know that having lived here all my life, I speak some of the native tongue. Still, there are various signs the Indians use for those who don't speak." The long barrel of his musket rested against his leg. "When an Indian lays down his weapon, it is an indication of peaceful intentions."

She stiffened. "Whacking off someone's hair is not what I consider peaceful."

He glanced at her, then returned his attention to the clearing. "Compared to losing your life, it is. They don't as a habit, though, chop off braids. I can only hope it's because he'd never seen red hair before."

"It's auburn."

"It's red, and I'm surprised he didn't kill you for shoving him down. The only explanation I can think of was that he was alone and no one witnessed his dishonor.

"We've had 'friendly' relations with the Powhatans for twenty years now, but there are several in our settlement, including me, who lost family members in the Massacre of '22. It will take many more peaceful years before the trust between the savages and the colonists is fully restored."

She stilled. He'd lost someone in the massacre? She pulled Sally closer. Now was most probably not the time to ask. "Are you saying I could have started a war because I didn't willingly give him my hair?"

"If he had killed you, yes."

She sat in shock, thinking of all the lives that could have been affected if the boy had brought another with him or if she'd provoked him beyond what was acceptable. A wave of vulnerability swept through her. "I want to go home. Better I do something dull-witted on a ship than here. That way, I've only my own life to answer for."

Withdrawing from the window, he moved to retrieve his hat from a peg. "You'll not be going anywhere, Constance. Now you know relations are supposed to be friendly . . . unless, of course, they come painted for war or they neglect to lay down their weapons."

"What does it mean when they poke your nose, chin, and cheeks?"

He paused for several moments before a smile tugged at his lips. "I imagine it means he had never seen freckles before."

Freckles. A pox on those wretched things. Then a smile hovered on her lips. No wonder the boy was so appalled when she poked his face. "Where are you going?"

"To get your cap and berries."

"All is well, then?"

From the shelf, he took a small charger filled with gunpowder that was secured to a circle of rope. Slipping it over his head, he opened the door. "I'll soon find out. Bar the door and window and stay inside until I return."

All hints of amusement fell from her face. Swiftly, she moved Sally from her lap and barred the door while Mary barred the window.

ELEVEN

The noon sun winked off the sea of tobacco, reminding Drew of his boyhood. Back then, he'd shared this task with his father while the tobacco plants towered above his and Josh's heads. Now, he stood surrounded by servants and the tobacco barely reached his shoulder.

A gentle breeze ruffled the crop set not in straight neat rows, but planted in what appeared a haphazard fashion, each plant in its own little mound of dirt a few paces apart from the others. The sturdy green plants had been snapped off at the top, allowing the strength of the plant to flow into its long broad leaves.

There was never enough time to weed the entire field, but Drew had gotten a pretty good jump on weeding the little area around each mound, having his men help him finish up last week.

Now, they were searching the massive plants for great horned worms about the size of Drew's little finger. Many a time had he walked these fields pulling grass-green worms off the leaves, snapping them in half, then dropping them onto the ground.

The task required a sharp eye but not a great deal of thought. And therein was the trouble, for his mind kept wandering, recalling Constance as she looked yesterday with her fear masked as indignation. With her arms about his baby sister. With her hair rippling over her shoulders. By Pharaoh, if the color of it wasn't starting to look downright . . . pleasing.

Still, when she actually ran her fingers through that thick, curly mane of hers, he'd been in complete control. Not a single carnal thought had crossed his mind. He nodded. Yes. That was what was important.

Now he needed to focus on suppressing the panic he'd experienced, for he'd been filled with an inordinate amount of it when Sally had half run, half stumbled into the fields out of breath, wide-eyed and crying that Constance was "scare-ed."

He rubbed the back of his neck. It was clear something would happen to Constance. It was only a matter of time. *Bolster my defenses, Lord, so when the worst occurs, I won't be affected.*

He sighed. Affected very much, that is. For the truth of it was, he would indeed be affected. Perhaps it was because he felt it his responsibility to keep her safe for her father. So maybe panic wasn't bad.

Yes. That was it. Panic was acceptable, for her father's sake. Desire was not. And if yesterday was any indication, he'd just about gotten the desire under control.

He'd found no trace of the Indians when he'd gone to find her basket nor had they been to visit—yet. They would, though. And when they did, Lord willing, it would be of a peaceful nature.

"You missed one, Isaac." Drew picked the worm off the tobacco leaf, snapped it in two, and tossed it aside. "The next one you miss, you eat."

"Yes, sir."

Drew smiled as Isaac searched the next plant more carefully. He would eat one before the day was through, just as Drew had eaten more than he could count when his father followed behind him during the worming of the fields.

None of those occasions was pleasant, but swallowing that first one was always the worst. Still, one worm could wipe out a whole section of tobacco within a day. The men must be made to understand the importance of killing every last worm.

The sun beat relentlessly upon them, the moisture in the air encasing them. Drew thrived on it. This was his legacy, and he could always find solace here, where he'd spent the largest amounts of time with those he now missed.

He wiped his brow. To his way of thinking, nothing could compare to laboring over his crop, tending to it with meticulous attention and vigilance while sweat sluiced down his body and the sun burnt into his skin. He inhaled deeply, his chest expanding with pleasure over all that was his. "Isaac?"

Isaac stilled, then turned back to the plant he'd just deemed worm free. Drew lifted a leaf, revealing a green worm about two inches in length clinging to the underside. "You missed one."

Isaac swallowed. "I'll be more careful, sir. Much more careful. Won't happen again."

Drew raised an eyebrow.

Isaac straightened. "Sir, I . . ." He looked at the worm and then back at Drew.

"In the past, I most often swallowed them whole. They're a bit on the crunchy side if you chew them."

Isaac wiped his hand across his mouth. The other men stopped to watch. "You, sir?"

Drew nodded. "My father used to follow me when I wormed the fields."

"They didn't hurt you none?"

"No, it's just a little worm."

Normally, you were a youngster when you ate your first worm. Being the eldest, Drew had had the pleasure of watching Josh eat his first worm. But never had he seen a grown man have to eat one.

Wiping his hand against his leg, Isaac peeled the worm from beneath the broad leaf. His Adam's apple bobbed several times, then he looked again at Drew. "Swallow it whole, you say?"

He shrugged. "I did. Of course, the risk is it might get stuck in your throat. Whichever way you prefer, it makes no difference to me."

"Would you be willing to let me have another chance, sir?"

"That worm could've wiped out a good portion of the field by this time tomorrow. There are no second chances when it comes to worms."

Isaac looked to the others. A couple appeared sympathetic, most displayed fascination. He again looked at the worm lying rather dormant between his fingers.

Drew lifted his hat and repositioned it on his head. He saw no reason to treat a grown man more delicately than he would a little tyke. One's first worm should be a memorable occasion. "I might ought to mention, the first worm I ate didn't stay long in my stomach. Of course, I was but a lad, barely out of wet pants. You, I'm sure, will have no such trouble."

What color there had been in Isaac's face left him. Drew chuckled. "Come, it's just a little worm. Eat it and be done so we can continue our work."

Squeezing his eyes shut, Isaac took a fortifying breath, popped the worm into his mouth, chewed two, maybe three times, and swallowed. A cheer rose up from the men. Drew whacked him on the shoulder. "Well done, man!"

Isaac turned as green as the tobacco.

Drew's smile widened. "Sweet saints, Isaac, don't cast up your accounts in the field. Run yonder if you must."

A great many chuckles followed Isaac as he clapped his hand over his mouth and sprinted to the edge of the field, heaving the moment he reached its edge. Upon his return there was much back slapping and congratulations all the way around.

The worming proceeded, but an air of festivity had taken over, and poor Isaac was the brunt of much ribbing for the rest of the afternoon. Drew smiled, thinking farming was indeed a wonderful occupation.

The sky rumbled and the air smelled of rain. Mary noted, however, that the men hardly seemed aware of it, so much fun were they having at Isaac's expense. As she served them their evening meal, she peeked over at Isaac, having by now heard in great detail of his initiation into farming. The men had been ruthless in the telling, each having his own slant.

She knew the poor man had never farmed in his life. Indeed, he had been the night watchman back home, shouting, "Past four o'clock of a fine spring morning. Past four o'clock, and all's well," as he made his way through London aside lifeless shuttered houses.

She'd felt a kinship to him, though, for one of the few signs of life displayed at such a time would be on Bread Street, where she and the other bakers of London worked. Their ovens glowing, they would withdraw piping hot loaves, the aroma filling their little bakeries and escaping out into the street. Isaac's cry would always be a bit more buoyant as he neared the end of Bread Street, knowing his duty for the night was almost over.

She'd heard his cry every morning for years, yet they had never met, nor even seen each other.

As fate would have it, though, it was Bread Street that caused Isaac's fall. One of the bakers down a ways from Mary's shop had started to make a habit of slipping a pinch of fresh bread to Isaac as he passed by. On one such morning, the store's owner caught them and had them both arrested. Isaac's sentence was deportment; the other man lost his life.

Such were not the ways here, not with Master Drew. Here, she was able to make an extra bit of bread for Isaac, glad to see he never went wanting again. It was a small thing, really, but it made them both feel they'd somehow cheated the hangman.

"Miss Mary, what's this green stuff in our carrot pudding?"

Chuckles reverberated along with the thunder. Isaac's

spoon paused on its way to his mouth, his face still looking a bit sickly.

The infectious mood tugged at her. "I'm not right
sure, Thomas. Master Drew brought them to me this
noon, he did. Said they would make better farmers of
any man who ate them and would I please mix them
into the evening meal."

Isaac made a show of digging through his pudding
before taking a big mouthful. "It's the best carrot pudding I've ever 'ad in me whole life, Miss Mary. Course,
it's the only carrot pudding I've 'ad in me whole life."

More chuckles. "Ho, that'd be the truth of it," Thomas
teased. "He'd been spendin' all 'is time eatin' bread,
he 'ad!"

Mary shook her head at their nonsense, while the
men murmured in agreement.

Constance came out to the yard to check on things,
immediately sensing a mood shift, caused by her presence, no doubt. Still, she could do nothing about it. Such
was the way of master and servant. She'd never much
thought about it before, but never before had she longed
to be included. It wasn't to be, though. There were strict
rules governing the relationship between master and servant. There always had been and there always would be.

The rain held off throughout the rest of the meal and
into the evening's chores. She and Drew didn't linger over
their time at the creek, though. The air was heavy and
mosquitoes swarmed about. Constance spent almost as
much time swatting them off of her as she did cleaning
the dishes.

After that first night of Drew's forfeit, never again

did she recline against the birch tree. She sat side-by-side with him as his helpmate, and to her surprise, when the week was up, he did not revert back to his old ways. Only after he had helped finish the dishes would he pick up his pipe and relax. It wasn't too long before she looked forward to the quiet walks with him where they shared this task, as well as time alone together.

Ever since her Indian encounter, he had carried his musket with him, and tonight was no exception. She smiled, remembering his blatant efforts last night to calm her lingering unease. He'd managed quite nicely by throwing her an unexpected mathematical challenge.

"Twenty-eight," he had said.

Muddy sand filtered through her fingers as she paused in her scrubbing. "Pardon?"

"Twenty-eight eggs. Seven hens would lay twenty-eight eggs in six days—at the rate you suggested, any-way."

She sat back on her heels. "Yes. You are quite right."

He quirked an eyebrow. "I know."

Suppressing a smile, she returned her attention to her chore.

"I've one for you now," he said.

She glanced at him. "Oh?"

Running his hand across his trencher, he laid it down and picked up another. "Sally and Sissy, four feet apart, walk side-by-side around a circular pond. How far does each walk if the sum of their distances is one mile?"

She bit the inside of her cheek. "Have you a solution already?"

He shook his head. "No. It occurred to me the other day when Sally regaled me with tales of daisy-chain crowns and meals by the pond, but I haven't given it much thought since."

She reached for a noggin. "I'll need to work in some soot. That's an algebraic problem."

"Humph. You need to work in the soot for all your problems."

She smiled. "We'll compare solutions tomorrow."

He winked. "Prepared I will be."

Droplets of rain found their way through the tree's covering, and the wind picked up speed, putting her recollections to a close. There would be no comparing of solutions this eve, not when the skies might open up at any moment. She sighed. She'd come up with an answer to his puzzle and had looked rather forward to lingering here with him.

A huge clap of thunder shook the very ground beneath them. Gathering up the dishes, the two hurried down the path toward the sanctuary of home.

Constance awakened at Drew's prodding. The cottage was still shrouded in darkness. "What is it? Has something happened?" she whispered.

"No. It's simply time for you to learn to milk the goat. I'm tired of doing it for you every morning. Come."

Wonderful. She rubbed her eyes. "I'm not dressed."

"See to it then. I'll meet you outside."

Rising from her pallet, she slipped on a dress and twisted her hair up into a cap. Maybe she would have time to go back to sleep after the milking.

Last night's rain had cooled things off but left a muddy mess to walk in. The mud oozed through her toes as she headed for the goat barn. Rubbing her arms against the chill, she saw Drew had already brought out the animal and stood conversing with it.

One hand held the stool and pail while the other scratched the goat's chin. She watched as he bent his head to its ear, whispering, nuzzling, chuckling. The animal bumped its nose against Drew's face in response.

Ruffling the area between its ears, Drew straightened and turned to find her watching him. Their gazes collided and her heart did something peculiar.

The animal nudged him. Without releasing her from his intense look, he slid his knuckles up and down the goat's jawline, yet it was her own body that did the reacting.

Had he done it a'purpose? No. She didn't think so.

Finally he set down stool and pail, then patted the ugly gray creature. "This is Snowflake."

Constance moved a little closer. She'd seen the goat many a time wandering about the area rummaging for food, but she'd kept well away from it. "Shouldn't we tie her up or something?"

"No. She doesn't mind the milking. Come and sit."

Rubbing her arms again, Constance took her place on the stool. Drew squatted and reached around her, grabbing one of Snowflake's teats. He squeezed and milk squirted into the bucket.

Fascinated, she watched the flexing and giving of the muscles along his arm, the sweep of short dark hairs decorating its surface. She closed her eyes, inhaling the morning's dew and dampness combined with a blend of man and beast.

Dawn touched the sky and, like some mighty conductor, cued a solitary songbird for the morning's prelude.

First a tentative chirrup from far away, and then another before it received a lonely trill in response. Next came a warble, and in the moments that followed a melody burst forth, grounded by the steady *pang, pang, pang* of milk hitting the bucket.

The panging stopped. "Now you try."

Constance opened her eyes, allowing her gaze to journey from his rolled-up sleeve to his muscular forearm. Her perusal leisurely progressed to his powerful hand coddling the goat's pink teat. He released it, resting his elbow on his updrawn knee.

Her leg muscles contracted, then she reached out and touched a teat, quickly withdrawing her fingers.

He chuckled. "It won't hurt you."

Wiping her hand on her skirt, she reached forward again, grasped one, and pulled. Snowflake jumped. Constance squealed and the forest quieted for a moment.

"No, no. You roll your fingers down her teat. Like this."

He reached around, magically making the milk flow out. She tried again. Snowflake turned her head and baahed.

"Baah, yourself." She looked to Drew. "This isn't working."

"Watch." He placed an open palm on the teat. "Roll your fingers down. First this finger, then this one and so on. You must set a faster pace, of course, but yanking is not what milks her."

She attempted to copy his actions, but still no milk.

He placed his arm alongside hers, cupping her hand in his, then guided her movements. Her skin leapt to life at every point he touched. It was most unnerving.

The milk hit the pail. "After you squeeze, cup her udder so more milk will flow in."

His chest now lay against her shoulder, his muscled arm still flexed against hers. And in a rush, the thought tumbled upon her. Sweet heaven above, she was falling in love.

TWELVE

In love? But how? How could that be? She paused while her breathing grew rapid and her heart pulsed. Then she made herself be completely honest, realizing it wasn't all that hard to believe.

He was, after all, a God-fearing man. He had agreed to her marriage terms, comforted her when she'd needed it, shown her how to survive in a new land, and at long last, he had believed her. He'd accepted she was Lady Constance Caroline Morrow, daughter to the Right Honorable the Earl of Greyhame. He'd accepted it because she had told him so. He also dallied in mathematical challenges.

Add that to a beautifully made body and a breathtaking face, and you have one lost battle before it ever began. She swallowed. The question now was what to do.

"Constance? Go ahead, you try."

She took a deep breath, throwing back her head. "Look at the sunrise, Drew. It's exquisite."

He glanced up at the sky. "It's exquisite every morning. If you'd like to watch the sunrise, I'll wake you early tomorrow. Right now, we need to milk the goat."

She gave him a sweet smile and turned back to Snow-flake. Cupping the udder, she rolled her fingers down the teat, ejecting a squirt of milk. She caught her breath and turned to him with delight. "I did it!"

He gave the slightest of nods. "Very good. Now continue with that over and over until the pail is filled."

Turning back to the milking, she tried again. Her expression fell. None was forthcoming. She tried several more times.

"You're squeezing too hard. Remember to let the milk flow in after you squeeze."

She tried again.

"No, like this." He placed his hand over hers, his whiskers grazing her cheek. Her insides fluttered.

"Relax your hand, Constance."

She relaxed. He repositioned her fingers.

"Cup the udder. Like this."

The pit of her stomach felt queasy. In truth, she needed to decide what to do about this and right quickly. She cupped the udder.

"Good. Now try to milk her."

He guided her hands. The concert playing through her veins drowned out all other sounds. Did he know? Could he tell? She angled her face to look at him. He was so close. He turned toward her then, which brought their lips near touching. What would he do if she tilted her head and pressed her lips against his?

The goat was forgotten, but their hands remained joined.

"Drew?" she breathed.

He jumped up and back like a sprung spring. The morning song within her slowed. Breathing became a challenge. An emotion just short of horror raced across his face.

He cleared his throat. "If you milk with two hands, it will go more quickly."

She waited a moment, letting him see her desire, before turning her attention back to Snowflake. She covered one hand with the other.

He tunneled his fingers through his hair. "No, Constance. I meant to milk two teats at once."

She moved to another teat. With very slow progress, she managed to extract some milk.

"We usually get a full pail from her each morning."

She nodded and continued with the task at hand.

He hesitated. "Constance, I . . ."

Stilling, she swept up her lashes.

"Nothing." He clamped his mouth shut and strode away.

Snowflake followed him, knocking the pail over on her way. Constance squealed and tried to save what little milk she had. There was only enough to cover the bottom of the pail.

The friendly elm held its shady arms over the teacher and her pupil in the yard. Constance leaned against the trunk and smoothed her skirts around her. "You are to keep *both* eyes closed during the prayer."

Sally's brow furrowed. "I just seeing if you eyes closed."

Constance quirked a brow. "Do you remember yesterday's verse?"

She nodded vigorously. "'J was a Jay, that pwattles and toys. K was a Key, that lock'd up bad boys.'"

Sally's bright eyes shone with pride, and Constance suppressed the urge to gather the child up and laugh with delight. "Your *Bible* verse."

"Oh!" she said, her eyes wide. "'Listen to me, my child-wen, for blessed are those who keep My way.' Boberb eight, thirty-two."

"Perfect. And the abecedarius?"

Sally jumped to her knees, causing a billow of dirt to rise around her. Squeezing her eyes shut, she chanted the alphabet.

"Oh, Sally, that was excellent. It's pleased I am with you." Picking up the gingerbread slate, she dusted it off and handed it to her. "Remember you what two and two added together make?"

"Foe!"

"Exactly." She leaned over Sally's shoulder as the moppet painstakingly wrote out the numeral with a piece of weathered oyster shell. It took up almost the entire slate. "What are one and two?"

"Thwee!"

Constance smoothed a hand down Sally's back. "My, someone I know will be eating a lot of this gingerbread slate if she continues in such an excellent manner."

Beaming, Sally continued with her work.

"What is the meaning of this?" Drew barked from the edge of the clearing.

Constance gasped. Sally hopped to her feet and ran to him. "Sissy learn me! Look!" Holding up her slate, she presented it to him.

He looked at Constance, his eyes conveying his fury. "What on God's green earth do you think you are doing?"

Although the words were not meant for Sally, she could see the child's anguish at his disapproval. "Sally, your verse for tomorrow is Proverb 14:17, 'He who is quick-tempered acts foolishly.'"

Tears welled up in the girl's eyes. "I do my numbers wrong?"

Constance opened her arms. "You did them perfectly. But enough for today. Let us close in prayer."

Sally crawled into Constance's lap, folded her hands, and bowed her head.

"Govern us with Thy grace, O eternal Wisdom, and direct our steps in Thy way. Amen."

"I keep my eyes shut, Sissy."

She brushed Sally's tears. "That's a good girl. Now run along inside and see if Mary is in need of any help." As soon as Sally made it through the door, Constance rounded on Drew. "How dare you! She's been working and working on her lessons, and you've no right to crush her that way."

"I will do much more than that if I ever catch you filling her head with such things again. She is to attend to tasks as belong to women, not meddle in things that are proper for men, whose minds are stronger."

"Stronger, ha! All your brains buttered would not fill two spoonfuls."

He straightened his spine. "You will heed me on this, Constance."

"How can you ask this? She's a bright child, her memory has no bounds, and already she's learned her tables. Her potential is incredible."

He took a step toward her. "I am the master, she is my sister, and I said *no*. That is the end of it."

"She is my sister too."

"Not for long."

She blinked. He was, of course, right. But more and more she'd been toying with the idea of staying. Certainly, life wasn't as easy here as it was in England, but when she was with Drew, easy didn't matter. For every color was deeper, every taste richer, every sacrifice sharper. He might be acting like a woodcock at the moment, yet, still, here with him, she was alive. Really alive. Even her home in England, her uncle, her math didn't compare to what she felt for Drew. She nodded her head. She wasn't toying with the idea at all. She had, in fact, made up her mind. She wanted to stay.

THIRTEEN

Of course, she need not give up her math. She could edit the journal from here almost as easily as she could back home.

She didn't think Drew would have any objection either, for he'd originally planned to accept their marriage. She was, after all, the one who'd insisted on the annulment. And if that weren't enough, he desired her. Hadn't he demonstrated such many a time throughout the last several weeks?

Yes. Yes, he had. And for the first time ever, she reciprocated the feeling. She took a deep breath. "No, Sally's not my sister. Not really. But I've been meaning to talk to you about that."

He waited, posture stiff, eyebrows drawn. Perhaps this wasn't the best of times. Still, she wanted the matter settled. She moistened her lips. "It's obvious you want to take me to wife, Drew. And since I'm already here, we're already wed, and there are no better prospects waiting for me in England, I agree to be your wife in all things. I will, of course, still need to edit the *La-*

dies' Mathematical Diary, since Uncle Skelly no longer can."

He said absolutely nothing. Doubts assailed her. Surely he wouldn't refuse her. He wouldn't dare.

"Do you see how schooling has ruined you? Listen to yourself. Think you I will fall at your feet the moment you crook your finger?"

She blinked, momentarily baffled. "What is it? You wish a financial settlement? It's a bit late for that, but I'm sure Papa would concede, and truly, I should have thought of it earlier." She pursed her lips. "You could probably get eight thousand pounds out of him, but I definitely wouldn't settle for less than seven thousand."

"That is as much vain bibble-babble as I've ever heard, and thank you, but no. I've no wish to be yoked to a woman of learning."

She sucked in her breath. Had she imagined those quiet moments that had passed between them? Imagined the desire she'd seen flare in his eyes? Placed more on them than was meant to be simply because she'd wanted to? Oh, sweet heaven above, she hoped not. That would be too humiliating by half. "What are you saying, Drew?"

"I'm saying I want you not as a wife. And even if I did, I certainly wouldn't allow you to participate in mathematical pursuits nor teach Sally anything improper."

Her heart pounding, she clasped her hands together, tried to swallow but couldn't. "I see. Please forgive me. I foolishly thought it was *my* idea to keep the marriage chaste. I was under the impression marriage was not taken lightly in the colonies and when a ceremony is performed, it is meant as a covenant with God until the couple's death." She lifted her chin. "Perhaps you are right. Perhaps I have been thinking entirely too much, for I'd even begun to worry about how our annulment would affect you after my departure, particularly in regard to the council. I had thought perhaps they might still banish you, or at least break an arm or two."

He opened his mouth then slowly closed it.

She took a step back. "No, no. Prithee, say no more. You've made yourself abundantly clear, and I should have known it without us having to undergo such an awkward scene." She blinked her eyes rapidly. "My apologies. I'll not bother you with it again, nor will I teach Sally anything other than religion and womanly type skills." She whirled and rushed into the cottage.

Heaven help him, he'd handled that badly. But what was he to do? He had no idea she'd ever consent to stay. Besides, he'd never had anyone propose to him before. It didn't help any that she'd all but said she would *settle* for him since the only clumberton waiting in the wings was fifty years her senior.

He rubbed his eyes with the palms of his hands. He was stunned she remembered so much of what he'd said to her when they'd frantically negotiated the terms of their marriage. But remember she did, and she had no trouble throwing it back at him.

Then all that diary business. How could she possibly think he'd let his wife involve herself in academics? He'd certainly been in the right there and didn't regret putting a stop to those tutoring sessions either. He sighed. He should never have encouraged her in that area to begin with. Should have, in fact, thrown out that diary back when she first got here. Words his father had taught him echoed within.

> Be to her virtues very kind;
> Be to her faults a little blind;
> Let all her ways be unconfin'd;
> And clap your padlock—on her mind.

Yes. He'd done the right thing by refusing her. But how was he going to walk inside that cottage as if nothing had happened?

He'd taken no more than two steps when he saw them. All were boys, all were naked, and one wore a bit of red braid around his neck. Drew took a deep breath. *"Comoneetop."*

The boys nodded and laid down their weapons. A good sign. That and the fact that they'd come without any fully grown men. Still . . .

"Constance," Drew called. "Bring the mats from inside the cedar chest."

She took forever. When finally she appeared with them, she went no further than the door, looking quickly to Drew, concern etched on her face.

"It's all right. Give me those, and we'll also need my pipe."

She glanced between him and the Indians, worrying her lip. "Where are your men?"

"In the fields. I came back early because a ship has come with cloth and other goods. Now go on. As of yet, there's nothing to fear, and I'm still in need of my pipe. Get the churchwarden."

Laying out the mats, he motioned for the boys to join

him. They had just settled in a circle when Constance, her eyes trained on Drew, returned with his churchwarden pipe.

He sighed. "It might help if it was lit."

She blinked. "I've never done such a thing in my life. I know not how."

He pierced her with his gaze. This gathering was of extreme importance, and the last thing he needed to deal with in front of these visitors was an unsubmissive female. "I'm sure you can figure it out since you are so very brilliant. Do it and do it now."

Nodding, she whirled around, then froze. "*My hair!*"

Drew jumped to his feet, unsure of her intentions. The boys responded in kind.

"He's wearing my hair."

"Ignore it and go light the pipe. Quickly."

She narrowed her eyes, pinning the youth with her displeasure. "I like it not."

The boy grinned and made a short statement to his friends. They all nodded in agreement, repeating what he said, as if to try it out on their tongues.

"What did he say?" she asked, tension radiating from her stance.

"He's given you a name."

"What is it?"

"I'll not tell you."

How she managed to make her back any straighter he couldn't imagine, but she did and the boys noticed it as well.

"What did he call me?"

Drew hesitated. "He said you will from this day forth be known as Red Spotted Wildcat."

He barely wrapped a restraining arm around her waist before she lunged. With a look of apology to his guests, he wrested the pipe from her hand, shifted her in his hold, slung her over his shoulder and took her into the cottage.

She was going to kill them both. First she'd do away with Drew, and then she'd deal with the Indian. She continued to struggle, but Drew held fast. There apparently would be no relief from this ignominious position until he was good and ready. And it appeared he wouldn't be ready until he carried her like so much baggage up to the loft and out of Mary and Sally's sight. That was just as well. What she had in store for him would not be appropriate for Sally's tender ears.

They were nearing the top of the ladder now, yet she continued with her struggle. He cursed and she gasped when his ascent faltered, but he managed to stay on.

At the top, he none too gently flung her onto the ticking. The force of the landing knocked the very breath from her and a wave of dizziness assailed her.

"In truth, Constance, you are pushing me beyond what any man should be expected to endure. Those may be youth out there, but do not fool yourself into thinking they are harmless. Their skills as warriors are not honed to perfection as of yet, but it's warriors they are, if a bit rough around the edges. Before you come racing back outside waving a broomstick above your head, you might, for once, consider the consequences. Is a useless lock of hair or a title you consider unacceptable worth your life, my life, Sally's life, and the lives of countless others?"

She raised a hand to her spinning head, keeping her eyes closed.

"Did you hear anything I said?"

"Every word."

"And?"

She considered his words. "I will not attack your *friends*, but neither will I play hostess to them. Go light your own pipe."

There was a moment of silence. The dizziness passed and she risked opening her eyes. He knelt on one knee, hovering above her. Close above her. She clamped her jaw against the direction of her thoughts. Had he not humiliated her, rejected her, tormented her? Oh, she wanted not to deal with this. She just wanted to roll over and escape in sleep. "Go away."

"You will stay in the cottage until they are gone?"

"I will stay right here in this tick."

His breath fanned her cheeks. "Very well. I will come tell you when they've left."

He stood. Rolling to her side, she closed her eyes and curled up into a ball, listening for his retreat. He took a few steps before returning. She felt a coverlet feather across her body and snuggled beneath it. Then he was gone.

"She still asleep?" he whispered.

Mary nodded. "Not heard so much as a peep from her."

Propping the bolts of cloth against the wall, he looked up toward the loft. Mary had already seen to the men's supper and had even cleansed the dishes. Constance should have wakened long ago.

Had her seasoning begun, then, so soon? Most of the servants went through a period of sickness where their bodies tried to adjust to this new world, a good percentage of them never making it past their first season here. It was so common, he and his fellow colonists had begun to call it "seasoning." But usually it happened within their first few months, not their first few weeks.

He swallowed. Would she be dead by morning, or would it be a long drawn out process? Thank God they hadn't consummated the marriage. At least there was no babe to worry about.

Placing one foot in front of the other, he forced himself to go up and check on her. The loft was warm and she'd flung off her covers. Her cap lay carelessly to the side of the tick, her mussed hair full about her head. He cleared his throat.

No response.

"Constance?"

Nothing. He frowned and knelt down to touch her forehead. Relief swept through him. No fever. Could it be fatigue and nothing more? He hoped to God that was the case . . . for her father's sake, anyway.

He brushed the hair from her eyes. "Constance? Wake up. You've missed supper."

Slowly, she twisted onto her back, stretching her arms and legs in a feline gesture. He didn't know where to look, or where *not* to look.

Open your eyes, Constance. Open your eyes and remember your anger with me before I forget myself.

Her eyes fluttered open. She smiled at him with an intimate I'm-glad-to-see-you, sleep-induced smile. His breathing became labored.

"God ye good den." The timbre of her voice could have melted butter.

He nodded.

She looked to the open side of the loft. "They've left, then?"

He cleared his throat. "Yes. Long since."

"What did they want?"

"To make peace."

"Just like that? He apologized, then?"

No. "Yes. You're feeling well?"

She propped herself up on her elbows. By trow, he would *not* look at the tension that caused in the fabric of her bodice.

"You say they've long since left? Why didn't you wake me?"

He shrugged. "I thought you might could use a bit of rest. How are you feeling?"

She sat up, noticed her twisted skirt, and turned a lovely shade of pink while quickly righting it. "I . . . oh, I'm fine. Thank you. You're sure it went all right?"

"With the Indians? Yes. Better than I'd hoped. Seems you made quite an impression. Or your hair did, anyway."

At its mention, she gathered her tresses up and shoved them into her cap.

He stood. "Come and share a trencher with me. It seems we've both missed supper."

Supper? She'd missed supper? Suddenly ravenous, she followed Drew down the ladder. Sally sat in a corner as Mary plaited her hair for the night. Smiling, Constance winked at her. Sally tilted her head and tried desperately to wink back, scrunching up her face in various contortions.

And so it was with a smile that Constance began her meal with Drew. As he made inroads into their food, though, she glanced at the fire and felt a pang of concern. There was no extra. When she looked back down, Drew's spoon was upon the last scoop of carrots.

She slammed her spoon down, stole the carrots from him, and stuffed them into her mouth.

He looked at her in surprise. "Those were mine."

She shook her head and swallowed them. "I had not even had one taste. Those were mine."

He frowned a bit but said no more, turning his attention to the meat. Again, he inhaled it, giving her little chance to do more than chew and swallow one bite to his four.

Looking to the window, she pointed and gasped. As soon as he turned his head, she snatched up the remainder of the meat, stuffing the whole of it into her mouth. He turned back to her, his eyes widening. "Constance! That was the last of the meat."

"I know," she managed around her mouthful.

He reached for the bread. She got to it first, tore it in two, and handed him half. After what could only be called a warning glare, he dipped his bread into the gravy, slopping up a goodly portion of it. She chewed faster but could only watch as the gravy and the greens began to disappear.

Shouldering him back some, she blocked his way and swallowed what was in her mouth so as to partake of some greens.

"Constance, what has gotten into you?"

She ate three spoonfuls before answering. "You do this every single meal. You eat twice as much as I do, leaving me next to nothing."

"I'm twice your size. It's only right I have the most. Now, scoot over and share the greens."

She hovered over the plate. "I'm fair to starving tonight. I'll only eat my share. You may have your half when I'm done. And no more gravy for you either."

"Constance, this is ridiculous. I'm still hungry and I want some greens."

"You'll have some greens, just as soon as I'm finished."

"I'll have some greens *now*."

She hugged the trencher to her, shoveling her share into her mouth. Placing his hands on her waist, he moved her to the opposite end of the bench, wrenched the trencher from her, and placed his back to her while eating what was left of the greens.

A good deal of her hunger had been appeased now, but the gravy was quite tasty and she only wanted her half of it.

She came up behind him and reached over his shoulder to dip her bread into the gravy. He snatched away her bread. She gasped. "Give that back!"

"Not likely. You ate all the meat, most of the greens, and the last bite of carrots. Your meal is over."

"I didn't eat all the meat. I ate only my share and that's *my* half of the bread. Now give over."

Slopping it in the gravy, he took a huge bite. Hunger had nothing to do with it now. She'd been a fairly good sport about her whole predicament. She'd tried her hand at cooking, she'd done her share of cleaning, she'd milked that wretched goat, and she'd even planned to face down

Mr. Meanie alone. To top it off, she'd offered to stay and had that offer thrown back in her face. The very least he could do was let her have her portion of the meals.

She yanked at his arm with no success and then re-evaluated her position. In order to eat that bread, he'd have to bring it to his mouth. And when he did, she'd grab it. She ceased to interfere yet stayed behind him, waiting to strike. And strike she did, but he anticipated her and blocked her move with his shoulders.

In desperation, she grabbed his elbows and jerked back, keeping the bread from reaching his mouth.

How they ended up wrestling on the floor, she wasn't quite sure. But there was really no contest. He not only had her pinned, but he still held the roll out far beyond her reach.

He didn't even attempt to hide his amusement. "No more naps for you. I think I prefer to share my trencher with you when you're a bit more tired."

She squirmed and writhed beneath him in an effort to get away. Then, wonder of wonders, that smug expression on his face transformed into what could only be tagged desire.

So she hadn't imagined it, after all? No, if the quickening of his breath and the tensing of his body were any indication, the man definitely desired her, but that yearning would go unrequited because she was educated and therefore unacceptable. Well, since he'd been so absolute in the making of his bed, she'd ensure the lying in it would be uncomfortable in the extreme for him.

Ever so slowly, she skimmed her nails up the length of his torso until her palms rested against his chest. "I'm still hungry, Drew," she whispered.

His gaze fell to her lips. She moistened them. He jumped to his feet, tossed her the bread, and made a hasty retreat from the cottage.

She closed her eyes, praying for God to grant her wisdom. It was then Sally jumped on her.

"Sissy, you're lots more fun than Gamma!"

Good heavens. She'd forgotten all about Sally and Mary. Opening her eyes, she sat up and put a calming arm around the child. Mary had made herself right busy at the fireplace.

Sighing, she kissed Sally's head. "To bed with you, my girl. I'll be up in a moment to tuck you in."

Constance watched her make her way up the ladder before standing. That entire episode had done much for her self-esteem, and she now had no need to cover her head in shame at her attempt to set their marriage aright. Certainly she was annoyed with him, but at least she hadn't imagined an attraction that wasn't there.

Moving to the table, she mopped up the last of the gravy, slowly chewed her bread, and hoped to heaven her *own* bed wouldn't be too uncomfortable.

FOURTEEN

Drew hurled the broken treenail across the yard. He should have finished making this cursed chair hours ago and yet here he sat, still trying to drive wooden pins through the last two joints. Now he only had one treenail left. If he broke this one, he'd be making *two* more.

He picked up the gimlet and checked the hole he'd bored through the joints. It was all her fault. Thanks to her, he needed a chair, for he would not share one more trencher with that shrew. Not after last night.

He sighed. He'd been doing so well, had almost conquered his traitorous thoughts. Setting down the gimlet, he worked the treenail into the hole.

If he didn't know better, he'd think she was doing it a'purpose. *I'm still hungry, Drew.* Hungry? What folly. She was foxing him, trying to lead him astray. Well, no more. No more would he leave this to chance. He was going to remove every last opportunity she might have for such mischief, beginning with the sharing of trenchers.

Picking up the hammer, he gently drove the treenail the rest of the way through. Many a master in the colony had a chair, and now he would as well. He would sit at the head of his board in his own chair, eating out of his own trencher. If it meant she had more to wash, then so be it.

And that was another thing. No more would he carry her dishes to the creek and help her clean them like some smitten half-wit. No, the tobacco looked ready to chop and cure. He'd have plenty to keep him busy there, and he'd also have Thomas and Samuel begin the brick-making. It was time to get started on the house.

The treenail went through, thank God. Picking up a small block of timber, he began the arduous procedure of carving one more wooden pin. At least he hoped it was just one more.

She chewed. The fish held no taste for her, and swallowing became more and more difficult. There was plenty of it, though. Her trencher was fair to brimming with food. She sighed, forced another swallow, and took another bite.

When he'd brought in his chair she'd been quite impressed. He'd made the thing within a day's time, and it was beautiful. It might not have all the spindles, cushions, and elaborate carvings as those back home, but it was handsome just the same. He'd come in without a word, set his thronelike chair against the wall, and turned and left. Sally had been mesmerized, touching it, crawling beneath it, and finally asking if she might sit in it "real quick."

Constance hadn't been much better. She'd stroked it too, surprised to find it so smooth. A simple carving of several large broad leaves fanned across the upper back and along the arms. She traced the leaves with her fingers, knowing his had been there first.

Never did it occur to her he'd made it so he would no longer have to sit by her. Imagine. Going through all that. The fish threatened to stick in her throat. She took a swallow of cider.

Breaking off another bite, she thought back to how she used to scoff at her friends, thinking them silly and feeble-minded to snivel and cry over what they claimed was a broken heart. She'd never dreamed of expending such emotions on a man.

Yet here she sat, barely able to eat, wishing she had the luxury of succumbing to such sentimentality. She stole a peek at Drew. He didn't seem to have any problem eating his supper. In fact, he seemed to be enjoying his meal with great relish.

It made no sense. She *knew* he desired her as a man desires a woman. She might not have been so sure if she hadn't endured that longing herself. But having experienced the feeling, she could certainly recognize it in him.

Yet he'd refused her. And all because she was educated. She frowned. Then why had he not only encouraged her mathematical games but actually participated in them? She shook her head. Something just wasn't right. She glanced at him again. Perhaps she'd confront him tonight at the creek.

The next bite was a bit easier to swallow. Yes, they were due to compare solutions to his puzzle tonight. Kneeling at the creek side-by-side would be the perfect opportunity to bring the subject up. Perhaps, just perhaps, she ought to tell him of her feelings then as well.

What did she have to lose? He'd already rejected her. The worst he could do would be to reject her again, and that was no different from what he was doing now. And there was, of course, the possibility he would change his mind. Hadn't Uncle Skelly always said there was nothing more attractive to a man than a woman in love?

With a sigh of relief, she finished the meal, if not enjoying it exactly, at least no longer choking on it.

Anxious to be alone with him, she wasted no time in dumping the trenchers and cooking utensils into the pots for carrying to the creek. Drew went to the fireplace, as usual, to light his pipe, then walked to his chair. But instead of setting it back against the wall, he placed it in front of the hearth and sat down.

She frowned. "Drew? Are we not going to the creek?"

Stretching his legs in front of him, he blew a stream of smoke into the air. "I think you've grasped the way of it now and no longer need my assistance. You may proceed without me."

A deep gripping pain seized her chest. He couldn't mean that. "I'll be happy to clean them, Drew, but won't you please help carry them for me?"

He stayed silent so long, she feared he might not answer. Surely he wouldn't make her voice the request again. Finally, he folded his hands against his chest and looked down at them. "I think not, Constance."

So soft were his words, she barely heard them. But the effect they had on her could not have been any stronger had he shouted them. Her throat closed, and she barely had time to pick up the pots and exit the cottage before all saw the tears quickly filling her eyes.

Stumbling down the path, she allowed her tears to

fall freely. How naïve she'd been to think a second rejection would be no worse than the first. Thankfully she hadn't proclaimed her feelings for him like some pitiful peagoose.

At the edge of the creek, she dropped the pots to the ground, her arms stinging. Sinking to her knees, she blindly reached for the dishes, scrubbing them with vigor one after the other until finally she doubled over and allowed the deep sobs to come forth, racking her body.

The embers in the fireplace had dwindled down to a dull glow, and his now cold pipe lay drying against the hearth. Mary and Sally had long since retired, and still she was not back. Anchoring his elbows on his knees, he propped his chin against fisted hands. Where *was* she? Surely it didn't take her this long in the mornings and the afternoons to cleanse the dishes.

Might she be trying to do mathematics in the dirt by the creek? Nay, it was much too dark, yet it was plain she'd been upset and he knew the math somehow soothed her.

He glanced at the chest. The diary was in there. She referred to it often, but he wasn't exactly sure what it was. Certainly, he'd flipped through it that first night she'd arrived, but he hadn't given it much thought since. Of a sudden, he could think of nothing else. Well, almost nothing else.

He leaned his head into his hands. She'd said she wanted to edit it because her uncle couldn't. It needed editing? He looked again at the chest. Oh, fie for shame. Standing, he strode to it and threw it open. There the pamphlet lay. Right on top. If it hadn't been so easily accessible, he might have talked himself out of digging through the chest in the dark. As it was, he saw its outline, clearly delineated in the shadows.

Picking it up, he returned to the fireplace, stoked the fire a bit, and sat down on the hearth. The compact volume of some twenty leaves lay squarely in his palm, just the size to tuck away in a lady's reticule. *The Ladies' Mathematical Diary* blazed across the cover in fancy gold letters beneath which was written *A Woman's Almanac Adapted for the Use and Diversion of the Fair-Sex*. Opening it, he took a much longer look at the booklet.

It appeared to be an annual publication, initially giving solutions to last year's puzzles, each answer accredited to a woman. He rolled his eyes as he noted one answer set to verse.

> When EIGHT fair shepherdesses to your view,
> Were altogether met beholding you,
> Who came to see their harmless flocks of sheep,
> Which daily they did on the common keep;
> The number just ONE HUNDRED, TWENTY-
> EIGHT,
> On which they did so diligently wait.
> Which numbers both do very well agree:
> The question's solved as you may plainly see.

The second half of the journal had about fifteen questions, all equally absurd. Still, he found himself wondering which was greater—three solid inches or three inches solid.

The last leaf posted the residence of one Skelly Torrence Morrow, to whom subscribers could send their solutions. The first women to submit correct answers would have their names published in next year's almanac.

He looked through it one more time and almost passed over the preface again before Morrow's signature at the bottom caught his attention. It was a lengthy address stating the English lady mathematician was of high distinction both at home and abroad. Further down, he encouraged the fair sex to attempt mathematics and philosophical knowledge once they saw here that their sex had "as clear judgments, as sprightly quick wit, as penetrating genius and as discerning and sagacious facilities as their male counterparts."

What a great bunch of tripe. Nevertheless, Drew found himself finishing Morrow's discourse, wherein the man admitted to having seen women cipher and was fully convinced the works in the diary were solved by members of the fair sex. He concluded by relating "all should glory in this as the learned men of his nation and foreign nations would be amazed were he to show them no less than four or five hundred letters from so many several women with solutions geometrical, arithmetical, algebraical, astronomical and philosophical."

Four or five hundred? The man was daft. Drew drug a hand down his face. *This* was Constance's uncle? The man she held in such high esteem? The man whose footsteps she wanted to follow? No wonder her head was so cluttered.

A distant clank of a pot signaled her approach. He bolted to the chest, tossed the book inside, and made it to the bed just before she entered.

He watched her from beneath half-closed lids, then

held himself still when she stopped mere feet away, staring at him. He couldn't see her face, but when she finally
moved to put the dishes away, her steps were heavy, her
shoulders slumped. He closed his eyes against her, convincing himself she was tired. After she settled onto her
pallet on the other side of the room, a great deal of his
tension eased. He was glad she'd made it home, tired
or otherwise.

FIFTEEN

The days grew shorter, the nights grew cooler, and Constance grew lonelier. The magnificent reds, oranges, and yellows of October had come and gone, yet she hadn't reveled in their glory, nor did she take any particular notice to the suggestion of winter just around the corner. She merely went about her duties, performing no more and no less than what was expected of her. Even Mr. Meanie ceased to draw her out.

The morning after *the rejection,* as she secretly referred to it, she had marched into the chicken coop, strode directly to Mr. Meanie, and said, "Do your worst."

The contemptible creature did nothing, so she sang, adding a jump and a jig to each verse for good measure.

> Here's to the man with a heart made of coal;
> Now to him who refuses to marry;
> Here's to the husband who hasn't a soul,
> And now to the man that is hairy:
> Let the toast pass,
> Break the long fast
> I'll warrant he'll prove an excuse for the glass.

Mr. Meanie charged. With a swipe of her hand, she snagged his legs and held him upside down, giving him the biggest dressing-down of his life. Since then, Mr. Meanie had kept his distance.

Drew had kept his distance as well. In the past four months, he and the men had cut all the tobacco, impaling their stalks onto slender sticks that they hung head down across beams in the ventilated tobacco barns to wilt and cure.

Her shoulders slumped. Those months had certainly taken their toll on the indentured men. Seven had been struck infirm; two did not survive. Still, time marched forward, and the surviving servants carried on.

The curing would last through winter, allowing most Virginia farmers to have a few months' rest. Not so on the O'Connor farm. The men worked from dawn to dusk on the big house, Drew at their side. He would leave before Constance awoke, only to return well after she'd retired.

In the beginning, she had visited the construction sight. Still not wanting to believe *the rejection* was final, she'd bounded up the mighty hill that overlooked the shimmering bay Fiddler's Creek fed into. The men had labored with shovels, carving out a massive cellar near the peak of the slope, their silhouettes sharp against a cloudless blue heaven.

But the higher she'd climbed and the closer she'd gotten, it was Drew her focus had honed in on as he stuck the blade into the ground, stomping on it with his boot. Shoulders, arms, and legs bulged and rippled while he loosened the dirt, bent over, grasped the shovel low, and slung the dirt to the side before repeating the ritual in its entirety.

How differently men moved than women. Smooth, fluid, and graceful, yet one hundred percent male. She'd come to a dead stop simply to feast on the sight before she'd realized what she'd done and pressed forward.

At first, she had offered suggestions concerning the length, breadth, and area of the house, the distance between its posts, and even the location of the house so one could walk the shortest distance possible from the house to the creek to the barn.

But Drew managed to find fault with every suggestion she'd made, openly hostile with his rebukes. Stung, she'd eventually not only quit making them, but quit going to the hill altogether.

If he didn't want to know where the hand stick must be placed so that the end of the wooden beam and the men at the ends of the stick carried equal weights, then so be it. If he didn't want to know what angle the ridge and what height the side walls must be so that the wind blowing from either of those quarters would have the least effect on the building, then so be it. It was of no matter to her.

Knotting her thread, she bit the end off and shook out the final pair of winter breeches she was fashioning for the men.

"Can we go now?" Sally asked.

Before responding, Constance placed the sewing implements in a small mahogany box, then hung the breeches on a peg. Her headache had returned this morn and what she'd really like was to rest here in the cottage. But she'd been promising Sally this outdoor meal for some time now, and the little thing's expression was too much to resist. "I suppose so."

Clapping, Sally skipped to the covered lunch basket while Constance fetched a cloth. "We won't be long, Mary."

Sally swept out the door, then turned to look at Constance while walking backward. "Let's go to the meadow and do chain daisies!"

"Oh, dearling, the daisies are all gone now. They only like warm weather."

"But it is warm!"

Constance caught up to her and took the basket. "I know, but it hasn't been. I fear the daisies wouldn't be there."

"Can we go see?"

A suggestion of pain stirred in Constance's lower stomach. Touching it, she sighed. It had been at least three weeks since she'd had these nagging head and stomach irritants. She'd thought she was over them. Well, maybe they would pass quickly this time.

"Can we?"

"What? Oh, no, Sally. It's simply too far. There's a nice spot a little ways up, though."

Sally's expression turned sullen, and she hoped the child wouldn't be in one of her tempers. She just didn't feel like coaxing her into a better mood.

They walked the rest of the way in silence, Sally kicking the dirt, Constance ignoring her spurt of assertiveness. Once there, she spread out the cloth under a big oak tree and made a concerted effort to be more cheerful and entertaining throughout the meal. Sally was having none of it.

"Can we go to the meadow after sweets?"

"No, Sally. We cannot. Oh, look! Mary's packed us some apple butter biscuits. Here."

Sally crossed her arms and furrowed her brows. "I don't want any."

Constance replaced the biscuit in the basket. "Let us away, then. I fear my head is spinning and you seem to be finished."

Sally huffed. "Oh, I'll eat one."

This last spell of dizziness sent a wave of nausea through her. "No, you may have it when we arrive home, but truly, I needs must return."

The child jumped to her feet, her eyes filling with tears. "That's untruth. You just not want to. You never go where I want. Never do what I want. Only we sew, sew, sew. Why don't you like me!"

Oh, dear Lord, please help. "Sally, come. I adore you and I'm sorry. I'm simply not feeling well."

She was sobbing now. "I only want go to the meadow."

Constance opened her arms and Sally crawled into them. The child had become restless and moody with the onset of winter. She had an active mind that needed to be engaged.

Constance sighed, then tightened her lips. A pox on Drew for refusing Sally her academic pursuits. She would have to confront him again, even if she had to go to the big house to do it.

Leaning back against the oak, she cradled Sally and closed her eyes. Sweet, sweet Sally. She must pay more attention to her, do more. Share more.

When she next opened her eyes, it took her a moment to place where she was. A brisk wind carrying the smell of rain whistled through her skirts, emphasizing the sudden drop in temperature. Tucking several stray tendrils under her cap, she glanced around. "Sally?"

No answer. Surveying the sky, she frowned. Dark clouds had moved in, and she could make no sense of the time. How long had she slept? "Sally?"

Quickly throwing the leftovers into the basket, she stood and shook out the linen, allowing the cloth to whip in the wind's flurry. "Come, Sally. We need to head back."

Still no response. An inkling of concern flittered through her. Securing the folded spread with the basket, she searched the area.

Sally answered none of her beckonings. Might she still be angry, even now hiding somewhere close but refusing to come forth? "Sally, come here this instant."

Nothing. Constance's frustration climbed. "Sally! There is danger for you unless you are with me. Now stop this silly game and come."

Light seared the sky just before a deafening crash of thunder reverberated through the forest. That should have brought the child scurrying. It did not. She frowned. Sally must have walked all the way home by herself. Still, Constance cupped her mouth with both hands and called again.

Her eyes narrowed. She had no doubt Sally knew her way home. The child could navigate the forest much as Constance could find her way about London. Well, she would not do so again. It would be to bed without supper for Sally this night.

Snatching up the basket and cloth, she hurried home, her irritation growing with each step. The first few drops of rain fell as she entered the cottage.

Mary, hands dusted in flour, looked up from pounding her dough. "Well, I was a'wondering about you."

Constance shook her head. "We drowsed a bit, me longer than Sally, though. Where is she?"

Mary paused. "What mean you?"

Constance set the basket down and glanced up at the loft. "Sally. Where is she?"

"She's not with you?"

Constance floundered. "She's not come back?"

"No, mum." Straightening, Mary wiped her hands on her apron. "I've not seen her since you left this morn."

Her throat tightened. "What time is it?"

"Why, the close of day will not be too long in coming now."

Constance shinnied up the ladder. "You're sure? You've not seen her at all? She's not in the tick?"

"No, mum. Should I check outside?"

Constance nodded, and the two of them searched the goat barn, the elm tree Sally liked to climb, the perimeter of the clearing, and then the cottage one more time. The ever-increasing shower tattooed the thatch roof, each rap heightening her anxiety. "Where's the bell?"

"The master took it a few days ago, he did. The clacker fell off."

Constance grabbed her shawl. "Stay here in case she comes, Mary. I'm going for Drew."

"Thomas! Get those braces up here, else all our hard work will be laying at our feet come storm's end!"

"We're here, sir!"

Drew motioned him and two of the others through

the house's skeleton as they barreled down the hall with all the spare lumber they could find. They'd just finished sheathing the second story but as yet had no roof nor chimney. Without the proper braces, a forceful wind could blow the whole house down. As it was, this sudden wind caused the exterior to whine and skirl.

With a rhythm established from months of working together, Drew and Thomas secured a length of timber at forty-five degrees across one wall while the other two men did the same to a second wall. Not for the first time did Drew feel frustrated with his father's sketch, which called for a huge house shaped like a cross. Now, instead of a mere four walls to brace, he had twelve.

Rain slid in rivulets from his hat's brim as he quickly checked the sturdiness of the brace, satisfied with its placement. "I'm going to see what's taking the men outside so long."

Thomas nodded before moving to help the others.

Hurtling down the stairs, Drew rushed out the front door's frame, then jumped out of the way as another crew forged inside with more bracing lumber.

A sheet of wind and rain struck him, knocking him a bit askew before he hunched over against its force. Body O'Caesar, but it was cold. He hurried around the house's perimeter, his boots sinking into the soggy ground as the water covered a good two inches of shoe with each footfall. They'd gotten more rain than usual throughout the season, so the ground had little use for this dousing and wasn't absorbing like it should.

No sooner had he spurred the remaining men on than he noticed the rain rapidly draining into the trench around the basement walls. He hurried toward it, surprised at the amount of water already accumulating. A fie upon it. Although the trench was needed to do all the exterior work on that lower level, if it filled up with water and sloughed in, the mud avalanche could collapse the bricked-in cellar and, subsequently, everything built on top of it.

Hastening back inside, he bounded down to the basement, chilled and suddenly fatigued. No water had seeped in yet, but if the rain continued with this kind of ferocity, it wouldn't be long before it did. Standing in the middle of the cool, clammy, soon-to-be kitchen, he pinched the bridge of his nose. There was not enough time to pack full the entire trench, but he had to do something. *Help me, Lord*.

The syncopated drumming of hammers above-stairs provided a bass for the monotonous roar of rain teeming outside the narrow barred windows that lined the top of the room. Moving swiftly from one to the next, Drew put up the shutters. By the time the last was secured, he'd formulated a plan, flimsy though it was.

Taking the stairs two at a time, he nearly collided with Thomas as he reached the first floor. "Collect half the men and help me embank the dig-out and divert the flow of the storm's runoff. Have the others continue to brace the interior."

Barely had they begun their labors when, for a moment, he thought he heard Constance call forth. Jerking his head up, he peered through the deluge but saw nothing. The perpetual downpour had not slackened but continued with its merciless assault, punctuated by ripple after ripple of distant thunder.

He waited a moment more, then wiped his face against his shoulder and returned to his task. Pouring a load of excavated dirt from the wheelbarrow, he began to develop a dike around the trench, then paused. There it was again.

Squinting his eyes, he just made out her advancing silhouette, then jumped to his feet and jogged toward her. What the devil was she doing out in this mess? Well, by trow, whatever it was, she'd have to handle it herself, for he could not leave the house.

It took him but a moment to take in her drenched clothing and the sodden shawl weighing her down. It wasn't until she was within reach, though, that he saw the dismay in her eyes. "What?"

"Sally," she gasped.

He could see her struggle to breathe, pulling vast amounts of air into her lungs. Saints above, had she *run* the entire way? "What? What of Sally?"

"She's gone."

Gone? *Oh, dear God.* Grabbing her arm, he jerked her erect. "What do you mean, gone?"

"I mean *gone*. We were having our midday meal out-of-doors, and I must have fallen into a light slumber. When I awoke, she was gone. I assumed she went home without me, but when I arrived home, she wasn't there. She wasn't there, Drew! Have you seen her?"

All too quickly, the flash of alarm he'd experienced turned to anger. He shook her hard. "By my life, Constance. *Gone* means *dead*. Never say to me she's gone. Do you hear me? Never!"

Tears filled her eyes. "Drew, you're hurting me. Stop."

He immediately released her, only to then catch her elbow, steadying her. Panic once again took hold as her words made their full impact. "You're sure she's not at the cottage? Never before has she run off."

Constance swiped at her eyes. "I know. I know. We had a disagreement. She wanted to go to the meadow. She was tired of—"

"I'll be right back."

Tearing back to the trench, he quickly found Thomas. "Sally's lost. Stay here and have the men do what they can to protect the house. Isaac, Samuel! With me!"

The flight back to the cottage with the two men following and Constance sludging along beside him was but a blur. All he could think was, *not Sally*. God wouldn't be so cruel as to take Sally from him too.

So many little ones. His sister Margaret, only a few months old when their cottage burned during the Massacre of '22. Drew had just turned seven, Josh was six, and Mama had left them in charge while she collected berries. Since Margaret was asleep, they decided to climb the big elm tree and carve their names into its branches with their new knives. It was from that vantage point they saw the Indians suddenly appear, invade their cottage, then set a torch to it. Flames clothed their thatched roof with a fiery cape in a matter of moments.

Josh mimed his desire to take on the Indians and save Margaret, pointing to his new knife. Drew, however, shook his head, some greater power alerting him to the folly of such an action.

The fire raged, its heat suffocating. Thick, swarthy smoke inundated them, parching their throats, stinging their eyes, and making the act of breathing near impossible. The Indians fled, and Drew wasted no time in shinnying down the tree.

The crackling and roaring of the fire blistered his ears, its scorching breath propelling him back, back,

back. Josh grasped his hand and Drew turned, his utter
helplessness and horror mirrored in Josh's eyes.

Mama told him afterward they were living on land
the Indians claimed and the natives had only been trying
to take back what was theirs. She also said he'd saved
both his and Josh's life, which would have been lost
along with the baby's, but never did his guilt lessen.
Margaret had burned to death, and she'd been under
his care. He should have left Josh up in that tree and
gone after Margaret alone.

His mother never blamed him, never scolded him.
Still, he'd heard her cry herself to sleep more times
than he could count, and he'd watched as Grandma
carried much of the load for the months following the
massacre.

Five years later, Nellie was born, followed by Alice.
Never would he leave their side when he was placed in
charge. As a result, he and Josh taught them to fish,
shoot, and swim. The girls taught them to prepare a
midday meal, chase butterflies, and pick wild flowers.

When Josh was eighteen and the girls were still in
pigtails, they all exchanged poignant embraces before
Drew boarded a ship bound for Cambridge University.

By trow, but he missed them. The newness of England
and the novelty of university life never quite extinguished
the dull ache his longing for home evoked. Then he met
Leah.

Everything changed. The landscape came alive, the
days passed more quickly, and his desire to lay the world
at her feet overwhelmed him. By the time his two-year
stint was completed, he'd talked her into going to Virginia to be his wife. She agreed only when he promised

to give her a few months to adjust to the colony before they spoke their vows.

Upon their arrival, he discovered little Alice had died some six months earlier. He'd never received Father's letter nor the news that he had twin siblings, Sally and Sister.

Still, he'd yet to hear the worst. The week before his ship docked in Jamestown, his beloved mother had been bitten by a snake, right there in the clearing. She'd died in a matter of days.

Leah nursed him through his grief, only to have pneumonia strip her of life three months later, a mere week before they were to wed. That left Grandma, Father, Josh, Nellie, and the twins.

Ah, the twins. So rambunctious were they, the family hadn't been given but a moment to consider their losses. Sally babbled nonstop, while Sister followed her like a shadow, never uttering a sound. Then the inevitable occurred. He lost Father and Sister to burning fevers, and now, Grandma and Nellie to his brother-in-law.

A crack of thunder pealed through the heavens. They'd just made it to the cottage, but with no sign of Sally.

SIXTEEN

Slipping a coiled rope over his head and shoulder, Drew perused her sodden clothes, drenched hair, and shivering body. "You're not going."

Constance straightened. "I am going—with or without you. So make up your mind. Do we leave separately to search for Sally or together?"

He sighed. If he let her go, she'd surely catch her death. If he didn't, she'd most likely do precisely what she claimed, and then he'd have two lost females to find.

Whirling around, she grabbed one of his jerkins from the peg. "Enough! I am away. Do as you will."

With that, she slipped the jerkin on and stomped out the door. He slammed his eyes shut, prayed for patience, then nodded to his men. "Let us away."

The wind, rain, and cold blasted him, immediately causing him to withdraw into his deerskin jacket. He hesitated only a moment before following Constance. His jerkin looked ridiculous on her, riding clear down to the backs of her knees, causing her skirt to bunch and billow out at the bottom. The sleeves of the jerkin weren't attached to it, but its heavy leather should at least keep her torso somewhat warm and dry. It was clear she was heading in the direction of the meadow.

He jogged to her, the men close behind. "Are you going this way a'purpose or are you just storming off for the sake of storming?"

She gave him no glance. "Sally wanted to make daisy chains, so I'm checking the meadow first."

"There are no daisies this time of year!"

That earned him a glance, searing though it was.

They trekked through the dark, wet forest, tripping on roots, loose stones, and slippery rocks while the crash and reverberation of thunder brawled above their heads. The trees protected them somewhat from the downpour, but not from the lashing of wet branches writhing in fury. Try as he would, he couldn't shield her from their vicious bombardment. There was nothing to do but forge ahead.

Somehow, he should have made her stay home. He'd just about decided to send her back anyway when they arrived. The meadow stretched before them, its dead browned blades flattened by the torrent hurtling ever downward while surrounded by trees whose tops twisted and whipped in the howling wind. He stopped and scanned the meadow, squinting against the darkness in hopes of finding a trace of Sally huddled in its barren expanse.

Constance did not stop, but waded right into its midst. Cupping her mouth, she called for Sally, the wind swallowing her cries. Her silhouette took on a desperate edge, her attempts to run to every corner of the patch thwarted by the greedy mud sucking her feet into its sticky muck.

Lightning seared the sky. He watched, his chest squeezing his lungs, as she turned 360 degrees, searching, searching, before covering her face and sinking slowly to her knees.

The oppressive rain exploded in his ears and onto his body before he even realized he was plunging toward her, desperate to pull her out of the mire. He grasped her arms, but she shrunk from him, shaking a vehement denial with her head. Falling to his knees before her, he tried again. "Come, Constance! We needs must get beneath shelter, for surely we are testing the fates to boldly sit here just daring the lightning to strike us!"

She raised her head. The desolation and despair he saw in her eyes frightened him with more intensity than he'd ever imagined.

"You were right! You were right, Drew! I never should have been educated. If I hadn't defied convention and Father and everyone else, I'd be home now, safely married. And you would be warm and dry and content in your home. Josh wouldn't be chasing all over a war-infested country, you wouldn't have a wife you never wanted, and Sally—" She choked, closing her eyes, and then forced them back open. "And Sally wouldn't be lost in this godforsaken forest. It's all my fault and I'm . . . so . . . so . . . soooooorry!"

He gathered her against him, not trusting the feelings rioting through his person. *Dear God, let Sally be safe. Let this woman in my arms not be forced to endure any misplaced guilt.*

Then, there in the midst of the storm, the cold, the blistering wind and the turbid muck sloshing against their legs, he experienced a quiet, calming, overwhelming peace. As sure as he knew that rain fell from the sky, he knew that, for now, Sally was all right.

Resting his lips against Constance's sodden hair, he closed his eyes, knowing, yet still not quite able to believe, what else had just been revealed to him. Raising his face to the heavens, he allowed the rain to beat against him. *Surely I can't be . . . in love with Constance? Can I?*

No confirmation nor denial from the omnipotent tranquillity flowing through him, only a suggestion of immense satisfaction.

Drew shook his head. *But she has red hair!*

The thought came to him, *And who do you think made that red hair?*

Well, fie. There was no arguing that. Pursing his lips, Drew nodded once. *Your pardon.* A pause. *And Sally? Where is she? Where?*

Nothing. No response. The sound of the rain returned, the cold seeped into his limbs once again.

He opened his eyes, not to find some parting of the heavens or the miraculous cessation of the storm, but to find something even better—Constance's warrior friend, standing not ten feet away and gesturing to him. Drew smiled.

Bracketing Constance's head with his hands, he tipped her face up toward him. "Ah, little Lady of the Realm, don't lose all your pluck now, just when I'm needing it the most. Come. I think I might know how to find Sally." Hooking her hair behind her ears, he lowered his mouth to hers, kissing her with the urgency of a man who loves his woman but has not the time to express it.

Clearly, Drew had gone mad. There was no other explanation. Why else would he be kissing her without so much as a by-your-leave in the middle of a rain-drenched field while Sally's very life was in danger?

She shoved him hard. He fell with a very satisfying splat onto his backside in the filthy water. She started to rise, only to have Isaac and Samuel appear at her side to offer her a hand. Accepting their help, she hauled herself out of the muck, whirled around and then she saw him. That awful, lily-livered Indian boy. He was clothed this time, in deference to the weather, she assumed. Still, she refused to look at the lock of auburn hair dangling from his neck, but it was there in her peripheral vision and it incensed her. "Sorry to disappoint you, Little Chief, but I'm rather busy right now and don't have time for any hair-cutting ceremonies at the moment. Perhaps another time?"

Picking her sodden skirts out of the mud and with every intention of walking in the other direction, a hand at her waist stopped her. "He knows where Sally is."

She spun around to look into Drew's eyes. "Where?"

"He didn't say where, only that she was all right."

The warrior turned and disappeared into the thicket. Drew grabbed her hand, and the group scrambled to follow. The young Indian made no concessions for her graceless and less than proficient attempts to keep up. She glanced at Drew, but he didn't seem annoyed. Neither, though, did he attempt to slow his pace as he dragged her in his wake. Stubbing her toe again, her cry escaped before she was able to stop it, a wave of dizziness sweeping over her.

"Here, Isaac. Take Constance and follow as best you

can. If you can't keep up, return home. Know you the way?"

"Yes, sir."

She felt Drew's release of her hand and Isaac's subsequent support beneath her elbow. "Wish you to return, Mistress?"

Shaking off the vestiges of her dizziness by sheer force of will, she tightened her resolve. "Not until we find her. Make haste! We're losing sight of them."

They continued on for what seemed hours when the sound of the rain changed. No longer was it pelting only the earth, but a source of water as well. A river? An extension of Fiddler's Creek? The ocean?

She inhaled but could smell no salt, and then they were upon it. A roaring, rocky, muddy stream tumbling toward some distant goal in a swell of rapids.

She could see where an assortment of large rocks provided a stepping-stone bridge of sorts when the stream was not high. And there, crouched in the middle of it, on a rock surrounded by a surging and billowing maelstrom, was Sally.

"I thought that wretched Indian said she was all right!" Constance screamed. "What's the matter with him, leaving her in the middle of all this? She might have fallen in and drowned before we ever got here!"

But the Indian was nowhere to be seen, and Drew was hurriedly wrapping his rope around a tree. The other end was already tied in a noose-like fashion.

"Hold on, Sally! We're coming!" she cried.

Sally looked up and her rock wavered. Squeezing her eyes shut, Sally groped for the edge of the rock just as a wave broke against it, cascading over her. She began to slip, and Constance threw a frantic look at Drew, noting he was now securing the knot.

Sally regained her balance, but the stream was vicious and if Drew's large body disturbed the precarious hold the soil had on Sally's rock, they might lose her still.

Constance eyed the location of Sally's rock, guessed at the velocity of the river, took into consideration her own weight and quickly calculated at what approximate point she needs must enter the water. Throwing off the jerkin, she grabbed the free end of the rope, slipped it around her waist, and plunged in several yards upriver.

"No, Connie! No! Oh, God, no!"

The icy water stole the very breath from her. She kicked, gasping while the current wrapped around her skirts, tangling her legs and sweeping her at a frightening pace toward the jagged stepping-stones. Regaining her breath, she kicked again with all her strength, paddling her arms toward Sally.

Help us, Lord. Help us.

Her feet skimmed the bottom and, though the pull of the water remained strong, Constance managed to forge bit by bit toward Sally, but the angle was wrong.

She hadn't counted on that initial depth of the water. She'd assumed she'd be able to retain a standing position throughout her flight. If she didn't correct her course, she'd miss Sally altogether.

The rock tipped once again. Sally held tight to the rock's edge, but her body had lost its traction. She now lay stretched out against the rock, hanging on only by her fingertips.

She was three. She was cold. She was exhausted. There was no way she could hold up her own weight.

From the corner of her eye, Constance saw Drew splash in downstream, probably in hopes of catching Sally if she tumbled into the water.

Whether it was strength borne from horror or God's own hand pushing her to their goal, Constance didn't question, but the next moment she was at Sally's side, wrapping her arms around the child's waist and digging her feet into the tumultuous soil. "Let go, sweet. Put your arms around my neck."

Sally whimpered, still holding fast to the rock.

Constance reached up to disengage her little hands just as another wave sluiced onto them. The rock gave way and they both went under.

Constance retained her hold on Sally, but the frightened moppet kicked and fought and squirmed for freedom. Their surge to the surface abruptly halted. Constance swirled toward the source of their constraint to find her skirt trapped under the rock.

Resisting panic's temptation, she tugged, but with no result. Should she let Sally go? Would Drew see the child? Catch her?

Poor Sally was frantic now in her bid for air. The rope around Constance's waist dug into her. Someone must be trying to pull her out.

She kicked. They pulled. Sally squirmed. How long had they been under? How much longer could Sally last?

Constance was about to release the child when she felt her bodice begin to separate from her skirt. Strong fingers dug into the hole, renting the skirt off and they were free.

She surfaced, coughing, sputtering, and hugging a

limp Sally to her. Drew took the child, then hesitated. "Connie?"

"Go on," she gasped. "I'm right behind you."

He stood in what must have been indecision for a moment before swimming with Sally to the water's edge. The current carried them well downstream before they reached land.

Isaac and Thomas began to reel Constance in. The nausea, the blackness, the shakes all descended at once.

Keep going. Keep going. Just a little farther. It was her last thought before water once again engulfed her.

SEVENTEEN

The fire popped and hissed, its heat cocooning the cottage with warmth. Brushing back her curls, Drew placed his palm against Constance's forehead. Was she a bit hotter now, or was it his imagination? Sighing, he rubbed his face.

"Her fever is rising again?"

"No. She's fine."

Mary touched Constance's forehead. "Mayhap it's more cool cloths I should be getting."

He whirled toward her. "It's not Constance. It's the cottage. This infernal room is like a tin foot stove."

Clasping her hands together, Mary started to move away.

"Wait. I'm sorry. I . . . it's just . . ." He gulped in a breath. "Did she feel warmer to you?"

Mary hesitated. "Yes, sir. Same as yesterday. Feels fine in the morn, but as soon as noontime arrives, up goes her fever, it does. I just hope it goes back down again this eve."

"Drew?"

He turned, the sight of his baby sister causing his heart to swell. "Sally Elizabeth. Come sit upon my knee and tell me a story."

Once in his arms, he withdrew a kerchief from his cloth pouch and held it to her nose. "Blow."

She did as instructed, not once, but several times. As he tucked away the kerchief, she wiped her nose on her sleeve. "Sissy gone to heaven?"

He tensed. "No. She's merely sleeping."

"But, I wake. Sissy need wake. Why Sissy not wake?"

"Sissy's taken ill—not from being in the water. Sissy's having her seasoning. That's all."

"Does she fever?"

"Sometimes she has a fever."

"Papa and Sister have the fever." Sticking her thumb in her mouth, she pinched his shirt between the thumb and finger of her other hand, rubbing the fabric back and forth. "Papa and Sister go to heaven."

Swallowing, he pulled her head against his chest. Back at the river, he had thought he'd lost this child. But she'd been spared, coming through the trauma with amazing resilience. She had lain limp on the tree-gnarled bank for agonizing moments before all the water she'd taken in had finally poured from her mouth.

At first she'd been cold, wet, and disoriented, but once home and bundled up in her tick, she'd slept the whole night through. Upon waking late yesterday morn, she complained only of "hurt fingers" and hunger—nothing else.

He'd laid those tiny little hands in his palm, carefully examining them. There was a cut or two, but mostly just bruising, probably from gripping the rock. She'd evidently made her way halfway across the stream, became frightened, and simply sat down on the rock. The longer she sat, the higher and more turbulent the stream became.

Thank God she was all right. Her appetite had returned full force, though swallowing caused some discomfort. No doubt the exposure had taken its toll in the form of a tender throat and blocked nose. But he'd had her inhale the vapors of steamed sage and thyme and then drink hot tea. No one would ever guess she'd nearly drowned just two days ago. "I thought you were going to tell me a story."

"Know not how."

"Um. Then maybe I'd better tell you a story. Which one would you like to hear?"

"Talk about the dog tree."

"The dogwood tree?"

She nodded, snuggling in for the well-known legend.

Mary approached with a bucket of water and a rag. Scooting his chair out of the way, Drew oversaw while Mary sat on the bed, wrung out the rag, and bathed his wife's face.

"I ready now, Drew."

He kept his eyes on Constance. "In days of old, it was said the dogwood tree grew large in size and as strong as an oak. Because of its strength—"

Sally pulled back. "You forgot the largest-tree-of-the-forest part."

Pausing, he looked at her. "It was among one of the largest trees of the forest." She settled back against him, and he looped his arms around her. "Because of its strength, it was chosen to make the cross from which

Jesus was crucified. This so grieved the dogwood tree that Christ, even amidst His great suffering, sensed it and made a pledge. Never again would the tree grow large enough or strong enough to be used for such a purpose."

Mary rinsed her cloth, then began on Constance's neck and chest.

"That not the end."

Drew stirred himself. "'Henceforth,' said He, 'the dogwood tree shall grow tall and slender, with its blossoms of white symbolizing the cross and their centers representing the crown of thorns. The outer edge of each petal shall be touched with brown, as with the rust of nails. And all who look upon the tree will remember the cross.'"

"Why it has no flowers now?"

"It's winter."

"Then how we know which one is the 'pecial one?"

"From its size."

Mary replaced the covers around Constance and started wiping down her face again.

"There no daisies too."

Drew slid his eyes closed. "No. There are not."

"Cuz it winner?"

"Yes. Because it's winter."

Sally slid off his lap and moved toward the bed. "Can she hear me?"

Mary paused and looked at Drew. He cleared his throat. "I know not."

"Sissy?" Sally said, her head tilted. "When you go to heaven, tell Jesus He should keep flowers all time. Even in winner."

Drew shot to his feet. *"She's not going to die."*

Sally turned to him, her eyes large and luminous. "Yes. She is."

Fisting his hands, he grabbed his jacket and stormed from the cottage.

Constance stirred and swept open her eyes. "Sally?"

Grandma looked at her feverishly drawn face and smoothed the edges of the coverlet. "She's fine. Only a scratch or two to show for her troubles."

"Thank the Lord." Her voice came from within. She closed her eyes. "What are you doing here?"

"I came as soon as the weather allowed."

"But, how did you . . . ?" she rasped.

"Drew sent one of his men the day it happened."

"Nellie—"

Grandma moved closer, wiping Constance's brow. "Is fine. Her baby's fine. Sally's fine. We're all fine."

"Drew?"

"He's running us all mad."

Constance strained to open her eyes. "Mad?"

Grandma tsked. "I was merely jesting. Here, take a sip of this."

Grandma cupped Constance's head and brought the broth to her lips. She groaned but swallowed once. "I must arise. Just . . . give me . . . a . . ."

She sunk back into the sweet oblivion of sleep.

Fists clenched, Drew towered over his grandmother. "Why did you not send for me?"

She handed him a cup of stew. "Raise not your voice to me, young man. She was only awake for a moment."

"She asked for me?"

"She asked for Sally."

He glanced across the room. Mayhap she'd wake again.

"Fetch more blankets, Grandma," he snapped. "The shivering's getting worse."

Grandma went to do his bidding while he sat on the bed, tucking the covers tightly around her body. It was nearing noon.

"So cccccold." Her eyes never even opened.

He jumped to his feet. "I know, love. I know. I've more blankets coming." He swiveled around. "Make haste! She's cold!" Grandma handed him a pile of blankets, and he layered them atop Constance. "Is that better? Constance? Can you hear me?"

Nothing.

"The fire," he said over his shoulder. "Stoke the fire! She's cold!"

Grandma didn't move.

"Make haste! Do you not ken she's cold?"

Grandma's lined face softened. "Her fever's coming back, Drew. In a moment she'll be burning up again. The blankets we can peel off. The fire is not so easy. We'll leave it as it is."

"A fie upon you, Grandma! She's going to shake right out of this bed! Now stoke the blasted fire!"

"When did you fall in love with her?"

He stopped, the last blanket hanging from his hands,

then returned to his task. "Will you *please* stoke the fire?"

"No."

He placed the blanket over Constance with meticulous care, sank onto the edge of the bed, and covered his face with his hands. "I thought you came to help me tend to her. Why are you not helping?"

Grandma gathered his unbound hair and smoothed it behind his shoulders. "I didn't come to *help*. I came to *tend* to her. I assumed you would be out working on the new house with your men. I never dreamed you'd leave that project for them to do unsupervised, yet you've ventured out only a handful of times and didn't stay gone for long at that. Why did you even bother sending for me?"

He turned his face, resting it on his fists while looking at Constance. "The shivering's stopped."

Grandma sat down beside him, rubbing her gnarled hand back and forth across his back. They stayed as such for several long moments.

Drew sighed. "I beg your pardon for cursing and raising my voice. I . . . I have no excuse to offer."

"The woman you love is seasoning. No need to ask my pardon."

"Will she die, do you think?" he asked, pinching the bridge of his nose.

Moving her hand to his waist, she gave him a brief squeeze. "It's too early to tell. Until these spikes of fever start to decline, we won't know."

"But there was next to no fever yesterday. And she's awakened several times. Long enough to drink a bit of broth, anyway."

"You know how the ague and fever are. One day good. One day bad. The bad days getting worse and worse until either the fevers peak and begin to decline or the fevers peak and . . ."

He lowered his forehead into his hands. "She wasn't to go in after Sally. When I heard that splash, I know not which I felt more strongly—anger or terror. But I didn't have time to reel her back in, plus go after Sally." He took a deep breath. "Then they both went under. By my life, it reminded me of . . . of Margaret. Of a sudden, I was seven again staring at that burning cottage, knowing Margaret was in there, knowing it should have been me instead."

Grandma stroked his hair. "Margaret's death wasn't your fault."

"She was under my care."

"You were a child."

"It makes no matter."

She paused. "I was there too."

He looked sharply at her. "What mean you?"

"I came upon the savages directly after they'd set the torch to the roof," she said, tears filling her eyes. "I thought all three of you were in there. Instead of confronting them, I ran for your father." She shook her head. "No, I should have been the one to save Margaret."

"They'd have killed you."

She nodded. "As they would have you."

He wrapped his arm about her. "Father never would have expected a woman to stand up to them."

"Constance would have." She swiped her cheeks.

"Constance has no power within her brain."

Grandma leaned back to look at him. "Constance is smarter than most men I know."

He allowed his arm to slide from Grandma's shoulder. Resting his elbows on his knees, he clasped his hands together. "Why say you I love her?"

"Because of your actions."

He stood and strode to the fire. Propping his hand against its frame, he studied into its leaping flames. It was true and he knew it. Not only because he'd like to have her between the sheets, though heaven knew he certainly craved that, but because of her very being. Her spunk. Her determination. Her devotion to her uncle. Her devotion to Sally. Her devotion to her Lord.

But, God help him, he didn't want to succumb to those feelings. For he knew only too well the pain it would lead to. Why, even now her life hung in a fragile balance.

"I've tried to keep her at a distance," he said. "I have."

"Ah, Drew. Have you not figured it out yet?"

He said nothing.

Grandma rocked a bit. Back and forth. Back and forth. "I know not why you thought to distance yourself from her. You've never even been able to distance yourself from the little ones. You were drawn to your baby brothers and sisters from the moment you laid eyes on them. So was Nellie. You should see her with that baby of hers. Why, you'd think that child was the king's heir.

"Yet Nellie's husband has given their little one no more than a second glance. Not even has he held that sweet boy. If, God forbid, they do lose the baby to this unsympathetic land, who do you suppose is the richer? Nellie, for having shared what precious moments God granted her with the babe, or Gerald, who would have lost the opportunity to know, hold, and love his first-born?"

"Gerald."

Grandma hooted. "Oh, Drew, you're missing the point on purpose." Slowly, she sobered. "But make no mistake. You've a wife here that you love, whether you like it or not. You might lose her and you might not. If you don't, I suggest you spend what additional time you have with her sharing that love to its fullest. Otherwise, you will die a very lonely man."

"Lonely men don't get hurt."

"Lonely men are the most bitter creatures of all." She rose and pulled a blanket off Constance, refolding it.

"What are you doing?"

"Her fever's back."

Drew reached for the bucket. "I'll fetch more water."

"You're sure you won't stay?"

Grandma shook her head. "There's no purpose. You've Mary here to cook for the men and for you. You have the men to labor on the big house. And since you refuse to leave Constance's side, there is really nothing for me to do. Besides, I miss my great-grandson."

"But what of Sally? You're sure she's fit for travel?"

"Travel!" Grandma snorted. "I'd hardly call a trek to Nellie's *travel*."

"Still, only a week has passed since her ordeal."

Grandma glanced down at Sally, her little face shining beneath the layers of clothing wrapped around her head and body. "She's fine, Drew."

"I see Nellie!"

Drew sighed. "Very well. Isaac will escort you." He gave Grandma a hug. "Is there nothing special I should do for Constance?"

Grandma patted his cheek. "Pray. 'For everyone who asks receives, and he who seeks finds, and to him who knocks it will be opened.'"

He nodded and lifted Sally into his arms. "You tell Nellie that if she doesn't give that nephew of ours a name, we'll be calling him . . . oh, what say you? Jael?"

Sally crinkled her nose. "I never heard that name."

Drew smiled. "It means 'mountain goat.'"

She barely suppressed a groan. Her head hurt. Her stomach hurt. Her whole blessed body hurt. Opening her eyes, she oriented herself, noting she lay in Drew's bed and he slumbered in that chair of his.

His hair was unbound, his face unshaved, his clothes wrinkled. He looked almost as bad as she felt. She turned her head a bit. Mary bustled around the fire as usual, but nowhere was Sally. Looking back at Drew, she discovered his gaze fastened upon her. She tried to smile but couldn't quite manage it.

"How do you feel?"

"Thirsty."

He rose then returned with some broth. She tried to lift her head, but he slipped his hand beneath her in assistance. The broth flowed down her throat but didn't set well within her stomach. "No more."

Setting the broth aside, he perched on the bed. "Are you cold? Hot?"

She gave a slight shake of her head. *Fine,* she mouthed.

He touched her forehead. "No fever right now. It was bad yesterday, though."

"How many days?" she whispered.

"About eight. You should start getting better, though. I'm thinking the worst is over."

"Sally?"

"She's fine. Gone with Grandma to visit Nellie and the new baby."

"Grandma. I thought I'd dreamed it."

He brushed her hair back from her face. "Is there anything you want? Anything I can get you?"

"It hurts."

He rubbed her arms. "What hurts?"

"Everything."

He leaned down and placed a light kiss on her head. "I'm sorry."

She smiled slightly, then closed her eyes. It was too much effort to keep them open.

The fever didn't drop as it usually did in the evening. Instead, it continued to climb higher and higher. He bathed her with cool cloths when she burned. Wiped her with dry ones when she sweat. Still, it did not cease.

Her limbs swelled and her pallor dimmed, causing even her freckles to lose their luster. She tossed her head, she moaned, she looked near death. It would happen tonight. She'd either survive or she wouldn't.

He'd never prayed so hard in his life. He barely noticed Mary refilling the bucket, replenishing the rags, subduing the fire.

If you let her survive, I'll allow her to educate Sally.

Her fever continued to rise. He threw the covers from the bed, bathing her arms and legs as well as her face and neck. Moments later, her nightdress was saturated with her sweat as was the bedding.

He stripped her nightdress from her, frantic to mop the perspiration from her body. Mary moved to his side with fresh linens. He lifted Constance into his arms, hugging her to him while Mary tightened the bed ropes and changed the linens.

If you let her survive, I'll never have another lustful thought about her.

He and Mary slipped a dry nightdress onto her. She was ablaze again, her skin now a deep bright red. He quickly laid her down and set to swabbing her with cool water.

Please. Please. Don't let her die.

The water all but sizzled against her skin. Her temperature couldn't go any higher. It couldn't. Yet it did. He slipped his hand into hers. She squeezed it in response.

Yes, Constance. I'm here. I'm here. And then he realized. She wasn't responding to him. Her whole body was tightening up. She was going into a convulsion.

Oh, God! Oh, God!

Her face tensed. Her body became rigid. He wrenched his hand from hers, quickly turning her head to the side.

Breathe, Constance! Breathe! Her body remained rigid, her chest still. He prayed and prayed and prayed.

All right! All right! If you let her survive, I'll honor my marriage vows and keep her to wife for the rest of my entire wretched life. Just let her live! I love her, Lord! I love her!

Her chest caught. Her body slowly relaxed. She began to breathe again. Jerking a cloth from the bucket, he proceeded to bathe her, prepared to continue doing so for as long as it took. He never noticed the tears coursing down his face.

EIGHTEEN

I lied, Lord. About the lustful thoughts part.

His eyes traced the curves beneath her covered sleeping form. She was resting peacefully, the fever, for now, subdued. It had come and gone in spikes for the last several days, each spike lower than the last. In another couple of days, it should leave her completely.

Then what? How, in all that was holy, would he tell her he wanted her for wife after giving her such a blistering rejection when she'd first offered to stay?

He sighed. He'd not had much time to think about his promises to God. Heretofore, he'd continued to care for her during her feverish bouts, trying to catch a bit of sleep in between.

He was wide-awake now, though, and thinking of all he'd said and done. That's when the lustful thoughts began. So worried had he been before, he'd barely even been cognizant of her as a . . . well, as a woman. But his subconscious had evidently been paying very strict attention. And now that the danger was over, it was reminding him with remarkable accuracy and frequency of her slim graceful arms. Her dainty curved feet. Her long willowy legs. Among other things.

He closed his eyes, trying to slow his errant thoughts. Instead, he recalled the moments he'd held her while Mary had changed the bedding. Her skin had been creamy and smooth, burning not only where he'd touched, but burning his very soul.

He took a deep breath. Yes, he'd definitely been lying about the lustful thoughts part. Still, she was his wife and now that he intended to make an honest go of it, surely it was permissible to have such thoughts about one's own mate. He frowned. He couldn't seem to call up one Scripture that said as such. Surely it said that somewhere. He grabbed his Bible and lowered himself into his chair.

"So husbands ought to love their own wives as their own bodies; he who loves his wife loves himself. For no one ever hated his own flesh, but nourishes and cherishes it."

Well, he certainly loved her body, but no matter how he manipulated the passage, he knew it had nothing to do with that. He continued to flip through the pages.

"Wives, submit to your own husbands."

An excellent verse, but not what he was looking for at the moment. He turned back toward the front.

Aha! *"Rejoice with the wife of your youth. As a loving deer and a graceful doe, let her breasts satisfy you at all times; and always be enraptured with her love."*

He slammed the Good Book closed. God would not hold him to the lustful thoughts part of his promise. As for the rest, he intended to keep to the letter his pledge.

He cringed at the thought of educating Sally, but perhaps that would work to his advantage. Constance would be very pleased at the prospect of tutoring her again.

After storing his Bible beneath his chair, he looked toward the bed. She was staring at him. Feeling color flood his face, he shifted in his chair.

"God ye good den."

He nodded. "Good afternoon."

She lay still for a few more moments. "I'm hungry."

He lifted the corners of his mouth a fraction. "That's wonderful."

"Might I have something to eat?"

"Certainly." He stayed where he was.

She frowned slightly. "Drew? Is everything all right?"

He cleared his throat. "Fine, fine. Everything's fine." He turned his head slightly but kept his eyes on Constance. "Mary? Might you bring Constance a bit of broth?"

Constance looked to the fire and then different spots in the cottage. "Mary isn't in here."

He twisted around. "Oh. So she isn't. Well, I'll get you something in a moment or two."

She moistened her lips.

His breath caught. "Or three."

Touching her hand to her forehead, she frowned again. "I also need to, well, your pardon, but I need to make use of the chamber pot. Um, *now*."

He shot to his feet and made his way hastily to the door. "I'll find Mary."

"Drew! Your coat!"

But he was already out the door.

Constance drank in the sight of his ruddy cheeks and nose, along with his wind-tossed hair. Peeling off his jacket, he shook the snowflakes from its folds and hooked it on a peg. "You look wonderful," he said, easing into a smile.

He was dressed for winter. He'd attached the sleeves to his leather jerkin with cording and donned thick woolen breeches. Stockings and shoes had been exchanged for boots. "Compared to what?" she asked.

He moved to the foot of the bed. "Compared to this morning, compared to yesterday, compared to last week, I don't know. You simply look wonderful."

It was a bald-faced lie, but she wouldn't argue with him. "Were you at the big house?"

He nodded.

"Did it suffer any from the storm?"

"What storm?"

She hesitated. "The *rain*storm, Drew. You remember the one? I believe Sally got lost in it?"

He raised a brow. "The house is fine."

She smoothed the coverlet's wrinkles. "Is the roof on yet?"

"Hardly. We only started on the chimney this morn."

Frowning, she looked up. "I thought you said I'd been ill for almost three weeks."

"You have."

"Then what in the world have you been doing?"

He stiffened. "The siding is on. The windows and doors are in. And the cornice boards have been completed. Is that all right with you?"

She shrugged. "I was simply worried about the snow. What with no roof, won't the snow cause problems?"

"No." He strode to the fire, rubbing his hands together in its warmth.

She sighed. "When will Sally be home?"

"I'll bring her home after the Christmas service."

Christmas. Sweet heaven, she'd forgotten all about it. "What is today?"

"The first day of December." Scooping some stew into a bowl, he brought it and a spoon to her. "Here."

She set them on her lap. "I'm tired."

"Just a few bites, then you can rest."

It took such effort to eat, and their conversation was already draining her. She stared at the steaming bowl.

The bed tilted from Drew's weight, then he took the bowl and spoon in hand. "Open up."

She wrinkled her nose. He grinned boyishly. "I promise not to miss, *if* you open up like a good girl."

She opened her mouth, the warm concoction pleasantly appeasing. He said nothing as she chewed, just watched her mouth until she swallowed. Before presenting her with the next bite, his gaze briefly touched hers. She skittered hers away.

She opened her mouth and again closed it around the spoon. He withdrew it much more slowly this time, then returned it to the bowl. Chancing another glance at him, she ceased to chew. His stare was bold and unabashedly direct. Something stirred deep within her.

He brushed her cheek with his finger. "Eat."

She finished the bite in record time.

His gaze, soft as a caress, touched her lips. "Open."

She hesitated, then opened her mouth. He fed her

another bite. Broth trickled from the corner of her mouth. Before she could wipe it, he was there with the spoon, scooping it up. His eyes then locked with hers as he drank from the spoon, cleaning it thoroughly within his mouth.

Her pulse pounding, she forced herself to swallow. "I'm all done. Thank you." She slid under the covers, turned to face the wall, then closed her eyes. But her heartbeat slowed not and her desire for him swelled.

She'd make certain he never saw it, though. Never again. Many tense moments of silence passed before he finally stood and moved away.

Upon awaking, she first looked to his chair. He wasn't in it, but neither was it empty. Rising up onto her elbows, she scanned the cottage. Mary was grinding with mortar and pestle, but Drew was nowhere in sight.

The chair had been pushed next to the bed, well within her reach. In its seat lay a gingerbread slate with a huge heart-shaped leaf resting atop it. On the leaf was inscribed a message.

A cylindrical bucket is 6 inches in circumference and 4 inches high. On the inside of the vessel 1 inch from the top is a drop of honey. On the outside of the vessel on the opposite side, 1 inch from the bottom, is a fly. How far will the fly have to go to reach the honey?

She studied the dry leaf, tracing its shape with her fingertip. What beautiful foliage this land produced. She'd never dreamed.

She reread the geometrical exercise, then sighed. He'd finally acknowledged her interest in mathematics again.

He must be feeling awfully sorry for her to have instigated such a thing. Still, she was pleased. Closing her eyes, she pictured the bucket, the honey, and the fly.

"You're home early today."

Drew shrugged out of his jacket. "We can only do about eight feet of bricking per day without squashing the mortar. So I'm having the men sheath the roof for now, then in the morn we'll do more bricking. How do you feel?"

"Better and better. I'm even beginning to miss my baths."

He tsked, waving his finger to and fro. "What would your father say?"

"He'd be scandalized."

Chuckling, he glanced to the fire. "Has she been eating, Mary?"

"It's lucky you are that you came home early, Master, for I fear there's a wolf in her stomach, I do."

Constance watched them exchange a smile, then looked at her hands. Things were different between Drew and Mary now. No longer was Mary meek and subservient around him. She looked him in the eye. She grumbled if he interfered with her chores. She laughed frequently and easily with him.

He was different as well. The barrier he'd always placed between him and others outside his immediate family was no longer there. He teased her. He whispered with her. He shared his laughter with her.

Constance refused to acknowledge the knot beneath her chest. She adored them both, and if they had found something special to share, she'd not sit here and moon over it. Lifting her chin, she blanched to find Drew standing behind his chair, staring at her.

"Have you decided how far the fly will have to go to reach the honey?"

Her gaze ricocheted from him to the untouched gingerbread slate and back up to him. "I've been toying with the idea in my head. Do *you* know the distance he must go?"

He took a deep breath. "I have no idea."

"I see." She bit her lip. "Well, I . . . it was . . . thank you. I really appreciate your giving me the puzzle. I've just been too tired as of yet to give it my full attention."

He picked up the slate and leaf, then lowered himself into the chair. "You must not be as well as you appear, then."

She gave him a tentative smile. "No, I do feel much better. Truly, I do. I simply tire very easily."

He nodded. "That will pass."

They sat in awkward silence—nothing like the easy silence that passed between him and Mary. This was tense and uncomfortable. She groped for something to say but could think of nothing.

He shifted. "The snow has ceased."

"Has it? Oh, Drew, I'm so glad. I did worry you and the men wouldn't be warm enough. Are you . . . uh . . . they warm enough?"

"Fine. Just fine. Everyone's plenty warm."

Another stretch of silence, this one worse than the last. She contemplated her toes, wiggling them underneath the coverlet. He studied his nails. Then they both looked at each other.

"Why don't you eat something, Drew? Mary made some wonderful—rack-coon, was it, Mary?"

Holding her arm above the fire to test its warmth, Mary shrugged her shoulders. "You needs must ask the master. My tongue has a time with those savage words, it does."

"Aroughcoune."

"Yes. That. Mary baked some today."

"Is there any left or did your wolf eat it all?"

"Mary exaggerates. There's plenty."

He continued to sit there. Saying nothing, just staring at her. *Say something, Constance. Quickly.*

She fingered the string that gathered her nightdress together at the neck. "Um, I think I can sleep on my tick again. You needn't give up your bed any longer. I'll—"

"No."

She stilled. "But, your bed."

"You need to stay quiet for many more days. I'll not risk your having a relapse."

"But—"

He leaned forward, close to her ear. "I like having you in my bed, Connie. Please."

Her eyes widened. His face turned a dull red. He shot to his feet. "I believe I'll have some dinner now after all."

Tossing the slate and leaf to the foot of the bed, he strode to the shelves and retrieved a trencher. She followed him with her gaze, dumbstruck. Her insides jangled, her heart pounded. He couldn't possibly mean what she thought he did. No, that's why he was so embarrassed. It had come out sounding different from what he'd intended.

Still, Connie? *Connie?* Where had that come from?

He had his aroughcoune now but did not return to his chair. He, instead, sat on the hearth, legs extended, feet crossed, eyes glued to the food he was devouring.

She allowed her attention to roam back to the slate and leaf. The *heart-shaped* leaf. Could it be? Might he actually be—no. Impossible. He was merely feeling sorry for her. Responsible for her. It was Mary who received all the soft looks. Mary with whom he was at ease. Mary who was uneducated.

The thudding of her heart slowly settled back to its natural rhythm. She must be very, very careful not to allow herself to misconstrue his actions to fit what she wanted them to fit.

Closing her eyes, she pictured the bucket, the honey, and the fly.

What a clodpate. Drew pounded another nail into the roof's sheathing, thinking of a thousand things he *should* have said but didn't. No, he'd just blurted out whatever thought happened to be in his worthless head. By trow, but his tongue did twang as readily as any buzzer's.

Holding two nails in his mouth, he withdrew a third and continued with his hammering. Treating the woman you were trying to court like some heifer at rut time was disastrous at best and irrevocable at worst. She'd barely gained the strength to feed herself. He should be coddling her, not pressing her with clumsy advances.

Pausing, he took a moment to look out over his land. At the bottom of the hill and several acres beyond lay the James River, where soon he'd build a huge wharf so the tobacco ships could sail right to his front door. This spring would be the last time he'd need to roll hogshead after hogshead to the public warehouses.

He felt a surge of satisfaction. Mayhap he'd build Nellie a barge so she and Gerald could row over for a visit. And Sally, wouldn't she love to run down and welcome Josh home from his factoring fresh off the ship? By trow, but it was going to be grand.

His elbow rested on his knee, the hammer hanging from his hand. Would Josh have little ones of his own racing down this slope? Most probably. He rolled the nails from one side of his mouth to the other. Would he and Constance have little ones racing down it as well? Did he even *want* babes of his own?

He looked to the half-finished barn. If they were to have children, he should probably go ahead and make a necessary. And a smokehouse. He sighed. And if Constance was to be the mother, he might as well construct a schoolhouse. She would surely want to educate not only the O'Connor offspring but every woman in the colony. Forsooth, his father must surely be spinning in his grave.

His grave. How many more would Drew be digging before he was laid in his own? More than he'd want. Some small and from his own seed, no doubt. Would it be worth it?

A cool breeze wafted from the river as he squinted against the sun's descent. What if just one of the babes survived? What if the child grew to adulthood? What would his dreams be? His pursuits?

He gripped the hammer. Yes. *Yes*. He wanted children. Lots and lots of them. But first, he must convince Constance to stay. And that was going to take some doing.

He thought for a moment, then straightened, slowly removing the nails from his mouth. He knew just the thing to get back in her good graces.

What in heaven's name was he up to? He'd been acting near giddy from the moment he'd arrived home. They'd eaten and visited, same as every night, but he was much like a young boy awaiting his birthday surprise.

Moments ago, he'd whispered furiously with Mary while she stoked up the fire and set several pots to boil. Now he stood on his chair, hanging a large sheet from several old ceiling hooks. When he was finished, the cloth completely enclosed a small portion of the room just in front of the fireplace.

She blushed with mortification. They wanted some privacy. How could she have been so addlepated? She would *not* lie here in his bed and force them to hide behind a curtain for . . . for whatever it was they were going to do. She would sleep in her tick tonight and she'd brook no argument.

Drew appeared from behind the curtain, his glance dashing away from her the same moment it found her. Saints above, how awful. She was about to tell him her intent when he whisked himself out the door.

"Mary, quickly. Get over here and help me up to my tick before he returns."

Mary peeked around the curtain. "Up to your tick? Whatever for?"

Constance threw back the covers. "Let's not make this any more embarrassing than it already is. Just help me up there and with haste."

"Mistress! Get back under those coverlets. You'll catch a chill for certain."

Mary bustled over, and Constance, her feet already on the dirt floor, held out her hand for help. "Come. I can't make it clear up there by myself. Now, make haste. He might return any moment."

"Of course he'll return, and he'll be plenty furious if I assist you with such a thing. I'd just as soon not have to deal with his wrath, I wouldn't. It's hard he is working to try and please. I'll not be spoiling it, I won't."

Constance stilled. Oh, dear. She was probably right. He'd be angered and then their little tête-à-tête would be ruined. Blast. She'd simply have to feign sleep. Immediately. "Perhaps you're right. Already I'm feeling weary. I think I'll go on to bed now. Dig you den, Mary." With that, she dove under the covers, turned her back to the curtain, and closed her eyes.

"Merciful me. What a pair the two of you are."

The door slammed open, a cold rush of air swooshing into the room. Constance peered beneath her lids just long enough to see him haul in a huge half-barrel of some sort.

She squeezed her eyes shut, willing herself to ignore their whispered giggles and the sound of splashing. He came and went from the cottage several times, chilling the room even more. *What in the world?*

Finally all was still. "Connie?"

She took the deep, even breaths of a slumbering person. He touched her shoulder. "Are you awake?"

"She's awake," Mary said from across the room.

Constance felt a rush of heat suffuse her cheeks. Thank the heavens it was dark. What could Mary be thinking?

"I've a surprise for you, Connie. Would you like to see?"

She stilled. A surprise? *For me?* She slowly lay back on the pillows. The darkness was even more pronounced than usual, for the curtain shrouded the fire and its light.

"Come. I've something for you."

"Right now?"

"Right now." He peeled back the covers and helped her sit before scooping her up into his arms.

"Drew! Sweet heavens, I can walk."

He said nothing but carried her to the curtain, then stepped inside it. Immediately, light and heat embraced them. And there, in the midst of it was a barrel of water, with a scent rising from its depths, the likes of which she'd never smelt before.

Setting her gingerly on the hearth, he allowed his hand to travel the length of her arm to the tips of her fingers, where his lips touched them. "For you, my lady. Enjoy."

Then he was gone, the closing of the cottage door loud in the subsequent silence, the gooseflesh on her arm still tingling.

Mary stepped forward. "Come. Let's get you into the bath so the master doesn't have to linger overlong in the cold."

A bath? *A bath?* She looked up. Mary smiled. "Come. It's just right."

As if in a dream, she allowed Mary to undress her and assist her into the barrel. The warm water swirled around her, encircling her as she lowered herself into it. The water came up to the slopes of her shoulders, teasing them as it lapped up over her.

Dipping hands and soap into the tub, Mary quickly worked up a lather from which the most delicate fragrance arose. Constance sat as if disassociated with her own body.

Closing her eyes, she felt Mary lather her arms, her back, and her hair, before pausing. "Wish me to continue?"

Constance stirred. "I've never before submerged myself in water. Have you?"

"No, mum. Is it as heavenly as it looks?"

"Even more. Do you suppose I'll be going to hell now?"

"No, mum. If it was to hell you'd be sent for such a thing, the master wouldn't have allowed it to happen to you. Wish me to continue?"

Constance opened her palm. "No thank you. I can finish."

Mary nodded. "I'm going to go check on Snowflake. It's time for her evening milking."

"Surely Drew has seen to it for you?"

"It's best I go check. You will be all right?"

"Yes. I'll be fine. Thank you. And Mary?"

"Yes, mum?"

"I'm sorry you're having to do my chores as well as your own."

A small shy smile touched Mary's features. "I'm happy to do them for you, Mistress. It's glad I am you're feeling so much better."

She turned and left, a soft whoosh and a click the only signs of her departure.

When he saw Mary leave the cottage, he'd assumed Constance had finished. Not so. He could see clearly her silhouette through the curtain with her head hung back over the edge of the barrel.

Mary should never have left her. Didn't she realize how dangerous it was for Constance to fall asleep in a tub full of water? He stepped inside the curtain and froze.

Constance's hair, still full of lather, was piled atop her head, her eyes closed, her face relaxed. The graceful curve of her neck gave way to delicate shoulders peeking above the water's edge.

"This is absolutely divine, Mary. You must try it next. But first, I needs must rinse my hair. Will you help me?"

He should turn around and walk out. He picked up the empty bucket. Dipping it beneath the surface, he filled it with water. Constance, eyes still closed, covered her face with her hands and bent forward. "I'm ready." Her voice was muffled and husky.

He poured the water over her hair. It took several more dousings before all the soap had washed out.

"A rag. Is there a rag I can use to dry my eyes with?"

He knelt beside her and placed a dry rag in her hand. She pushed her hair back, drug the rag down her face, peeped over the top, then squealed and sunk deep into the water.

"Will you be my wife, Connie?"

The fire crackled. She said nothing. Only stared at him through those long lashes spiked with water.

"I mean, my *real* wife. Till death do us part?"

The rag came further down her face, revealing her nose, mouth, and chin. "Why?"

Because I love you. Because I want my children to be your children also. He remained silent.

"What about Mary?"

He frowned. "I wouldn't sell Mary. She could stay."

"Oh, Drew, please. I like it not that you can buy and sell Mary, or me, or anyone else at your whim. And that's not what I meant. I thought, well, things between the two of you are . . . different."

He relaxed some. "We worked long and hard to care for you while you were ill. I'll always be grateful to her. But I've never had any feelings for her. Besides, I'm married to you. Even if I had interest elsewhere, I would never pursue it while married to another."

"And do you have interests elsewhere?"

"No."

"And do you have . . . feelings for me?"

"Yes."

"What kind of feelings?"

He should have known she'd demand it all. He took a deep breath. "Love feelings." Reaching for her hand, he flattened it against his chest. "Deep inside here."

Her expression softened, and she moved her hand up to comb a piece of hair back from his face. The tip of one shoulder rose above the water's surface. He kept his eyes on hers, but there was nothing amiss with his peripheral vision.

"Five inches," she said as she continued to comb her fingers through his hair.

He frowned. "Your pardon?"

"The fly," she whispered. "He has only to go five inches to reach the honey."

He was silent for a moment. "He'd have gone much, much further if he'd had to."

A mere hint of a smile touched her lips. "What think you if the honey meets him halfway?"

He lowered his eyes to half-mast. "Is that a yes, Connie?"

She nodded once. "I would be very honored to be your wife, Andrew Joseph O'Connor, until death do us part."

Cupping her face with his hands, he leaned forward and brushed his lips against hers.

NINETEEN

His kiss was gentle and achingly sweet. Her own calm, however, had long since shattered.

Love feelings. Until death do us part. He didn't want Mary! He wanted *her*. And she, most definitely, wanted him. Burrowing her fingers into the thick hair at his nape, she returned his kiss.

He'd asked her to stay. Forever. She would be the real Mistress O'Connor. She would live in his big house. In his chamber. With him.

His caress moved down her arms, his callused thumbs brushing her inner wrists. The pit of her stomach whirled. Every nerve stood on end.

He raised his mouth, his breathing ragged. "We needs must stop."

She shook her head. "Why?"

"It's too soon. You're not well."

"Oh, but I am. I am!"

Resting his forehead against hers, he closed his eyes. "Ah, Connie-girl. I'll not indulge in a piece of stair-work here aside the tub when Mary could walk in at any moment."

Her water-slicked skin cooled as air engulfed the chasm between them. She settled back against the barrel. He was right, of course. But when? When would Mary not be here? She didn't have the fortitude to ask.

Rising to his feet, his gaze roved leisurely over the swell of her breasts peeking just above the surface. With a delayed sense of modesty, she sunk a bit deeper into the water. Eyes dark with desire, he turned and disappeared behind the curtain.

A maiden is 27 steps ahead of her sweetheart and takes 8 steps while her sweetheart takes 5; but 2 of his steps are equal to 5 of her own. How many steps will he have to take before he can capture the maiden within his arms?

Smiling, Constance laid the leaf back upon the chair, then swept her hair to the side. It was a gnarled mess, for she'd fallen asleep without braiding it.

Dragging her fingers through tangle after tangle, she recalled last night's events, relishing each exchange, each revelation, each touch. After he'd left, Mary had bustled into the cottage, helping her from the barrel and into a clean nightdress. Then he'd returned, removed the curtain, stoked the fire, and settled her onto a pallet while he brushed her hair. When next she stirred, it was to wake up in his bed with another heart-shaped leaf at her side.

She paused, closing her eyes. *Mistress O'Connor. Mistress Constance Caroline O'Connor.* She still couldn't quite believe it. She must concentrate on regaining her health so that very soon she could wake up next to the man instead of his love letters.

It was a length of fine green wool that lay at her bedside this time. Fingering it, she chided herself for being disappointed. Not with the fabric, of course, but with his absence. It had been three days since his address and she'd not seen him once.

Picking up the material, she drew it into her lap, almost missing the heart-shaped leaf wedged within its folds.

You may make yourself a new Christmas Day gown, and though I look forward to seeing you in a lovely confection, I shall be jealous of it and wishing it were me that hugged those luscious curves. Make haste, my love, in your pursuit to good health.

Heat stole into her face and she darted a quick glance at Mary. But Mary paid her no mind, just continued to knead and punch the lump of dough beneath her fists. Constance reread the missive, his words provoking a scandalous reaction in her.

"Mistress?"

Constance jerked guiltily, her face burning. Stuffing the leaf under the coverlet, she attempted a casual smile. "Good morrow."

"How feel you this day?"

She took a fortifying breath. "I'm tired of laying abed, Mary. I wish to break the fast at the table."

Wiping her hands on her apron, Mary reached for a trencher. "You're sure you feel up to it? It's early yet, it is. The master left word you were to stay abed for another fortnight."

"You've seen him?"

"I see him every morn."

"Did he say what has kept him away from the cottage?"

"It's anxious, he is, to finish the roof. Seems it's time to be putting the tobaccy leaves in those great barrels."

Constance bit her lip. "And he thinks to keep me abed for another fortnight?"

"Those were his words, they were."

Fluffing up her pillow, Constance leaned back against it. Was that truly what needed to be done? She didn't want to take ill again, but still, she couldn't possibly lie abed the entire two weeks. "Very well, Mary. I'll break my fast in bed, but if I continue to feel fit, I might sit in his chair for a short while this afternoon."

And so the week went. Constance worked in her diary, she sewed on her gown, she sat for spells in his chair, and she slept quite a bit. She'd just woken up from one such nap when Drew burst into the cottage.

"We're dried in!" His tall, raw-boned body exuded triumph edged with self-satisfaction as he swaggered to the bed, planting his feet on the dirt floor like some captain at the helm of his ship. An open, honest smile spread across his face, wreathed in dimples.

She couldn't help but respond with a smile of her own. "The roof is on, then?"

"The roof, the chimney, the siding—everything! All that's left is the interior."

She held up both hands. "Congratulations."

He strode forward, grasped them in his, and brought them to his lips. "Thank you."

They stayed as such, absorbing the first sight they'd had of each other since making their pledges. My, but he was handsome. Massive shoulders beneath his coat, cheeks and nose red from the chafing wind, and his eyes. Eyes the color of a robin's egg—frank, admiring, and deliriously pleased.

"What's next?" she asked.

Releasing her hands, he removed his jacket, his movements hardy and robust. "The tobacco. I should have been well into the packing of the hogsheads by now, but I'm behind."

"Because of the house?"

He gave her a crooked grin. "Among other things."

She flushed. "But I thought you didn't send the tobacco back until spring."

"It depends on when a ship comes through. One year we had a ship come just after Christmas and half the colony wasn't ready. Those that were, reaped the bigger profit."

"And those that weren't?"

"Waited for the next ship, which didn't arrive until March."

She frowned. "But what about Josh? Isn't he supposed to factor the tobacco for you?"

"Hopefully he'll be on whichever ship comes through first." He eased down onto the bed, taking her hand into his lap. "How do you fare?"

"Very nicely. Mary won't let me do a thing, so I've no choice but to be a slug-a-bed all the day long."

He hooked a stray tendril behind her ear. "Good for Mary."

She lowered her lashes. "Thank you for the wool. It's beautiful."

"Is there enough for a proper gown?"

"Oh, yes. Plenty." She smoothed the blanket over her legs. "But, Drew, I'm unsure of the styles here. Are they the same as in London? Precisely what *is* a proper gown?"

"Whatever you make will be perfect."

"And you'll let me attend the Christmas service?"

He nodded. "As long as you continue to improve, I think it will be all right."

"There will be other women there?"

"Every woman from this part of the colony will be there."

"Grandma too?"

"Grandma too."

She leaned against the wall, and he reached behind her to adjust the pillow. "Did you get my note?"

She smiled. "Yes. The sweetheart didn't have to take any steps to capture the maiden within his arms."

His eyes widened. "How did you figure that?"

Leaning forward, she glanced at Mary tending the fire, then whispered, "The maiden turned 'round and ran straight to him!"

Chuckling, he hooked her chin with his finger. "Such shocking behavior from a maiden? I think not. You'd better check your work again. It was thirty steps he took."

"Yes. You're quite right. But I still think if the maiden had any sense at all, she'd have never run away."

He, too, shot a glance at Mary before leaning forward

and briefly touching his lips to hers. "What about my other note? Did you find it?"

Liquid honey poured through her. "I most certainly did," she whispered. "What were you thinking to write down such things? Why, anyone could have seen it."

He grazed her lips with his thumb. "I didn't write down the half of it. Besides, Mary can't read."

Her pulse skittered. "Oh, Drew. I'm feeling ever so much better."

His eyes darkened. "Are you?"

She nodded.

After a slight hesitation, he picked his jacket up from the chair and pulled it on.

"Where are you going?"

"I've hogsheads to pack, my sweet. I won't be back until well after nightfall."

"For how long?"

"Until they're done."

"The whole crop?"

"Pretty much."

Her shoulders drooped.

Drawing the strings on his jacket tight, he gave her a tender smile. "I'll try to check in when I can."

"Can't you take your meals here? The tobacco barn's not as far away as the big house."

He shook his head. "It uses up precious daylight to come back here for meals. We've little enough light in the day as it is." His gaze lingered on her lips. "I'll be thinking of you, though, Connie-girl. Rest assured, I'll be thinking of you."

And think of her he did, for every day something new greeted her when she awoke. A length of fine silk ribbon the color of oyster shells, a real wax candle to read by after dark, several more mathematical puzzles, and yesterday, a pair of soft homemade leather shoes—one shaped for the right foot, one shaped for the left. Ah, such luxury.

When she opened her eyes this morning, a large blackened cooking pot sat in his chair. Frowning, she peered over its edge, then squealed. Covering her mouth with her hand, she looked to Mary. "What . . . ?"

"It's Mr. Meanie, it is. The master said he'd be home for supper this night and he says to me, *'Mary, it's something special I'm wanting to give my wife for supper.'* A few minutes later, he comes back with Mr. Meanie hanging limp in his hand. He was going to put the cock right in the chair, but I stops him, I did. Thought he best set it in a pot first."

Sliding her hand to her neck, Constance peeked into the pot once again. The gray and white rooster lay at an awkward angle, a sad reflection of his once proud demeanor. Mr. Meanie. *Mr. Meanie.* Drew had killed his precious rooster. For her.

Tears welled within her eyes. The ribbon, the candle, the shoes, as sweet and special as they were, all paled in comparison, for this, without a doubt, was an act of genuine love.

Swiping at her eyes, she flung the covers back and slid her feet to the floor. "I want to cook it, Mary. Can you tell me what to do?"

"Oh, Mistress. You needn't do that. I'll be happy to cook that old rooster for you."

Shaking her head, Constance moved to Mary's side. "You don't understand. I *want* to cook it. Please? Will you teach me?"

Mary blinked. "Why, of course I will. Just don't tax yourself. If you start feeling woozy, promise to tell me?"

Smiling, Constance threw her arms about Mary. "Oh, thank you! I will, I will." She pulled back. "And don't worry. You've seen how I'm more out of bed than in these days and getting stronger by the minute."

Mary didn't look convinced but argued no further. "You'd best put on an old dress, then, for you've some plucking to do."

Drew knew she'd be pleased, but he wasn't prepared for the sight greeting him now. Constance stood beside the board dressed in Nellie's remade frock, with all that glorious hair tucked beneath her cap. Her cheeks were flushed, her smile captivating and her eyes brimmed with life, pleasure, and unmistakable warmth.

Sweet heaven, but she was beautiful. She glided around the board toward him. "Welcome home, Master Drew."

Her low, silvery murmur so distracted him, he almost missed the significance of her words. *Master* Drew? He searched her eyes, then felt his chest expand a good two or three inches. She was pleased with him. Very pleased.

Pressing her skirt against her thighs, she poked out the toe of one shoe. "Look, they're perfect. Much better than Nellie's discards."

His gaze moved down the length of her. "I can't see much of it. Perhaps you could lift the hem of your skirt a bit more?"

Withdrawing her foot, she tsked. "Such suggestions, good sir."

Their eyes met.

"Thank you," she whispered. "I'm saving the ribbon for Christmas, I haven't had to make use of the candle yet, and as you can see, the shoes serve me well. Where did you get all these things?"

"That'd be telling."

Her features softened. "Did you make the shoes?"

He nodded once.

"There's a left one and a right one. You'll spoil me." Leaning toward him, she placed a hand against his chest. "Thank you."

His blood pounded. He covered her hand with his. "I should have done it long ago."

She twined her fingers within his. "You killed Mr. Meanie."

He swallowed. "Yes."

Taking another step forward, she stood on tiptoes and touched her lips to his. "I love you."

He froze for a mere instant before propelling her to the door, slinging his jacket around her shoulders, and pushing her outside. The door hadn't thumped to a close before he'd crushed her against him, his mouth claiming hers.

Running his hands up and down her spine, his mouth strayed to her ears, her neck, her shoulders. She threw her head back, her cap floating to the ground as mountains of hair spilled atop his arms.

It was then he saw the coat no longer covered her but lay crumpled at her feet. "Your jacket."

"Leave it."

Snagging the coat, he again settled it about her shoulders, scooping her hair from beneath its confines.

Her lids fluttered open, eyes smoldering with desire. "When?"

His heart slammed against his ribs. "I will arrange it."

She fisted her hands, wrinkling his shirt within them. "When?" she whispered.

"Tomorrow."

She couldn't eat a thing. Her body hummed, her nerves stood on end, her skin prickled.

Drew ate like a starved man. "This is wonderful, Mary. Absolute perfection."

"The mistress made it, she did."

He paused, drumstick halfway to his mouth. His attention swerved to her. "Wanted to roast the little roister yourself, did you?"

Constance pulled her focus away from his lips, suppressing a smile. "Such wit. I wanted to learn to cook. For you. I thought it was a good place to start."

Tearing a piece of meat from the bone with his teeth, he held her gaze and chewed. "Very tasty."

A quiver surged through her, pooling at the pit of her stomach. "Thank you."

"Aren't you going to try it?" He wiped his sleeve across his mouth.

She studied the wing and thigh on her trencher. She hated Mr. Meanie. But she'd gotten to know him and they'd reached an understanding of sorts. Now she was to have him for supper.

"Don't tell me you're feeling guilty?"

Breaking off a piece of the wing, she brought it to her lips and took a bite. It did taste good. Very good. "I wonder if all grouchy males are this palatable."

Drew choked.

She looked up, tilting her head. "Are you all right?"

He turned a dull red. "Eat your supper, Connie."

TWENTY

She couldn't do anything right. She'd been clumsy in the milking of Snowflake—which resulted in a near miss from the goat's hoof, she'd knocked her shin against the bench, she'd sewn a sleeve on inside out, and now, she'd kicked over the sand bucket they kept for extinguishing cooking fires.

Falling to her knees, she scooped handful after handful of sand back into the bucket. The more she scooped, the bigger the mess. In a few short hours it would be nightfall, and she'd be Drew's wife in every way.

Her face heated. How ever did one make it through their own wedding party? She'd never much thought about it before, but every guest *knew* what was going to happen between the couple come sunset. She paused, looking at the sand. How awful!

Mary knelt down beside her. With expert hands she corralled the scattered sediment and returned it to the bucket. "Mistress, I'll do this, I will."

"No! *I'll* do this. I made the mess; I'll clean it up."

Mary slowly withdrew her hands, then stood. Constance sat down on her heels. "Your pardon, Mary. I didn't mean to snap at you."

"What ails you, Mistress?"

The door opened. Constance jumped to her feet.

"What happened?" Drew asked.

Constance stood mute. Mary resumed scooping the sand.

Surely it wasn't time yet! It was still light outside. Drew closed the door. "Connie?"

She started. "Oh! I, uh, I kicked over the sand bucket."

"Are you all right?"

"Fine! Fine. Just fine. How are you?"

A slow smile spread across his face. "Very, very fine."

She blinked.

Mary paused and slowly stood. "I think I'm going to see if there are any eggs in the hen house, I am. I'll be back in a . . . while." Grabbing her shawl, she slipped out the door.

Drew raised an eyebrow. "What was that all about?"

Constance clasped her hands together. "I think she must need some eggs."

"She's going to have a hard time finding any in the middle of December."

"Will she?"

He hesitated, then slowly stalked toward her. "I haven't been able to get a thing done. I forgot to attach the bottom head to a barrel before filling it with tobacco, I mislabeled two hogsheads, I strode straight into the tobacco press, and I let go of the packing lever before it was time."

She moved backward. "Oh, Drew, you peagoose. Are you nervous? You've nothing to fear."

A charming grin split across his face. "Well, that's certainly a relief."

Her back connected with the wall. "You're laughing at me."

He narrowed the distance between them. "Never."

"It's still daylight!"

He propped his hands on either side of her, bracketing her in. "I couldn't wait another minute."

She ducked underneath his arms, flitting to the other side of the cottage. "Drew! You can't possibly be serious."

Pushing away from the wall, he headed toward her again. "No, but a kiss would be rather nice. Just to hold me over."

Her pulse leapt. She glanced at the door. "Well, maybe a quick one."

He shook his head from left to right, coming closer, closer.

Her heart beat painfully against her breast. "Drew, maybe we'd best . . ."

He laid his hands upon her shoulders, running his palms up and down her arms. "You're so unbelievably beautiful."

He kissed her forehead, his hands moving, moving, never staying still. Her eyes drifted shut. Up her arms, across her shoulders, down her back and up to her shoulders again.

Slipping an arm about her waist, he traced her lips with tiny kisses. "Ah, Connie-girl."

She slid her hands inside his coat, cataloging the strength of his waist and back. His mouth covered hers, weakening her resolve.

The door flew open.

They jumped apart, Drew spinning to face the intruder, Constance hiding behind him.

"Josh!" Drew surged forward, leaving Constance where she stood. "Well. This is certainly a surprise."

She was too mortified to move. Surely the earth would be merciful and swallow her whole. It didn't. She had mere seconds to compose herself while Josh dropped his cloth bag and the brothers embraced.

"You're back! How did you get here so quickly? I'm not even finished packing the hogsheads!"

"I came over with a group of settlers who were heading to that new colony, Maryland." He pulled back from Drew's hug. "You say you've not finished with the hogsheads? Why not?"

Drew reddened. "I've been busy."

Josh lifted a brow. "I'll just bet you have." He moved to her. "Lady Constance. You're looking lovelier than ever."

Disregarding the high color she felt in her cheeks, she strode for a sense of normalcy. "Welcome home, Josh."

He bowed low and deep, drawing her hand to his lips. "I must say what an honor it is to have a *real* lady as my sister-in-law."

Her gaze flew to Drew. Lifting a corner of his mouth, he winked. She slowly exhaled. So he really had believed her.

Josh straightened, then stared at the locket hanging about her neck. "What's this?" he asked, gathering the locket into his palm.

It had completely escaped her mind. Drew had left it for her this morning, and in all the confusion she'd forgotten to thank him. "Drew gave it to me."

Josh's eyebrows raised. "Did he? And when did that happy event occur?"

"This morning," she said, blinking in confusion.

Josh froze, swerving his attention to Drew. *"This morning!"*

Drew reddened again, saying nothing. Josh turned back to her. "Do you know what this is?"

"It's a locket."

Josh released his hold on it, watching it settle against her throat. "It was my mother's locket. Father gave it to her on their wedding night."

She felt the color in her face intensify, and she searched Drew's face. He stood stiffly, saying nothing. She clasped the gold ornament within her hand. "Oh, Drew." Sidestepping Josh, she moved to him. "Thank you."

He nodded his head once, the silence crackling. She took a deep breath. "I think I'll go check on Mary. I'll be right back."

The door clicked softly behind her.

"Body O'Caesar, Drew! I've been gone since June and you're just now getting around to bedding her?"

"Watch your tongue."

Josh rolled his eyes. "Your pardon, Drew, but I'm, well, just . . . amazed."

"Well, you're testing my temper."

"Your temper must be at the very breaking point. Six months!"

"You overstep yourself, Josh," he growled.

"But am I reading this situation correctly? Tonight is to be your wedding night?"

"Not anymore."

Josh threw back his head and laughed. "By trow, but it's good to be home, big brother."

The women reentered the cottage. Constance looked between the two of them—Drew was obviously agitated, Josh delighted. *Same old Josh,* she thought, then watched him refocus on Mary and come forward with another courtly bow.

Capturing Mary's fingers, he brought them to his lips. "Ah, my sweet, gentle doe, what pleasure to again behold your wondrous charms. Did you miss me, for you did lie upon *my* heart with a most alarming frequency."

Constance frowned. His words lacked the light tones she was used to hearing from him.

Astonishment touched Mary's face. She snatched her hand out of Josh's. "Where's your bride?"

Josh took on a wounded expression as he pressed a fist to his heart. "Though Hannah once declared her undying love for me, it seems another had the greater part of her fickle heart, and all her fair words to me were but lies."

"She cast you out, did she?" Drew asked.

Josh looked back at him. "With brutal haste."

Had she not been studying Josh so intently, she would have missed the pain that flashed within his eyes. She quickly glanced at Drew, but he didn't seem to have noticed.

Pasting a grin upon his face, Josh slapped his stomach. "Ah, Mary, 'tis starving, I am. Have you anything for me to eat?"

Mary bustled to the fire. Josh waited, then gravitated to Drew's chair. "What's this, big brother? Have you a sudden need to establish yourself at the head of the table?"

Constance watched Drew's expression turn stony. Josh looked at the two of them and grinned before, bold as you please, settling into the chair. He ran his hands along its arms and pushed himself against its back. "Well done, *Master*. It seems it should serve the purpose it was made for. Does it?"

Constance held her breath. The edge to Josh's voice was unmistakable.

Drew arched a brow. "Kindly remove yourself from *my* chair and come with me. I wish to show you the big house."

"Your pardon, Master." Springing from the chair, Josh brushed nonexistent dust from its seat. Mary handed him a hunk of bread.

Tearing off a bite, he chewed and slowly scanned the cottage. Constance watched him swallow, sober, and take a deep breath. "Where's Sally?" All pretense had vanished from his expression.

Drew offered him a small smile. "She's fine. She's with Grandma at Nellie's."

Josh's shoulders visibly relaxed, and he stuffed the rest of the bread into his mouth. She blinked as his charm reappeared and he bowed once again to Mary. "Thank you, my lovely creature. I shall count the moments until I may return to the cottage and partake of your delicious meals."

Drew grabbed him by his coat sleeve and shoved him toward the door. "Out." He looked at Constance, shrugged, then followed Josh out the door.

Drew's chest swelled with pride when they rounded the bend and the house came into view. Josh stopped short, a slow whistle coming from his mouth. Magnificent and impressive, its newly whitewashed exterior gleamed against the artistic sky lines. Its enclosed porch and stair towers gave it the shape of a cross, curving Flemish gables springing from its eaves. Triple chimneys protruded from both the east and west ends, unique in their very nature.

Patches of snow surrounded the house, lying like miniature lakes in every direction. Neither spoke as they climbed the slope, ice crunching beneath their boots. On the front steps, Drew threw open the doors, allowing Josh to enter first.

The interior had yet to be completed, of course, but the window casements with lead glass panes were in place, minus the trim work. Josh moved from the enclosed porch to the great room, looking out one of the windows facing the James. "I'm overwhelmed. What will you call it?"

Closing the paneled front doors, Drew shrugged. "I haven't decided yet. Any suggestions?"

"I'll have to think on it." Josh peered at the fireplace. "The tile backing turned out well."

"Yes. I'm very pleased with it."

Josh walked into the huge barren opening, testing the sturdiness of the expensive Dutch tiles with his hands. "I'd forgotten about bringing them over for Father, it's been so long."

"Come, I'll show you the rest."

Drew took him through the parlor and up a flight to the two chambers, one directly above the parlor, the other above the great room. "This will be my and Constance's bedchamber. Yours is there across from us."

Josh walked over to his chamber, a mirror image of Drew's. The fireplace, though a bit smaller than the ones downstairs, still dominated the vacant room. "I was not expecting so much."

"Why ever not?"

Josh shrugged. "I'm hardly ever here. It seems a waste of space."

"It's not as if I've *bestowed* something upon you. We are partners, and there would be no new house if it were not for your factoring skills. You may be gone a good bit of the time, but this is your home, and this chamber is no less than what you should have. Besides, when you marry, your wife will not be with you on your trips, but here with us."

There. He'd given Josh an opening to speak of the broken betrothal.

"What of children?" Josh asked. "Constance will be wanting a nursery close at hand."

Drew allowed the opportunity to pass. "True. But I would imagine she'd want to keep the little ones in the chamber with us until they are older. Then when she's ready to move them, we've plenty of room up in the garret. Come, I'll show you."

Along the way, he pointed out the beamed ceiling supporting the next story's planked floor and the staircase's newel-posts with a half baluster set into it.

"With what will you finish the walls?"

"I'm going to panel the great room and parlor, then

plaster everything else. Did you check on the furniture I ordered?"

Josh nodded. "A ship should come through in March with your beds, chairs, tables, chests, and all."

Drew took a deep breath of satisfaction. "Excellent. Now, come down to the cellar and see the kitchen."

The thumps of their footfalls echoed in the stairwell. Josh slapped Drew on the back. "Her father really is the Earl of Greyhame, you know."

"You tracked him down, then?"

"There was no need, for he was still at his manor. He's an old gaffer, Drew, well into his seventies, I'd say, and too old to take part in the fighting. So he furthers the cause by giving his silver and other valuables to the king, as well as sending his sons into service—those that weren't for parliament, that is."

"How was your reception?"

"Very good until his relief was replaced with anger. The Lady Constance has evidently been a bit of a trial for him. And when he found you'd married her, I feared he would expire on the spot. I sought to pacify him by giving him her missive, which evidently contained her plans for an annulment. That, however, only caused him more anxiety. He claimed her reputation would be in tatters if word got out, especially since he'd recently found a suitable match for her."

"A suitable match?"

"Um. Some young, handsome aristocrat he felt would appeal to her."

"And wouldn't do him any harm either, I'd wager."

"Quite so."

"So what conclusion did you reach?"

"The earl can't leave his home right now, but he's making plans to fetch her this spring."

Drew raised his eyebrows. "I thought you said he was seventy-something."

"Oh, he's old, all right, and substantial in both paunch and pouch"—Josh hinted at a smile—"but mark you, he'll be here come spring. You can count on it."

Drew raked his fingers through his hair. *Lord help us all.*

They reached the bottom of the stairs. Sleeping ticks littered the cellar's brick floor, and a pile of lifeless ashes lay heaped in the huge fireplace. Josh turned a questioning glance to Drew.

"The indentured men. I saw no need to make them stay in the tobacco barn once we'd dried in the house."

Josh nodded then moved through the room. "Not only brick walls but a brick floor? Was that in Father's plan?"

"Not the floor. I thought it might make for a happier cook, though, if she had a brick floor rather than a dirt one."

Josh lifted one corner of his mouth. "Might provide your bottomless belly with a few more succulent dishes as well, eh?"

"Couldn't hurt." Sucking in his stomach, Drew made a concave area. "I'm always in need of a hearty meal." The brothers shared a smile. "Come. The milk closet is over here."

They examined the dairy and another room filled with empty wooden kegs for storing fruits and vegetables. Finally, they stood at a door with a bulkhead entrance while Drew expounded on how easy it would be to transport food from the garden and such without having to traipse through the main house.

Josh leaned against the brick wall, crossing his ankles, and looked the room over before returning his attention to his brother. "It's a fine plantation home you have here, Drew. Father would be very proud."

Drew pulled the door shut, latching it with a rope. "The men you recommended have worked out better than I'd dared to hope. I couldn't have done it without them."

"They survived the seasoning, then?"

Drew shook his head. "Not all of them. Seven suffered at one time or another and we lost Browne and Payne. Still, I never expected to have eight men come winter. So I'm grateful."

"What about the women?"

Drew moved toward the stairwell, heading up to the front door, Josh at his side. "Mary never had so much as a sniffle. Constance nearly died."

Josh stopped. "My sword, Drew. What did she get?"

"The ague and fever."

"When?"

"In November."

Josh blew a stream of air from his lungs. "Yet Mary had nothing?"

Drew shook his head.

"Do you think Mary's still likely to take ill?"

"I don't think so, but one never knows." They continued on to the front door, where Drew paused, his hand on the knob. "I'll not have you trifling with her, Josh."

"Her husband's dead."

"Is he?" He expelled a breath of air. "I guess I'll have to tell her this eve."

"No!"

Drew lifted his brows.

"I'd like to tell her."

"As you wish. But that changes nothing. Widow or not, she's under my care and she's an indentured servant, which means she can't marry until her service to me is over."

Josh stiffened. "She could marry if someone bought out her contract."

"She was transported by the court's command, Josh. If I were to release her before her sentence is up, it would mean her death."

"Only if she went back to England."

"Do you wish to wed her, then?"

Josh blanched. "Mary? Well, no."

Drew opened the door. "Then I'll not swap arguments with you. She's under my care, and if you or any other man trifles with her, it will be my temper they face."

"Do you credit me with so little scruples, then, that you think I'd force myself upon our own servants?"

"I've no concern whatsoever that you would even consider force. I said I'd not have you *trifling* with her."

"And if she's willing?"

"You're her master, Josh. She won't say nay to you whether she wishes to or not. If you want her, you'll wed her first."

Josh's lips thinned. "Hear me well, Drew. Because you are the firstborn, I am willing to cooperate with you—up to a certain point. But I'll not let you nor anyone else tell me who I can *trifle* with and who I can't."

Drew narrowed his eyes. "She's under my care and as long as she is, that means you are a protector of her also. I will not have her put into a position where she must fend off the very person who's supposed to be protecting her."

"Thus, any man can trifle with her but me?"

"*No* man can trifle with her, *especially* you, and that's an end to it. Have I made myself clear?"

Josh held himself erect. "Rest assured, you've made yourself perfectly clear." Spinning around, he stormed down the front steps. Drew hesitated, then pulled the door shut behind him.

He disliked being in a chair at the head of the board when Josh was home, particularly after the exchange they'd had at the big house. Their father had certainly never seen the need to establish himself in such a way. But there'd really been nothing left for Drew to do. So he'd just pulled the chair up and taken his place.

He glanced over at Josh. His brother, never one to stay angry long, was back to his old self, entertaining the ladies and telling them of the news from London. He gave them updates on the skirmish and answered Constance's endless questions about her family and friends.

Drew ate his last bite of rabbit, its tender, juicy texture setting well within his stomach but not improving his disposition. He'd planned for this to be his wedding feast, not Josh's homecoming.

Mary rose to collect the trenchers and take them to the hearth, Constance following her lead. He and Josh shoved the board against the wall, then moved his chair and one bench to the fire.

Picking up his pipe, Drew leaned back and took great pleasure in observing his wife as she scrubbed a trencher with sand from the sand bucket.

He sighed. He, of course, was pleased to have Josh safely home, but for the first time in his life, he resented Josh's presence and the lack of privacy the cottage provided. Still, he was loath to send him packing off to Nellie's on the very day of his return.

The women made short work of the trenchers, then stacked them on the shelves.

"Come join us, ladies," Drew said. "I've a need to look at something other than this ill-mannered brother of mine." He watched them return, Connie taking a place on the end of the bench farthest from his chair. Stifling his disappointment, he focused on the fire.

"Well, Lady Constance, you've asked after everyone in your family, you've asked after several of your female companions, but you've yet to ask me of your father's reaction to your nuptials."

Drew stilled.

Constance laid her hands upon her lap. "Only because I'm quite certain of what his reaction was once he read my letter."

"Are you?"

She nodded. "Anger. A great deal of it."

"I didn't give him the letter right away, but once I did, you're quite right. His anger was something to behold."

She bit her lip. "And?"

Josh stretched out his legs, crossing them at the ankles. "We had a bit of a discussion, and then he said he'd come and fetch you back this spring."

Constance's back straightened. *"Spring!"*

"Yes. Is that too long to wait, my lady? I'll take you back on the next boat if you wish it."

Drew furrowed his brows as her face filled with color and her jaw tightened. Quickly thinking back to the summer night he'd brought her home from the ship, he remembered with clarity her confidence that once her father received word, he would immediately come for her. That bounder. That she wanted to stay now was not at issue here. Her father's indolent attitude was a slap in her face. "Enough, Josh. We'll discuss this later."

Josh sent him a hard look, full of resentment. "I'll have it from her own lips that she desires to wait. Otherwise, I'll take her back. We wouldn't want her to feel obligated to you simply because you're her *protector*."

Drew lurched to his feet. "Outside."

Josh immediately stood.

Constance jumped between them. "Sit down, the both of you. Sit down. And of course I want to wait—I mean, stay. I've already made that perfectly clear to your brother, Josh, but I appreciate your giving me the opportunity to return home right away if I'd wished. Now *sit down*."

Drew slowly sunk back into his chair, his temper barely in check. Josh walked to the shelf, slipping the courting stick out from where it had been wedged. He thrust the stick toward Drew. Drew straightened himself in the chair. What was the matter with Josh? He was acting like a princox. Drew looked at Connie. She gave him a slight shrug of her shoulders. Clearly, she was baffled as well. He made no move to take the stick.

"Do you not wish to woo your lady? You remember how it's done. Just think back. Gerald certainly had no problem wielding it."

Drew narrowed his eyes. Josh was intentionally trying to provoke him. He knew the subject of Gerald was a sensitive one. He knew Drew felt responsible for Nellie's indiscretion, for Drew had had no previous experience with courting rituals.

But it didn't take much intelligence to figure bundling a young woman, bundling up her beau, and then allowing them to lie abed and whisper love words to each other was anything other than a recipe for disaster.

Leah had refused to bundle with him, and Josh had never taken advantage of the custom, so Nellie had been the family's first.

He'd held serious doubts about the wisdom of it, but Josh had made little of those concerns, Nellie had badgered him and everyone else in the colony did it. Even Grandma hadn't objected to the practice. So he'd given in.

When Nellie finally admitted to her condition, he'd been furious—with Gerald, Nellie, Josh, Grandma. Everyone. But most especially with himself. And it had all started with that blasted courting stick.

His lips thinned with irritation. It was pure folly Josh was up to.

Drew watched Josh present one end of the stick to Mary. "Sweet maid, be so kind as to hold this against your ear."

She glanced at Contance and hesitated before lifting the stick's end to her ear. Josh placed his lips at the other end of the hollowed out log and whispered something into it.

Color flooded Mary's face as her gaze collided with Josh's, and she quickly lowered the stick to her lap.

Drew surged forward, wrenching it from him.

Josh bowed to Drew. "No need to grab it from me. I had planned on letting you use it." He sat on the bench. "Go ahead. Mary and I will chaperone."

Drew clasped the stick with both hands, then slammed it against his thigh, slinging the broken halves into the fire. "You've overstepped yourself. Be gone from my sight."

Josh rose, the muscle in his jaw pulsing. "Certainly."

He watched Josh climb up the ladder to the loft and descend with two cumbersome ticks slung over his shoulder. "Come, Mary. It is time."

Mary scrambled to her feet, heading to the door.

Drew curled his fists. It was nothing short of an open challenge. He'd made it clear where he stood on the matter of Mary, yet Josh was flaunting that directive. Not only flaunting, but from the way Mary had responded to his call, Josh had obviously made some kind of arrangement with her.

Josh opened the door.

"A moment, you two!"

Mary froze, and Josh impaled him with his glare.

"Where go you?"

"From your sight, I believe the instructions were."

"Those *instructions* were for you, not Mary."

"She's going with me. We will spend the whole of this night in the big house. But do not worry. I will see to her *protection*."

"She goes nowhere."

"On the contrary, Drew. It is your wedding night, if you will, and I, for one, fear that if you don't have total privacy you might never manage it."

By my troth! He pierced Josh with his gaze. "Mary, get yourself up to the loft."

Mary quickly tried to acquiesce, but Josh encircled her arm. "Nay. She goes with me."

"She will not."

Keeping a loose hold on Mary, Josh dropped the ticks and squared his shoulders. "She will."

Lord help me! It would serve no purpose whatsoever to come to blows with him, other than to possibly relieve him of whatever devil was in his craw. With supreme effort, Drew reined in his temper and calmed his voice. "I'll have your word about the concerns I shared with you earlier."

They stood in silence for several moments before Josh lifted his chin a notch. "I give you my word, none of the concerns you have will come to pass this night. Get your shawl, Mary."

Mary looked up at Drew. He nodded once. She grabbed her shawl and flew out the door, Josh right behind her with their ticks once again slung over his shoulder.

TWENTY-ONE

The door swung back open, unable to latch itself after Josh had slammed it. Constance moved nary a muscle. Drew, with a heavy tread, pushed the door shut. "This isn't exactly the way I had the evening planned."

She clasped her hands together.

He turned around and leaned against the door, resting his head back as well. He surveyed the beam work supporting the thatched roof. "He's changed. I haven't seen him act this way since he was ten and three. He said not a word to me about his broken betrothal, but whatever happened has obviously affected him greatly."

"Hannah Eastlick is a vicious woman."

His gaze snapped to hers. "You know the lady Hannah Eastlick of Bowden?"

She nodded. "Quite well. Her father and mine dealt together often, and I must confess those business dealings were not as forthright as they should have been. Regardless, Hannah often accompanied her father to our home and I was responsible for her entertainment."

"How did you know she was betrothed to Josh?"

"The day of our marriage, he spoke of it to Governor Hopkin."

"Why say you she's vicious?"

She took a deep breath. "I've both witnessed it and been the recipient of it. She's deceitful, manipulative, self-centered, and cruel."

His eyebrows shot up. "All that?"

"Well, according to my brother Foley, she also plays the part of the maiden quite well but is, in fact, without discretion."

"He told you that!"

"Certainly not. He told my other brother and I was . . . I uh . . . overheard it."

He shook his head. "Josh is usually very good at discerning a person's character."

"She's a master at deception. It was quite some time before I realized her true nature as well."

"Then it's glad I am he's rid of her." After a moment, he rubbed his hand across his mouth. "About your father, Connie. Josh didn't tell you everything. The earl not only wants you home, but he has—"

She held up her palm, stopping his flow of words. "I want to stay, Drew. It will be wonderful to see him this spring, but he'll return home without me."

"But, he—"

"Not another word. My mind's made up."

He appeared to think that over, then pulled away from the door. "Are you cold?"

She rubbed her arms. "Um. A little."

He moved to stoke the fire, then indicated the bench with his hand.

"It will be a cold walk for them this night," she said, settling her skirt about her.

Drew nodded but clearly his mind was elsewhere.

She tried again. "I wish I could see the new house. Now everyone but me will have seen it."

He sat down beside her, took her hand in his, and rested them atop his thigh. "Not just yet. Though you're well, I want you to stay that way so you can attend the Christmas service with me next week. The meetinghouse is quite a trek from here. I would that you were rested for it."

"How far away is the meetinghouse?"

He pursed his lips. "If we walk at the rate of 3 miles an hour, we shall be 10 minutes late, but if we walk 4 miles an hour, we shall be 20 minutes too soon. Know you now how far it is from here?"

She arched a brow. "You thought that up ahead of time."

"Maybe."

Suppressing a smile, she cleared her throat. "I've a question for you too."

He nodded once.

"I ask you, sir, to plant a grove, to show that I'm your lady love. This grove though small must be composed of 25 trees in 12 straight rows. In each row 5 trees you must place, or you shall never see my face."

His eyes flickered. "How long will it take you to solve my puzzle?"

"How long will it take you to solve mine?"

"I already have."

She choked back a laugh. "You lie."

"How long will it take you?" he asked.

"Fifteen minutes."

His gaze caught and held hers. "Care to place a wager on it?" He skimmed a callused thumb across her knuckles. "And this time, there will be no bargaining over dish-washing."

Her heart fluttered. "Then what will we wager upon?"

"A kiss. A kiss freely given."

"And if I win?" she said, swallowing tightly.

His eyes darkened. "I'll forfeit much, much more than just a kiss."

She fingered the locket about her neck. "I'll need my slate."

He bent toward the fire, scooping up a handful of cold soot and spreading it out on the hearth. "Sketch away."

For a space of several beats, she considered him, then found herself on her knees beside the pile of soot. She quickly scratched several numbers into it before glancing back over her shoulder. "Clock's ticking. You'd better get over there with your own soot."

Chuckling, he moved to the opposite end of the hearth. Twenty-five minutes later, she sat back. He was leaning against the hearth, one leg extended, one bent, his face propped atop his palm. He removed the pipe from his mouth. "About time."

She narrowed her eyes. "You're awfully sure of your-self."

A slow smile stretched across his face.

"What's your solution?" she asked.

"Come see."

She rose to her knees, shuffling over to his drawing. He had indeed laid out a grove in which 25 finger inden-tions were placed in such a way that each row held 5 indentions for a total of 12 rows.

"What's the answer to my puzzle?" he asked.

She sat back on her heels. "Church is a five-mile walk from here."

He smiled. It was a two-dimple smile. "Wrong. You lose."

Her eyes widened. "How so?"

He smoothed the soot beside him, effectively erasing his grove, then scribbled numbers into the ashes. "If d is the time it takes to walk to church at 3 miles per hour and 4 miles per hour respectively and the difference is half an hour, then d over 3 minus d over 4 equals one-half. Multiply both sides by twelve to eliminate the fractions and you have $4d$ minus $3d$ equaling 6. Church is a *six*-mile walk from here."

She studied his figures. Oh no. How could she have miscalculated something so elementary?

"What formula did you use to come up with five miles?" he asked.

Her eyes drifted closed. "The wrong one."

He brought his hands together with a clap, a tiny cloud of soot tickling her nose.

She opened her eyes, but he'd already moved to resettle himself upon the bench. Spreading his knees, he rubbed his thighs. "I'm ready for my forfeit."

Heat stole into her face. Looking one more time at his figures, she pulled her trapped skirt from beneath her knees, then slowly stood.

His gaze roved boldly over her. A flash of self-con-sciousness threatened her resolve before she reined it in. Gliding toward him, she moved between his knees, stopping just short of touching him. His Adam's apple bobbed.

"Close your eyes," she whispered.

He immediately acquiesced. She pecked him on the nose, then whirled, darting back to the fireplace, but not before he snagged a portion of her skirt.

"I don't think so." His voice had dropped two octaves.

She looked behind her, watching as he wrapped her skirt about his fist, effectively reeling her in. "I gave you the forfeit! One kiss. Freely given."

"That was not a kiss and well you know it."

"It most certainly was. That you neglected to specify where and how the kiss was to be administered is no fault of mine."

He had her between his knees now and gave a quick jerk, causing her to drop onto one of his legs. He touched a finger to his lips. "Right here, Connie. I'll have one right here."

She bit the insides of her cheeks. "Really? Or else . . ."

A glint of mischief entered his eyes. "I dare not threaten to make you sit here all night until you do so, or you might very well take me up on it."

A giggle worked its way up, then she sighed with an exaggerated sense of resignation, wrapped her arms about his neck, and pressed her lips to his. That was the last bit of control she exerted over the kiss, for he immediately took charge. All thoughts of forfeits and challenges fled from her mind. She parted her lips, he deepened the kiss.

Shifting, she sought to slow the pace a bit. He pulled her closer, but the bench made his movements awkward, threatening to unseat them at every turn.

Tearing his mouth from hers, their eyes met, a flurry of butterflies brandishing their wings within her tummy.

"Are you frightened?" he asked.

She swallowed. "I didn't think I would be. I thought I'd be . . . oh, I know not. The only word I can think of is, well, *anxious.*"

He became very still. "*Anxious* as in *impatient?*"

Heat flooded her face.

He squeezed her waist. "It's not a shameful thing to be feeling, not for your husband."

"How do you know?"

"I looked it up in the Bible."

She covered her mouth with her hand. "You didn't!"

"I did. And it's very biblical to be wanting your mate. As a matter of fact, it says to rejoice in the sharing of your flesh—to relish it, even."

She smiled behind her hand. "It does not."

"It does too. Proverbs 5:18."

Laughter bubbled up from her throat. She knew perfectly well it said no such thing, but she'd never expected him to soothe her in such an outrageous way.

He frowned. "I'll show you."

She tightened her grip on his shoulder, stopping him. "Where are you going?"

"To get my Bible."

"Right now? You can't get your Bible out right now! I'm, I'm, we're just about to, to . . . ." She'd never be able to go through with this if he got out his Bible. She wiped all humor from her face. "I believe you. Proverbs 5:18. 'Rejoice, relish, and romp with your husband.'"

He chuckled. "I'm serious, Connie, and I won't have you feeling ashamed or unclean over anything we do in that bed, tonight or any other night."

"I won't. I feel unashamed and very clean. I promise. But please don't get out that Bible."

"What? Think you God can't see us right now?"

Groaning, she slid off his lap and covered her face with her hands. He sunk to his knees in front of her, drawing her hands down. "I love you. You love me. We are man and wife. God is watching, Connie, and He is very, very pleased."

I love you. It was the first time he'd ever said it to her. She'd known it, of course. Known it since he'd killed Mr. Meanie, but she hadn't realized how much she wanted to hear the words. A warm glow flowed through her.

And, truth was, she *didn't* feel ashamed. And she *had* in the very back of her mind worried over it. Smiling, she tilted her head to the side. "Shall we rejoice?"

He grinned. "By all means."

Lifting her into his arms, he carried her to their marriage bed.

TWENTY-TWO

A cacophony of voices filtered up from the cellar, punctuated by short barks of laughter. Josh dropped the ticks, quietly closing the front doors behind him. "Wait here."

The clamor grew louder as he made his way down the stairs. Standing on the bottom step, he watched as one-by-one the men noticed him, stopped speaking, and jumped to their feet.

He advanced into the room. "Dig you den."

Thomas stepped forward and they clasped hands. "Welcome home, Master Josh."

"Thank you, Thomas. It's good to be back. I can see the lot of you have been enjoying Mary's meals. You men were but a big bag of bones when we first arrived."

A few chuckles and murmurs of agreement answered him. He made a point of greeting each man with a handshake, a slap on the shoulder, and a comment or two. He mentioned his sorrow over the loss of Browne and Payne, as well as his pleasure that everyone else was in such good health. They relaxed some, but none resumed their seats on the floor.

"I decided to try out my new chambers and thought I'd best come down and warn you of my presence. I had no wish to confront any of you in the midst of the night thinking I was a cutpurse of some kind."

More chuckles and murmurs. He scanned the bricked-in room. "You've been busy. The house is spectacular, and Drew says the tobacco crop is one of the best we've ever had. It's pleased I am to come back to such news."

All but Thomas lowered their chins and shuffled their feet. "Thank you, sir."

"'Tis I who should be doing the thanking." Josh slapped Thomas again on the shoulder. "Well, I'm going to borrow some of the split wood I saw outside and then retire. Good night, men. I'll see you in the morning."

Flames cavorted among the logs, devouring the pine kindling before taking the slow-burning oak into its embrace. Josh poked at the fire, trying to maximize the amount of heat it put forth, for the barren chamber was cold, as well as quiet and very still.

Nary a sound reached them from belowstairs. Josh glanced at Mary's form hovering just inside his doorway. He hadn't wanted the men to know she was here, aware of what the implications would be if they had. He'd planned to have her sleep here in his chamber while he slept in Drew's with no one the wiser. But the more he thought of it, the more impractical that became.

What if one of the men did come abovestairs? How

could he even begin to protect her when he lay in a completely different room? There weren't even any doors yet. And those men had been without women for a very long time. She'd be lying alone here much like a lamb waiting for the slaughter.

Besides, it was deuced hard to warm these huge chambers, and he had no desire to lug up another stack of lumber. No, it would be best if they both slept in here together, where he could keep his eye on her. "Come, Mary. Warm yourself."

She did as he instructed, but with obvious hesitation. He gave his full attention back to the fire, thinking it might put her more at ease if he were to be engrossed with its care.

When the fire became too hot to tend, he retrieved the ticks from across the room and threw them in front of the hearth. "Sit down, Mary. Please."

She wrung her hands, then did as he asked, looking much like a newly placed fence post—stiff, sturdy, and rigid. He settled onto the other tick, propping his elbow on his bent knee while fingering the toothpick in his mouth. Silence permeated the room while each watched the flames paw at the thick pile of logs.

It was highly improper what they were doing. And both knew it. The emptiness of the house and room only added to the feeling of isolation and seclusion. A room even as bare as the cottage at least had a bed, a board, benches, and chests. This room had absolutely nothing except two ticks, a man, a woman, and a very large wooden floor. To pretend the atmosphere wasn't wrought with tension was ludicrous.

He glanced at her, feeling sure she was cognizant of

it. She still held herself perfectly erect in the midst of her tick, arms wrapped around knees that hugged her chest beneath her skirt. He rolled the toothpick to the other side of his mouth.

Adding to the impropriety of it all was the risk of being caught by one of the eight men only two stories below them. If they were to be discovered, the men might think Mary was free game from then on. He sighed. He should have left her at the cottage and come here alone. "Do you wish to go back?"

If possible, her body stiffened even more. "Needs I?"

He slowly removed the toothpick from his mouth. "I'll not be making any advances on you, if that's what you mean."

The grip she had on her hands relaxed some. "I see no need to return until morning, I don't. Not unless *you* wish it."

"No. No, I don't."

She looked at him then, but didn't ask. Didn't ask why he'd baited Drew. Didn't ask why he'd whispered inappropriate words through the courting stick. Didn't ask why he'd been making such an idiot of himself. But she didn't need to. Those huge eyes of hers said it all.

He clamped down on the toothpick. "I found your husband."

She pulled her attention away from him.

"He was already six feet under, though, so I couldn't tear him apart for you. Seems somebody else beat me to it."

Laying her forehead against her updrawn knees, she made no comment.

"Wish you to hear the details?"

"You are sure it was Obadiah?" Her voice was muffled but very distinguishable in the vacant room.

"I'm sure."

She shook her head. "I care not for the details, I don't."

Look up, Mary. Are you crying? Or are you simply relieved? Look up and let me see. She remained as she was, hiding within the folds of her skirt.

"I saw where you lived. Where you worked. Met your neighbors."

The burning logs shifted, spitting out tiny flickers of fire before settling into a new position. His gaze moved over the nape of her neck, exposed by her position and tickled by a few fine dark hairs slipping from beneath her cap. "Ruth Parker sends her greetings."

She turned her face toward him while keeping her head against her knees.

"She's expecting her eighth. Might well have had it by now."

He watched in fascination as she slowly blinked her eyes, a leisurely down sweep of lashes, tarrying for a moment before swinging open again. She asked nothing and, indeed, he had nothing more to tell. Her neighbors had been very reluctant to talk to him at all. If it had not been for this Ruth woman, he might never have found Obadiah—or his remains, as the case may be.

"Why didn't you marry her?"

So jolting was her question that it took him a moment to realize she wasn't talking of Ruth but of Hannah. He took a deep breath. He hadn't spoken about it to anyone. Not in England, not here, not anywhere. He'd simply posted the announcement and left.

Yet with Mary, he didn't have to be the successful tobacco factor from the colonies. He didn't have to be the
I'm-okay-even-though-I've-been-jilted younger brother.
He didn't even have to be the *master,* as Drew implied.
With Mary, he need only be Josh. He snapped his toothpick in two. "I found her between the sheets with my
best friend."

He heard her quick intake of breath and chuckled
humorlessly. "Know you what the saddest part is? I regret
the loss of my friend more than I do the loss of Hannah."

"I'm so sorry, Josh, but it's glad I am that you found
out before the wedding day."

"I'm still incensed about it, Mary. The humiliation
was beyond words."

He tightened his lips. "I had intended to remain in
England once I married and simply receive Drew's ship-
ments and fill his orders from there. I'm the only factor I
know of who travels back and forth and have only done
so to help Drew with the harvest. But he has men to help
him with that now. So even though the marriage is off,
I'm leaving when the next ship comes through."

She slowly lifted her head up off her knees. "He'll be
heartbroken, he will. He cares for you very much and
speaks of you often."

"He has a new wife, a new home, and a new life. He'll
get over it."

She said nothing for a long, long time. "Know you
how to read your Bible, Josh?"

He humphed. "Between my mother, my father, and
my grandmother, they made sure I read the thing front-
ward, backward, and upside-down. Alas, I've memorized
half of it, I think."

"Lucky, you are. I know not how to read and have only heard what the Father offered on an occasional Sunday morn."

"I would be happy to read to you, Mary. Any time you'd like."

She offered a hint of a smile. "Do you believe what it says?"

He squinted into the fire. "Yes, I suppose I do."

"Hmm."

He slanted her a glance. "What does that mean?"

"Oh, I know not," she said, lifting her shoulders. "Just thinking of how I believed as you did, yet still Obadiah robbed my happiness."

Frowning, he shook his head. "What are you talking about? One has nothing to do with the other."

Unraveling her hands, she turned her face toward him. "That's what I thought. I thought if I was clever or careful I could save my babies. But in the end, I couldn't. I realized I had no power at all. So I gave God complete control over my life, I did."

"When was that?"

"When Obadiah killed the babies."

He was silent a moment. "I mean no disrespect, Mary, but since that time your husband was press-ganged and murdered and you have been tried for perjury, deported, indentured, and sold. If that's what you can expect by giving God 'control,' then I think you'd be better off handling things on your own."

She turned back to the fire. "Just be careful that you don't let Lady Hannah rob you of your home, your family, or your very soul."

He shifted, seeking a more comfortable position. "I

had decided to leave Virginia long before I discovered Hannah was a bedswerver."

"I speak not of your leaving, I don't. I speak of your easy and caring nature."

"You refer to a glass-gazing, knotty-pated, naïve Josh. He exists no more."

Silence. "Then I will mourn the loss of him."

She stretched out on her tick, and after a moment's pause, he followed suit. They now lay feet-to-feet along the front of the fireplace. After a long while, her deep, even breathing reached his ears.

He, however, didn't sleep but for snatches at a time, finally rising in the predawn hours to stoke the fire.

He had wanted Drew to have the pleasure of waking with his bride in total privacy. With that in mind, he'd brought corn pone over yesterday and left it in the storage room belowstairs, and he intended to have the men fed and packing hogsheads by the time the sun touched the horizon.

For Mary, it would mean a morning off from her ever-present task of feeding the multitudes. Opening the cloth pouch on his belt, he removed a battered chicken feather and ran his fingers along it for quite some time before brushing it across his lips, laying it beside her, then moving downstairs to wake the men.

Christmas Day dawned bright and sunny. Constance smoothed her hand down the waist of her new dress, anxious for Drew's reaction. He'd been quite busy the past week, and she'd not seen much of him after that first day.

She hadn't seen much of Josh either, for that matter. He'd continued to sleep in the big house, though Mary returned to the loft, and he only took the evening meals with them, opting to stay in the fields the rest of the time.

She wondered how Sally and Grandma were. They would see them at the service today. Grandma planned to stay on with Nellie, but Sally was to come home with them afterward. Constance couldn't wait. She'd missed the little moppet terribly. Her only regret was she hadn't been able to personally give her the green dress she'd made from her leftover fabric.

But Josh had insisted on taking it to her yesterday. He'd wanted to see Grandma and Nellie and then stay the night with them, meeting Drew and Constance at church on the morrow.

Well, the morrow was here, and she couldn't wait to embark on her first outing as Mistress O'Connor. The walk to church would totally wet the bottom of her skirt and soil her shoes, but it mattered not. It was Christmas Day, she'd meet new friends and Drew would be at her side the whole day through.

A great deal of noisy crunching heralded the approach of Drew and his men on the icy ground outside the cottage. She tightened the bow at her chin, ran a hand down her stomach, then glanced at Mary. "Are you ready?"

Mary nodded, her only concession to Christmas being a beautiful lavender ribbon tied about her waist. Constance had oohed and aahed over it before Mary finally confessed that Josh had given it to her.

The door opened, and Constance's heart stopped beating. Drew had dressed for the occasion as well. She'd grown so used to seeing him in the same type of garments day in and day out she'd never imagined him wearing anything else. But, oh, what a sight he was in his burgundy doublet slashed along the sleeves to accommodate the full white shirt bulging from its slits. Fine linen had been sewn to the cuffs and front opening, shown to fine effect against his camel-colored jerkin. His loose maroon breeches matched his doublet and were fastened below his knees. He reached up and removed a stiff beaver hat. He looked from Constance to Mary, then indicated with a nod of his head for Mary to leave. Mary scurried out of the cottage, grabbing her shawl before closing the door behind her.

"You said you had enough material for your gown."

Constance blinked, glancing down at her dress. "I did."

"Then what happened to the bodice?"

"Nothing happened to it. Why? What's wrong?"

His face filled with color. "What's wrong? What's *wrong*? The upper swell of your breasts are exposed!"

She laid a hand across her chest. "Is it lower than what the women here wear?"

"By trow, Connie, look at it!"

She jerked her hand down to her side. "I *asked* you what the fashions here were, and you said anything I made would be fine! Scooped bodices are all the rage in London and usually cut much, much deeper. But this one is perfectly decent. Am I to believe *no one* here wears scooped bodices?"

"Of course not!"

She swallowed hard, holding her tears in check. "I see. Well, I'll just wear one of my everydays, then." She turned her back, moving to retrieve one from a peg.

Softening his voice, he took a couple of steps forward. "Haven't you a neckpiece or something?"

She shook her head, silent tears now pouring down her face.

"Are you crying?"

She shook her head again, but he'd moved behind her, turning her to face him.

"Oh, Connie. Maybe the other women do wear scooped bodices. I honestly know not. All I know is, when you try and pack yourself into a bodice of that sort, well, it worries me. What if you had to sneeze or something? You'd be in jeopardy of . . ."

Her shoulders wilted. "That is the most addlepated thing I've ever heard. This neckline barely dips below my throat. I'm not in jeopardy of anything."

He looked unconvinced. "I suppose you could leave it on. The meetinghouse doesn't have a fireplace, so we'll all be in overcoats. No one will ever know."

"What about afterward?"

He rubbed his palms up and down her arms. "The men's military exercises are all out-of-doors, and any indoor activities will be in the frigid meetinghouse. You can simply claim you're not used to these Virginia winters and wish to keep your overcoat on. The bottom of your skirt will still be visible."

Bitter disappointment pushed more tears from her eyes.

"Now what's wrong? I said you could wear it."

She drew in a shaky breath. "I w-wanted you to l-like my dreeessssss."

He moved his gaze over her. "The gown makes my mouth water, love."

She swiped at her tears. "Drew, will the other women take off their overcoats?"

He nodded. "Yes."

"Then I want to take mine off. I can't possibly keep it on all the day long."

He glanced at her neckline. "Oh yes you can. Now wait here and I'll be right back."

Moments later, he returned with a beautiful fur draped across his arm. Constance stroked the soft orangish-red fur, cool to the touch from being outside. "Fox?"

"Yes."

"When did we eat fox?"

"We didn't. I made the Indian boy who chopped off your braid give me something in return. He decided fur the color of your hair would be a fair exchange."

She buried her fingers in it, running them against the grain. "It's stunning."

"So is your hair."

Looking up at him, she smiled. "Oh, Drew, you're such a peagoose."

He opened up the fur, placing it across her shoulders.

"It's a cape! And calf length! I thought it was a lap robe."

He smiled, pulling the hood up over her head and tying the front closed.

She preened, looking down at the lovely contrast it made against the green of her skirt. "Perhaps I won't need to take it off after all."

He pulled her against him and gave her a swift, hard kiss. "Merry Christmas, love. Now, we needs must go. The others wait upon us."

Outside, the eastern sun delved through the barren

forest, scattering a profusion of tiny rainbows from the ice-covered branches to the earth's crystal floor. A handsome young bird wearing a leaf-brown jacket and a white bib at the throat fluttered to a branch, emitting a lovely series of descending halftones in a clear, loud voice.

Cool air bathed Constance's face, bringing the crisp, clean scent of winter with it. None of it, however, had the effect on her that the chair sled did.

Constructed of wide oak boards, the sled itself was nothing more than a chair on runners with a handle attached to the back for someone to push. But strewn across its sides and back were a series of yellow wild flowers woven together to form a garland of sorts. The daisylike flowers were no more than an inch in diameter but grew in clusters and were very numerous.

She fingered one, a delicate petal breaking off into her hand. "They're beautiful. Wherever did you find them?"

"Josh spotted them on his walk home from the wharf. He only mentioned them because they don't usually bloom this late in the season."

She brought the petal to her nose. "What are they called?"

When he failed to reply, she looked up at him, noting the mixture of humor and consternation in his expression.

"What?" she asked.

"They're called *sneezeweed*."

A smile tugged at her lips. "You're jesting."

"I wish I were."

She bit the insides of her cheeks. "Do they make people sneeze?"

He hung his head, but suppressed laughter caused his shoulders to bounce. "For some."

Laughter rippled from her lips, his low and throaty chuckle harmonizing with hers.

In that moment, when his crystal blue eyes held hers, when his straight white teeth contrasted pleasingly with his tanned face, when those deep dimples framed his smile, she knew once again. Knew there was no other place she'd rather be on Christmas Day or any other day than right here with Andrew Joseph O'Connor.

He extended a hand to her.

"I would have been happy to walk."

"I don't want you to take ill again."

"Where did you get the sled?"

"I made it."

"For me?" she asked, running her hands along its smooth surface.

He nodded.

"When?"

"Over the last month or so. Come. We needs must go."

She put her hand in his and allowed him to settle her into the seat. He handed her a small pile of blankets, which she secured on her lap, then he placed a tin foot stove with fired charcoal at her feet. Removing one of the blankets from her lap, he draped it over her and the stove, effectively creating a cocoon of warmth.

Had she been in London, it would have been less than what she was accustomed to. But here, in this wilderness, with Drew the one attending to her, she felt much like the queen herself.

"Warm enough?" he asked.

"It's wonderful, Drew. Thank you."

He seemed to remember their audience then, and handing a musket to Thomas, positioned himself behind the sled. With him pushing, they, as well as Mary and the men, began their six-mile trek to church.

TWENTY-THREE

So much had changed since she took ill six weeks ago. Winter had well and truly set in with remnants of snow here and there, icicles dangling overhead, and a frigid temperature numbing her cheeks. She saw no wildlife other than a few birds, but was once again humbled by the profusion of trees this land offered. Around every bend, there were more, reaching for the heavens with bare, knobby, ice-covered limbs.

And the sky. Lord have mercy, she'd never seen such a bright, rich blue stretching for miles with nary a cloud in sight. The absence of leaves on the trees stripped away all obstruction, allowing the blue wash overhead to envelop her within its magnificence.

The men all offered to help push her sled, but Drew wouldn't hear of it, so they instead centered their attention on Mary, an air of festivity injected into their tones.

Constance smiled. So effectively had the men encircled her friend, each trying to outdo the other with clever remarks, that she was completely hidden from Constance's view. At one point, Isaac walked backward in order to better catch her attention, only to stumble on a root and fall down with a resounding splat.

The other men made much of this display until Mary rushed forward to assist and ask after him. Through that one stunt alone, he had out-maneuvered every man there, and Constance delighted in watching their exasperated expressions, obviously wondering if Isaac had done it a'purpose.

They'd covered much ground now, and she expected to come upon the meetinghouse and perhaps other church-goers at any time. She was laying her head back to question Drew when she realized he had slowed their progress to not much more than a crawl, falling well behind Mary and the others.

"What?" she asked.

He looked down, wiping the unease from his expression. "What?"

She twisted around in her seat. "What worries you?"

"Nothing!"

She smiled. "Do not pretend with me, Drew. Something is amiss. What is it?"

He allowed what little momentum they had to fizzle out.

She waited, but he shrugged and then set to the path again. "It was nothing. Really."

Placing a hand on his, she gave it a gentle squeeze, and he stopped.

"Of what were you thinking?"

He swallowed, avoiding her gaze. "Everyone will be there."

"And . . . ?"

"And, everyone will see the chair sled."

"And . . . ?"

He looked down at her. "And I can't ever in all my days remember anyone arriving at church in a chair sled covered with sneezeweed."

She bit her lip. "Would you like to take it off? I mind not." She hesitated, then furrowed her brow. "I was, however, looking forward to Sally's expression when she saw the flowers. Perhaps if we leave the garland here, we could retrieve it on our way back? She could see them then. What think you of that?"

It was clear he was still vacillating.

"I truly do not mind, Drew."

He lifted his hat up, then resettled it upon his head. "Well, actually, I've . . . uh . . . never seen anyone under the age of eighty arrive in a chair sled."

She widened her eyes. "Oh, my. Perhaps I'd best walk the rest of the way."

He scowled and began pushing the sled again. "No. It matters not."

She heard the others backtracking, most likely to see what was keeping them. "Drew, this is my first time to meet the community. I really have no desire to arrive in the same fashion as a grandmother. Pray, let us leave the sled here and I'll walk."

"Ho, there!" Thomas called. "All is well?"

Drew paused and Constance threw off her covers, scrambling out of the sled. "Actually, Thomas, I'd very much like to walk the rest of the way. Would you be so kind as to carry the foot stove? And perhaps some of you others could assist with these blankets?"

She had the blankets dispersed and all in readiness before Drew had a chance to object, then watched him glance at the abandoned chair sled and Thomas. "Perhaps we should push this up behind the brush here so it won't be in anyone else's way if they happen along."

Thomas lifted his brows but said not a word as he helped Drew hide the chair sled. Constance made sure she not so much as batted an eye. When they were on their way again, Drew slipped his hand into hers.

She looked up at him. "Thank you. I would have been most disconcerted to arrive in such a manner if it was inappropriate. I very much want to make a good impression."

He pulled her against his side. "You could have arrived atop a wildcat and no one would have said a word. They will adore you."

That was a gross untruth, but it mattered not. Only a man in love would say such a thing, and it warmed her through and through. She leaned against him, and he gently squeezed her waist.

The steady beating of a drum reached Constance's ears well before her first sight of the meetinghouse. About six times the size of their cottage, the long wooden structure commanded attention, mighty oaks and locust trees flanking its sides. From its yard came the mingled sounds of children shouting, loved ones greeting, the church drummer summoning, and that hum of life that denotes civilization.

Constance took stock of the assembly of people, immediately noting the scarcity of women. Two she recognized from the boat, while a smattering of children ran betwixt and between those gathered. Her gaze ground to a halt on one particular man, the likes of which she'd never seen before.

He stood within a group, laughing and conversing together with them, dressed much in the same fashion as Drew, with doublet, jerkin, and matching breeches. What held her attention, though, was not his attire but the beautiful deep ebony color of his skin.

Having been cursed with freckles, she remained ever fascinated with people whose skin was smooth and flawless. This man's was not only smooth and flawless but rich and glowing.

"Who's that?" she whispered to Drew.

"Where?"

"The man with the black skin."

"'Tis Adam Lucas. He came to Virginia as an indentured servant some years ago. He has since completed his service and owns a good piece of property north of here." He glanced at her. "I suppose you've never seen a person with black skin. Most of the blacks haven't been here as long as Lucas. In fact, he's waiting for one particular woman to finish her indenture so he can marry her. He offered to buy out her contract, but her master wouldn't sell it to him, much like I wouldn't sell Mary's if someone were to ask."

"But he's the only black-skinned person I see. Where are the others?"

"There aren't that many, actually. The Royal African Company usually takes them to the West Indies or Brazil, where they bring in more money as slaves. We've not much use for slaves here. It's less risky to buy an indentured servant's labor for a few years than to gamble a lifetime investment in a slave who might die a few months after purchase."

"Oh, Drew. I like not the idea of anyone being purchased, whether it's cost effective or not."

"Well, with indentured servants, we're not really purchasing the person but their labor. Though, probably, you're right about the other." He moved her hand to the crook of his arm. "Lucas is a good man, a good farmer. Honest and well respected amongst us. It would have been terrible for him had he been sold into slavery."

"Drew!" Sally suddenly burst from the crowd, projecting herself straight toward them. Constance could see the green of her new outfit, soiled and wet beneath her overcoat.

Drew caught her up into his arms and swung her about. "Ah, pumpkin! How I've missed you."

She locked her arms and legs about him, and the two remained tight within their embrace while a young woman approached, a babe nestled in her arms. "Happy Christmas."

"Happy Christmas, Nellie. How do you fare?"

Constance watched Drew bend to plant a kiss upon her cheek. Her eyes were the same clear blue as Drew's but framed with light brown eyebrows and lashes. Her hair lay neatly tucked up inside her cap. Nellie immediately made an opening in her bundle, exposing the babe's face, which scrunched up the moment the crisp air struck it. "Look. Isn't he beautiful?"

Drew's expression softened. "Ah, Nellie. He's bald, pink, and has no teeth. What's so beautiful about that?"

Nellie's laugh tinkled out like musical chimes while she covered the babe back up and turned to face Constance. "Hello. I've heard much about you. Your cape is exquisite."

"Thank you. Drew surprised me with it this morn." She clasped her hands together. "Your son is, indeed, quite handsome."

Sally lifted her head from Drew's shoulder. "You woke up. I thought you go to heaven, but Gramma said no."

Constance touched Sally's leg. "And Grandma was right. I'm planning to stay here for a very long time. And look at you! I think you've grown a whole inch, and I see you're wearing your new dress."

"Can I pet your coat?"

Constance reached out, and Sally went straight into her arms, rubbing her face and hands against the fur. The child's weight felt so good, so right. Constance hugged her a little more tightly, then smiled to see Grandma emerge from the peripherals.

"Well, it looks as if this will, indeed, be a very happy Christmas," the old woman greeted. "How do you fare, Constance?"

She answered positively while Grandma linked her arm around Drew's waist. "Thought you didn't like red hair."

One of Drew's dimples kicked in as he draped an arm about Grandma's shoulder. "Must have me confused with someone else, but I'm not surprised. Seems to happen to most of the older set at some point or other."

That was the last exchange made before they were sucked into the crowd. Drew took Sally from her arms, all the while introducing her to farmer, after farmer, after farmer. Nellie eventually commandeered her away from Drew's side and introduced her to some of the women.

All nodded politely and allowed her to stand in their circle, but she found she had not much to say as they discussed cooking and babies and the tobacco seedlings they evidently nursed within their cottages. She wondered where Drew's were and if she was supposed to be nurturing them.

She scanned the crowd for him and found him staring at her. My, oh my, but he was easy on the eyes. She gave him an intimate smile. With Sally no longer in his arms, he excused himself and headed her way.

He'd made it almost halfway when behind her the word *sneezeweed* caught her attention. She turned an ear to the group of men.

"You jest! Why would Apperson put sneezeweed on their chair sled?"

"Perhaps it doesn't affect Apperson's granny and she wished to have her chair bedecked."

"But Apperson hates the stuff. Can't get near it without sneezing his head off," a new voice interjected.

"No, it wasn't Apperson's sled. It looked brand new."

"Who else would need one?"

"What about you, Josh? You've got a granny."

"Wasn't us," she heard Josh reply. "You know how Grandma loves to hike through these woods. Besides, she'd never do such a fool thing. Sneezeweed on a chair sled. What rubbish."

"Then who else would need one?"

"Maybe it wasn't for a granny," someone suggested. Silence fell amongst them. "What mean you?"

"Well, it was hidden, I tell you. Would've missed the thing if it hadn't been for little Henry stumbling upon it by accident."

"But why?"

"I'm thinkin' one of the men with a new tobacco bride sought to impress his maid and wanted not to be discovered."

Murmurs rippled. "Impress his maid? With sneeze-weed?!"

Many guffaws. "Who do you suppose it was?"

Constance stiffened, recognizing that Josh had voiced the question.

"Perhaps it was your brother, O'Connor. He has a new bride."

"Sensible Drew? Unflappable Drew?" Josh responded. "I hardly think so."

Constance threw a look at Drew, words of warning on her lips. But it was too late. The men had waylaid him, greeting him and pulling him into their midst.

"You'll never guess what we discovered, O'Connor. A chair sled."

"My, what an exciting morning you've had, Caskie."

A few chuckles reverberated before the Caskie fellow continued. "No, no. Not just *any* chair sled. But a newly constructed one . . . covered with *sneezeweed*. Now, you wouldn't be knowing anything about that, would you?"

"Caskie, it's addled you are. Why would anyone put a garland of sneezeweed on a chair sled?"

"A garland?" piped in another voice. "Who said anything about a garland?"

Constance slid her eyes shut, mortified as the men closed in on their prey, all speaking at once. "Was it a garland, Caskie?" "Look, O'Connor's turning red, he is." "By Pharoah, Drew, did *you* do that?" "What's amiss, O'Connor? Yer lady love need a'sweetening?" "She must, for 'tis a new fur cape she's a'wearing today as well."

"Fur and sneezeweed. You sure know the way to a lady's heart, O'Connor."

And on it went, the laughter and jesting growing louder by the moment. Constance shifted her feet. The women within her circle, she noticed, had at some point begun to listen as well and now all looked at her, their expressions fraught with curiosity.

Nellie cocked her head. "Well, Constance. It's pleased I am. Grandma told me he fancied you, but I believed her not. I've been feeling quite guilty, for it was because of me that Grandma left, forcing him to purchase a bride. I see all those hours of worry were for naught. Did he push you in that chair sled all the way here?"

Constance nodded, noting some of the women's expressions softened, while others were tinged with a bit of good-natured humor. The men behind them teased Drew mercilessly, all of which he seemed to take in good sport, turning their jests about until he'd managed to move the focus to someone else.

In the next moment, he stood by her side, placing his hand against her waist. His face was still rather flushed, and Nellie didn't let it go by. "Sneezeweed, Drew?"

He grinned. "Jealous?"

"Surprised."

"Remind me, and I'll have a talk with Gerald. Give him a few tips."

"Promise?"

"Absolutely."

"Then tell him I want a real crane in my fireplace instead of just a lug pole, I'd like a pudding pan and . . . a fur cape."

He chuckled. "Done. And what of you Goody Trible? Need I speak with Seward?"

And so the conversation went, each woman telling Drew what she wished her husband would provide for her—all of whom included within their list a desire for a fur cape—and Constance realized he was not merely being polite, but very cleverly arming himself with ammunition for the time when those gentlemen teased him about the sneezeweed. After a moment he turned to the woman next to Constance. "Now, who might this be?"

Nellie introduced the woman, Kendra Woodrum, explaining some Francis Woodrum had purchased her as a bride at the same time Drew had purchased Constance.

"I see. You know my wife, then?"

"I remember her very well. She came to the ship not with the rest of us, but just before we sailed wearing a green gown the likes of which took my breath away."

Surprised, Constance looked at the girl more closely, for she had no recollection of her. Thick brown brows stretched above her doelike eyes, while a mouthful of teeth dominated her kind face.

Then she remembered. This girl had been ill the entire voyage, miserably seasick. At the time, Constance had thought only of herself, of rebuking the captain, and of returning home. She'd not concerned herself with the other women in that hold nor with what had become of them—other than Mary, of course. Now she wished she'd not been so apathetic.

Kendra offered up no complaints concerning her husband.

"Come now, Mistress Woodrum," Drew implored.

"I've known Francis my entire life. Am I to believe he's a model husband?"

"'Course I am, O'Connor. Wouldn't catch me giving my wife sneezeweed." A young round-bellied man with a full black mustache and beard slipped his hand beneath Kendra's elbow. It was the same man who'd kept Emmett from pawing Constance during the auction.

"I see you've not given her a fur either," Drew said.

"So I haven't. Where the devil did you get it?"

Drew straightened his spine. "Why, I caught the first fox with my bare hands. Wrestled him to the ground, only to have more pounce on me. But when the dust settled, it was only I who remained standing."

The other women tittered, Nellie rolled her eyes, Francis hollered. "Ho! Wise men say, 'He who hath not a good and ready memory should never meddle with telling lies.'"

Drew smiled. "I have a good and ready memory."

The steady drumbeat changed in tempo to a *rat-a-tat-tat*. The crowd silenced and turned to the door of the church, where the preacher, Morden, who'd performed their wedding ceremony, stood. "Come, my children. Receive God's Word and blessing."

TWENTY-FOUR

She hadn't brought any food. As soon as the service was over, every other woman had hurried to retrieve their precooked contributions while some of the men laid boards on the backless benches and others built a huge bonfire outside. Drew had left almost immediately to help, the others of the family doing the same.

She stood alone and unmoving in the sea of activity as it took on an almost abstract quality. People swarming in different directions, but each with a sense of purpose in their steps. The room transformed from a church with its uniform rows of benches into a social whirl complete with food, ale, and suppressed excitement.

She jumped to the side to avoid being rammed with a bench, moved back a step or two to make room for three women carrying earthen pots, and circled around a tub of ale, until finally she had been driven into a corner, an island of self doubt.

Why hadn't Drew told her she was to bring something? She'd had no idea. Christmas was so different at home.

Of course, with the war and all they wouldn't have observed the full rites of Christmas with mummings and dancing about Maypoles and processions. Still, a Yule log would have been lit, carols sung, a service attended, and Christmas boxes exchanged, culminating with a feast of Christmas pies, plum pottage, oranges, spices, figs, wine, and more, all displayed around a mighty boar's head sporting a lemon within its ferocious mouth.

Why, just last Christmas she'd organized the celebration for her father. Yet she'd never prepared the actual food, brought in the Yule log, nor hunted down the boar. She'd simply orchestrated the events.

The torrent of movement had ebbed somewhat, now replaced with a hum of conversation, the women and girls around the table, the men and boys outside. Constance glanced out the arched doorway, trying to catch sight of Drew but without success.

She watched the hub of women chattering and communing amongst themselves. She hadn't realized how artificial and coy the ladies in London were, herself included, until she watched these colonials. They were sincere, unaffected, and freely touched one another—something unheard of at home.

Two women shared a hug. Another squeezed the arm of a friend with affection. A couple of younger women pressed shoulder-to-shoulder, heads together, whispering animatedly before breaking apart in laughter.

No guile. No wielding of fans. No subtle insults. Just open, honest expressions of friendship. Her heart filled with longing. Her stomach twisted into knots. How was she ever going to fit in? For she was only now beginning to realize much more than an expanse of dirt flooring separated her from these women.

The longer she cowered in this corner, though, the harder it would be. She tried to summon up the confidence that allowed her to move with poise and certainty in elite ballrooms throughout London. Yet poise and certainty were not what she needed here.

Here, she was expected to drop all pretenses and expose herself as she was. She'd never done such a thing in her life, at least not with anyone other than her immediate family and Drew, of course.

As it ended up, Sally took the matter into her own little hands, breaking away from Nellie and running to Constance, commanding everyone's attention at the same time. "Sissy!" she hollered. "Come see what I bring!"

She allowed Sally to pull her to the table, the other women opening their ranks to make room for her. Sally pointed to a basket of shelled pecans. "Look! I made myself!"

Constance oohed and ahhed, praising the child for her efforts.

"What did you make, Sissy?"

She surveyed the oysters, fish, wild fowl, corn puddings, pumpkin fritters, dried apricots, and spoon bread displayed around several dressed turkeys. Heat rushed up her neck and face. "I . . . I didn't realize." She looked at the others. "Drew didn't tell me. That is, I—"

An older woman tsked and shook her head. "Now, isn't that just like a man? Doesn't tell his new wife Christmas dinner was to be eaten here. Why, you've probably a whole spread waiting to be put on the coals at home."

The other women mumbled in understanding. Constance didn't correct their misconception and glanced at Mary. Obviously Drew hadn't told her either.

"Worry not about the food, Mistress O'Connor," one of the women offered.

"It's Constance."

The older woman nodded. "Yes, we know. Not a female over the age of twelve that wasn't wishing she could have Drew O'Connor to spouse."

Good heavens. Her cheeks blazed with embarrassment.

The old woman moved forward, grabbing Constance's hand within her shaky grasp. "I'm Granny Apperson. You go on and take that fancy cape off and sit with us a while."

The men had started filing in, complaining for food. The women ignored them.

Nellie transferred her babe into another woman's arms. "Oh, yes, Constance. I've been wanting to try your cape on all morning. May I?"

Constance paled. The day had warmed up considerably and most had discarded their overcoats. All were attired in simple homespun dresses. They weren't faded or well worn, but freshly dyed and very carefully ironed. Obviously their best.

They weren't anywhere near as fine as the wool Drew had given her, and their styles were homogeneous. Not a scooped neck in sight.

The room had quickly filled, the men looking over the food, but now in a rather subdued manner, as if curious to what the women were puttering about. Constance scanned the faces for Drew. No luck.

She bit her lip. There was nothing for it. No matter what she did, disaster would be the result. If she didn't remove her cape, she'd appear selfish and self-centered. If she did remove her cape, she'd not only upset Drew but alienate every woman there. Her gown was one of nobility, and these women would know it the moment they saw it.

Still, if she was going to offend the women, it would probably be best to do so with her apparel rather than with a condescending attitude. Besides, she wouldn't dream of disappointing Nellie by refusing her request. She slowly released the loops on her cape and slipped it from her shoulders.

An overwhelming silence descended. All movement suspended and every eye—male, female, and child alike—was fixed on her.

After a lifetime of agony, it was Nellie who responded with a near swoon. "Oh, Constance! Is this what they're wearing in London now?"

Bless her sweet soul, Nellie had, in her unaffected way, shown awe and genuine feminine appreciation for a lovely piece of frippery, totally disregarding the out-of-place design and neckline. Constance would not dare to explain that she'd have been laughed right out of church had she worn something so simple and unadorned back home. "Yes, but I'd much rather have a gown like yours."

Nellie's gaze, marked with amusement, flew to hers. "If I thought I had a prayer of filling yours out, I'd trade with you right here and now."

Constance felt color rush to her cheeks again. Honestly, these colonists said anything, anywhere, anytime.

She barely suppressed her urge to jump back when

Granny Apperson stuck her hand into the side of her neckline, fingering its border. "Did you make this, girl?"

She nodded.

"Look here at this fancy needlework, Nellie. She's embroidered green tobaccy leaves all the way around. Would have missed it if I hadn't been standin' so close."

Nellie, as well as a good dozen others, leaned forward to examine her work.

Releasing her hold on the gown, Granny clucked. "I sure would be likin' a dress like this 'un." She again eyed the dress up and down. "Think you could show me how to make one?"

"Me too!" Nellie exclaimed, echoed by several of the others.

Overwhelmed, Constance could only nod. That they showed no censor nor ridicule for the gown, but instead embraced it, humbled her. How different they were from those she associated with at home. Never would they have allowed an opportunity like this to pass without using it to make themselves seem superior. Even she had caught herself doing so to others. She didn't deserve such consideration—was unworthy of it, in fact. She didn't belong.

"It's done, then," Granny announced. "Before we leave today, we'll decide on a time to gather at the O'Connor's for sewing lessons. It'll have to be after we've all had time to order some fabric, though."

"Best we not act too hastily." All eyes shifted to Jonathon Emmett. "Never would *my* wife garb herself in such a manner."

Constance stiffened.

Granny narrowed her eyes. "Well, Goodman Emmett,

no need to get your breeches in a twist. I'd be worryin' about gettin' a wife before I worried about what she would or wouldn't wear." She clapped her hands together. "Say grace, Morden, and be quick about it so we can eat!"

Morden gave a brief blessing, and then pandemonium broke out. There were no plates. People just picked up what they wanted and ate it. Communal spoons were left in the puddings and other foodstuffs that required utensils. The turkeys, torn apart piece by piece, were eaten with fingers. The oysters dropped down people's throats.

Constance stood in mute fascination.

"Ale, Connie?"

She turned to find Drew at her elbow, a noggin of ale in his hand.

She shook her head. "Your thanks, but I drink not spirits. I'll just have what the children are having."

"They're having ale."

"You jest."

He nodded his head toward the cask where a young boy of no more than five stuck his face underneath the spigot to catch a mouthful of the brewed liquid.

She took the noggin from Drew, sipped from its contents, then shuddered, pressing it back into his hands. "I'm really not thirsty." Their fingers brushed and she glanced up. "I'm sorry about the gown, Drew. I wanted to leave the cape on, but—"

"We'll discuss it another time." His eyes flashed, and then he turned. A heaviness centered in her chest as she watched him stride from the meetinghouse.

Moments later, Josh touched her sleeve. "Worry not,

sister. He's fighting his own demons right now, and there's naught you can do. Meanwhile, partake of some supper, else your actions might be misconstrued into something they are not."

She quickly blinked back her threatening tears, giving Josh a hesitant smile.

He gently squeezed her elbow. "Easy, now."

"I didn't know," she whispered, frantically searching his eyes for understanding.

"About the demons?"

"About the gown. When he gave me the fabric, I asked him what the women here wore, but he said naught. I didn't even make an evening gown, but a very average day gown, thinking that would be most appropriate. You know the fashions in London. Can you see I wasn't trying to—"

He increased the pressure on her elbow. "Hush. You look exquisite."

"I look like a freak."

He bussed the top of her head, turned her toward the table, and nudged her forward. "Go fetch something to eat. I'll be right back."

"What's the matter with you? Can you not see she's scared to death?"

Drew thought this would be a remote enough spot for some privacy. Evidently not. "What do you want, Josh?"

"I want you to go to your wife. Can you not see she's entirely out of her league?"

"Oh, I can see that, all right. I was a fool to think otherwise. She's not only out of our league, she's from a different world altogether." He threw a pebble into the surrounding forest. "She's no colonist, and I've known it all along. I simply chose to ignore it." He rubbed the back of his neck. "No, she belongs in a blasted palace made of gold and platinum with jewels around her neck and servants at her beck and call."

"What a great bunch of tripe. She's not the queen. She's your wife and she needs you."

"It's of no use, Josh. These women have essentially asked her to be a seamstress. Can you imagine? An earl's daughter as a seamstress. And did you see her face when everyone started eating? Did you see how shocked she was? She's used to eating at tables with cloths and porcelain and silver candelabras. Not some pine board with a bunch of dirty farmers shoving food into their mouths. She doesn't belong here any more than Her Royal Majesty would."

"Is that what she told you?"

"She didn't have to. I have eyes."

"You have a pickled brain is what you have. I'll allow she might have been taken aback for a moment, but she's not so shallow that she would judge people simply because of their eating habits."

"You've blinders on where she's concerned, Josh. But, pray, step back for a moment and reflect. Her father has some wealthy young aristocrat waiting at this very moment to give her everything she wants and deserves. And she does want those things, whether she realizes it or not. Take her gown, for instance. You saw it. She couldn't have better illustrated to others she was a member of the privileged class had she screamed it from the rooftops."

Josh lifted his shoulders in a gesture of confusion.

"So, her attire's a bit fancy. What has that to do with anything when it's so obvious it's you she adores?"

"For how long? How long will that last, do you suppose? I might be amusing now, but am I worth giving up the entertainments of London, the sprawling manor she's used to living in, the family she'll never see again? For what? For some paltry house with a parlor and a great room? For a life where she socializes with others on Christmas, Whitsunweek, and court days, isolated on a farm the other forty-eight weeks of the year? I hardly think so."

"She told me, rather emphatically as I recall, the first night I returned, that she wanted to stay."

"That was before."

"Before what?"

Drew pulled his hat from his head, spinning it to the ground with a flick of his wrist. "She was lonely, Josh. I had just helped her recover from a life-threatening illness. She probably imagined me as some romantic knight of old that saved fair damsels." He blew out a puff a breath. "And I took shameless advantage of it."

"And now it's too late."

Drew peered into the thicket. "I know not. What think you would happen if she went back? I could secure a divorce for her here, and she could tell those in England that I'd died. God knows, it happens all the time out here. No one would doubt her." Drew turned to Josh when he did not respond, surprised to see his brother's face red with anger.

"You worthless piece of horse dung. Does she mean so little to you that you would discard her like some worn out boot?"

Drew took no offense, but instead slumped his shoulders in defeat. "Nay, Josh. God help me, I love her. I love her enough to see I've no right to ask her to stay."

Josh's rigid stance relaxed. "Does she love you?"

"Oh, she thinks she does."

Josh retrieved Drew's hat, wiped some condensation from it, and handed it back to him. "Then why borrow trouble? As long as she isn't asking to leave, and she *thinks* she loves you, why not wait and see what happens?"

Drew thumped his hat's rim, the impending sense of loss so acute it was that of a physical pain. He sighed heavily. "Because I'd rather her leave now. The longer she stays, the harder it will be to let her go."

"Be not false with yourself, Drew. It would tear you apart no matter when she left, now or later. Might as well ride it out for as long as you can. Who knows? Maybe she'll think you're worth staying for." He slapped Drew on the shoulder. "In any case, you're her husband now and she's foundering. Why not show up on a white steed to save her? Might buy you a few more days—and nights."

Drew raked his fingers through his hair. He couldn't believe this was happening. Couldn't believe he'd done this to himself again. Anger rippled down his spine and he clinched his jaw. But done it, he had, for he'd allowed himself to be vulnerable, and this time, this time was by far the worst. Assailed by an overwhelming fear over his impending loss, he settled his hat upon his head.

She wasn't good enough for him. How could she have been so naïve? Drew needed a woman like . . . well, like any of these dear ones around her. After listening to them talk, she realized they not only cooked but they made their own soap, their own candles, their own baskets, their own preserves, their own home remedies, their own spirits, their own . . . everything.

Back home, her father either purchased those items, or she had the servants make them. She had a rudimentary idea of what was required, but never had she been involved in the actual process.

She sighed. The only thing the women talked of that she had any skill at was sewing and quilting.

What a shallow existence she'd held. Even her lofty goals for her mathematical pursuits were frivolous compared to what these women did. Why, some trapped and dressed their own wildlife, while others went into the tobacco fields and worked side-by-side with their husbands.

She could hardly tend the garden, much less harvest tobacco. It had taken weeks before she'd even collected the eggs by herself. And she'd made a muck of her most important job, Sally, nearly costing both of them their lives and endangering Drew's.

He was bound to be having second thoughts. And who could blame him? So she could read Latin, speak French, write in a lovely script, and spell like a master. What good was it?

No wonder Drew had scoffed at her education. She truly hadn't needed it. She certainly hadn't used it—not here nor even in England.

It was a waste. She was a waste. How long would it be before he tired of her and her inadequacies? How long before he lamented being forced into marrying her?

Already he showed signs of displeasure, storming off earlier because she'd disobeyed him and removed the cape, thus exposing her ignorance for all to see.

And, as she now realized, her shortcomings were a reflection on him. Were the other men at this very moment making jests about poor Drew being saddled with an ignorant wife?

Would these women be forbidden by their husbands to associate with her? Would she be seen as a bad influence? Would Drew lose his place in their society, for there were places, as she'd begun to realize. Nothing as elaborate as England's hierarchy, but a hierarchy nonetheless.

There were slaves and indentured servants. Then, the small farmer, known as *Goodman*. The larger land owners became *Master*, often taking a place of office in the community.

There was no professional army but rather a local militia. The captain accepted his rank as entry into the gentry, and everyone addressed him by his title. There was also the crown-appointed governor, of course, and his council.

The women cleared away the remains of dinner, replacing it with a dessert course of Indian meal pudding, syllabubs, seedcake, and small tarts.

"I wonder who will win first rights to the mistletoe this year," someone said from near her elbow.

Now there was something familiar. Constance always enjoyed the scrambling and confusion that ensued as soon as Papa suspended a huge branch of mistletoe from the center of the ceiling. She smiled as she recalled herself and other young ladies running into corners screaming and struggling, threatening and remonstrating. In short,

they did everything but leave the room until such a time
as they found it useless to resist any longer and submit-
ted to being dragged to the center of the room for a kiss
from some charming gallant.

Of course, Papa would merely stand directly under
the berried bough, arms open wide, until he was surrounded by the whole body of young ladies and kissed
by every one of them!

"First rights?" asked the woman with all the teeth—
Kendra, she believed.

She voiced the question of many who were attending this celebration for the first time. Of the fifty or so
brides who'd shared the voyage with her, about a score
were present. Of those not in attendance, some lived too
far away to come, while many others had died. Still, the
veterans seemed to enjoy the task of introducing their
colonial customs to all the newcomers.

"We've a shooting contest between the unmarried
men," Nellie explained. "A keen shot can sever the mistletoe right off the tree outside. The one who retrieves a
cluster from the loftiest point on the tree gets first rights.
The losers save their clusters, then try to make use of
them on the sly."

"The women," another girl chimed in, "gather together as the winner walks amongst our ranks. He then
holds the cluster above the lady of his choice, who must
forfeit a kiss."

"After the kiss, she picks off one berry," Nellie added.
"Once the berries are gone, so ends the kissing."

"Granny Apperson made up rules after the year Jor-
die Bacon kept claiming kisses from the same girl over

and over—each kiss a bit longer than the last—and she already married to another!"

The women tittered, and Granny Apperson took a long pull on her pipe before blowing out a slow stream of smoke, content for now, it seemed, to let the younger set do the telling.

A woman with skin browned from the sun nodded her head. "At first she wasn't going to allow any of the married women to participate, but that only left two girls. So then she set down that the men could claim no more than three kisses from any one girl."

A matronly woman took a sip from her noggin. "It went on like that for several years until the O'Connor boys came of age."

A collective sigh rippled through the group. Nellie turned to Constance. "Jonathon Emmett had won three years in a row when Drew first came of age. They're both crack shots, and it was neck-and-neck there for a while as the two of them knocked cluster after cluster off the tree. Drew finally tired of the game, aimed a good ten feet above Goodman Emmett's last shot, and picked one clean off, proving to all he'd only been toying with his competitor. Emmett couldn't match him."

Another woman several years older than Constance smiled in what appeared to be fond remembrance. "I'll never forget standing with the other girls that day as young Drew looked us all over, each of us hoping to be chosen." She chuckled. "He didn't disappoint a one of us, did he, Granny?"

Granny Apperson smiled. "No, he didn't. Of course, the next year Josh came of age and after that either one or the other of those two won. Call it the O'Connor era, we do."

"Who finally beat them?" Constance asked.

The group stilled, no one answering. Granny Apperson stirred, smiling sadly. "Leah."

The hairs at the nape of Constance's neck prickled. "Who's Leah?"

Again, no one answered. Granny sighed. "Drew's betrothed."

Blood drained from her face. Nellie reached over, patting her hand. "It was a long time ago."

"Tell me."

Nellie turned her attention back to her sleeping baby. Constance looked at Granny Apperson.

The old woman removed the pipe from her mouth. "Drew had never before shot like he did that day, nor has he since. It was something to see. The contest had just begun when he walked up, aimed, and felled a cluster from the very top of the boughs. No one else came close."

"I thought Leah won."

"No, child, that's not what I meant. Certainly, Drew teased not the women as he usually did. When they had assembled, he walked straight to Leah and claimed three kisses. Then slipping his knife from his scabbard, he sliced the end of her cap string off, tied it onto the remaining cluster, and hung it above the meetinghouse archway, announcing to all that he was through and any female caught under the mistletoe was free game."

Another woman sighed. "It was the most romantic thing I'd ever seen."

Constance furrowed her brows. "Then why did you say Leah beat him?"

"I meant Leah beat down his youthful exuberance, for she died a few weeks later," Granny said, melancholy touching her features. "Every Christmas since, Drew has still won the contest, but he never again titillated the girls to whom he would award his favor. He's simply claimed one kiss from his grandmother, then hung the mistletoe above the archway."

Constance swallowed. "How tragic."

Granny Apperson lifted her brows. "He seems to be doing mighty fine this year."

Constance kept her face free from expression, not wishing to disillusion the old woman with what she had begun to suspect was the real truth.

TWENTY-FIVE

Constance watched colonel Tucker lead the men in musket drills. By the time they were through, instead of taking a minute and a half to load their muskets, it took only three-quarters. They practiced many of the rank speeds the men back home did, but Nellie explained it was only so the men could load without thinking, for the Indians didn't come straight at you the way Englishmen did. Instead, they took advantage of cover, often surprising their quarry.

"I thought relations were friendly."

"Oh, they are," Nellie assured her. "But it's still important to practice. One never knows."

Constance turned back to the assembly of men who were now breaking up in preparation for the mistletoe ceremony. She'd enjoyed watching Drew go through the choreographed movements with the others as the Colonel called out commands, "Shoulder your musket!—Poise your musket!—Cast about your musket!—Draw forth your scouring stick!—Ram down your charger!" and so on until finally giving fire.

Even in a crowd, his presence commanded attention. He'd discarded jerkin and doublet, bringing the muscles of his arms and back into prominence as they rippled beneath his white shirt.

She'd seen him shoot the musket before, for several times he'd brought it with them to the creek for target practice after cleansing the dishes. And she'd enjoyed watching him then as well.

Leaning his musket against a tree, he shrugged on his doublet and jerkin, then moved to her, sweat lining his brow. "How fare you?"

She pushed back the hood of her cape. "Well."

"Are you tiring? Need we leave?"

"I'm growing a little weary, but I'd like to stay and watch the mistletoe ceremony. May we?"

He nodded. "Very well, but we'll leave as soon as it's over. You've had a long day."

He placed a hand beneath her elbow, catching up to the others as they moved down a path toward a rather sturdy oak. In the midst of its leafless branches, mistletoe shot from the trunk with boughs of brilliant green, decorated in an abundance of white berries, its richness a precious gem in the otherwise barren surroundings.

Granny Apperson grouped the women together and then the unmarried men. Constance and Mary gravitated toward each other to stand side-by-side for the ceremony.

Shots echoed throughout the forest as men applied their musket drills to loading and aiming for the mistletoe in record time. Within minutes the competition had narrowed to three—Josh, Goodman Emmett, and the man they called Caskie.

Young Caskie wiped a palm against his breeches.

Emmett cackled, his scrawny beard quivering. "Just imagine you're having yer sights on one of them red-skinned savages, Caskie. That'll make yer aim true."

Constance frowned. Caskie raised his musket, fired, and missed.

Emmett pounded him on the back. "Well, son, step back now and take a good look at how it's done." Emmett prepared his weapon with exaggerated slowness, drawing attention to each of the forty or so steps it took to prime. "Now, where you fell short, boy, weren't in your aim but in the picture you held inside yer head. You got to actually *see* them beggarly devils, naked but for a covering acrost their loins and heathen paintings of all kinds profaning their bodies."

With what few teeth he had, Emmett uncorked one of the apostles around his neck, pouring powder down the barrel of his gun before replacing the cork onto the little bottle. "Of courst, it's important to remember those whoresons fight not with honor. Oh, no. They slither like vile snakes behind tall grasses and trees just waiting fer a chance to strike at us God-fearing Christians. And all because they think we're the fulfillment of some heathen prophesy about whites coming to take their lands." Snorting, he opened the gun's cap. "Why, everybody knows God meant for us to have this land so we could Christianize them barbarians. Ain't that right, Preacher?" Shouldering his musket, he took aim and fired at a particularly lofty cluster, bringing it to the ground.

Disgust for his uncharitable words and attitude was soon replaced with a flicker of anxiety as Constance realized his shot was well above the ones Caskie and Josh had felled before. If Emmett won, she could be subjected to his kiss—possibly even three.

Josh took less than a minute to prepare his piece, aim, and fire. He said nary a word. Relief swept through her as a clump of mistletoe bounced from branch to lower branch before finally making its way to the ground.

Emmett rocked back on his heels. "That's it! That's what I'm talking about." Joining his musket to his wrist, he loaded with remarkable speed. "Did you see that, Caskie? Why, O'Connor here was prob'ly thinking about the time them bloodthirsty savages came in '22 and set a torch to his family's cottage, even while his baby sister lay inside, helpless in her cradle. Story has it ol' Josh here watched the whole thing from up in a tree, his knees a'knocking and doing nary a thing to save her."

A black silence descended over the crowd. Constance's gaze flew to Drew, her breath momentarily cut off. Every muscle in his body exuded tension, his face cold with fury.

Josh took a menacing step forward. Emmett quickly shouldered his musket and fired. A cluster of berries tumbled to the ground.

Panic took hold of Constance. What was the range of these muskets? What if Josh couldn't reach a higher point due to the limitations of his firing piece? Josh loaded his musket with carefully controlled movements, then held the gun loosely within his grip, his attention pinned on Emmett.

Emmett's smug expression slowly slipped as he looked between Josh and the primed musket. "Meant no offense, O'Connor. Just giving Caskie a few pointers."

"It's Christmas day, Emmett, and need I remind you that without the Indians we wouldn't be here, for our grandfathers would never have survived?"

Emmett's lips thinned. "Oh, those lily-livered curs *saved* our grandfathers all right, but only to fatten 'em up for the kill in '22."

"All was fine until your father murdered their leader."

Emmett's face reddened. "He was openly wearing Morgan's cap! And after Morgan had been missing for days!"

"Morgan went with Nemattanew on a friendly trading expedition. Nobody knows what *really* happened. Morgan could have been attacked by a wild animal for all we know, but Nemattanew the Immortal was never given a chance to explain, was he? He was simply killed out of turn by a lowly Englishman whose 'patience had been tried' because he didn't like Nemattanew's hat."

Josh's grip on his gun tightened. "The result was a massacre, famine, and epidemic that killed hundreds upon hundreds, then a ruthless counterattack by us where even more perished." He leaned into Emmett's face. "I'd just as soon avoid having my loved ones put through that again. Wouldn't you?"

Emmett took a step back, his eyes taking on a fanatical light. "Seems we've an Indian lover in our midst."

Constance gasped.

Governor Hopkin stepped forward, placing himself between the two men. "Enough, Emmett. We are at peace with the Indians and, God willing, will remain that way. O'Connor, it's your shot."

Constance looked back to Drew only to discover he

had moved up to the front, very close to his brother's back. She started at the explosive report of Josh's musket, then swung her gaze back to the tree, but saw no mistletoe descending. She scanned the tree's boughs. Maybe it had gotten caught in another branch. The crowd murmured and her pulse beat erratically. Had he missed?

Anxiety spurted throughout her body. She knew, in the deepest core of her being, that Jonathon Emmett would come to her, not once, but all three times. Bile rose in her throat. With extreme effort, she swallowed.

Josh's face looked grave as he stepped back, and Emmett reloaded his piece, silent now. So Josh hadn't missed after all. She folded her arms against her waist. *Thank you, God.*

Emmett once again took aim. Constance held her breath, tension tightening every muscle. A loud discharge. A miss. A roar from the crowd. Josh had won.

Her limbs went buttery with relief. She shook, she gasped for air, she barely managed to remain standing. Mary grabbed her elbow. "Mistress! Are you all right?"

Drew strode through the crowd, then encircled her waist with his arm. Josh rushed to them.

"Your pardon, Josh. She's overdone today, I fear."

Josh nodded. "Best take her home, then."

The brothers exchanged intense looks, communicating on a level she couldn't begin to broach. Josh tipped his head once, turned to Mary, and paused for a moment before approaching Granny Apperson. He suspended his mistletoe above her head, and the startled old woman looked up as he hooked a thumb beneath her chin, awarding her a gentle kiss right on the lips.

Straightening, he winked at her as she plucked a berry

from the cluster. "I hereby start a new tradition, Granny," he proclaimed in a voice that reached every person present. "I say the winner claims one kiss and one kiss alone, then hangs the mistletoe above the meetinghouse entry, giving all a sporting chance."

The single and married men alike roared their approval, and Granny Apperson held up her hands for silence before announcing, "Let it be so!"

Drew held Constance still, allowing the revelers to swarm past them as they followed Josh back to church.

Emmett sauntered by, his gun resting against his bony shoulder. "Too bad yer not feeling well, Mistress, or you might have been able to catch me under the mistletoe and seen just what could've been yers had yer *husband* not cheated me out of yer hand in matrimony."

She felt Drew tense, but before he could respond, his grandmother approached. "Run along, Emmett," she said, "for 'he who envies admits his inferiority.'"

Drew quirked a brow. "You'll have to speak more plainly, Grandma. *Inferiority* is too long a word for Emmett here to grasp."

"You hush up too, Drew, and get your woman home." Grandma gave Emmett a push, prompting him to proceed forward. When he and Grandma moved around the bend, Drew nuzzled the top of Constance's head. "Are you all right?"

She rested her cheek against his chest. "I am fordone. I want to go home."

I want to go home.
How prophetic had that statement been? Drew thought.

Had she meant England? No, of course not. She'd meant the cottage, but still, that wasn't her *real* home.

He hammered a head onto the barrel of tobacco, effectively sealing it. Home for her was something he couldn't begin to reproduce. Even if he built some huge manor house, it would be for naught. The manors in London were made for entertaining, and no one "entertained" here. There were no dances, no balls, no teas. There wasn't even a city.

Lifting one shoulder, he wiped his brow against it, then continued hammering. If only he hadn't gambled that long ago summer night. But then, Emmett would have her.

If only he hadn't married her. But he'd had no choice.

If only he hadn't loved her, bedded her. But he did and had.

The only thing to be done now was to send her back, for she was as misplaced here as a rainbow trout in a school of gasper goo. Jamestown was nothing more than a harbor for their tobacco trade. They had no theater, no roads. They didn't even have horses.

He shoved the hogshead onto its side, then rolled it to the barn. She didn't belong here. It had all become so clear on Christmas. And ever since, nothing had been the same.

She'd slept almost solid for those first few days after the celebration, and he'd begun to grow concerned. But she'd evidently just been taxed. Once she caught up on her rest, she'd immersed herself in the running of the cottage like never before, starting with that ludicrous sneezeweed she and Sally had draped across the bedposts.

What worried him, though, was how she insisted on cooking the meals. It had caused some tension heretofore absent from the cottage, for Mary, of course, resisted relinquishing her duties to her mistress, but Connie insisted. And once Connie dug in her heels, Mary hadn't a prayer.

With assistance from Isaac, Drew heaved the barrel up on its end, wedging it next to other hogsheads lining the outside of the barn. Only a few more to go, and his shipment would be ready to roll down to the public warehouse near the wharf.

He watched Isaac move back to the tobacco press. It wasn't just the cooking either. For some reason, Connie had decided to launch into all kinds of domestic projects. She'd tried to make candles out of the old bayberries she and Sally had picked last fall, but not only were there not enough berries, but neither could she get the temperature of the fire quite right. At first, the candles came out lumpy, so she added fuel to the fire. Then the paraffin became so hot it melted the already deposited wax right off the candles she was re-dipping. She ended up with a huge mess, a bunch of wasted wicks, and about four questionable-looking candles instead of thirty. The yard sure smelled good, though.

Drew returned his attention to the task at hand. Pulling the knife from his scabbard, he carved the O'Connor identity mark and the grade of tobacco into the barrel's side. Connie's attempt at soap-making hadn't gone much better. She'd managed to drip the lye all right, but when it came time to mix it with lard, she'd used the leftover candle wax instead, got the proportions wrong, and could never get it to harden. The yard sure smelled good, though.

He moved to the next hogshead and reached inside to break off a piece from the top leaf, testing for quality. The thing to do was to let her go back to England. Right now she was young, and this domestic role of hers was new. But she'd grow older and wiser, and the newness would wear off. And that was the crux of the whole problem.

When that happened, she'd compare the life she could have had in London to the life she had in the colonies. It wouldn't measure up. *He* wouldn't measure up. He needed to send her back.

He could never marry again, of course, but what was that compared to this torture of knowing his wife was miserable?

Satisfied that the grade and quality were good, he picked up a new head for sealing the barrel. Yes. He'd send her back as soon as the next ship came through. It was the decent thing to do. The responsible thing to do. Weariness engulfed his body in tides. It was the only thing to do.

He hammered the head's rim. Meanwhile, he'd have to address her endless questions about the tobacco seedlings. He'd planted his close to Halfway Creek in a patch of sunny new ground with a southeastern exposure. He'd covered his seedbed with oak leaves and straw, then laid oak boughs on top for protection. Now that the weather was mellowing and the frosts appeared to be gone, he'd planned to remove the debris and expose his tender plants so they could grow strong and large enough to be transplanted come May.

He couldn't possibly tell Connie of his precious seed-bed. She'd insist on helping and ruin it for sure. And if anything happened to those plants, there would be no crop and he'd be in great trouble.

He lifted up his hat, then resettled it on his head. He still had some seeds left, though. Every planter worth his salt saved many more seeds than he needed in case some were lost or mildewed or didn't sprout. Mayhap he could collect some of those extras and make a flat-bed for her to keep in the house. If she killed those, no harm would be done. If she didn't, he'd take her out to the fields come May and show her how to plant them in little mounds.

He stopped, disgusted with himself. What rubbish. He would have no earl's daughter working in his fields. She wouldn't even be here come May. The ship with his furniture was due in a few more weeks, and he'd see that she sailed back to England aboard it.

He again swung the hammer down onto the barrel, catching the tip of his finger. Cursing, he yanked back his hand, then hurled the hammer across the yard. Josh and the men paused, then continued with their packing.

With his finger throbbing, his teeth grinding, and his heart breaking, he pulled his hat low and strode after the hammer.

Constance aroused herself from the melancholy that weighed her down. Drew had insisted she tutor Sally, even though she now knew how ridiculous that pursuit was. The child would be much better off hanging on to Mary's skirts and learning of what *really* mattered. Drew had been adamant, though, so here she and Sally sat at the table.

The child was, as usual, quick and eager to please. They'd concluded their reading lesson and now practiced rules for behavior at the table.

With a spoon, Sally scooped some imaginary food from her empty trencher ever so slowly. "Eat not with greedy bee-haver." She sipped from the very tip of the spoon.

Constance gave a slight shake of her head. "Make not a noise with your tongue, mouth, lips, or breath in your eating."

Sally scooped up more invisible victuals, stretching her mouth wide in order to poke the spoon inside without making any noise.

"Very good. Now watch me." Constance demonstrated with her spoon, stretching her lips like Sally had. Sally clapped a hand over her mouth, giggling.

"What do you find amusing?"

"You open too much."

Constance smiled. "Do I? Please show me how to correct it."

Sally demonstrated, this time placing the spoon in her mouth with decorum and without noise. And so the morning went as they practiced breaking imaginary bread instead of biting it, sloping the knife instead of holding it upright, and drinking to the health of Sally's elders.

As she watched the child's efforts, tears threatened at the back of Constance's eyes, and a nauseating sinking despair overcame her. She'd decided she must go back to

England, just as soon as the next ship arrived. It wasn't what she wanted to do but what she had to do. Drew had all but told her outright he no longer wanted her for wife. Why, he'd completely withdrawn his affection after Christmas.

What a disaster that day had turned out to be. She'd left the cottage with hopes high and outlook bright, only to have her expectations dashed time after time throughout that fateful celebration.

Her many inadequacies had become glaringly apparent, but exactly which of those had caused Drew to retreat from her so completely she did not know. Up to then, he'd loved her. He had.

Was it that pox-smitten dress? Her ignorance of their customs? Her physical weakness—which prompted the whole chair-sled mess?

Whatever it was, it was major.

At first, she'd thought to soothe his fears by showing him she could be a good colonial wife. Yet the harder she tried, the more obvious it became that she didn't belong.

And worse, he didn't even want her to perform those wifely duties for him. He wanted Mary to. Mary, who should have been his wife in the first place. Or Leah. Now there was an appalling discovery.

She swallowed. All this time and never had he mentioned his long lost love. He wouldn't even speak of her now. When Constance had questioned him, he'd only said, *"It's done and no longer an issue."*

No longer an issue! Why, Leah was not some tobacco bride he'd bought on a whim. Oh no. Leah was a young woman he had met, fallen in love with, and *brought* home—clear from England. Nellie had told her so.

What a fool she'd been. She should have accepted the first marriage contract her father had ever presented her with. Only now, after it was too late, did she finally realize why brides were left out of such negotiations. Because they had no idea what was best for them.

Constance reached over, tucking a stray curl into Sally's cap. What a pair she and Sally made, both wanting to make daisy chains from a field that no longer produced them. Her daisy chains, though, were of becoming the perfect colonial wife for Drew while editing the *Ladies' Mathematical Diary* for Europe.

What ignorance. What arrogance. And not only the "perfect colonial wife" part. What made her think she could edit the *Ladies' Diary,* especially from here? And what made her think the world would stop spinning simply because the *Diary* quit publication? Why, for all she knew, Aunt Katherine had already returned this year's submissions, disclosing to all that the *Diary* was no more. And even if she had not, Drew would most likely have forbidden it.

"Look not earn-ist-lee at any other that is eating."

Constance blinked.

Sally looked at her expectantly.

"Your pardon." Kissing the top of the child's head, cap and all, she gathered up the trencher, noggin, and spoons. "All done for today. Let us pray."

As soon as the prayer was over, Sally shot out the door to enjoy the springtime sun finally beginning to warm the land. Soon, new life would burst all around them.

Constance stacked the utensils on the shelf. Spring wouldn't bring new life to her, though. The new life she sought here in the colonies was not to be had. At least not for her.

She watched him cradle the handkerchief as if it held hundreds of precious gems instead of tiny seeds. "Would you like to help me start a seedbed for my next tobacco crop?" he asked.

She pulled her gaze away from his hands—callused yet gentle, loving, wonderful. "I thought you were supposed to have started one already."

"You don't have to help. I merely thought . . ."

They were alone in the cabin. He had come home in the midst of the day, an unusual occurrence. Mary had wasted no time in taking Sally outside to feed the chickens.

"No, I want to help. What do I do?"

"Hold out your hands."

She cupped her hands as he gingerly transferred the cloth. Their fingers connected, and a shiver of longing spread through her. The seeds blurred.

God help her, she would not cry. Not again. She'd done enough of that to last her a lifetime. She rapidly blinked back her tears.

Placing one hand beneath hers, he removed some seeds from the cloth she held. She allowed her eyes to flutter closed, relishing the feel of his touch.

"Before sowing, you test the seeds by throwing a few into the fire. If they sparkle like gunpowder, they're good and should produce."

She gave him a curt nod, keeping her head carefully
bent. He removed his hand, then tossed his seeds into
the fire. They immediately popped, shooting sparks
outward.

She looked up, surprised to find his attention not on
the fire but on her, an odd heaviness and a twinge of
pain lurking in their depths.

She closed her fingers over the handkerchief, nestling
its contents within her grasp and pressing it against her
waist. "The seeds are good."

"Yes. Mix a fair amount of them with some ashes
and we'll sow them."

"Show me."

He retrieved an earthen jar and filled it with soot. "Put
some in here," he said, holding it out for her.

She carefully siphoned a number of seeds into the jar,
then laid the handkerchief on the table.

"Good. Now stir it."

Allowing him to retain hold of the jar, she sunk her
finger into the mixture and slowly whirled it around.
And around. And around.

She needed to go ahead and tell him. Tell him of her
decision to spare him from any more of her bumbling
ways. Tell him of her decision to release him from any
misplaced responsibility he might have for her. Tell him
of her decision to leave.

"Why are you crying, Connie?" he whispered.

She jumped back, wiping her finger against her apron.
"I'm not."

It was a foolish statement, of course, for even now,
she felt fresh tears fall from her eyes.

"You don't have to help me with the tobacco. I thought you wanted to. I mean, you had asked, and . . ."

She swallowed. "I very much want to care for your seedlings. I know not what's wrong with me. I've never been such a watering pot in all my life."

"Are you in pain?"

Not like you mean, but yes. Oh, yes. My heart is rending in two. "No."

"Then what is it?"

Tell him. A frenzied desperation infiltrated her body. *No.* She didn't want to leave. What she really wanted was to stay. Stay and be his wife. And maybe an editor on the side?

What would he do if she voiced such a thing? What would he say? She searched his eyes. What if he said yes? She felt her throat closing up.

But he wouldn't. He'd say no. "Why have you not taken me to the big house, Drew?"

After a moment, he averted his gaze, the tension within him palpable. Then, as clearly as if someone had lifted blinders from her, she saw. Saw what she'd been oblivious to all along.

Her decision to leave or not to leave was inconsequential, for clearly Drew had already made up his mind. *He* was going to send her back, and she had no say in the matter whatsoever.

Her cheeks burned. And here she thought she was being so noble, so sacrificial. Yet all the while, he'd intended to send her back regardless.

An internal roaring resounded in her ears. "Don't answer that." She turned and found a shallow wooden crate. "Is this what we plant the seeds in?"

He hadn't moved, but his attention had now honed in on her.

She took a deep breath. "I'm sorry, Drew. Forget I spoke. Is this for the tobacco?"

After another long pause, he set the jar down on the hearth. "We need to talk."

Her composure slipped a notch. "No we don't. Everything's fine, truly. Come. Let's plant the tobacco. You get the crate, I'll get the seeds."

She hustled forward and reached for the jar, only to be halted by a gentle grip on her wrist. "We tried, Connie, we did. But we both know . . . it just isn't going to work."

No. Not yet. She wasn't ready. She needed more time! She broke free from his grasp, picked up the jar, and plopped down onto the hearth. Swishing the ashes inside with her finger, she dug a small hole. "How much dirt is there in a hole the dimensions of which are an inch, do you suppose?"

He squatted down beside her, his knees cracking. "I haven't taken you to the big house because, all things considered, I thought it best not to."

She jumped to her feet. "Let's go plant the tobacco."

He stood and closed his hands over her shoulders. "Connie."

Tears surged to her eyes, tumbling down her cheeks. "Please, Drew, please. Can we please just plant the tobacco?"

Maybe if she did a good job with the seedlings he wouldn't send her back. If he would give her a chance, he'd see. She would water them, nurture them, set them in the sun. Whatever it took. And it would be the best blessed crop he'd ever had in all his days.

A tiny niggling voice reminded her he'd be better off without her. She drove it from her mind, convincing herself that if she could just do this one thing, it would be a start. Her heart thumped madly as she waited for his answer.

Backing up a step, he let his hands fall. "Very well. We'll plant the tobacco, for now."

TWENTY-SIX

I t was her favorite time of day, and for a short while it managed to chase her oppressive sadness away. During this early morning hour, the world belonged to her, for though she was up, hundreds more throughout this primitive land still snuggled in their ticks, resisting the moment they must arise.

Not Constance. She and her dear companion, Snowflake, took in nature's concert every morning. They had standing reservations, with the best seats in the house. She rested her cheek against Snowflake's coarse hide, working milk from the goat's teats by rote as they waited for the concert to begin.

Sweet heaven, this country had taken her by surprise. It was lovely in the summer, a virtual painter's palette in the fall, a marvel in the winter, and an absolute Eden in the spring. She wished she'd paid more attention to her art lessons. How glorious it would be to capture this place and keep a piece of it with you always.

She breathed in the freshness of dawn, picturing in her mind the multicolored spectacle spring made of itself here. Many of the unfamiliar trees and shrubs she'd learned of last summer now clad themselves in blooms that took the very breath from her body.

Dogwoods crowned with thick, lush clusters of white looked as if snow covered their boughs. Spicebushes filled her senses with fragrance while simultaneously awarding a charming yellow floral display. Wild trumpet creepers in blossom festooned the trees. And trimming these exquisite ensembles were iris, lilies, poppies, peonies, larkspurs, hollyhock, and more.

The concert was in full swing now, bursting with twitters, whistles, cackles, and fluting. Some short and staccato, some with crescendo, some with irregular haphazard rhythms.

The milking was done, her hands lax against her knees. Yet Snowflake stood still, cushioning Constance's upper body as she rested against the gentle beast. She opened her eyes. A hare, no bigger than the coneys back home, sprang across the clearing. She smiled as she followed its progress until it disappeared into the thicket.

A movement captured her attention, and finding its source along the perimeter of the yard, her eyes widened. *What in the world is that?* A slow-moving, furry black creature with a wide white stripe from its head to its tail lumbered into the yard. Constance slowly lifted her head from Snowflake's side. The goat fidgeted, backing up a step or two.

Constance quickly grabbed the pail and pulled it out of harm's way. Snowflake turned and headed toward the front of the cottage. Constance stayed on the stool and looked again at the fascinating animal moving toward her.

"Good morrow. And what might you be?"

"*Eeeeth, eeeeth, eeeeth, eeeeth.*"

"I see. And might you be hungry? I can give you not the milk, but I might be able to round up some chicken feed. Would you like that?"

The animal paused and, nose twitching, examined Constance with its marblelike eyes. Reaching into her pocket, she tossed some feed to the animal. It froze, erecting its white-plumed tail into the air.

Constance sat very still, sensing she'd frightened it. After several long moments, it lowered its tail and ambled forward, snatching up the feed before scurrying back into the safety of the forest.

She sighed. Oh, how she loved this country. Thoughts of smelly, crowded, confining London crept into her musings. She didn't care to ever see it again. She missed it not. Not at all.

She did miss her family, though. Still, Uncle Skelly, God rest his soul, and Aunt Katherine had been her real family, and she'd been taken from them years ago. Her siblings were busy with their own lives and, of course, the war. And Father, too, for that matter.

But here, here she felt . . . well, free. Free in that she had no tedious social obligations to fulfill. Free in that she could venture forth alone without putting her person or reputation in jeopardy. Free in that everyone was quite expected to be unconventional. Even now she wore no shoes.

She burrowed her toes into the grass. Why, she'd never realized how cumbersome the numerous garments and undergarments she wore at home had been until she'd come here and discarded all for one simple gown. And now that the weather had warmed, everyone put away their shoes, not wanting to use them when there was no need.

She dipped her finger into the milk, then brought its creamy taste to her mouth. Yet while she felt free, she also felt so vulnerable. She always seemed to be sabotaging something, her relationship with her husband included.

But today was a new day. Maybe this would be the day the tobacco seedlings would nose their way to the surface. Maybe this would be the day Drew took her to the big house. Maybe this would be the day he decided to keep her.

Please, Lord. Let this be the day.

The seedlings didn't come forth that day, nor did Drew. But a week or so later, a tiny suggestion of green grazed the surface of the soil, and now her plants had reached about an inch in height. Drew had been pleased. She had been ecstatic.

Still, he hadn't shown her the new house. She could have gone and seen it for herself. She certainly had the time and the desire. But she'd fantasized so often about going there with Drew, being carried over its threshold in his arms, wandering through its corridors together, that to go there now without him would be the same as admitting defeat.

And she was far from admitting defeat. Her cooking was improving. Her seedlings were thriving. And she had a new pet she called Blackberry. He visited her most every morning during the milking and many an evening at the creek while she washed dishes. If the animals here accepted her, then surely it was a sign from God that Drew would too.

Please Lord, let it be a sign.

The sun had gone down, so Constance brought her treasures inside. They now stood two inches tall, and a new one had just sprung up this morn.

Placing the flat carefully on the shelf, she picked up her diary and recorded a puzzle that had come to her when she'd watered her flat this afternoon.

A seed is planted. At the end of two years it produces a seed, and one each year thereafter. Each of these, when two years old, produces a seed yearly. All the seeds produced do likewise. How many seeds will be produced in twenty years?

The salty air whipped Drew's hair against the side of his face. He stood on the shore before the weather-beaten *Myrtilla,* sitting low in the water, anchored some one hundred yards out on the Chesapeake Bay. In its hatch rode, among other things, enough furniture to fill his house. Soon, that furniture would be replaced with tobacco. He should be pleased. Drew was anything but.

Crewmen crowded the deck, continually coming and going, their step quick, their ribald laughter carrying across the water. A lusty tune of a milkmaid and her lover cut through their den of exchanges. A sturdy sailor came into the bows, dumping a bucket of refuse overboard.

Screeching, the seagulls swooped down, their squawks drowning out all other sounds.

Maybe he could keep the ship's presence from her. It wasn't out of the realm of possibilities. Only men came to shore for the unloading and loading of ships, none of whom would have any reason to make a social stop at his cottage.

So, if he could ensure that Josh and the indentured men remained quiet, he might could secret the furniture off and the tobacco on, then allow the *Myrtilla* to sail again before Connie was ever the wiser. But, no, Josh would be on board with the tobacco, and he'd not leave without saying good-bye.

Drew wasn't sure how much longer he could stay away from her anyway. He helped not with the washing of dishes, he came home for only one meal a day, and he'd created a handful of extra projects to keep him busy until she fell asleep each night.

He'd repaired the old raft that they never used at the creek and even now had begun to whittle a new hickory handle for an ax whose handle still had plenty of wear left.

He'd considered relinquishing their bed to her completely but could never quite bring himself to do so. He'd be sleeping in an empty one soon enough. Still, he mustn't join with her, for the risk of pregnancy was too great. They were lucky she wasn't already breeding. Sending her home a "widow" was one thing; sending her home a "widow" with child was something else entirely. Something he wouldn't do.

Constance stared at Mary, then sunk down into Drew's chair. "You cannot be serious."

Mary continued to stir the pudding. "You know it to be true, you do."

Constance placed a palm against her stomach. She'd kindled? Surely not. She would have known. Wouldn't she? "But I've not been ill."

"Consider yourself lucky."

She took a deep breath. "Now, Mary. I've been through quite a lot these past several months, what with the kidnapping, the marriage, the seasoning. It could simply be my poor body is a bit abused and confused."

"Your body knows exactly what it's doing."

"But how can you be certain?"

"You're tired all the time, you are."

"Of course I'm tired. I did not but collect eggs before. Now I do much, much more."

"You cry all the time."

Constance lifted a brow. "I've never been married before."

"You cannot eat large meals, yet you're continually nibbling on everything in sight."

"That's part of learning how to cook. I must taste so as to see what the concoction needs. Then, when the meal's finally ready, I've tasted so much, I'm too full to eat."

"Your breasts are tender?"

Constance said nothing.

Mary turned, amusement touching her eyes. "You're with child, all right. And soon, me thinks you'll be feeling the wee one squirming around in there, you will."

A warm glow flowed through her. Tears rushed to her

eyes. She was going to have a baby! Drew's baby! She hugged her stomach. *Oh, thank you, thank you, thank you.* A baby. Imagine that.

She couldn't wait to tell Drew. She stilled. Drew. What would he think? Would he be happy?

Of course he'd be happy. But . . . but what about their marriage? She knew in the deepest core of her being that once she told him, he wouldn't send her back.

Would he be bitter? Resigned? Would he feel trapped? But what could she do? Go on to England and never tell him he had a child? Of course not. That would be unthinkable.

"How far along do you suppose I am, Mary?"

"How long has it been since your last monthly?"

Constance blushed. "Since December."

"I'd say you're close to four months, then."

"How long before I show?"

"Within the next few weeks, I'm thinking."

Constance bit her lip. "Mary, I'm not going to tell Drew right away."

Mary stopped stirring midmotion, looking sharply at her.

"Please. Don't say anything."

After a moment, Mary nodded. "Yes, Mistress."

A sure sign of her displeasure, the use of *mistress* was. But it couldn't be helped. The babe changed everything.

Constance would have to stay now, but it would be ever so much better if Drew thought it was his own idea. Men were so very testy when they felt pushed into something.

She clasped her hands together. Yes, she must make

certain he insisted upon her permanence here—before
he found out about the babe. And she had very little
time.

She pursed her lips. Winning his adoration by performing wifely duties around the cottage had reaped
nothing. She must think of something else.

A slow smile crept upon her face. There was one thing
he'd never been able to distance himself from, even in
the beginning. She smoothed her apron down. And of
that, she had plenty. Plenty with which to use in the
seduction of her husband.

"Drew! Drew! We bring you lunch!"

Drew gave one last push against the lever, wedging
an opening in the large crate, then looked to the west.
Sally bobbed across the grass with cap, caught by its
strings around her neck, flopping against her shoulders,
her long black curls fluttering free. Constance followed
a few paces behind.

She carried a large cloth-covered basket in one hand
and reached high above her head to wave with the other.
His senses leapt to life. Propping his lever against the
crate, he moved to the edge of the shipment.

Sally reached him first. "What's in the boxes?"

"Furniture."

Sally darted off to investigate before Constance even
reached them.

Drew wiped his forehead with a handkerchief as he
watched Connie's progress. The sun splashed onto her
shoulders, and his gaze traveled to the gentle sway of
her hips.

He stayed as such until she stopped mere inches in front of him. She raised a delicate freckled hand to her chest, marking the swells of her labored breathing. "My, it's been a while since I've walked out here."

A while? It had been a blasted century. As far as he knew, she'd not been here since Sally's mishap. So what was she doing here now?

He stood rigid as she scrutinized the house.

Her eyes filled with an indefinable emotion. "Oh, Drew. It's magnificent. I had no idea." She turned to him. "Will you show it to me? I've so wanted to see it."

He waved his hand toward the structure. "Help yourself."

A small intimate smile crept onto her lovely sunburned face. "I'd prefer a guided tour. From you. Please?"

"I'm rather busy."

She peeked around his shoulder, exposing a nice portion of freckled slender neck. "So I see. What have you in the crates?"

"Furniture."

Her eyes widened. "Furniture! You told me not the house was finished. When did you complete it?"

"A fortnight ago."

Her face lit with pleasure. "Why, that's wonderful! Congratulations! We must have a celebration."

He had to put some space between himself and her. His blood was pumping, his heart was hammering, and his senses were reeling. "What are you doing here?"

She hesitated, then held up her basket. "I decided to bring you something special for your midday meal."

He frowned. Had her voice taken on a husky quality, or had he imagined it?

She raised the basket higher, pressing its handle against her chest. "Go ahead, take a peek."

He quickly lifted a corner of the cloth.

"Trout," she whispered. "I caught it and made it myself."

"Caught it?"

Her entire face spread into a smile, dazzling him. "With a frying pan! You've never seen such a thing, Drew. The trout are so plentiful, I needed only to scoop my pan into the water and up came enough fish for dinner and supper too!"

He couldn't help but smile at her enthusiasm. "I know. So you fried it up too?"

She hugged the basket closer to her, nodding her head proudly.

There may have been trout in the basket, but it was the scent of Constance that filled his senses. Lilacs and woman. A lethal combination.

He gave himself a mental shake. Her ticket home was floating right down by the wharf, and he'd not stand here billing and cooing in the meanwhile. He glared at her. "I already have a meal."

Turning, he moved back to the crate he had been working on. He'd meant to hurt her feelings, but he'd not done a very good job of it, evidently, for she followed him to the crate and rested her shoulders and back against it, flinging her chin up toward the sky. Long cinnamon-colored lashes lay against her cheeks as he moved his gaze along the enchanting profile she displayed.

Grabbing the crate's side, he wrenched it off, jostling her from her position. It mattered not. She settled right back against it.

"I'm not leaving, you know."

His heart stopped beating. *Did she know about the ship?*

"At least not until you've eaten my trout."

Lips thinning, he grabbed the basket from her. "Then by all means, let me eat."

She jumped from the side of the crate, laying a hand against his. "No, not here. Not like this. Take me inside, Drew. Take me inside, show me the house, and we'll sit down and eat in there."

He jerked his hand free. "Why?"

"Because it's important to me. I want to see what you've worked for, what you've sweated for, what you've forsaken your family for."

He whipped himself up to his full height. "Forsaken my family for? Just what is that supposed to mean?"

"Sally and I never see you anymore. You leave before dawn and return well after nightfall. You've even quit taking meals with us. She misses you." She fingered the laces at her neck. "We both do."

He scoffed. "It's a lonely life, the life of a farmer's wife."

"Only if that wife is a widow. Which I'm not. What keeps you out so long?"

"Somebody's got to work around here."

She took a deep breath. "And that somebody's got to eat." She lifted a brow. "I went to a lot of trouble to fry that fish for you. So you'd best just resign yourself to taking me inside, showing me my new home, and eating your midday meal."

He spun on his heel, heading toward the house. "Well, don't do me any more favors."

He didn't want her in the house. It held no memories of her within its walls, and he'd wanted to keep it that way. But she was going to ruin that for him too.

Well, so be it. He would take her inside. He'd show it to her. He'd eat her pox-smitten trout. Then he'd kick her fancy backside out.

He slammed open the front door, moved into the great room, dropped the basket of trout onto his new hardwood floor, and plopped down to eat. He'd taken no more than two bites when her voice reached him from the front steps. He looked up to find her hovering in the doorway.

"Will Sally be all right out there?"

"Of course," he replied. "The men will look after her."

She hesitated. "I've never been in before."

He ripped off another bite of fish with his teeth. "Well come on, then. Otherwise, go away and leave me be."

Her shoulders straightened and she stepped across the threshold, pausing there before entering the great room. Removing the bones from his mouth, he said not a word as she circled the room, touching this, running her fingers along that.

He found some spoon bread in the basket and shoved it into his mouth. "You obviously made the bread too. Mary sure didn't."

She sighed. "No, she didn't."

"Well, I wish you'd let her. That's what she is, Connie. My cook. And I like the way she does it." He tunneled around in the basket. "Is there anything to drink?"

"Yes. There's some cider in the wine skin there on the left."

He dug through the contents, purposely abusing the

other prepared foods, then yanked out the wine skin, squirting a stream of cider into his mouth.

She settled across from him, her skirts billowing out around her. "The workmanship is exquisite, Drew. I had no idea the house would be so fine."

He wiped his hand across his mouth, then burped. "Even we colonists have some skills."

"That's not what I meant," she said, loosening the top of her bodice. "I meant—"

"What are you doing?!"

She froze, eyes wide. "What?"

He jumped to his feet. "Don't *what* me! You know exactly what I'm talking about."

She looked down at the basket. "Is something amiss?"

He ground his teeth together. "Your bodice, Constance."

She snatched her hand away from her laces. "I was merely warm."

"Well, it's spring and Virginia gets much, much hotter come summer. So if you're hot now, you'll be miserable in the summer."

Tears filled her eyes. "I don't mind."

He fisted his hands. "Well, I do! Now lace your bodice and get out of here."

She fumbled with her lacings. "But I haven't seen the house."

"Out!"

She stumbled to her feet. "Why are you shouting, Drew? Why are you angry?"

"I'm not shouting! I'm not angry! I'm just ready for you to be gone from here, and as soon as the ship in port is loaded with tobacco, I will put you on it and be done with all this!"

Her gaze flew to the window facing the water, but of course, she wouldn't be able to see the ship from here. "Right now? There's a ship out in the harbor right now?"

Bitter cold swept through him. Was that eagerness tingeing her voice? He couldn't quite tell. "Yes."

"And . . . and you want me on it?"

He felt his chest heave in order to take in enough air. "Yes."

She moved toward the window, her back to him. "Why?"

Because I love you and I want you to be happy, not miserable. "You don't belong here, Connie. And you know it."

She bent her head down. "Because of my math?"

"Among other things."

"But we're married, Drew. We said a handfast, to Morden, to God, and to each other."

"Consider yourself a widow."

She spun around. "But you're not dead!"

"No one will know."

"I will know! God will know! Surely you do not think I would return home and take another husband when I already have one?"

His temper began to climb. He said nothing.

"Well, I'll not do it, Drew. I'll never take another. Not ever." She bit her lip. "I want not to go. I want to stay."

By my troth, must she rip his heart from his very chest, leaving nothing in its wake? "So you think, but years from now you'll be thanking me."

She wrung her hands. "You're attracted to me, Drew. I know you are."

His heart slammed against his ribs. "It matters not."

Tears spilled over and onto her cheeks. "How can you say so? It matters. It does."

"It doesn't. Not in the long run."

"When did you decide to send me back?"

Forsooth, why couldn't women have been given the foresight of men? Why couldn't they see what was best for them? Why must they always fight it? "You know when."

"Christmas Day."

"Yes."

"Yet you're still attracted to me."

He clinched his teeth together. "Yes."

"Then take me to wife, Drew. Just one last time before you send me away. Please."

Heat shot straight through him. "Absolutely not."

A new flood of tears. "Why? *Why?*"

Because it would kill me, it would. His mind scrambled for another answer, then zeroed in on one equally as important. "Because my seed might take root, and I do not want you to have my child."

ome *on,* Sally!" she snapped, turning around for the umpteenth time.

Sally pumped her pint-size legs but gained little ground. For the first time, resentment reared its ugly head. If it hadn't been for Sally, Constance could have made if not a dignified, then at least a swift, exit from the big house, then given herself over to the vanquishing weight bearing down upon her heart.

Instead, she'd had to go out to where Josh and the men were eating their meal and exchange pleasantries before collecting Sally and heading toward the cottage as if her very life hadn't just been wrenched from her body. But it had. And if she succumbed now, Sally would no doubt report it all to Drew in vivid detail.

Compressing her lips, Constance marched back toward the child.

Sally's steps faltered, her eyes widening. "I hurry!" she implored.

She hauled Sally up and off her feet, propping the child against her waist as they moved toward home.

Sally wrapped her legs and arms around Constance, whimpering.

Constance hardened her heart, offering no comforting word or gesture, for she had nothing within her but anguish. Nothing. By the time they reached the clearing, Sally had exchanged whimpers for actual sobs. They were minor compared to the sound Constance made upon the sight that greeted her. Screeching in horror, she barely kept herself from dropping the child. "*Noooooo!*"

Letting Sally down with a thud, Constance ran toward her seedbed, waving her arms. "Shoo! Shoo!"

The goat looked up inquiringly, a tobacco stem still in its mouth.

"No! Oh, no! How could you! *How could you?!*"

The goat shied away, then bolted when Constance struck its flank with every bit of force she could muster. Pain shot through her hand, surging up her arm. She paid it no heed but spun to face the damage, then fell to her knees, covering her mouth.

The flat of tobacco seedlings was no more. Snowflake had nipped the buds off all but two plants. Short stubby stems no more than a quarter inch tall stuck up above the imprisoned earth. An agonizing wail slowly escaped from her as she grabbed her stomach and rocked back and forth.

Mary rushed outside. Looking at the scene, she quickly captured Sally in her arms, carried her into the cottage, and left Constance to grieve alone over the ruined seedbed.

Constance plunged her fingers into the fertile soil, tangling them in the roots beneath the surface. Curling her fists, she yanked the fibers out, crushing them within her hands.

She squeezed harder, harder, her arm muscles quivering, her fingernails drawing blood. The desolation within her strained against the boundaries of her being until like a great serpent of the deep, she roared to her feet, hurtling the roots at the seedbed.

They hit with a very soft, dissatisfying thump. She booted the flatbed with her foot, jamming her bare toe and moving the flatbed not one mite.

Fury clawed through her. *Blast these infernal seeds. Blast Drew. And blast him for making me care!* With quicksilver movements, she grasped the flat's edges, pulling it up and over. Dirt spilled out into a huge jumble, and she let the crate fly.

You want me not to bear your child? Well, you're too late, you three-suited knave! You're too late! She kicked the dirt, stomped the roots, and cursed with renewed vigor.

"Sissy? Your di'ry make you feel better?"

Constance jerked her head around to see Sally tentatively holding out the diary, her tiny chubby hands extended.

It wasn't until she tried to focus that she realized tears obstructed her view. Mopping her eyes with a hard swipe, she lost sight of Sally and beheld only the diary.

The pamphlet took on a life of its own, growing larger and larger in Constance's eye, until she perceived it as a laughing, mocking, heinous creature.

She snatched it from Sally's hands. The child gasped and stumbled backward, her lower lip quivering. But

Constance merely spun and raced away. Away from the cottage. Away from the seedbed. Away from Drew.

For nothing would she slow. Not for the sharp stitch in her side, not for the tearing flesh on the bottoms of her feet, not for the nausea swimming in her stomach. She noticed not the blooming dogwoods, the colorful phlox sprinkled alongside the path, nor the stillness of the forest. She simply plunged forward, eyes straight ahead.

She heard the creek before she smelled it, smelled it before she saw it, and then she was there, racing toward it. With legs whizzing over the ground beneath her, she cranked her hand back, squeezed the diary tight, then launched it through the air.

The momentum of her action slammed her to her knees. With nothing short of sheer determination, she caught herself on her hands, never losing eye contact with her journal as it arched above the water then somersaulted into it with a splash.

Sunning turtles slipped from their logs. Unsuspecting ducks squawked and flapped their wings, painting ribbons of water in their wake. The *Ladies' Mathematical Diary: A Woman's Almanac Adapted for the Use and Diversion of the Fair-Sex* bobbed to the surface before swirling downstream.

Constance stayed on her hands and knees watching until it turned from a booklet, to a speck in the distance, to nothing. Then she curled up into a ball and wept.

Drew worked like a man possessed, driving his brother and the other men with excessive pressure. They tore open crates, unloaded furniture, and hauled it into the house. But the satisfaction, the fulfillment, the exultation he had expected to accompany this moment were sorely lacking.

In their place was mirthless, pathetic dejection. He cared not about the superior craftsmanship of the pieces they unloaded. He cared not if any had been damaged during their shipment. He cared not if he even had furniture.

Sunlight poured through the huge diamond-paned windows, exposing a jumble of chairs, tables, and assorted pieces crowding the great room. The men jostled about, lugging bits of a bed abovestairs, stacking chests against the walls, fitting drawers into an elaborate secretary, none of them talking, none of them exhibiting the relaxed air that usually permeated the atmosphere.

Drew gave Josh a nod, then moved back outside to the few unopened crates remaining. The physical demands of tearing open wooden boxes suited his mood. Picking up the pry bar, he wedged it into a seam.

Connie's reaction to his words had surprised him. Shock, acute anguish, then blazing anger had played across her features in a matter of seconds. He'd realized immediately she'd misinterpreted his words. Typical of a woman.

He didn't mean he thought her *unworthy* of bearing his children, only that it was *unwise*. Yet he chose not to clarify his statement. Let her think what she would.

As strong-willed as she was, any crack he revealed in his defenses would soon be a huge crevice if she discovered it. No, it was best to let her think the worst.

The crate resisted his efforts to open it. Cursing, he moved the bar down to another point in the seam. The rest of the furniture should be in the house well before sunset. As soon as the job was done, he'd walk over to the public warehouse and see how the loading of tobacco progressed.

They'd spent the last week rolling their many hogsheads there and collecting the crates of furniture. With no animals for pulling, the transfer of crates over the pock-ridden terrain had been long and arduous, with Drew, Josh, and the men all dragging borrowed flatbed wagons back and forth more times than he cared to remember.

He'd decided that would be the last time he did any dragging of that magnitude. He would have a couple of extra weeks before planting commenced, and he'd use those weeks to build himself a dock right at the bottom of the slope here.

A tight bubble formed in his stomach, growing larger and larger while he tried to dismiss the fact that Connie would be gone and would never see his new dock, nor anything else, for that matter.

He glanced up, the Indian boy's rapid approach giving him pause. The boy had filled out since he last saw him, his arms and chest taking on a more refined edge. But that wasn't what held his attention.

It was the manner in which the boy approached. Ordinarily, he stood at the perimeter of the yard and waited until he was noticed.

Of their own volition, Drew's feet moved toward the Indian, each step quicker than the next until he matched the boy's hurried lope. They met halfway. "What is it?" Drew asked in the native tongue.

The young warrior hadn't yet learned to guise his

emotions as well as his adult counterparts. Still, it was hard to decipher other than the fact that the boy was troubled, maybe even torn.

"What?" Drew repeated.

The boy's nostrils flared with each rapid intake of breath. His lips thinned. "My leader, Opechancanough, grows old. And with age, so grows his bitterness. He speaks with great hatred for the white planters as they turn ancestral land into sot weed. Again and again Powhatans die from white man's disease and from white man's anger."

A shadow of alarm touched Drew as he translated the words within his mind. "White man's anger? Someone has died from white man's anger?"

A steely light entered the boy's eyes. "One of my brothers take ground nuts and tuckahoe from land once ours but now claimed by your John Emmett."

Unease swept through Drew. "And did Emmett detain the next available Indian for the paying of compensation as agreed upon between your chief and mine?"

The young warrior's jaw tensed. "John Emmett killed the next Powhatan he see."

Needlelike pricks spread from Drew's scalp to his toes. "Sweet, merciful God."

"Opechancanough set forth big plan. My brothers fan out through our overtaken land and approach the white planter with no weapons or war paint. Upon entry into the homes, they attack with whatever implement at hand, slaying all, then burning their dwellings with the dead and wounded inside."

Drew's heart slammed within his ribcage, then accelerated in tempo, each beat faster and harder than the next. "When?"

"Now."

No! Panic surged through him, gnawing at his throat. He grasped the boy's forearm, squeezing. *"My wife?"*

"You must go to her. Quickly. My brothers move toward there even now."

Drew whirled around, barreling up the hill toward the big house.

"White Coon?" the youth called after him.

Drew spun back to the boy, his chest heaving.

"We are enemies," the young warrior said in his guttural language. "If we meet again, it will mean death for one of us."

Drew nodded. "So be it. And thank you." Turning his back again, he sprinted to the house.

"Josh! *Joooosh!*"

His brother and the other men poured out the front door.

"Indian attack! Quickly, to Grandma and Nellie!"

Without another word, Josh grabbed a pry bar and raced toward his sister's home.

"Thomas! Take two men and get to the public warehouses! Hurry!" He tossed the remaining men pry bars, hammers, and anything else he'd happened to grab on his flight up the slope. "Isaac, sound a warning to the east!"

Isaac caught a hammer and headed out with a companion.

"You two, to the west! And make haste! There's not a moment to spare!"

No one asked him how he knew, no one asked him for details—they simply took the orders and executed them.

Denouncing himself a fool for having no guns in the new house, he clutched the remaining pry bar in his hand and outstripped the wind in an effort to reach Connie and Sally. He leapt over tree roots, plowed through overgrown brush that whipped against his legs, arms and face and focused on reaching the cottage rather than on what might take place if he were too late.

Please, God, please. Let me not be too late!

The distance between the big house and the cottage had never seemed so far. He pushed himself even harder, unaware of the protests his body made.

He was closer now and neither saw nor smelled smoke. A good sign. *Please, God, please. Let me not be too late!*

Pebbles sprayed from beneath his boots, sweat plastered his shirt to his chest, his hair fell loose from its leather binding. *Almost there, God. Almost there. Hold on, Connie!* He accelerated, thoughts of Connie and brutal Indians consuming his mind.

Just one more bend. He made no effort to disguise his approach but exploded into the clearing, a bloodcurdling scream on his lips as he sighted the Powhatan ready to torch his cottage.

He rushed the Indian, driving the pry bar against the warrior's wrist, sending the torch flying. Drew followed the lever's momentum, whirling around with it full circle before slamming it into the Indian's head. The pry bar swung from Drew's grasp upon contact, shooting white heat up his arm.

The Powhatan careened and then fell to the ground. Drew checked his temptation to run into the cottage, forcing himself to first make sure the Powhatan would not rise again. He reached down for the Indian's neck. The warrior's arm flashed up, grabbing Drew, kicking him, and tossing him backward before he had a chance to react.

Then the Indian was there, on top of him, encircling his throat with a vengeance. Drew butted the Powhatan's arms. The pressure against his throat increased.

He clawed at the Powhatan's face, flesh collecting beneath his nails. The pressure increased.

The warrior's tight-lipped grimace hovering above him faded in and out of view. Drew gasped for breath. His ears began to ring.

He was going to die. *Connie! Sally!* No. Not yet. He couldn't die yet. He had to breathe. *God, help me! Help me!*

The crackling of the fiery torch penetrated the fog within his brain. The torch. The torch. The fire from the torch. He could hear it. Feel it. Almost taste it upon his lips.

Drew flailed his legs. Bucked his hips. And with supreme effort, rolled to the left, reversing positions with the Indian while plunging his enemy into the spreading fire.

The viselike grip around his neck loosened only slightly, and Drew sucked in a trickle of air while driving his knee into the Indian's chest and yanking against the warrior's wrists. The acrid smell of singed flesh teased his impoverished lungs. The sizzling of human skin resounded in his ears.

The Powhatan acknowledged none of it. Drew sucked in another paltry breath. He couldn't begin to imagine the torment the Indian must be undergoing. Even Drew's own body smoldered from the searing heat.

The warrior held firm to Drew's neck, though, glaring at him and squeezing, tighter, tighter. Apprehension twisted within him. What manner of man was this? *Let go, you fiend!*

The Indian dug his nails into Drew's neck, then shoved him back and off. They broke apart, bounding to their feet, channeling their focus onto each other instead of the torturous pain racking their bodies.

Drew circled to the left. The Powhatan mirrored his moves, a slow, satisfied smile creeping onto his face. If it came down to a bare-handed struggle, Drew would die. And they both knew it.

Drew's gaze swept the area where the pry bar had fallen, then quickly returned to track the Powhatan. The pry bar would be of no use. It now lay in the midst of the spreading fire, flames engulfing it. A trail of flames tickled the base of the cottage. He must kill the Indian before the fire reached the thatch roof or all would be lost.

The Powhatan lunged, making a swipe at him. Drew jumped back and free. He glanced at the ax buried in the tree stump. The Indian saw it as well. The Indian was closer—just barely.

They both broke and ran for it, but Drew detoured, snatching up the new hickory handle he'd been whittling, which was still a good six feet long and stood propped against the mulberry tree.

The Powhatan whirled to face Drew with the ax. Drew rested on the balls of his feet, bending his knees and facing the Indian with a hickory handle turned quarterstaff. The Indian smiled, swirling the ax above his head, then tossing it from hand to hand.

Drew cocked a brow, spinning the quarterstaff within his grasp. An earsplitting shriek pierced the air as the Indian rushed Drew with an overhead swing of the ax.

Drew swept his quarterstaff up with both hands, blocking the half-moon slash toward his head. The moment the ax handle connected with his dense pole, he jerked the staff backward, whipping the ax out of the warrior's hands to fly harmlessly behind his own back.

In less than a heartbeat, Drew snapped his right hand forward, slamming the right butt of the staff into the Powhatan's left temple, stunning him. Capitalizing on his advantage, Drew dropped to his left knee, sweeping the quarterstaff behind the warrior's knees, knocking him off his feet and hard onto his raw back.

He heard the Powhatan's breath rush from his body and followed up with a sharp jab, thrusting the end of his staff into the Indian's throat, crushing his voice box.

Drew jumped back. The Indian's eyes bugged. He clawed frantically at his throat, rolling onto hands and knees while he choked. Drew dropped his weapon and grabbed the warrior by his hair, jerking him to his knees. The Indian grasped Drew's arms, but the pressure behind his grip faded even as he made contact.

With the same detached passion he used to destroy wild game, Drew placed the Indian in a headlock and snapped his neck, dropping the Powhatan's lifeless body onto his face in the settling dirt.

He knew he'd wrestle with it later, but there was no time to think of what he'd just done. Flames now licked two sides of the cottage. He had to get in there. Now.

He didn't allow himself to hesitate. But he knew. Before the end of his struggle with the Indian, he knew.

Knew what he would find once he set foot inside that cottage. For if anyone had still been alive, they would have come outside to assist him in destroying the enemy. But maybe, just maybe in the Indian's rush to move on to his next prey, he had merely knocked them unconscious.

Drawing the neck of his shirt up over his mouth and nose, he plunged into the cottage. Scorching heat and dense smoke blasted him in the face. He dropped to his knees. A layer of murky but navigable air hovered about three feet deep over the cottage floor.

He found Mary and Sally immediately. Both lay prone on the dirt floor. Both were dead.

TWENTY-EIGHT

Drew watched himself as if from afar as he placed Sally atop Mary, then gathered them both in his arms and staggered back out of the cottage in a crouched position. The anguish, the grief, the misery had to be moved someplace else. There was no time for it now. He needed to find Connie.

Settling the girls well beyond both the cottage and the Indian, he whipped out his handkerchief, tying it about his face as he pitched himself back into his beloved home, now filled with billowing clouds of black, uncompromising smoke.

Narrowed into slits, his eyes burned, while his throat, raw and chapped, sucked in air. She wasn't on the floor, or he'd have seen her when he first came in and found the others. Dropping to his hands and knees, he scrambled toward the bed.

The thickened smoke and shortage of air made his head spin. Was he still moving in the right direction or was he going in circles? He couldn't see a blessed thing.

He cracked his temple against the bed frame, blinding himself for a moment. At least he'd found the bed.

Rising up on his knees to check the mattress, thick, heavy smoke strangled him. He ran his arms along the tick. Nothing. He sunk again to the floor. Where *was* she? The board. Maybe she lay on the board.

The roof had caught now, and bits of fire rained from above. Whipping the tick off the ropes, he covered his back with it as he slithered on his belly, so impermeable was the smoke. His lungs ceased to function. He was losing awareness. He had to find Connie.

Then he heard it. A soft, mourning, heart-wrenching wail from far, far away. Had he imagined it? No, there it was again and she was calling him. Calling his name.

Hold tight, Connie! I'm coming! I'm coming! Keeping his face close to the dirt, he pulled his knees up beneath him and moved toward the sound. The roaring of the fire blistered his ears, but her high-pitched plea cut through it all. He shuffled toward it, praying desperately as he went.

Her throat was dry, her eyes parched from crying when she finally pushed herself to her knees and wiped her face with her apron. Thick, moist clouds had moved in front of the sun, threatening rain.

What held her attention, though, was Blackberry. The striped animal stood a stone's throw away, facing her, his body tensed, his ears flattened, his tail erect. The hairs on Constance's nape tingled.

Blackberry drummed his front paws on the ground with an astonishingly loud *thump . . . thump, thump*. He repeated the long, short, short rhythm two more times.

After a taut moment, he lowered his tail, then turned toward the forest. Constance scanned the thicket as well but could see nothing. The forest lay eerily quiet. Blackberry sniffed several times, his nose prodding the air around him, before finally dismissing whatever had concerned him and ambling toward her.

She ran a hand over his downy coat and long, fluffy tail. "What's the matter, young fellow?"

She perused the forest again but could see nothing amiss. Blackberry climbed up her torso with his front paws, nudging her chin with his cold nose. She sniffled and lay back down, the animal flopping over onto his back as she did so.

She massaged Blackberry's tight tummy and forced herself to confront the weighty slab of desolation inside her. She might not have a congruous marriage anymore. Her interest in scientific pursuits might have lost its allure, but she had a God. And He'd given her a baby. Drew's baby. And for that reason, she must prepare herself for the long journey back to England. She cuddled the black and white animal, fresh tears filling her eyes. "Oh, Blackberry. I don't want to go."

Pearls from her time here strung together in her mind. The graceful deer poised outside the clearing on her wedding day. The smell of Drew's pipe when they washed dishes at the creek. Surprised delight after submerging herself in a tub of deliciously warm water. Learning to milk Snowflake. Taming Mr. Meanie. Berry-picking with Sally.

Sally. Regret, spiced with sadness, sprinkled through her. Oh, but she was going to miss the little moppet. Her actions toward that sweet, precious child this afternoon had been inexcusable. She must apologize to her, with not only words, but with a great display of affection.

Blackberry rolled onto his feet, burrowed closer, then turned in circles until finally settling in the crook between Constance's stomach and legs.

"And you. I'm going to miss you too." She scratched behind his ears. He tucked his head underneath and wrapped his tail around himself.

I've been a fool, Lord. A fool. I've placed myself, my marriage, and my mathematics above you. I've made them my gods, and as you can see, I've made a huge muck of things.

She ran her hand down Blackberry's coat. *Still, you've blessed me. You knit a babe together with your own hands and placed it to nest inside of me. Thank you, thank you, thank you.*

Because I know you will tolerate no other gods before you, I give you my marriage, my mathematics, myself, and this sweet, precious babe inside of me.

Her eyes drifted closed.

How long she slept, Constance was unsure, but when she awoke, Blackberry was gone and something was . . . burning?

Frowning, she sat up, wincing at the stiffness of her limbs. What was burning?

Then she saw it. Black, ominous smoke curling in great gusts toward the heavens.

"Fire!" she screamed, scrambling to stand up. A biting pain tormented the soles of her feet. She ignored it as thoughts of a fire took hold.

Hiking up her skirt, she ran pell-mell for the cottage. Her foot caught on a root, and she sprawled to the ground, the impact knocking her senseless. Shaking her head clear, she hoisted herself up, barely giving her body a chance to fully rise before her feet dug into the ground again as she ran and ran and ran.

Blood drained from her head. Her mind swam. *No! I will not swoon! I cannot swoon! Sally! Mary! Oh, sweet Lord! I cannot swoon!* Nausea churned in her stomach. Breathing became an exercise in futility. The smell of fire spurred her on.

The crackling and roaring of flames reached her ears, the cottage's demise, her eyes. *Oh, Lord!*

She saw the Indian first, then Sally slumped atop Mary. A wrenching pressure ripped throughout her body, starting deep in the pit of her being. It spiraled up into her chest, suffocating her. Her knees buckled. "No!" she screamed. "Noooooooo!"

Falling to the ground, she tried to crawl to them but got tangled in her skirt. She wrested it from beneath her knees, finally reaching the woman and child. "Oh no. Oh no. Oh no," she sobbed.

Scooping Sally into her arms, she drew the limp body to her own, rocking it, patting it, murmuring to it. "Wake up, Sally, wake up. Don't go. Please, pumpkin, don't go!"

Sally's head toppled like a rag doll from one side to the other as Constance rocked. She burrowed her fingers into the child's hair, bracing her little head and feeling a huge sticky lump at the base of it.

Nausea rushed up Constance's throat, and she bit her tongue to keep it at bay. She couldn't succumb to it yet. She had to wake up Sally first. She had to apologize to the dear little thing.

She reached out and grabbed Mary's arm. "Mary,

Mary. Fetch me a cool cloth. I can't get Sally to wake up." But Mary only lay there.

Constance shook her. *"Mary!"* She'd injected her most severe tone, one she'd used back home when dealing with recalcitrant servants but had never before used on Mary. "Get *up,* I say. I need help. I hurt Sally's feelings, and I need to tell her that I'm s-sorry. That I d-didn't mean it. That I l-l-love her!"

But Mary would not get up and Sally would not wake. Constance squeezed her own eyes shut, then squeezed Sally to her heart. "Drew!" she screamed. "Drew! Sally w-won't w-wake uuuuuuup! Dreeeeeew!"

How many times she screamed his name, she didn't know, but suddenly he was there, wrapping his arms around her, Sally trapped between them. He ran his hands up and down Constance's back, neck, and hair, kissing her forehead, her eyes, her cheeks, her mouth with quick, frantic pecks.

The stifling smell of charred wood engulfed his shirt, smothering her. She pushed at him. "Stop it! I can breathe not! You're going to hurt Sally!"

But he didn't stop and anger twisted inside her. She released Sally long enough to shove him away. But when he fell back, so did Sally, her body contorting in an unnatural way.

"Now look what you did!" She gathered Sally to her again, this time cradling her like an infant. "I'm trying to wake her up, not squash her to death." She looked up at Drew through tear-streaked eyes. "She won't wake up!"

Tears were pouring from Drew's eyes as well, and he looked like death itself. Dried blood lay in streaks down the left side of his head and matted his long hair. His face was plastered with black soot. Blue and purple imprints crisscrossed his neck. "What happened t-to you?"

He licked his parched lips, then moved them, but no sound came out. He tried again but only croaked. Impatience flickered in his eyes, and he jerked his head toward the cottage.

Constance looked at it dispassionately as flames consumed all four sides and the roof. She became vaguely aware of an immense heat pressing against her body. "It's on fire," she stated.

His expression changed. He stood, plucking her to her feet. Holding fast to Sally, Constance crumbled back to the ground. "Stop it, Drew. I need to stay with Sally."

His hands bit into her arms, and he hauled her to her feet again, his mouth working, guttural sounds emitting from it. He pointed to the cottage, to Sally, and then to the forest.

"You want me to take Sally away from the fire?" she asked.

He nodded and pointed to the path.

"Take her to the creek?"

He nodded again and spun her toward the path, giving her a push. She started to fall, but he grabbed hold of her skirt, propping her up again. When he let loose, her feet wavered but she stayed upright. She turned back to him once more and said, "Please tell Mary to come too."

He leaned down and swung Mary into his arms.

He knew not what to do first. Tend to the burning cottage or to Connie. He decided on Connie, for by himself there was not much he could do about the spreading of the fire, and Connie was in no shape to fend for herself.

He would get her to the creek and follow it to the James River and on to the ocean. For if the forest were to catch fire, he wanted to be far, far away.

He hoisted Mary to his shoulder and trotted to catch up with Connie. She was still talking to Sally. Talking about showing her some friendly blackberries. Forsooth, he hoped she wouldn't catch the mind sickness.

He remembered some who'd lost everything in '22 and how mind sickness took over their bodies. And this surprise attack was exactly like the other one. The last had killed near four hundred. He wondered how many this one would claim.

His thoughts gravitated to Josh. Had he reached Grandma and Nellie in time? What about his new baby nephew? Would he be orphaned . . . or worse? He blacked the thoughts out, refusing to consider the possibility of losing them too. As far as Sally and Mary went, he would not, could not, dwell on it now.

Connie was alive and he had to keep her that way. To think of anything else would undermine his ability to do so. He tuned out her sentimental blabbering and started planning for what he would do if they encountered more Indians. Or what he would do if the wind picked up and the fire spread so rapidly they became cut off from an escape route.

His throat ached, his lungs burned, his heart remained resolutely numb. Connie's progress was slowing with each step, her hold on Sally more and more precarious. When she snagged a toe and lurched to the ground, she refused to release Sally. Both fell with a thud.

Quickly lowering Mary, Drew dropped to his knees. Connie lay face down in the dirt, her shoulders shaking.

"Get up, Connie." His throat barely croaked out the words. "We need to keep moving." He placed a hand on her arm. "Come."

She reacted like a wild animal, jerking herself up with teeth snarling and claws barred. "Touch me not! Just leave me be! I see not what the hurry is anyway. In case you haven't noticed, Drew, she's dead. Did you hear what I said? Sally's dead! *They're both dead!* Don't you even care?"

Tears spilled down her cheeks, and he watched her crawl to Sally's side, straightening the child's dress into neat folds.

A raw and primitive anguish seeped into his soul. He had tried to tell her. One should never, ever allow himself to get too close to the children. The odds were too high against you.

But Connie had scoffed at such advice and now look at her. So torn up with grief she didn't even recognize the peril her own life was in this very moment.

This was why she must go back. This was why she couldn't stay. He would not have her go through this again with her own children. And she would. As sure as the sun, she would.

And it would rip her sweet, tender heart from side to side, top to bottom, corner to corner. He knew it for a fact, for his at this very moment lay in tatters. Again, curse it all. *Again.*

"*Drew,*" Connie screamed, grasping Sally's face and rapidly patting her cheek. "Oh, sweet saints above! Did you hear that?" She snapped her head up to look at him. "Did you? I think she moaned!"

But, of course, she hadn't. Connie was delusional. Still, it would be more expedient to recheck Sally than to try to convince Connie otherwise.

He moved closer and held Sally's wrist with one hand while placing his other hand against the lifeline located in her neck.

Connie stilled, waiting for his reaction. Sitting back on his heels, he slowly shook his head. "I'm sorry, love. I feel no heartbeat. Now, we really needs go. The wind is blowing this way, and we need to keep moving."

He looked down again at Sally, then ceased to breathe. Had her little chest risen and fallen, or had it been a trick of the wind?

"But I *heard* her, Drew. I know I did!"

He grasped Sally's wrist again and leaned over her inert body, lifting one eyelid and then the next. He could neither feel nor see any sign of life whatsoever, yet he heard it too. As soft as a butterfly's wings, it was. The slightest of whimpers.

Oh, my Lord! Have you spared her? Have you?

Eyes wide, he looked up at Constance. "Yes! Yes! I heard it!"

"Mary! Check Mary!"

He rushed over to Mary, checking her and checking her again. "No. We've lost her, Connie. I'm sure of it. But we must move now, quickly. We must get Sally to the creek."

He scooped up Sally and laid her in Connie's waiting arms.

"You're sure you can manage her?" he asked.

"Yes, yes. Get Mary. Make haste! Make haste! Oh, hang on, Moppet. Hang on."

By the time he picked Mary up and laid her over his shoulder, Connie had already started scurrying to the creek, Sally held tightly across her breast.

The fire was gaining ground. He could hear it. Smell it. Feel it. He knew Constance's pace was awkward and slow not only from fatigue, but also to keep from jarring Sally too much.

The wind whipped, picking up momentum. Fiery sparks floated all around. Thick smoke chased their heels. The braying of the fire sounded menacingly close. They had to reach the water. And quickly.

He hastened his steps, prodding Connie from behind. She increased her speed.

The wind surged, flattening their clothes against their backs. Flames leapt ever toward them, gaining so fast the smoke and heat soon became overpowering.

He opened his mouth to tell Connie to run. Smoke swirled into his lungs. He swallowed and tried again. "Run, Connie."

She didn't respond. He moved past her and turned around, jogging backward. "Run."

Mary's body jostled against his shoulder while Connie's eyes conveyed a message of heartbreak and commiseration. She couldn't run. Her skirts would trip her for certain. He opened his free arm.

She grasped Sally's waist and lifted her up to him. Folding the child into his embrace, he tried to bore a message of urgency into Connie. "Run."

She glanced back, then lifted her skirt, picking up speed.

He increased his backward lope. *"Run!"*

She ran. He whirled around, keeping pace beside her. The wind rose yet again. A swelling of fire crashed at their heels. They weren't going to make it.

At that moment, when the heat became unbearable, when he realized they were going to perish in nature's furnace, when he thought of all he still had to live for, an indomitable desire to survive burst upon him. Mary was gone, and maybe even Josh, Grandma, and Nellie too. And Sally's life still hung in the balance. But Connie was alive, and he wasn't ready to give her up.

God forgive me. Without ever breaking stride, he released Mary to Him, allowing her to tumble to the ground. His heart lurched, his breath caught, then he repositioned Sally and called out to Constance.

She turned to him. He swooped down, flung her over his shoulder, and sprinted. Sprinted toward the creek. Toward life. Toward salvation.

TWENTY-NINE

The wind changed. And with it, the fire's direction. One minute it nipped at their heels, the next it receded into the distance. Drew kept running.

They reached the water. He plopped Connie down onto her feet, handed Sally to her, and splashed into the creek, swimming toward the raft.

He swiftly untied it, swam back, and pulled it up onto the shore. "Quick!" The two of them laid Sally onto the raft. Connie flopped down next to her.

He pulled the raft back into the water, wrapped the tie cord around his hand, and scissor-kicked his legs, pulling them downstream. His leg muscles prickled, his lungs labored, his head throbbed. He concentrated solely on moving them farther and farther from the fire. When it became too much, he veered to the water's bank.

His feet finally touched bottom, the mud suctioning each step. Constance jumped off the raft, went completely under, then popped back up, holding tightly to the bound logs until her feet touched and she could help pull the craft in.

The water shallowed, and they fell to their knees, tugging the raft behind them. Flopping back over onto the grass, arms flung above his head, he closed his eyes and sucked in air.

"She's alive, Drew," Connie said between breaths. "She twitched once and moaned twice."

When he could summon enough energy, he lifted one lid. By trow, Connie was a mess. Her cap had long since fallen off, leaving her hair plastered to her head in a wet tangle. Her face was pale, her clothes sodden, her posture dejected. But she was alive. Alive. Never had a sight been so sweet.

He reached for her hand, gathering it into his, their water-shriveled skin finding solace together. He gave a slight tug and she tumbled over, half on top of him, half on the grass.

"I love you." It was all he could manage at the moment, though he wanted to tell her more. Much more. But he needed to save his strength, for it was a good distance yet to the bay.

"Did you hear what I said about Sally?"

"Yes." But he was afraid to dwell on it, for at any moment her life could be snuffed out.

More minutes passed, and he knew they'd tarried as long as they dared. Forcing himself up, he rose. "We need to keep going. The fire's still spreading."

She shook her head. "You and Sally go ahead. I think I'll stay right here."

He bent down on one knee, combing a swath of hair

from her eyes and hooking it behind her ear. "We needs must go, Connie."

Her weary gaze traveled over the water. Heavy clouds billowed overhead, darkening the sky.

He rose again, helping her to her feet. "Come."

She crawled back onto the raft, collapsing onto her stomach next to Sally instead of sitting. Connie groped around with one hand until she found the child's, then clasped it within her own. He swallowed, then pushed the crude vessel into the water. Kick, pull, breathe. Kick, pull, breathe. They were making progress, but it seemed so slow. So very, very slow.

Images of leaving Mary behind hammered against the periphery of his mind. Her hair uncovered and matted, her body contorted. He shoved the images away, forcing himself to concentrate on moving downstream.

He lasted longer this time before having to move to the water's edge. He was no less exhausted, though.

Not so Connie, for she found her voice as soon as he pulled the raft to shore. "What are you going to do?" she asked, sitting next to him on the bank.

About what, he wondered. Sally? Mary? The fire? Her? Their lives together? He slid his eyes closed. "Sally and I are going back to England with you. You can be the king's accountant for all I care, but if you go, I go."

When he'd made that decision, he didn't know. Somewhere between the fire and this creek bank, he supposed.

Surprise lit her voice. "But you're a tobacco farmer. We grow not tobacco in England."

He rubbed the muscles in his legs. She pushed his hands aside and took over the massage. Sweet saints, how could something feel so good and hurt like the dickens all at the same time? "I'll be a factor, like Josh. The O'Connor Tobacco Agency. And you can just forget about that 'young, wealthy aristocrat' who's waiting for you. I'm not sharing."

"What young, wealthy aristocrat?"

"The one your father's contracted for you."

"Oh. Well, that's good, for I want him not anyway, whoever he is." She paused in her labors. "Drew, do you really want to go to England?"

"I want to stay with you."

"Forever?"

"Forever."

She started to work on his other leg. "I want to stay with you too."

Such simple words, yet they sluiced through his system, restoring energy where moments before he'd been flagging. He peered at her from beneath his lashes, but she was concentrating on her task, her tongue captured between those pretty white teeth.

Her brow furrowed. "If we stay here, would you have to fight in a war against the Indians?"

He winced, and she lessened the intensity of her massage. "No. Usually the second and third sons, or those who lost everything, do the fighting. The rest will stay and continue to cultivate tobacco, thus ensuring permanence in the colony."

She moved her attention to one of his arms, kneading it like a roll of dough. "I want to stay here."

He fully opened his eyes. "Stay here? Why would you want to do that?"

She pressed her thumbs into his palm, then worked

the joints in each of his fingers. "I like it here. No, I *love* it here."

He closed his fingers over hers, halting her administrations. "We just went through a massacre and you *love* it here?"

She looked at him, crystals of the creek's water still dancing on her lashes. "I want to stay."

His heart pounded. "What about that editing work of your uncle's?"

She swallowed, tears springing to her eyes. "It's a bit insignificant when you consider what's taken place these last few hours, think you not?"

A seed of hope buried within struggled to burst forth. He suppressed it. "Connie, it could happen again, along with any number of other things. Have you considered the well-being of our children?" His eyes darkened. "For there *will* be children."

"And?"

"And their chances of survival would be much better in England."

"Horse dung."

He blinked.

She moved to his other side, setting to work on his right arm. "There are hard times in England. Disease. Why, even a war." She shook her head. "I want to stay here."

He pulled himself up to a sitting position and scanned the band of forest around them. "Connie, look at it from a mathematical point of view. I come from a family of nine, and Sally and I just might be the only ones left today. You come from a family of twelve. Eleven of you are left."

"Uncle Skelly died."

"That doesn't count."

She cocked a brow.

He ran his fingers through his hair, rivulets of water collecting between them. "Okay. So he counts. Still, the odds are better in England."

Her expression drooped, disappointment evident within her eyes. "Oh, Drew. You are not God. Think you if the Almighty has need of one of our offspring, He will not be able to find them in England?"

He rested his forehead in his hands. He didn't want to think about God right now. What kind of God allowed a child to be savagely attacked? He stood. "It's time to go."

Without resistance, she returned to the raft, checked on Sally, and lay down, once again entrusting her life to him. He splashed into the water.

The skies rumbled, and a hint of smoke drifted across the water. The fire had not spread this far as yet, but its smell still clung. He hated to think of the damage the fire would do, for in spite of his words to Connie, he loved it here too.

Still, to raise a family in this primitive land was another matter. Foolhardy at best, a death wish at most.

"Drew?"

He grunted, pulling them through the water.

"I'm with child."

All motion stopped. Had she grown wings he'd have been less appalled. With child? *With child?!* He spun the raft so that she lay next to him instead of behind him. Only when she glanced down, frowning, did he realize he was paddling neither his legs nor his arms but was standing upright. They'd hit a shallow.

She rolled onto her side, propping her head in her hand. "Surprise."

He looked at her stomach. *With child! God help him.* "When?"

"I think it will arrive in about five months. Maybe sooner. I'm not really sure."

Stark, vivid fear hit him full force.

She must have seen it, for she placed a hand against his cheek and gave him an affectionate smile. "'Fear not, for I am with you; Be not dismayed, for I am your God. I will strengthen you, yes, I will help you, I will uphold you with My righteous right hand.'"

It was Isaiah 41:10. The very same verse he'd recited to her during their wedding ceremony. Why did it fail to bring him comfort?

She smoothed his hair back from his face. "You must not worry, Drew. You must simply let God and nature run their course."

That terrified him even more. "I don't like the way God and nature run their course."

Tenderness touched her face. "There is naught you can do. Why, think of Sally. It is God who has spared her life and who still holds that life in the palm of His mighty hand."

Oh, Lord. Up to now, he'd managed to avoid those thoughts. But before he could stop it, pain crashed into his heart as his gaze drifted to Sally. So still she lay, each breath a miracle. And he could do nothing to wake her. To heal her. To ensure that she survived. Not one blessed thing.

Unbidden, long sable curls framing sparkling eyes and a mischievous smile filled his vision. He recalled with clarity the powerful, instantaneous feelings he'd experienced the first time he'd held her. She in one arm, her twin sister in the other, identical in appearance. And now, there was a very real chance that he could lose her. Even still. Just like that. He wasn't ready to give her up, was never ready. He felt so infernally helpless.

Moisture rushed to his eyes while tears swelled in Connie's. He tried to swallow but couldn't. Like a trembling volcano, the pain, the grief, and the horror erupted without warning. A cry of agony burst from his lips, his groan echoing across the water even as Connie rolled from the raft into the creek and wrapped her arms around his neck. He cinched her to him and cried. For Sally. For his family. For himself.

Only after some time did he realize Connie was crying too. Eventually, their sobs turned to silence, a silence of nothing. Still, they remained in the middle of the shallow, clasped to each other, waiting for the emptiness to cease and for the healing to begin.

But it already had. For somewhere in the furthest corner of his heart was a little worm, wiggling with excitement about the overdue realization that Connie really did desire to stay. About the tremendous mercy God had shown by sparing Sally, so far. And about the news of a baby. *His and Connie's* baby.

I give up, God. You made me. You know how I am. I cannot keep my distance. Nor can I keep those I love alive. Only you can do that. Only you are God.

I give over. I fall prostrate before you. What you see fit to bless me with I will rejoice over. When you takest

*away, I will turn to you for solace. For you are the One
and Only God.*

He lifted his head. The smoke had begun to thicken
again. The fire was still spreading. "We need to keep
going." Slipping a hand between them, he rested it against
her stomach. "How do you feel?"

"Like I've run the length of this country and back,
then swallowed the entire river."

His eyes widened in alarm.

She lifted a corner of her mouth. "I'm fine, Drew.
Truly, I'm fine."

He believed her not, but there was nothing he could
do. So he lifted her back onto the raft, and they once
again headed toward the bay. They'd traveled no more
than a few feet when a ball of light zinged the air above
them, followed immediately by a deafening peal of thunder. He quickly propelled them to the bank, grabbed Sally,
and hurtled both Connie and himself out of the water.

The crack continued to resound, each clamor a tiny
bit less in volume than the last. No sooner had it stopped
than the heavens opened up. It was as if God had sent a
legion of angels to scoop the contents of the ocean into
buckets and dump them onto Virginia.

In mere moments, the ground was afloat and the great
fire was surely no more than a smoldering mist. They
scrambled to the forest's interior for protection from
the pelting shards until, finally, the rain began to slacken
into a steady drizzle.

He scanned the area around them, untouched by fire,
and got his bearings. Though they'd traveled what seemed
like miles in the winding creek, if he wasn't mistaken,
they were just a short walk from the big house.

"Hold out your arms."

Connie cupped her arms, and he gently placed Sally in them, then scooped the both of them into his.

"What are you doing?!"

He took a fortifying breath. "I'm taking you, Sally, and our baby . . . home."

THIRTY

It looked as if Drew would carry her over the threshold after all, and Sally as well. Enormous relief and thankfulness had swept through Constance when the big house came into view as fresh and untouched as a young maid. And now, Drew took the front steps two at a time, pushed open those great double doors, and carried her across the threshold before climbing up the stairs to the master chamber.

A chill from being wet and suddenly indoors took hold of her. She must get Sally and herself out of these sodden clothes haste, posthaste.

The child was still breathing but lay heavy against Constance and had not yet made any signs of awakening. Constance had seen nothing of the house but the great room the last time she was here but didn't have the luxury of savoring her new surroundings. Her attention was centered on Sally.

Still, when they entered the master chamber, there was no avoiding the bed. Large enough for an entire family, the high post mahogany bed stood on four stately legs and was closed in at the head and foot by ornately decorated wooden panels. Though it had poles for bed curtains on the two open sides, none had been hung yet and no tick lay on the ropes.

She tightened her hold on Sally as Drew set them down in a chair.

"There's some dry wood belowstairs in the kitchen," he said, "and as soon as I get a fire going up here, I'll tighten the ropes and put the tick on the bed. You will be all right for a moment?"

"Yes, yes. Go ahead."

He looked around the room and snatched a wool coverlet off a stack of folded linens on a nearby dressing table. He shook it out and draped it around Connie's shoulders like a cloak, arranging its folds so that Sally would be covered as well. "I'll be right back," he said and hurried out the door.

She could barely see the top of Sally's head peeping through a gap in the coverlet. The sweet body heat they shared warmed Constance. Swaying from side to side, she hummed a lullaby while allowing her attention to wander across the chamber.

It was huge. The cottage could have fit into it two times. Furniture was planted haphazardly throughout. Two drop-leaf tables, several chairs, trunks, and a dressing table as fine as any back home took up much of the space.

A sapling broom stood propped in one corner, and a chest of drawers with butterfly pulls received an elaborate walnut Bible box complete with lock and key.

The beautifully plastered walls held three window casements with diamond-shaped lead glass panes, along with two additional windows in the attached alcove that would serve nicely as a nursery.

A brief movement below her feet caught her attention, and she could just barely discern Drew through the minute cracks in the plank flooring that set upon beams and served as a ceiling for the great room underneath.

Footfalls on the stairs reached her ears seconds before he strode into the room, dumping his load of wood into the fireplace that took up two-thirds of the west wall. "I've some heart of the pine to mix in with the regular pine and oak, so the room should heat up quickly. Are you all right?"

"Yes. As soon as you're done, though, I need to get Sally out of these wet things."

He nodded, igniting the wood with some flint, then quickly pressed fingers and thumbs to his lips, blowing a steady stream of air through the tiny hole he'd formed. The fire responded immediately, devouring the kindling and enfolding the dry logs.

He stood. "Let me tighten the bed ropes and throw the tick on first, so you'll have someplace to put her when she's dry." He grabbed the bed key, and starting at one end, wedged the large wooden peg between the rope and bed frame, twisting, then releasing. From section to section, his movements were quick and sure until he'd made it all the way around.

The tick lay beneath the bed, and she knew it must weigh a tremendous amount. How he had any strength left with which to wrestle it onto the ropes amazed her.

"There," he said, blowing a puff of air from his lungs. "She'll be able to sleep tight now, and the tick is feather instead of straw, so there'll be no bed bugs to bother her."

A feather bed. Oh my.

Together they worked silently, she disrobing and drying Sally, he covering the tick with linen and fetching water from the kitchen. When all was ready, she carefully laid Sally on the mattress, covered her with wool, then finger-combed her hair away from the swollen bump at the base of her scalp. Dipping a rag into the bucket of water, she began to wash the blood from the wound.

"I've no garden here yet, nor any comfrey," Drew said. Leaning forward, he tenderly touched the gash. Sally moaned. He sent Constance a look filled with hope and relief. "A good sign. Perhaps she'll waken soon."

When they'd done all they could, Constance wrung the rag out into the red-tinted water, a shiver going through her.

"You next," he said. "Out of those clothes and into bed."

She nodded but didn't move from Sally's side. The thought of undressing exhausted her. Where would she find the strength such a task would require? "I'm filthy. I'll ruin the new bed."

"I'll bring you some fresh water."

"I've no clothes to change into."

His grin was downright wicked. "I know."

A short laugh escaped her, yet still she made no move. He leaned down to place a light kiss on her forehead before grabbing the water bucket and leaving the room.

He returned to find her exactly where he'd left her, sitting on the edge of the bed, shoulders slumped, eyes closed. Surely she hadn't fallen asleep like that.

As he drew nearer, though, he saw tears pouring from her eyes and streaming down her cheeks, jaw, and neck, then trickling into the folds of her neckline. Yet she made no sound nor any move to wipe them from her face.

He set the bucket down. "Connie? What's wrong? Are you all right?"

She raised her gaze to him, her eyes swollen, red. "*Mary.*"

She'd barely whispered it, yet that one short name held immense anguish and misery within it.

"Oh, Connie." He reached down and pulled her up into his embrace. "I know. I know."

"She had such a hard life." Her voice was muffled and broken against his shirt.

He cupped her head, holding it against him.

"And yet she was so giving and unselfish. She showed me how to survive on that ship, you know, when she could have easily left me to flounder or perish, even." She hiccupped. "She comforted me when Uncle Skelly died. She offered encouragement here when I was having such trouble adjusting. She taught me so much. Listened. Shared. Even prayed with me. Oh, Drew," she wailed, "how am I ever going to manage without her?"

Sobs racked her body. Tightening his hold, he stroked her hair, kissed her head, rubbed her shoulders. Mary had come to mean much to him as well. He'd not thought of her as a servant. Hadn't for quite some time. He'd thought of her as a friend. A sister. An angel.

Oh, Lord. Why? Why would you take sweet, sweet Mary from Connie? From Sally? From me? Have you really such an urgent need for her to be with you? I don't understand. Will never understand.

Connie trembled, and he knew he must get her warm and safely tucked into bed.

Tilting her head back, he kissed the tears from her cheeks and placed a soft, tender kiss on her lips. Then scooping her hair off her face and shoulders, he began loosening her skirt and bodice. She stood mute and dejected as he peeled the sodden clothing from her frame and washed the mud, sand, and debris from her person, all the while supporting her lest she crumble to the floor.

Thank you for giving me this woman.

He patted her dry, careful not to hurt her bruised and battered body, then wrapped her in soft linen.

Please protect her and the baby. Please, Lord. It is my heart's deepest desire.

He lifted her into his arms and laid her next to Sally. Connie rolled to her side, curled her knees up, and sucked in a choppy breath.

She was asleep before he'd finished tucking the wool coverlet beneath her chin. After spreading her clothes in front of the fire, he shucked his garments off and splashed water over himself. He paused to stoke the fire and then crawled onto the tick beside his beloved family.

The dowdy, scrubbed, heavily laden ship rested peacefully on the blue water. It carried the usual three masts, the fore and main square-rigged, the mizzenmast lateen, while her poop deck graduated into three different levels up over the stern.

Drew had seen many a ship just like it over the course of his life, but this one, this one he would never forget. "You won't change your mind?"

Josh shook his head. "I've been wanting to do this

for a long time. I was waiting only for you to acquire enough help so as to run the farm without me."

Drew looked from the *Myrtilla* to his brother. "If I'd known, I never would have bought the indentured men."

Josh's mouth tipped up. "That's why I told you not of my intentions."

"But why must it be so final?" Drew removed his hat, tapping it against his thigh. "What was so bad about coming back and forth with each shipment?"

"Nothing. It's just not what I *want* to do. I've never liked or excelled at farming the way you have. It's the factoring I enjoy. If I live in England, I can factor not only our tobacco, but many others'. I can factor full time, Drew. I . . . I'll be my own man." He pursed his lips. "The best part, of course, is I won't have to answer to Grandma anymore."

Drew attempted a smile but could not muster one forth. "You'll get dragged into the war. You know you will."

"I'm the second son here, Drew. If I return to help you farm this summer, the colony will have by then organized a counter force against the Indians in which I would be expected to participate." He shrugged. "It seems no matter where I go, I'll be fighting a war of one kind or another."

Drew studied his brother. Something wasn't quite right. Everything he said made sense. But, still. Drew narrowed his eyes. "Mary. Is that what this is all about?"

A mask descended over Josh's face. "Not to worry, Drew. I'll send you a *replacement*." His inflection made the word sound heinous.

Drew angled his head. "Mary could never be replaced,

and that's not what I meant. Nor am I worried about a cook. Connie learned more than I realized about food preparation, and when her time approaches, Grandma will come and see to the cooking for her." A salty breeze disturbed the hair against his shoulder. "No, I wasn't speaking of cooking at all. I was speaking of *Mary*. Did you perhaps have deeper feelings for her than you let on?"

His brother's jaw tightened. "I'm going to stay in England because I like it there. I want to live there. I can be a successful factor there." He picked up his bag. "I needs must go."

Drew's throat thickened. "Your pardon. I spoke out of turn."

After a tense moment, Josh's shoulders wilted. "No, it's your pardon I must ask for. My-my feelings for Mary are jumbled within me and I—" the telltale tick in his jaw pulsed—"I'm not yet ready to think much less speak of them."

Pain congealed within Drew. "I'm sorry I was too late for her. I-I'm sorry we couldn't give her a proper burial. And if it makes you feel any better, I loved her too."

Josh took a deep breath. "It wasn't your fault." He scanned the shoreline. "I'm just glad Sally is mending and showing no signs of head weaknesses." He turned back to Drew. "And, of course, I'm vastly relieved that Nellie and the rest are all right."

Drew nodded, a spurt of anger replacing the hurt of just moments before. "I'd give anything to get my hands on Emmett."

"So would the Powhatans."

"You don't think the Indians kidnapped him and took him back to their camp for . . . retribution?"

"I don't. It's not their style. I think if he'd been home they'd have been very deliberate in killing him and careful to leave what remains there would have been for all of us to see."

"Then where is he? Every man in this settlement wants a piece of him."

"I know not, Drew. I know not. But his life here is over—one way or another."

"Still, I—"

Laying a hand on Drew's shoulder, Josh squeezed. "Our losses were great, but it could have been worse. We could have lost additional family members and we could have lost the big house." He compressed his lips, the tick in his jaw pounding. "Is it callous to be relieved the house was untouched?"

Drew took his time answering. "If it is, then I am calloused as well, for I was not only thankful the house still stood, but also that the seedlings were unharmed and the cured tobacco was safely intact within the ship's hull."

His brother nodded.

"I want not to anger you, Josh, but Grandma had some parting words she wished me to give you."

Josh gave him a sideways look. "That sounds ominous. Why didn't she say them to me herself?"

"She's distraught." He shook his head. "This massacre was so much like the last one, I'm sure she's reliving it some. In any case, she asked that I place a Bible in your bundle."

Josh glanced at his bundle. "I thought it burned in the fire."

"It did. Morden gave her two more—one for each of us."

"Why, Drew? She knows I've read it already."

"Yes. I'm aware of that. We both have read it." He sighed. "Still, I'm glad she insisted on it, for I confess I have turned to it and the One who inspired it often of late and have discovered this . . . this freedom—from guilt, from failure, from the responsibility of keeping everyone alive."

Josh rubbed the back of his neck. "I know not what to say. You've caught me a bit off guard."

"I know and I'm sorry. I wish we had more time. I wish I were better with my words. But will you read it over again? With a perspective of freedom instead of as a book full of rules? Mayhap starting with the New Testament this time?"

Josh took a deep breath. "I could try, I suppose."

"Thank you."

Josh extended his hand. "Take care, brother."

Drew grasped his hand and pulled him into an embrace. "I'll continue to refer to the second bedchamber as yours. So if you ever have a need or desire to return, know that it waits in ready for you."

They held tight, then broke apart, neither bothering to hide the sheen in his eyes. Turning, Josh walked out to the end of the pier and jumped down into the dinghy. Drew placed his hat on his head and watched the sailor row his brother to the *Myrtilla*.

The dinghy pulled alongside the great boat, and Josh climbed its wooden steps along the sloping side of the flat, holding his bundle over one shoulder. He swung up onto the deck, then leaned against the port bulwarks looking out to his brother and home.

Drew inhaled. The salty air smelled good. Fresh. Not

like the acrid air of decay permeating the desecrated land over so much of the area. Too soon the bosun's voice traveled across the water. "Let fall your main! Bring your cable to the capstan! Break out anchor!"

Young sailors with shirts open to the waist scurried to and fro across the deck. Josh remained a still figure in the midst of the chaos.

The fore and main topsails flew up, as did the square and lateen sails on the poop. With a creak and a moan, the weather-beaten girl moved slowly out of the harbor.

Drew watched the seagulls dip and swell in her wake until the squawking birds were mere dots, the ship but a toy boat, and his brother a poignant memory.

THIRTY-ONE

Answering the knock, Drew yanked open the front doors just as an earsplitting scream from above-stairs rocked the house. In an effort to remain upright, he squeezed the door handles with an iron grip, though he felt all circulation drop to his toes.

The haggard, overdressed old gaffer in front of him straightened his spine and turned as red as his doublet. "By my life, what goes here!"

Drew scowled. "Who are you?"

The portly travel-worn man narrowed his eyes. "I am the Right Honorable the Earl of Greyhame, Lord Randall Christian Morrow, and if that was my daughter, *you* are a dead man."

Another scream from abovestairs descended into the hall, but this screech was nothing like the one before. This one was the unmistakable bawl of a newborn baby.

The blood rushed back up from Drew's toes to his head in a whirling mass, causing Connie's father to appear in triple. *It's here. The baby is finally here.*

Fighting the urge to run up the stairs and into their bedchamber, he blinked. Only two fathers stood before him now. Drew felt a slow smile spread across his face as he took a wobbly step back. "That first scream, my lord, was indeed your daughter, my wife, and if you kill me, your grandchild will be quite without a father. Won't you come in?"

Lord Randall barreled inside, brandishing his cane in Drew's face. "You beggarly knave, I was told this marriage was in name only! Who gave you permission to consummate the vows?"

"Theodore Hopkin, governor of this colony, representative of the king, and it's going to cost you plenty, for that daughter of yours is nothing but trouble. What in the blazes were you thinking to allow her an education?"

Drew bit back his smile at the man's shocked expression. Nothing like landing the first punch.

Lord Randall furrowed his bushy gray brows. "I knew not about her education until it was too late."

Drew straightened the cuffs of his shirt. "Well, be prepared to pay dearly for it. No man should have to suffer through what I do with the constant spouting of the most addlepated word puzzles you could imagine." He took the man's bag, then extended a hand toward the great room. "Please, have a seat."

The poor man's bluster dissolved, a look of resignation on his face. "Blasted chit." He shuffled into the room, settling his substantial girth into Drew's chair.

The game had begun. Drew poured them each a noggin of ale and took the chair across from him. "I require fifteen thousand pounds."

Lord Randall spewed ale across the floor. "What! Surely drink has tickled your poor brain. You're a *farmer,* you impudent rascal. I'll give you five thousand."

Drew plopped his drink onto the table at his side, its contents sloshing over the rim. A satisfied smile broke across his face. "Excellent." He stood. "When will you take her back to England with you? Today? Tomorrow?"

The old man's red-rimmed eyes widened. "I cannot take her back. Why, she's already birthed a child!"

Drew shrugged. "Fifteen thousand or I send her *and* the babe back, with or without you."

Lord Randall opened and closed his mouth several times, then shifted uncomfortably in the chair. "Well, is she . . . is she happy?"

Drew arched his brows. "What, in the name of the sword, has that to do with anything?"

His father-in-law scowled. "It has everything to do with it, you impudent knave."

He slanted Lord Randall a glance. "My price is still fifteen thousand."

Her father surged to his feet, the blood vessels in his face fair to bursting. "You'll see not a blessed shilling until I've spoken with my daughter."

Drew moved to the secretary, withdrawing a fully written and prepared marriage contract. "Feel free to peruse this in the meanwhile."

Lord Randall whipped the document from Drew's fingertips, then bent his way to his bag, pulling out a bundle of correspondence. He shoved it against Drew's chest. "And *you* feel free to peruse these."

Drew took the bundle, loosening the bow secured about the numerous packets. All were addressed to one

Skelly Torrence Morrow, all were from women. Drew slowly lifted his gaze to his father-in-law's smug one.

"They were willed to her." The old gaffer patted his round stomach. "Enjoy."

Hurried footfalls from the stairwell interrupted any response Drew might have had. He spun around. Sally, now four years old, bounded through the door.

"Drew! We have a baby!"

He scooped Sally up into his arms, his heart accelerating as he barely retained hold of the correspondence in his hand. Grandma entered at a more sedate pace, then came to an abrupt halt. "Well, by heaven, if this isn't a surprise. God ye good den, Randall." She turned to Drew. "It's a girl and Constance is fine."

A girl. Connie was fine. Oh, thank God. *Thank God.*

Excitement, jubilation, and triumph exploded within him. He wanted to shout from the rooftops. He wanted to bang on his chest. He wanted to rush abovestairs and see for himself.

Instead, he turned to his father-in-law, but before he could say a word, Lord Randall whipped himself to attention, adding a good two inches to his height. "Lady Elizabeth!"

Drew blinked. *Lady* Elizabeth? He studied his grandmother with narrowed eyes. "You *know* him?"

She smiled. "Why, of course. I broke Randall's heart once many a year ago."

Drew regarded Lord Randall. Broke his heart? The old man looked as if he'd been poleaxed.

Drew's focus snapped back to the issue at hand. "Connie's fine, you say?"

"Oh, yes. Just fine. Go on. You can go see her now."

He hesitated, glancing at the stairs.

Grandma smiled. "Go on. Randall and I have things to discuss, and she's asking for you."

He looked at Sally, gave her a huge smile, and spun her around until they reached the stairwell. Her delighted squeal filled the hall. After setting her on the floor, he ruffled her hair, took a deep breath, and raced up the steps two at a time.

Constance pivoted her head toward the door in time to see her husband hovering about its threshold. "Hello."

He moved into the room, his well-muscled body hesitant, his thick onyx hair mussed, his face showing signs of fatigue. He surveyed the disarray within their chamber, then focused his attention back on her. "Are you all right?"

She patted the tick beside her. "I'm wonderful."

He inched closer, stopping just short of the polished mahogany bed. His attention was fastened to the squirming mass swaddled in her arms. "Grandma said it's a girl."

"Yes." Constance moved the blanket away from the babe's face so he could better see her.

His eyes widened, his Adam's apple bobbed, his face paled. "Oh, Lord."

Constance suppressed a smile. "What are you hiding behind your back?"

He looked startled, then nodded toward the babe. "I want a closer look first."

Constance laid the bundle against her shoulder. "And I want to see what's behind your back."

He glanced between her and the babe, then pulled his hands in front of him. "These are for you."

He handed her a stack of correspondence, tattered and worn along its edges. The moment she read Uncle Skelly's name inscribed across the first one, she knew what it was. Her gaze snapped to his. "Where did you get these?"

"They were willed to you. It appears you are now the official editor of *The Ladies' Mathematical Diary*."

Confused, afraid to allow even the possibility to cross her mind, she flipped through the many packets. "But . . . how?"

Drew answered not and she looked up at him again.

"Would you like to be the editor of *The Ladies' Mathematical Diary*?" he asked.

She held her breath. "You wouldn't mind?"

His expression softened. "No. No, I wouldn't."

A kernel of excitement stirred within her. "But what will everyone say? What if they disapprove and take you to task for my presumptuousness?"

He waved his hand in a dismissive gesture. "Oh, they'll never believe a woman could solve such puzzles. They'll just assume I'm humoring you by editing it myself and allowing you to put your name to it."

She raised her eyebrows. "But you wouldn't be."

He humphed. "They'll never hear me admit it."

"I will," she said, a smile curving her lips.

He shrugged. "They'll believe me, not you. Now let me see our baby."

She allowed a soft chuckle to escape.

"Daughter?"

Constance turned toward the voice in the doorway, and the world came to a halt. "Papa?"

He nodded his head once.

She handed the babe up to Drew, then opened her arms wide. "Papa!" He entered, bending over to return her embrace.

"Oh, Papa! Whatever are you doing here?"

He straightened, pulling at his doublet. "I received a rather frantic message from my daughter some time back. This message contained tales of kidnappings and forced marriages"—he quirked a brow—"and annulments."

She slanted a glance at Drew, but he was paying them no mind, his attention totally captured by the infant cradled in the crook of his arm. She took a moment to relish the picture they made before turning back to her father. "I changed my mind."

"You were kidnapped not?"

"I was kidnapped."

"You were forced not into marriage?"

"I was forced into marriage."

"You want not an annulment?"

"I want not an annulment."

"Why?"

She now had Drew's full regard. She smiled tenderly at him. "Because I love my husband. I love the colonies. And there is nowhere on God's green earth I'd rather be."

"He wants a fifteen thousand pound settlement."

"Fifteen thousand!"

"He says you're a great deal of trouble."

She hesitated for one startled moment before choking back a laugh. "I am."

"I thought so." He leveled Drew a look. "If I pay you the fifteen thousand, do you swear to keep her?"

Drew reared back his head. "Forever?"

Her father scowled. "Forever."

"Oh, I suppose." He gave a long-suffering sigh. "If I must."

She bit the insides of her cheeks to keep from laughing outright.

Her father turned to her. "You will sign the papers this time?"

With an effort, she sobered her expression. "I will sign."

Seemingly satisfied, he indicated the babe in Drew's arms with a tilt of his head. "I advise against educating her. Will cause you nothing but grief if you do."

Drew nodded gravely. "I quite agree." He followed her father to the chamber door, closing it behind the man. When Drew turned back around, his shoulders shook and a smile wreathed his face.

She returned his smile. "That was really quite awful of you."

He moved forward, blithely unrepentant. "He deserved it. He shouldn't have been near so lax with your well-being."

"He did the best he could."

"I disagree. But I don't really want the money. I say we settle it on our children."

Her breath caught. "Oh, Drew, that would be lovely." She patted the tick. He settled down next to her, laying their daughter in her lap, then peeled back the layers of swathing. He examined her tiny toes, rubbed her little tummy, and smoothed her eyebrow with his fingertip. "She's beautiful."

Love swelled within her, filling every corner of her being. "She has red hair."

He ruffled her startlingly bright downy hair, then cupped her head, placing a kiss on her nose. "It's auburn."

"It's red."

Their daughter scrunched up her hands and legs, waving them wildly in the air. He opened his palm, allowing the babe to kick his hand. "Is she like a puppy?"

Constance choked. "What!"

He looked up. "Will she get her spots later?"

Laughter bubbled up from within her as she playfully whacked him on the shoulder. "Yes. Yes, I'm afraid she will. As soon as the sun touches her skin, the freckles will appear."

A delicious two-dimple grin spread across his face. "Good. I find I'm rather partial to freckled redheads." The babe squalled, and he shushed her while rubbing her tummy. "I want to give her a name now. I want not to wait until she's three."

Her heart full, she fingered the bluish-black curls covering his bent head. "Then let's name her Mary Elizabeth O'Connor, after Mary and Grandma."

His gaze collided with hers and, after a beat, he smiled. "And so it shall be."

Leaning over, he captured her lips with his, and she encircled his neck, rejoicing in the love God had bestowed upon them.

She was a woman who had it all. A bit of her past through Uncle Skelly's diary, an anointed present through her fine marriage, and a promise of future blessings through the fruit of their love, even now wiggling within the shelter of their embrace.

And sending up a heartfelt prayer, she thanked Him, for behold, it was very good.

AUTHOR'S NOTE

Many Virginia colonists truly did secure themselves a bride for a payment of 120 pounds of tobacco. The purpose of this practice was to induce the men of the colony to remain, build homes, and raise families—thus ensuring England's presence in the colony. At first, "young and uncorrupt maidens" (usually spinsters and widows) volunteered for this unique duty. But the Crown was only able to round up a hundred or so volunteers, while the demand was for significantly more. So they eventually resorted to transporting female prisoners. Every so often, an unethical ship captain would kidnap an innocent woman of high moral fiber, transport her, and sell her. Thus the premise for *A Bride Most Begrudging*.

The first edition of *The Ladies' Diary* was compiled by Englishman John Tipper, a schoolmaster who taught science and mathematics. Inexpensive and compact, it was the first almanac on the market expressly targeting a female-only audience and wildly popular. Though

I have Constance using it in our story, the real *Diary* did not make an appearance until 1704. Many of the puzzles and solutions used in our novel were taken verbatim from the *Diary*, as was the *Diary*'s preface—which was written by Tipper's successor, Mr. Henry Beighton. Other puzzles were taken from *Mathematical Wrinkles*, by S.I. Jones.

As so often is the case in the history of our nation, battles over the land upon which we encroached took many lives. In 1622 and again in 1644, the Powhatans rose up to protect their sacred home. And the colonists fought back. I very carefully researched these particular events and portrayed them as accurately as possible in the fabric of my novel. The massacre of 1622 cost the lives of almost 350 settlers and contributed to a famine and epidemic that killed another five or six hundred. It also brought on a counterattack against the Indians, in which scores of settlers and hundreds of Indians perished. The massacre of 1644 was almost as destructive as the first. These confrontations might have lasted for many years if Sir William Berkley had not captured Opechancanough. Berkley planned to take the Indian chief to England as an exhibit of the healthiness and long life of the American natives, but one of the soldiers shot him in the back. In 1646, Opechancanough's successor made a bid for peace and renounced title to the land between the James and York rivers below the falls.

And lastly, I have a confession to make. It would have been much more historically accurate to have used the King James version of the Bible when quoting Scriptures throughout the novel. However, I personally have a bit of a time understanding that translation and chose, instead, to use the New King James version because I understand it better and am more familiar with it. Forgive me?

In Him,
Deeanne Gist

More Historical Romance

You May Also Like . . .

The lifeblood of the village of Ivy Hill is its coaching inn, The Bell. When the innkeeper dies suddenly, his genteel wife, Jane, becomes the reluctant owner. With a large loan due, can Jane and her mother-in-law, Thora, find a way to save the inn—and discover fresh hope for their hearts?

The Innkeeper of Ivy Hill by Julie Klassen
TALES FROM IVY HILL #1
julieklassen.com

When Brook Eden's friend Justin, a future duke, discovers she may be an English heiress, she travels to meet her alleged father. Once she arrives in Yorkshire, Brook undergoes a trial of the heart—and faces the same danger that led to her mother's mysterious death.

The Lost Heiress by Roseanna M. White
LADIES OF THE MANOR
roseannamwhite.com

❖ BETHANYHOUSE